PROPHET ™

② BROTHERS

PROPHET, VOL. 2: BROTHERS TP.
ISBN#: 978-1-60706-749-8
First printing

Published by Image Comics, Inc. Office of
publication: 2001 Center Street, Sixth Floor,
Berkeley, California 94704. Copyright © 2013
Rob Liefeld. Originally published in single magazine
form as PROPHET #27-31 and 33. All rights
reserved. PROPHET® (including all prominent
characters featured herein), its logo and all
character likenesses are trademarks of Rob
Liefeld, unless otherwise noted. Image Comics®
is a trademark of Image Comics, Inc. All rights
reserved. No part of this publication may be
reproduced or transmitted in any form or by
any means (except for short excerpts for review
purposes) without the express written permission
of Image Comics, Inc. All names, characters,
events and locales in this publication are entirely
fictional. Any resemblance to actual persons (living
or dead), events or places, without satiric intent,
is coincidental.

PRINTED IN USA.

For information regarding the CPSIA on this
printed material call: 203-595-3636 and
provide reference # RICH – 489098.

For international rights and foreign licensing
contact - foreignlicensing@imagecomics.com

STORY Brandon Graham
with Giannis Milonogiannis
and Simon Roy (chapter 1-2, 4-6)
with Farel Dalrymple (chapter 3)

ART Giannis Milonogiannis (chapters 1-2, 4-6)
with Brandon Graham (chapter 4)
Farel Dalrymple (chapter 3)
Simon Roy (chapter 2 title page)
Fil Barlow (chapter 3 & 6 title pages)
Helen Maier (chapter 4 title page)
Boo Cook (chapter 5 title page)

COLORS Joseph Bergin III
with Brandon Graham (chapter 4)
and Giannis Milonogiannis (chapter 4)
COLOR FLATS Charo Solis (chapter 2, 3)

LETTERS Ed Brisson

EDITS Eric Stephenson

COVER Giannis Milonogiannis

PROPHET created by Rob Liefeld

1

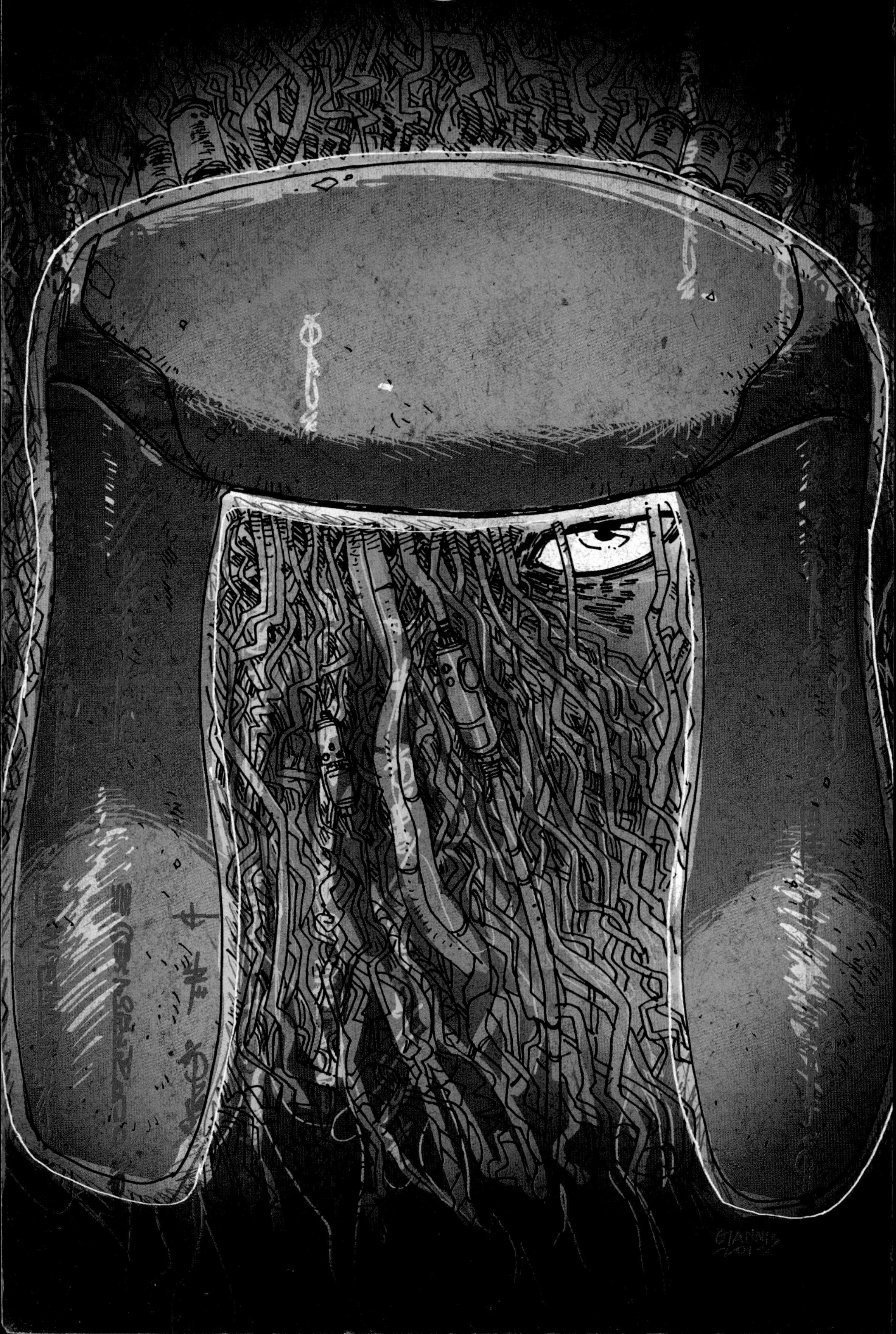

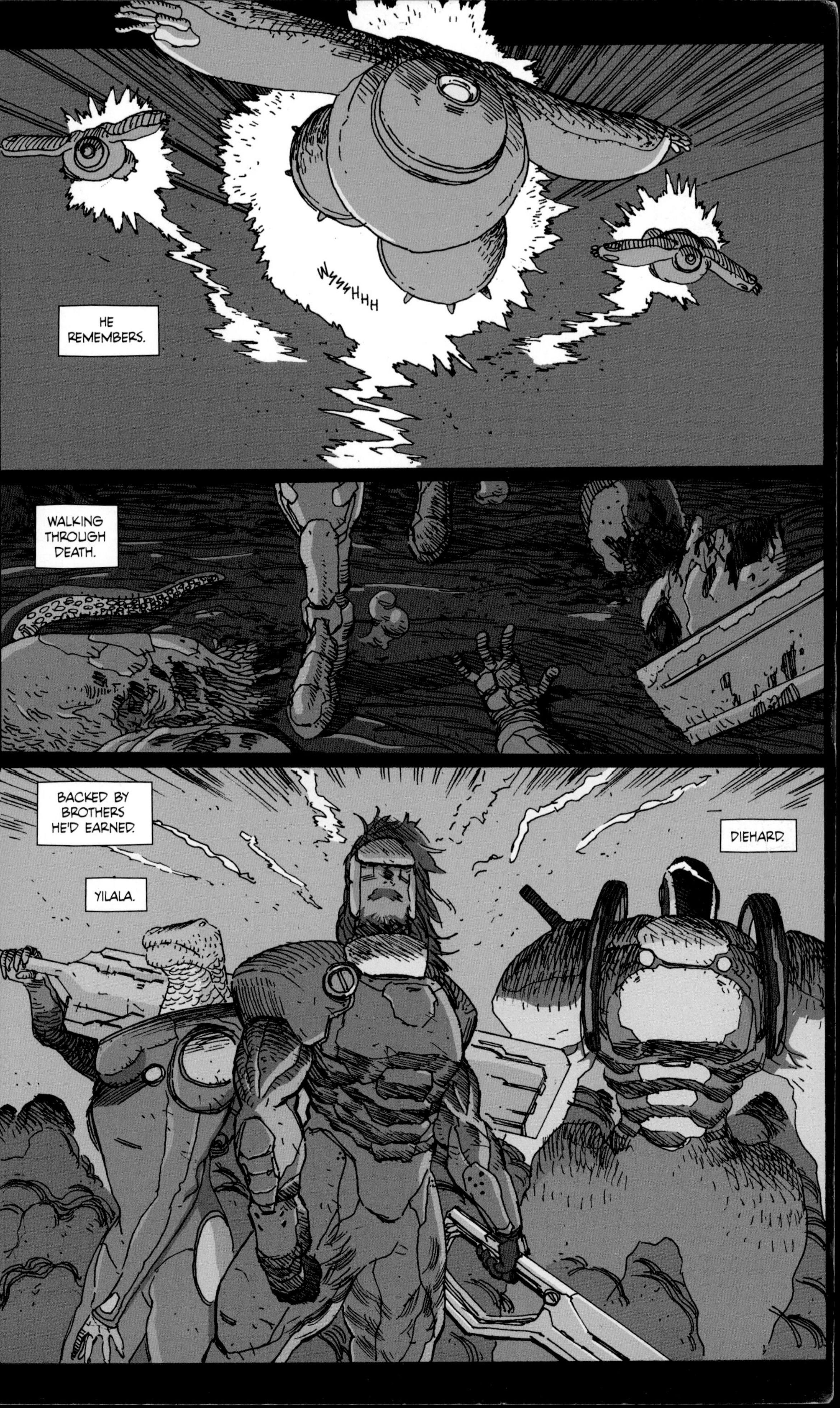

WYYYHHH
HE REMEMBERS.
WALKING THROUGH DEATH.
BACKED BY BROTHERS HE'D EARNED.
YILALA.
DIEHARD.

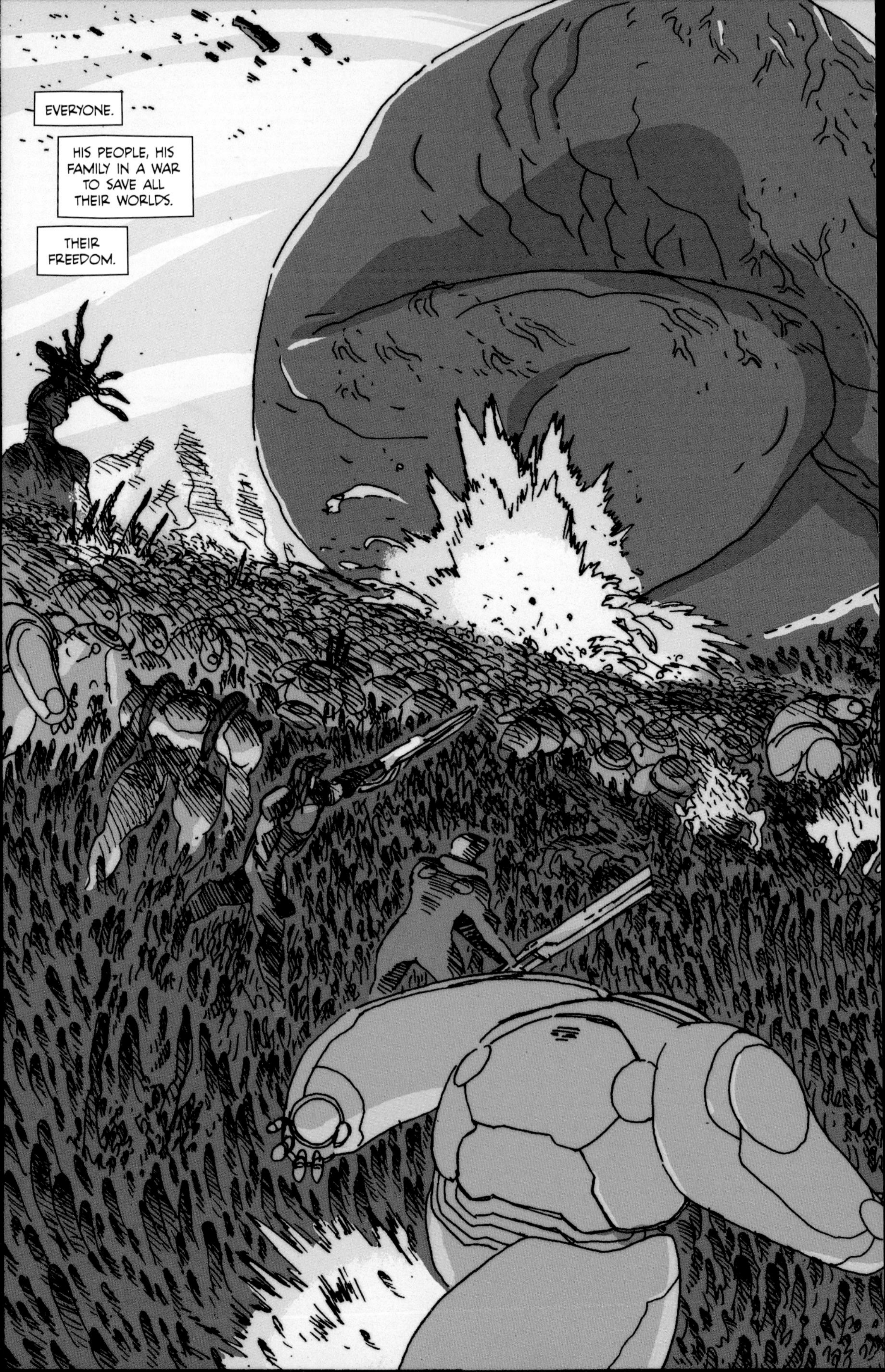
EVERYONE.
HIS PEOPLE, HIS FAMILY IN A WAR TO SAVE ALL THEIR WORLDS.
THEIR FREEDOM.

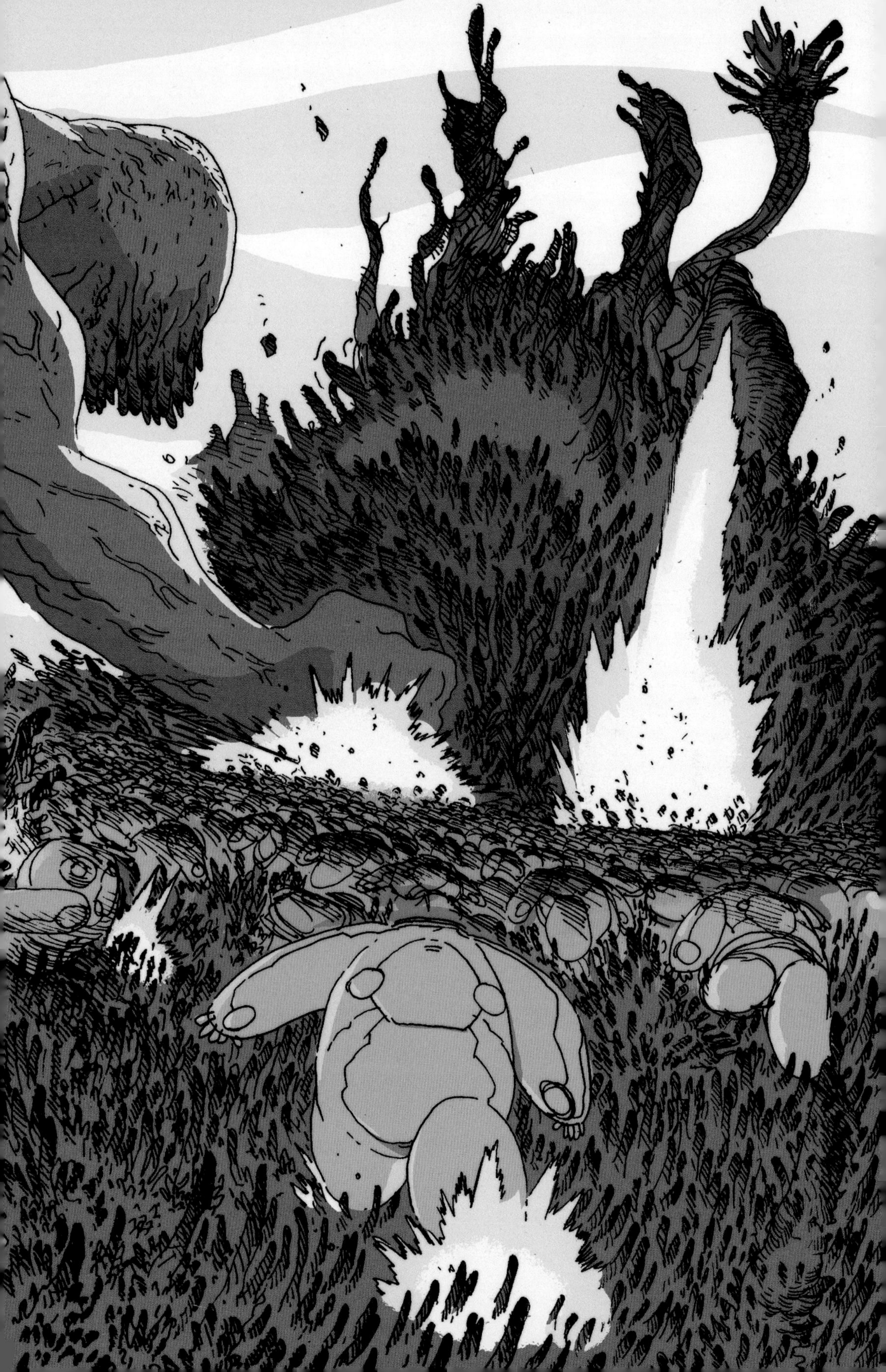

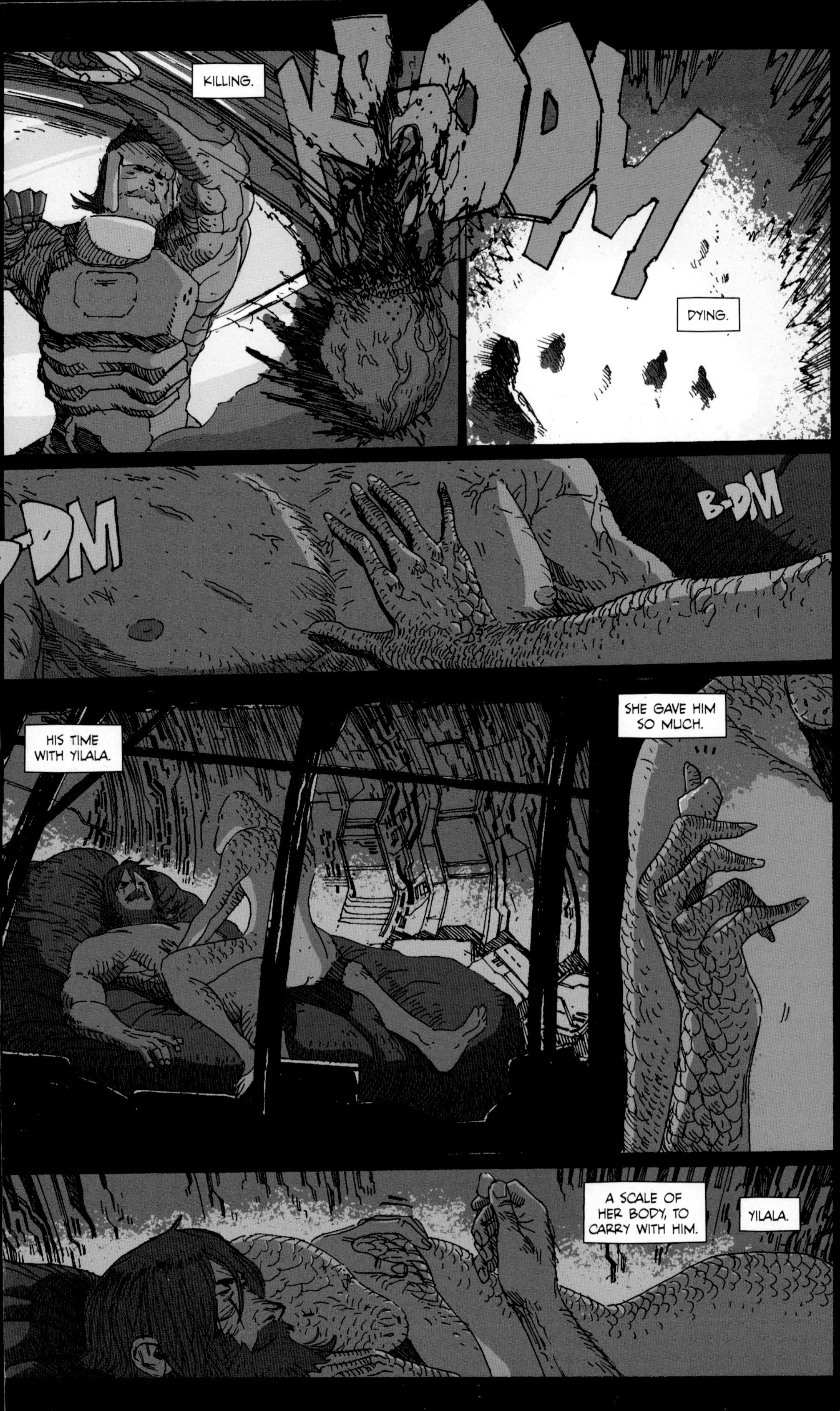
KILLING.
DYING.
B-DM
HIS TIME WITH YILALA.
SHE GAVE HIM SO MUCH.
A SCALE OF HER BODY, TO CARRY WITH HIM.
YILALA.

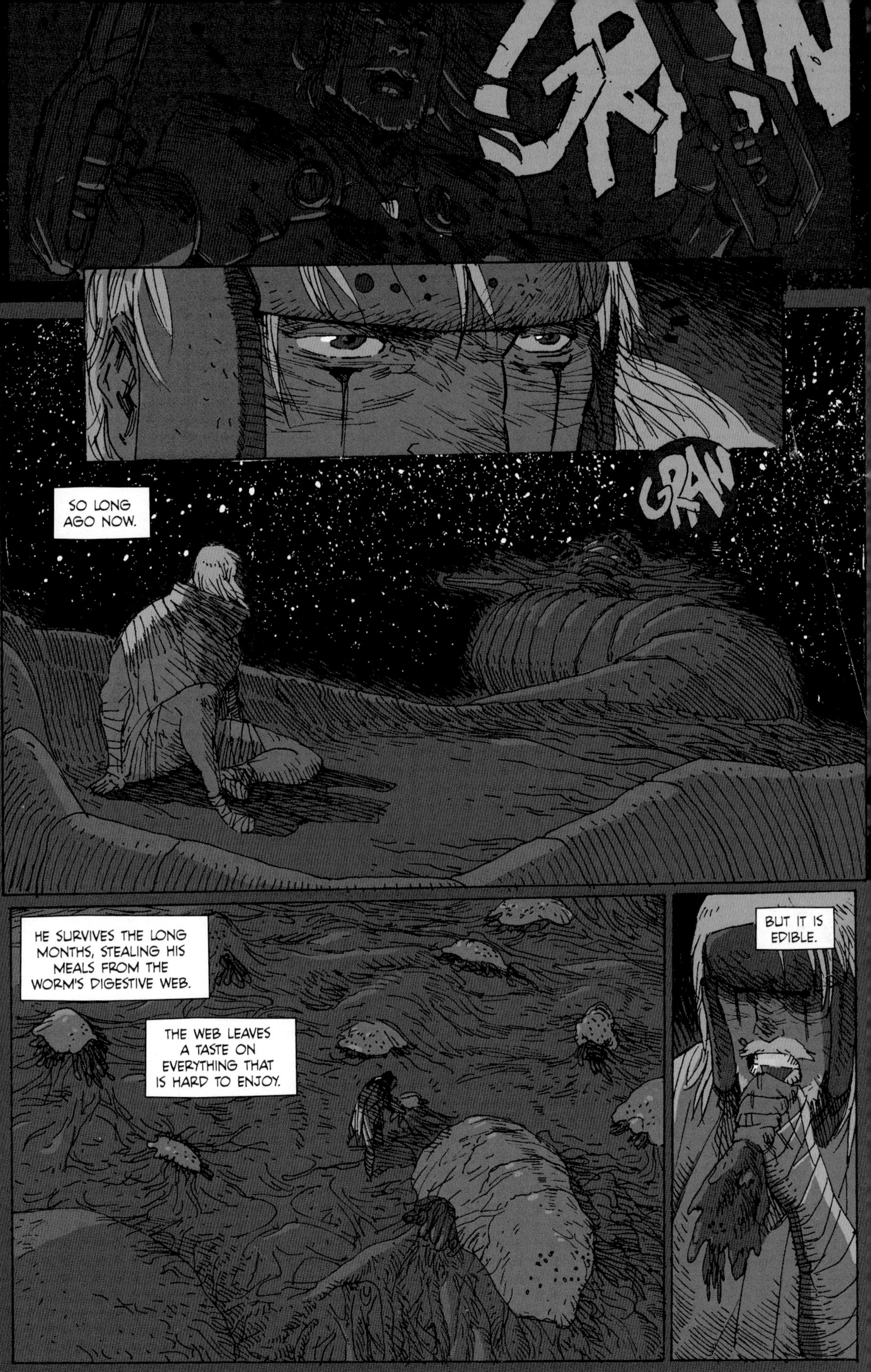
GRAWN
GRAN
SO LONG AGO NOW.
HE SURVIVES THE LONG MONTHS, STEALING HIS MEALS FROM THE WORM'S DIGESTIVE WEB.
THE WEB LEAVES A TASTE ON EVERYTHING THAT IS HARD TO ENJOY.
BUT IT IS EDIBLE.

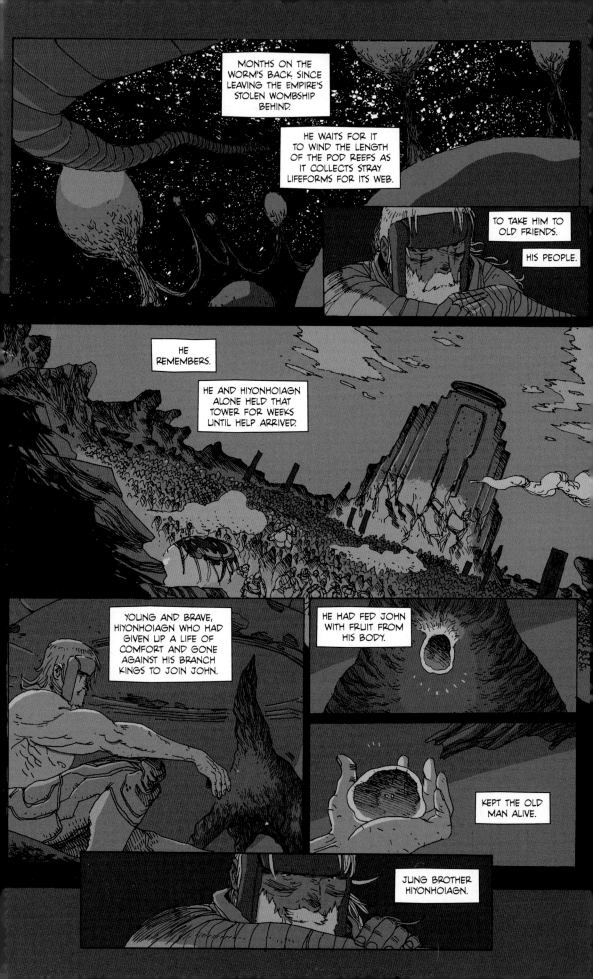

MONTHS ON THE WORM'S BACK SINCE LEAVING THE EMPIRE'S STOLEN WOMBSHIP BEHIND.

HE WAITS FOR IT TO WIND THE LENGTH OF THE POD REEFS AS IT COLLECTS STRAY LIFEFORMS FOR ITS WEB.

TO TAKE HIM TO OLD FRIENDS.

HIS PEOPLE.

HE REMEMBERS.

HE AND HIYONHOIAGN ALONE HELD THAT TOWER FOR WEEKS UNTIL HELP ARRIVED.

YOUNG AND BRAVE, HIYONHOIAGN WHO HAD GIVEN UP A LIFE OF COMFORT AND GONE AGAINST HIS BRANCH KINGS TO JOIN JOHN.

HE HAD FED JOHN WITH FRUIT FROM HIS BODY.

KEPT THE OLD MAN ALIVE.

JUNG BROTHER HIYONHOIAGN.

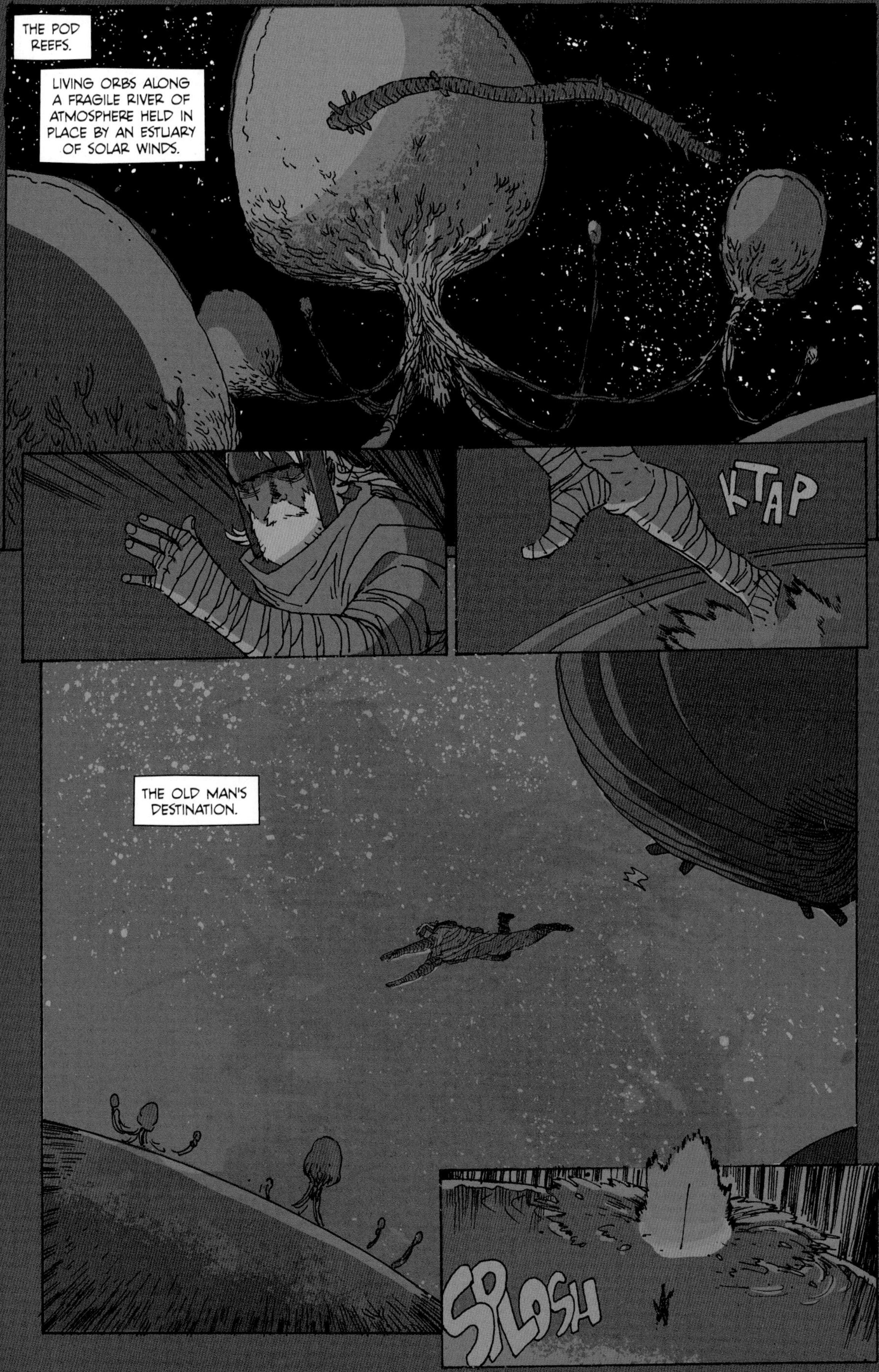
THE POD REEFS.
LIVING ORBS ALONG A FRAGILE RIVER OF ATMOSPHERE HELD IN PLACE BY AN ESTUARY OF SOLAR WINDS.
KTAP
THE OLD MAN'S DESTINATION.
SPLOSH

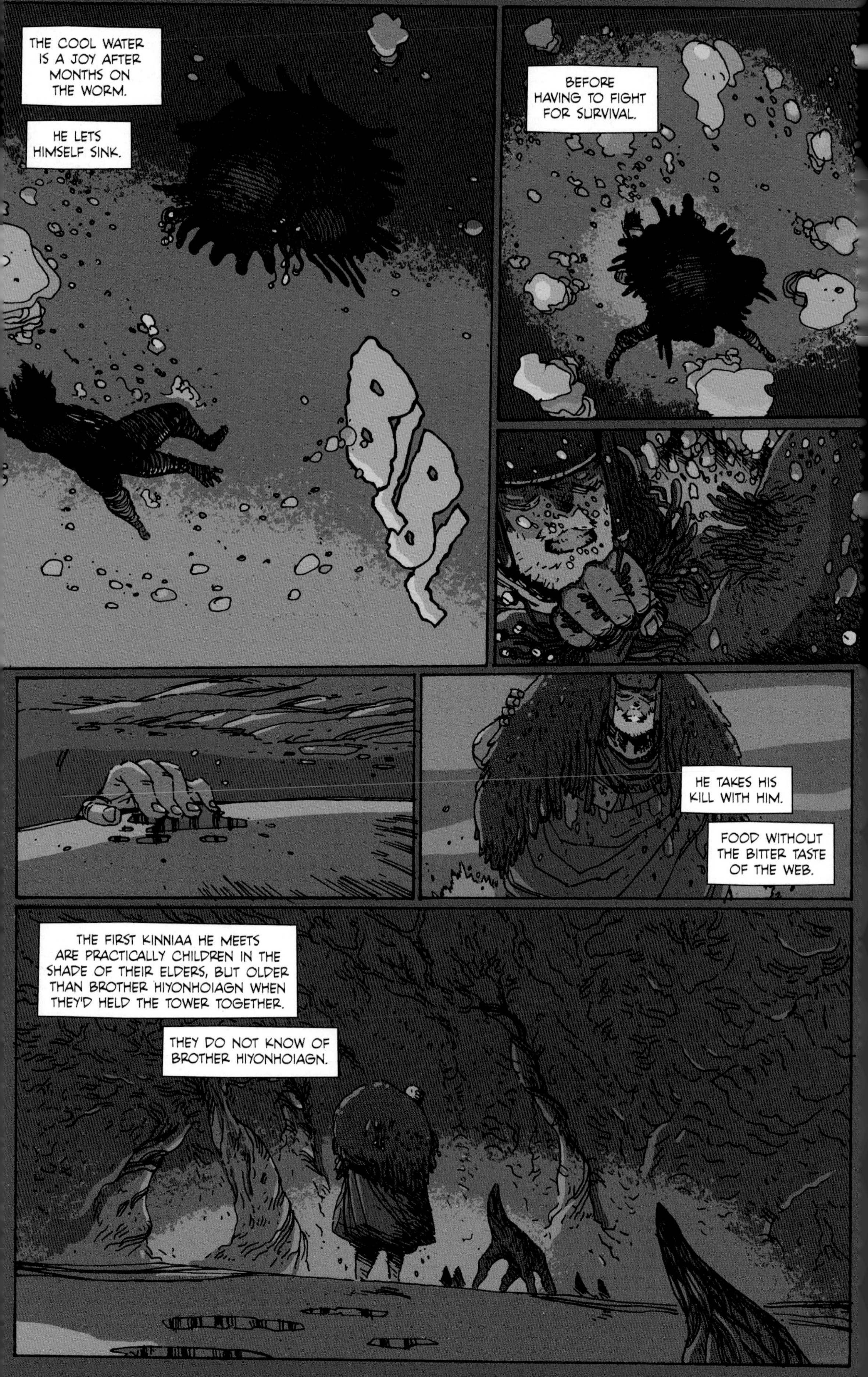
THE COOL WATER IS A JOY AFTER MONTHS ON THE WORM.
HE LETS HIMSELF SINK.
BEFORE HAVING TO FIGHT FOR SURVIVAL.
HE TAKES HIS KILL WITH HIM.
FOOD WITHOUT THE BITTER TASTE OF THE WEB.
THE FIRST KINNIAA HE MEETS ARE PRACTICALLY CHILDREN IN THE SHADE OF THEIR ELDERS, BUT OLDER THAN BROTHER HIYONHOIAGN WHEN THEY'D HELD THE TOWER TOGETHER.
THEY DO NOT KNOW OF BROTHER HIYONHOIAGN.

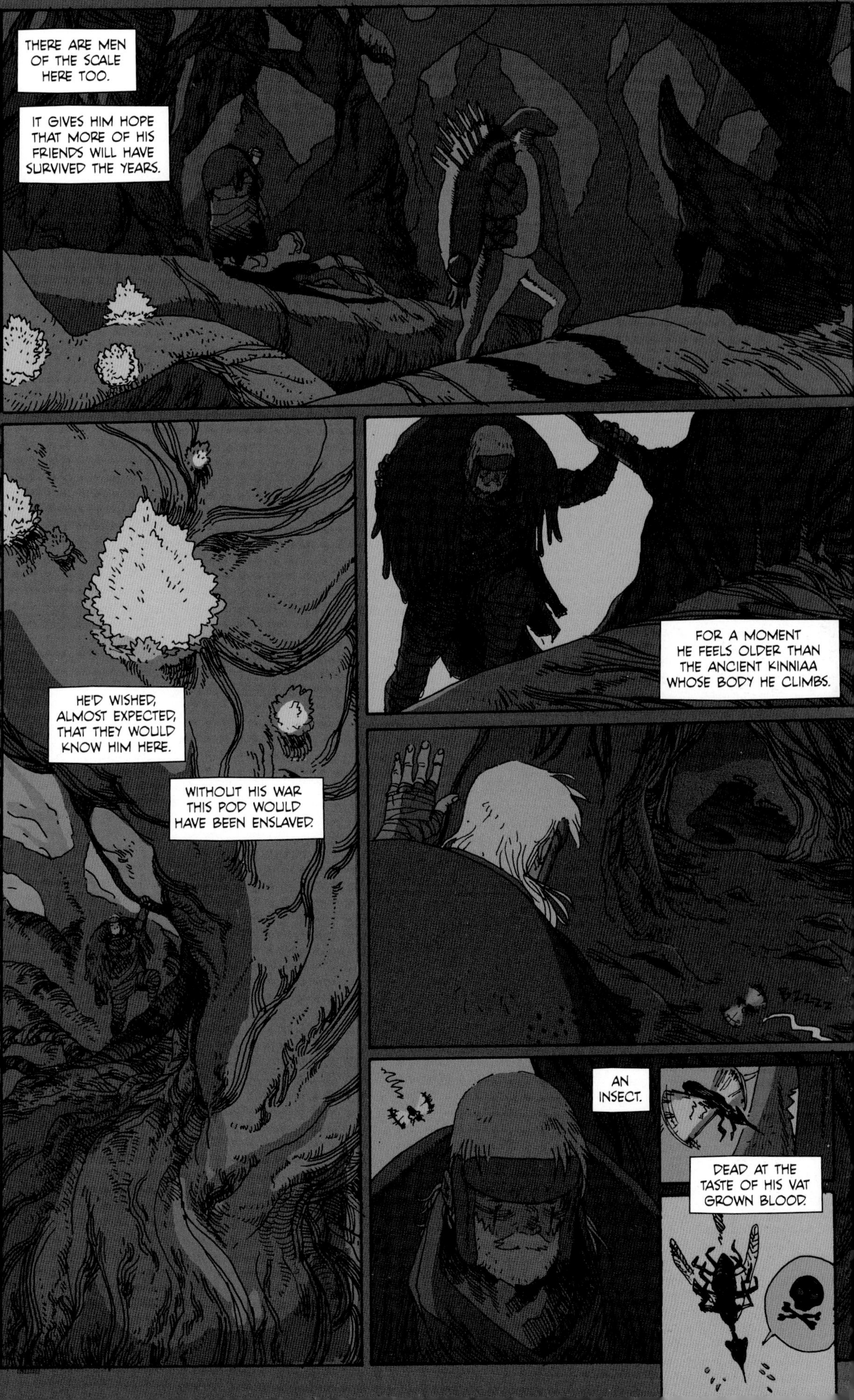
THERE ARE MEN OF THE SCALE HERE TOO.
IT GIVES HIM HOPE THAT MORE OF HIS FRIENDS WILL HAVE SURVIVED THE YEARS.
HE'D WISHED, ALMOST EXPECTED, THAT THEY WOULD KNOW HIM HERE.
WITHOUT HIS WAR THIS POD WOULD HAVE BEEN ENSLAVED.
FOR A MOMENT HE FEELS OLDER THAN THE ANCIENT KINNIAA WHOSE BODY HE CLIMBS.
AN INSECT.
DEAD AT THE TASTE OF HIS VAT GROWN BLOOD.

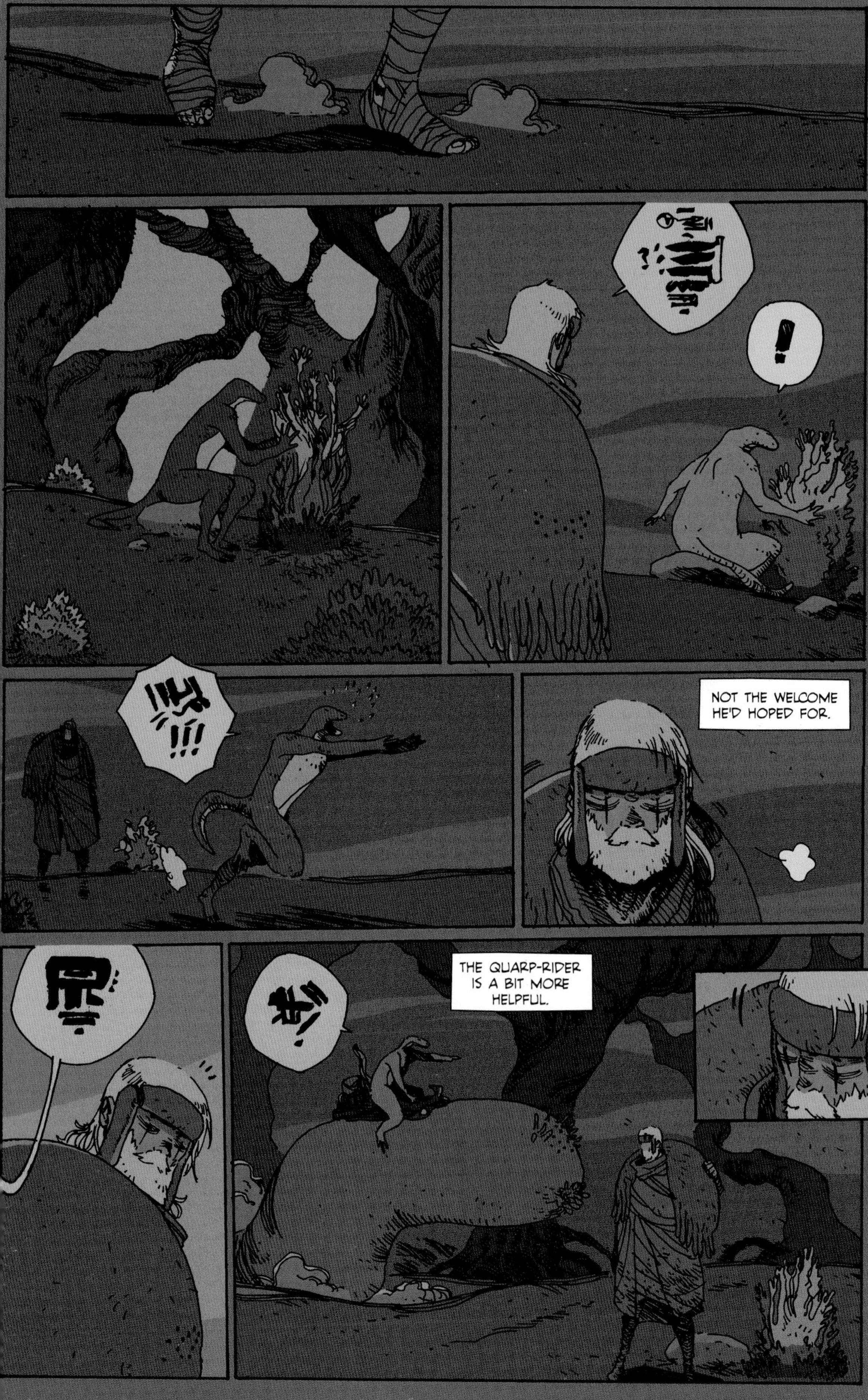
NOT THE WELCOME HE'D HOPED FOR.
THE QUARP-RIDER IS A BIT MORE HELPFUL.

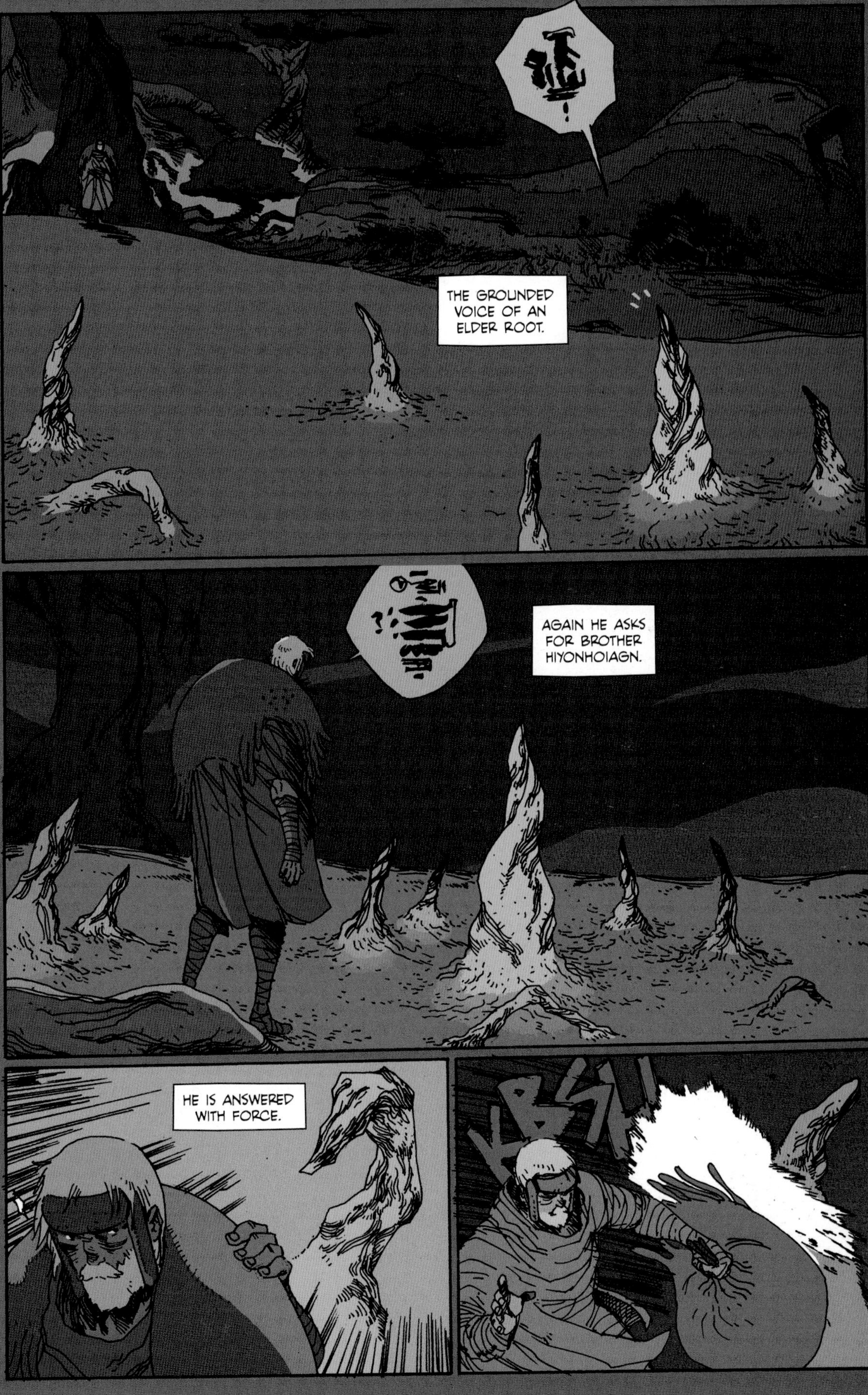
THE GROUNDED VOICE OF AN ELDER ROOT.
AGAIN HE ASKS FOR BROTHER HIYONHOIAGN.
HE IS ANSWERED WITH FORCE.
KBSH

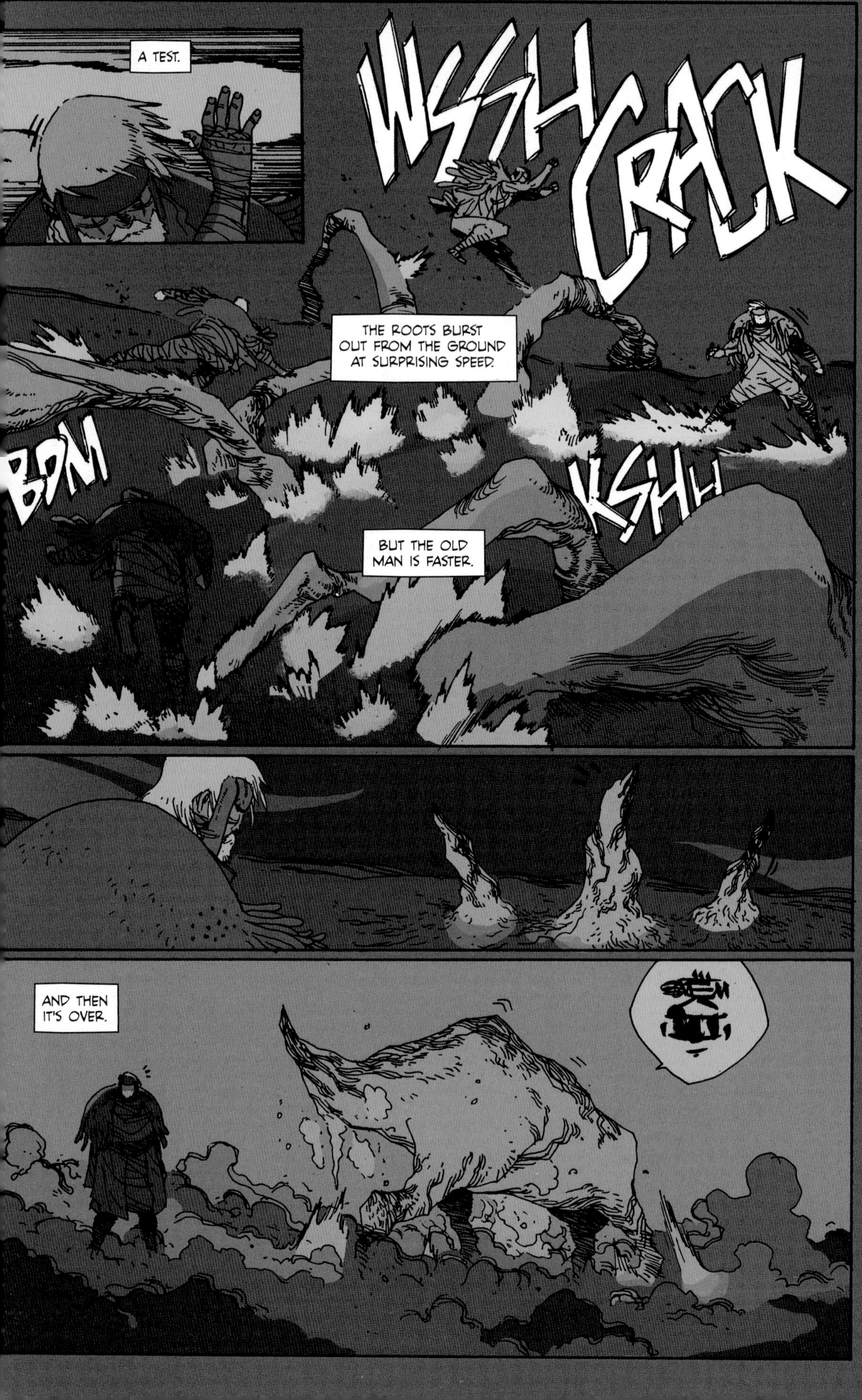
A TEST.
WSSH
CRACK
THE ROOTS BURST OUT FROM THE GROUND AT SURPRISING SPEED.
BDM
KSHH
BUT THE OLD MAN IS FASTER.
AND THEN IT'S OVER.

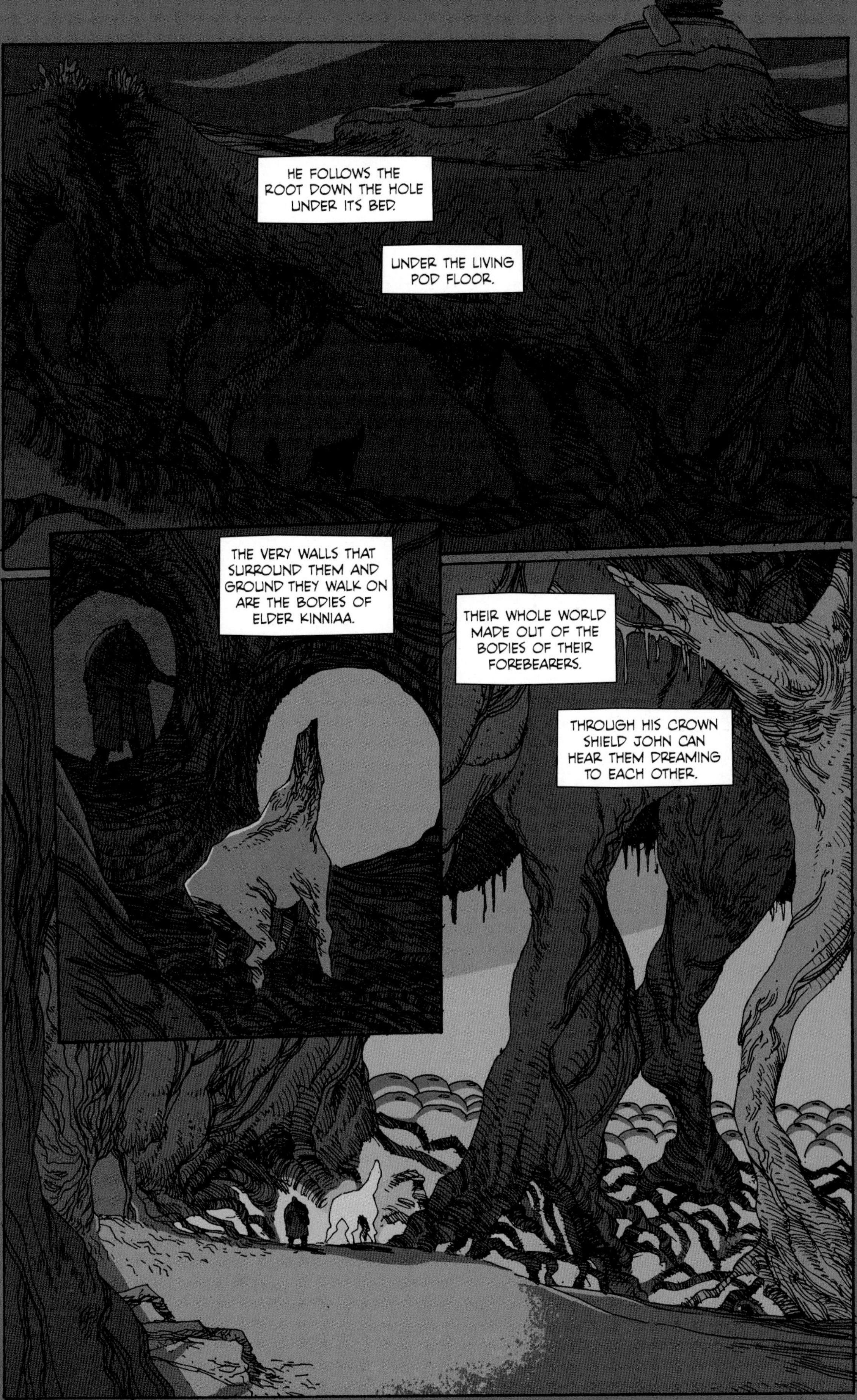
HE FOLLOWS THE ROOT DOWN THE HOLE UNDER ITS BED.
UNDER THE LIVING POD FLOOR.
THE VERY WALLS THAT SURROUND THEM AND GROUND THEY WALK ON ARE THE BODIES OF ELDER KINNIAA.
THEIR WHOLE WORLD MADE OUT OF THE BODIES OF THEIR FOREBEARERS.
THROUGH HIS CROWN SHIELD JOHN CAN HEAR THEM DREAMING TO EACH OTHER.

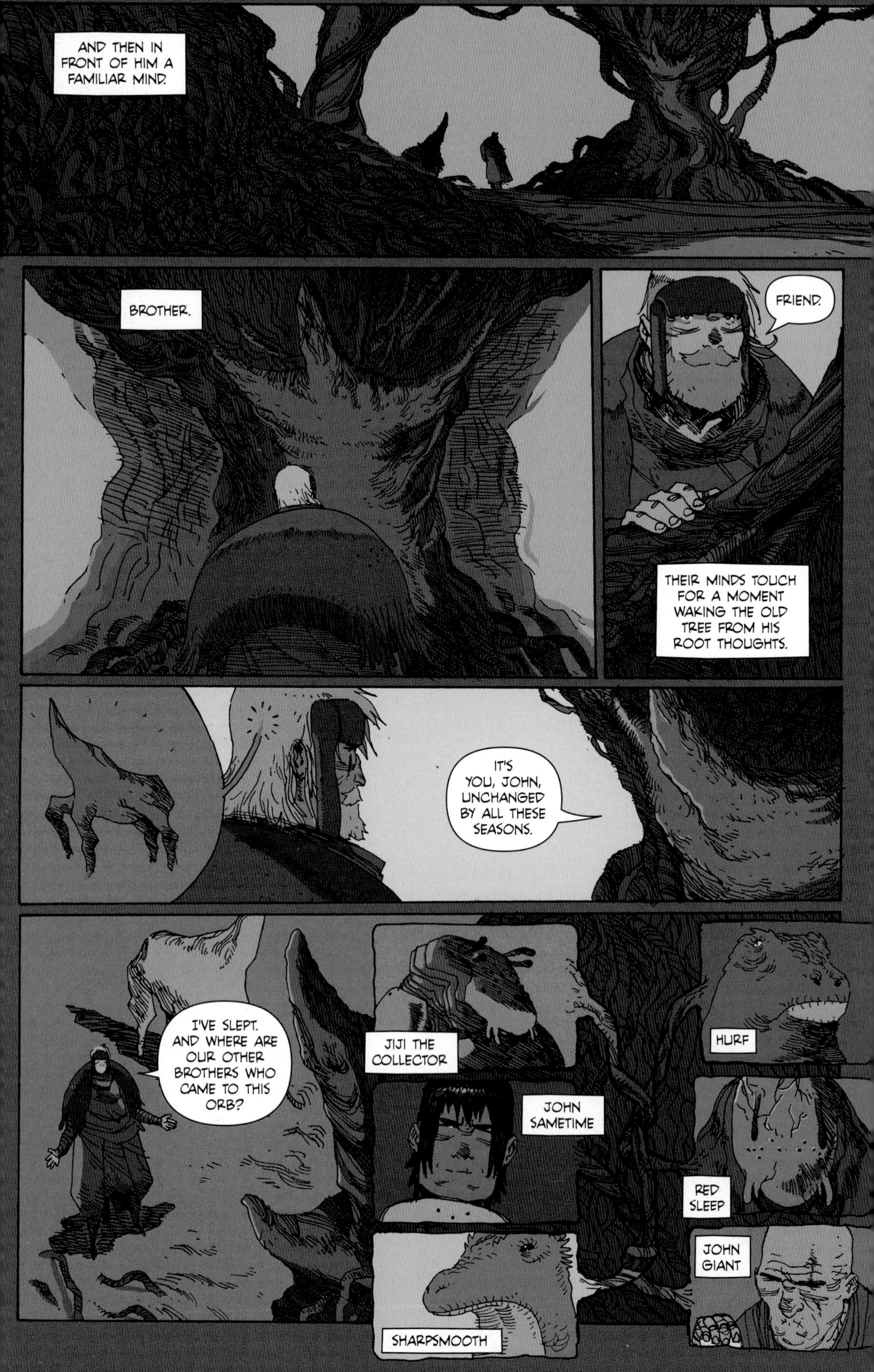
AND THEN IN FRONT OF HIM A FAMILIAR MIND.
BROTHER.
FRIEND.
THEIR MINDS TOUCH FOR A MOMENT WAKING THE OLD TREE FROM HIS ROOT THOUGHTS.
IT'S YOU, JOHN, UNCHANGED BY ALL THESE SEASONS.
I'VE SLEPT. AND WHERE ARE OUR OTHER BROTHERS WHO CAME TO THIS ORB?
JIJI THE COLLECTOR
HURF
JOHN SAMETIME
RED SLEEP
JOHN GIANT
SHARPSMOOTH

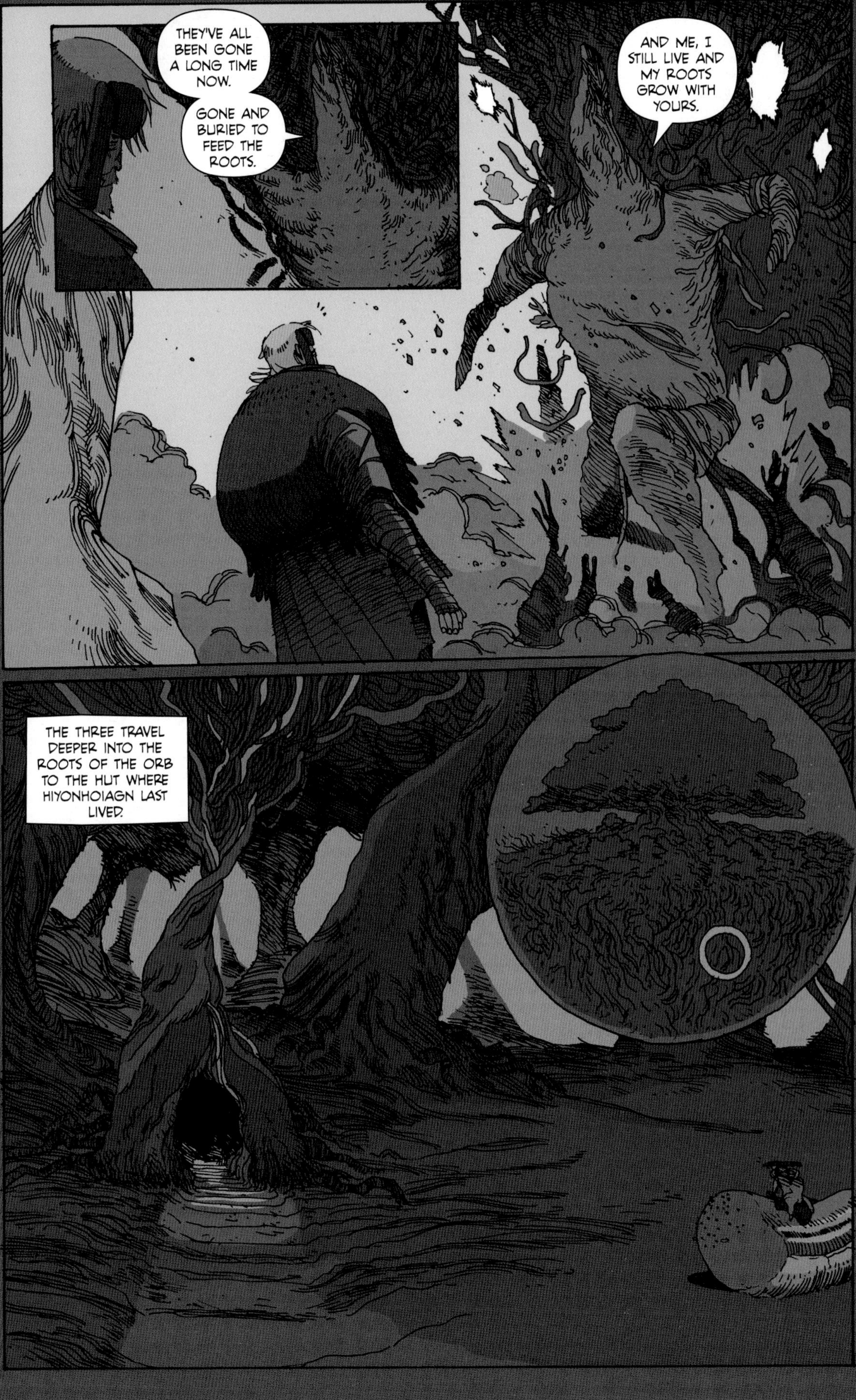
THEY'VE ALL BEEN GONE A LONG TIME NOW.
GONE AND BURIED TO FEED THE ROOTS.
AND ME, I STILL LIVE AND MY ROOTS GROW WITH YOURS.
THE THREE TRAVEL DEEPER INTO THE ROOTS OF THE ORB TO THE HUT WHERE HIYONHOIAGN LAST LIVED.

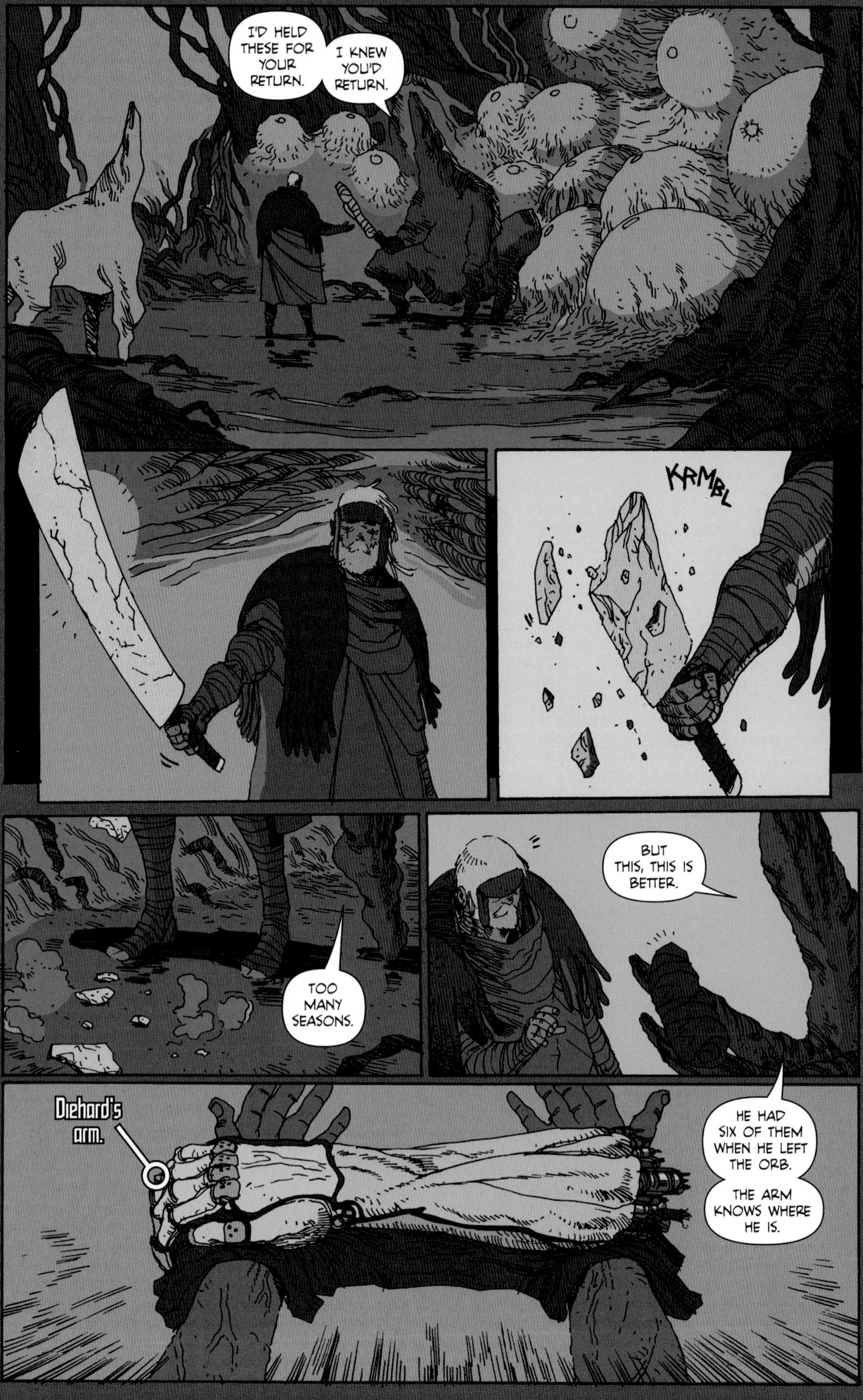
I'D HELD THESE FOR YOUR RETURN.
I KNEW YOU'D RETURN.
KRMBL
TOO MANY SEASONS.
BUT THIS, THIS IS BETTER.
Diehard's arm.
HE HAD SIX OF THEM WHEN HE LEFT THE ORB.
THE ARM KNOWS WHERE HE IS.

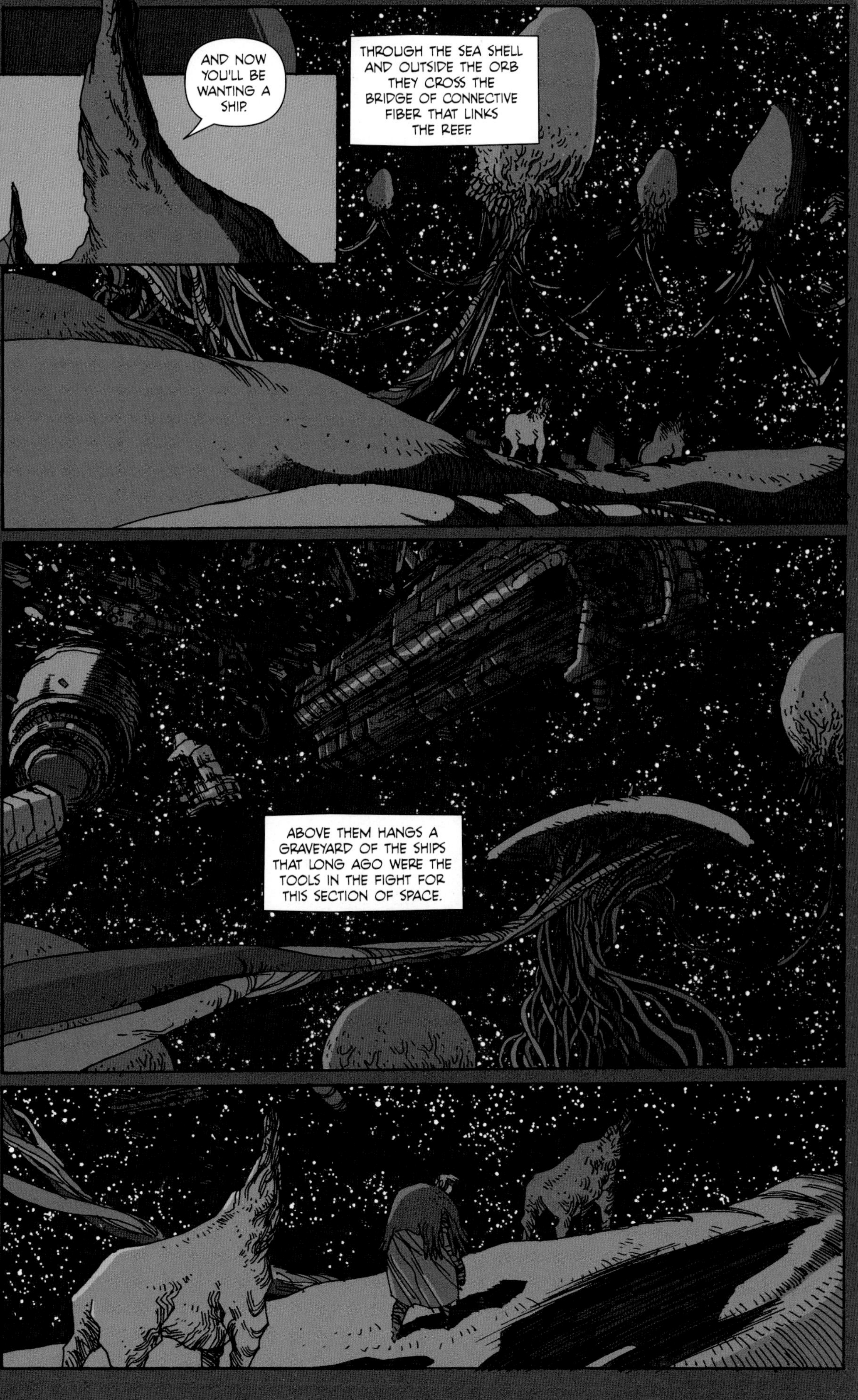
AND NOW YOU'LL BE WANTING A SHIP.
THROUGH THE SEA SHELL AND OUTSIDE THE ORB THEY CROSS THE BRIDGE OF CONNECTIVE FIBER THAT LINKS THE REEF.
ABOVE THEM HANGS A GRAVEYARD OF THE SHIPS THAT LONG AGO WERE THE TOOLS IN THE FIGHT FOR THIS SECTION OF SPACE.

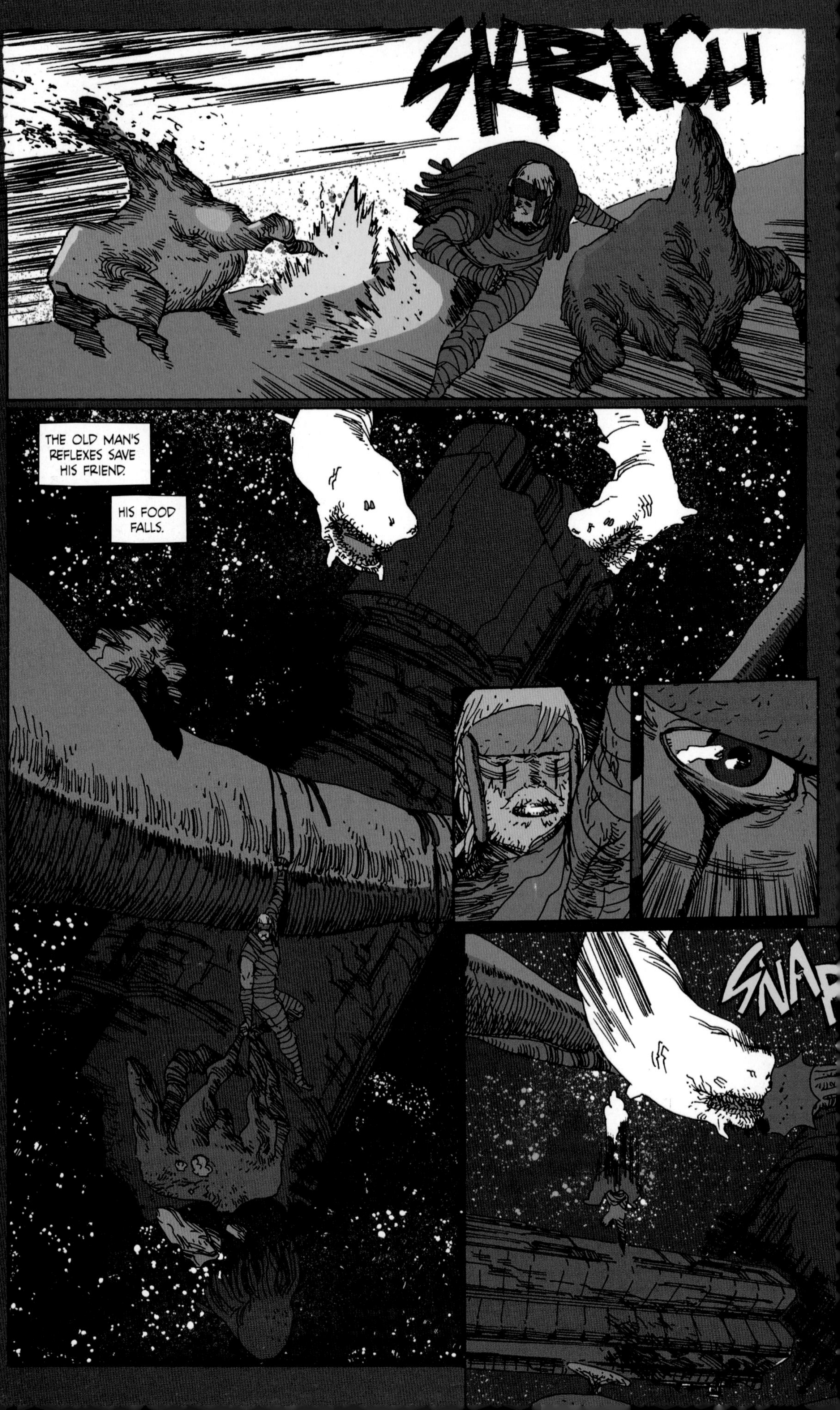
SKRNCH
THE OLD MAN'S REFLEXES SAVE HIS FRIEND.
HIS FOOD FALLS.
SNAP

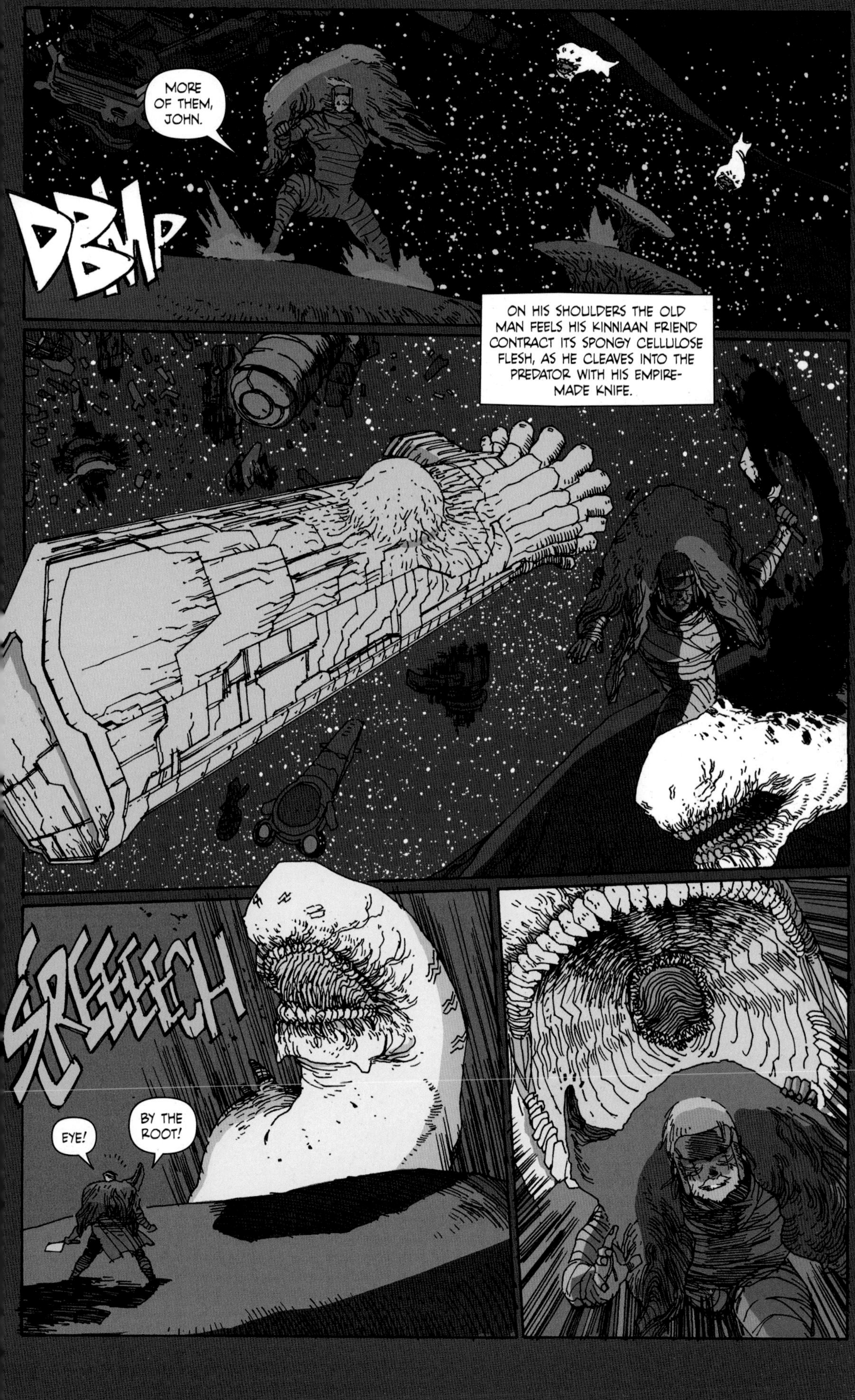
MORE OF THEM, JOHN.
DBUMP
ON HIS SHOULDERS THE OLD MAN FEELS HIS KINNIAAN FRIEND CONTRACT ITS SPONGY CELLULOSE FLESH, AS HE CLEAVES INTO THE PREDATOR WITH HIS EMPIRE-MADE KNIFE.
SREEECH
EYE!
BY THE ROOT!

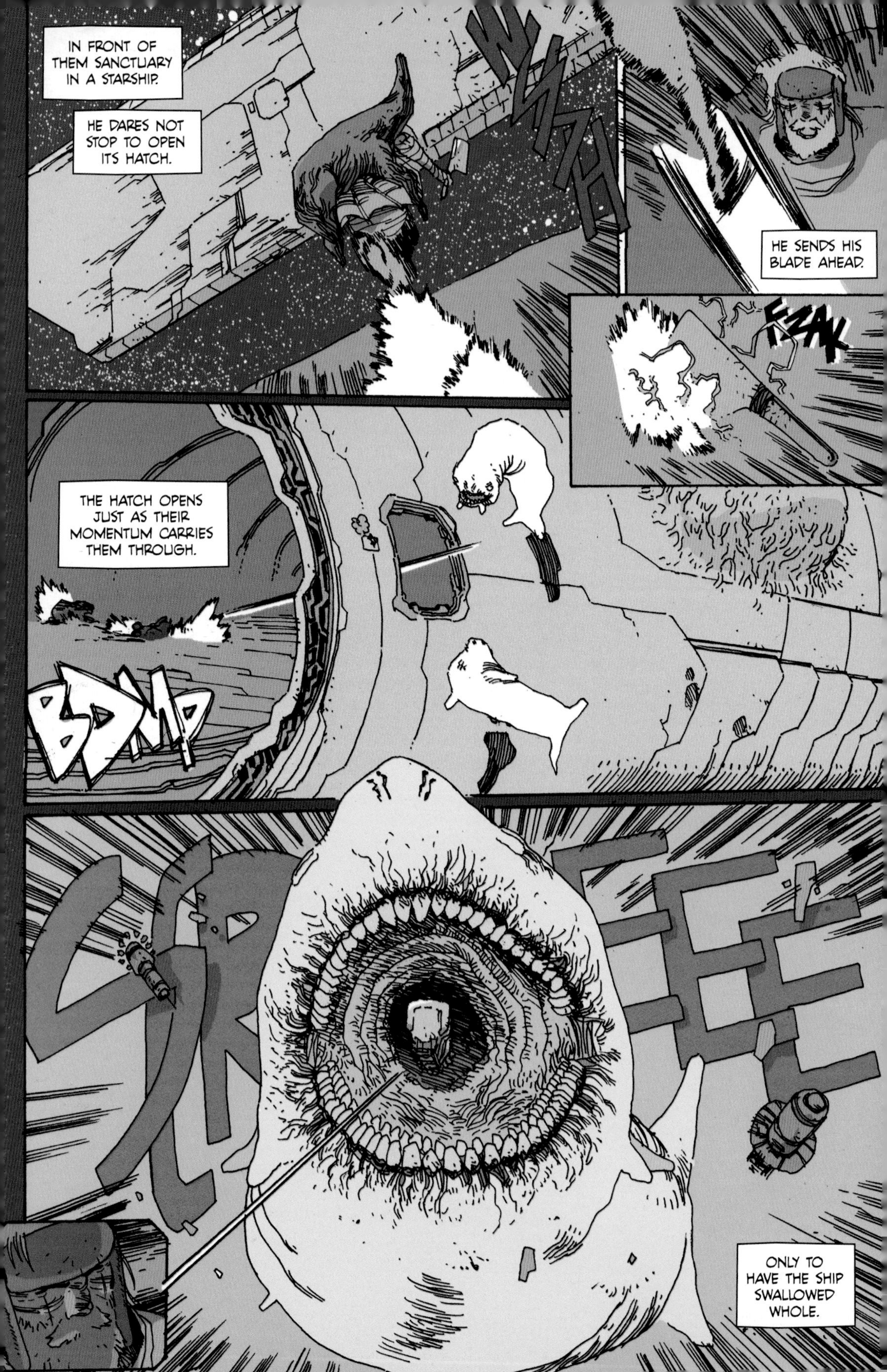
IN FRONT OF THEM SANCTUARY IN A STARSHIP.
HE DARES NOT STOP TO OPEN ITS HATCH.
WHSSH
HE SENDS HIS BLADE AHEAD.
FZAK
THE HATCH OPENS JUST AS THEIR MOMENTUM CARRIES THEM THROUGH.
BDMP
ONLY TO HAVE THE SHIP SWALLOWED WHOLE.

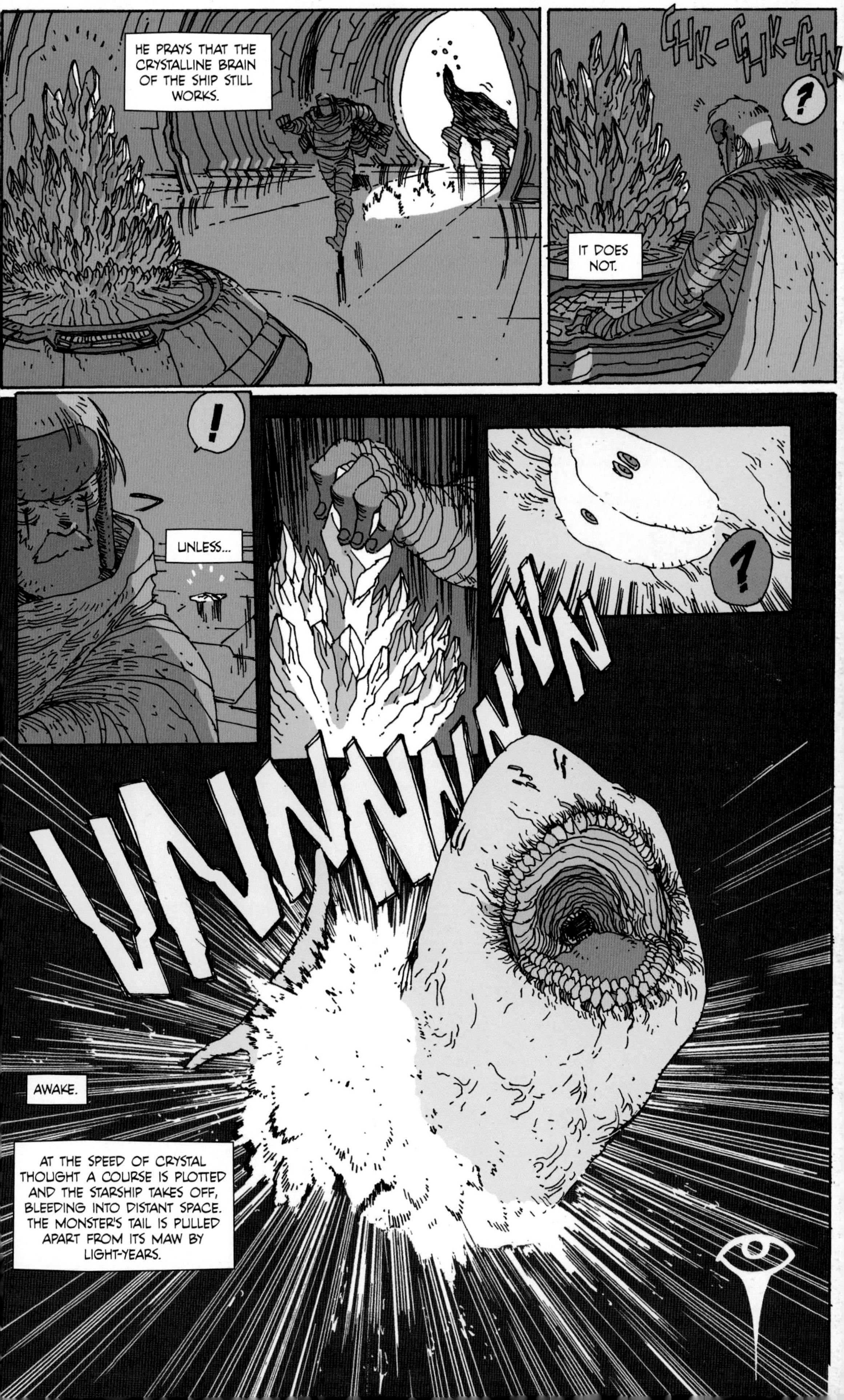
HE PRAYS THAT THE CRYSTALLINE BRAIN OF THE SHIP STILL WORKS.
CHK-CHK-CHK
?
IT DOES NOT.
!
UNLESS...
?
VNNNNNNNN
AWAKE.
AT THE SPEED OF CRYSTAL THOUGHT A COURSE IS PLOTTED AND THE STARSHIP TAKES OFF, BLEEDING INTO DISTANT SPACE. THE MONSTER'S TAIL IS PULLED APART FROM ITS MAW BY LIGHT-YEARS.

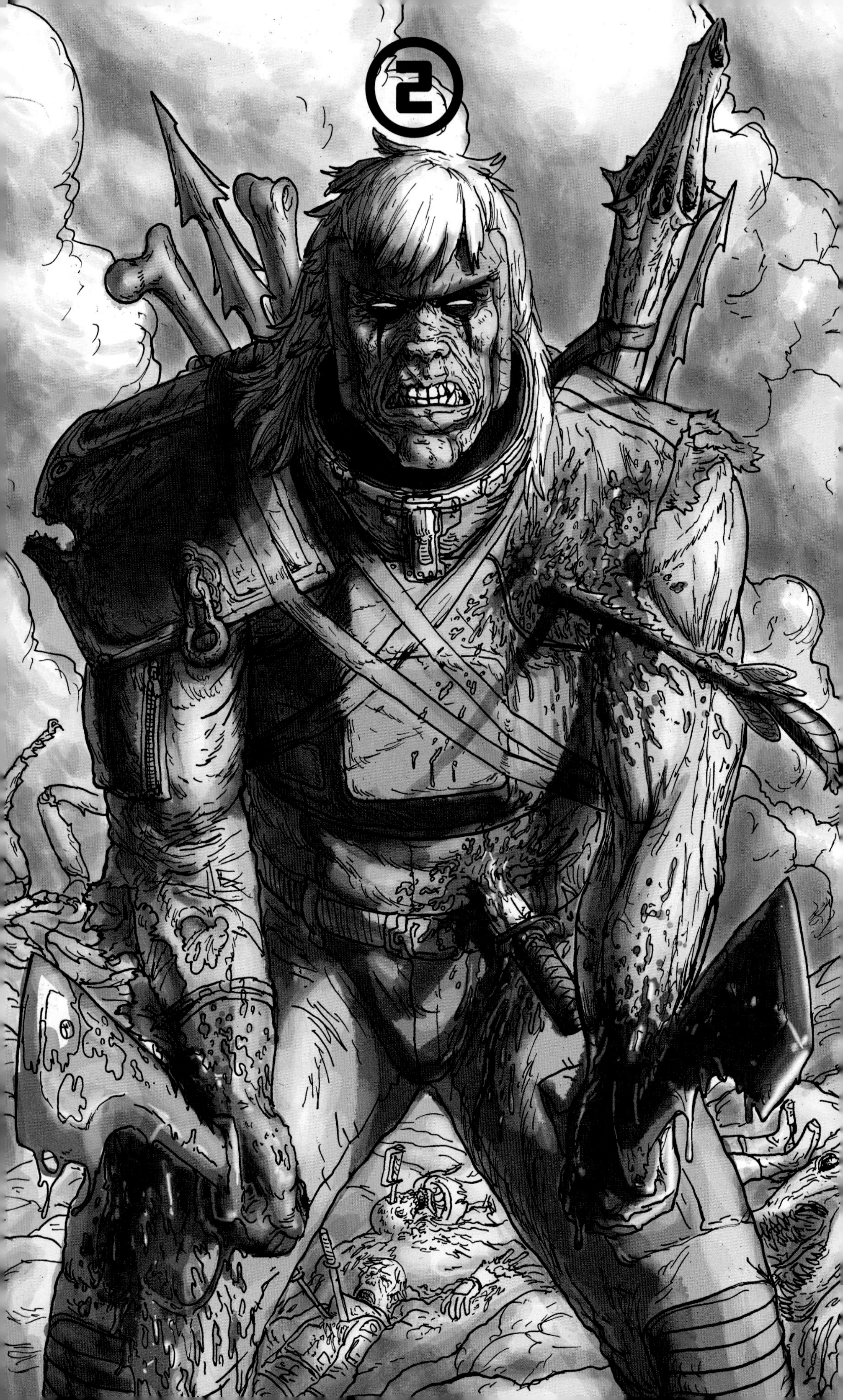
2

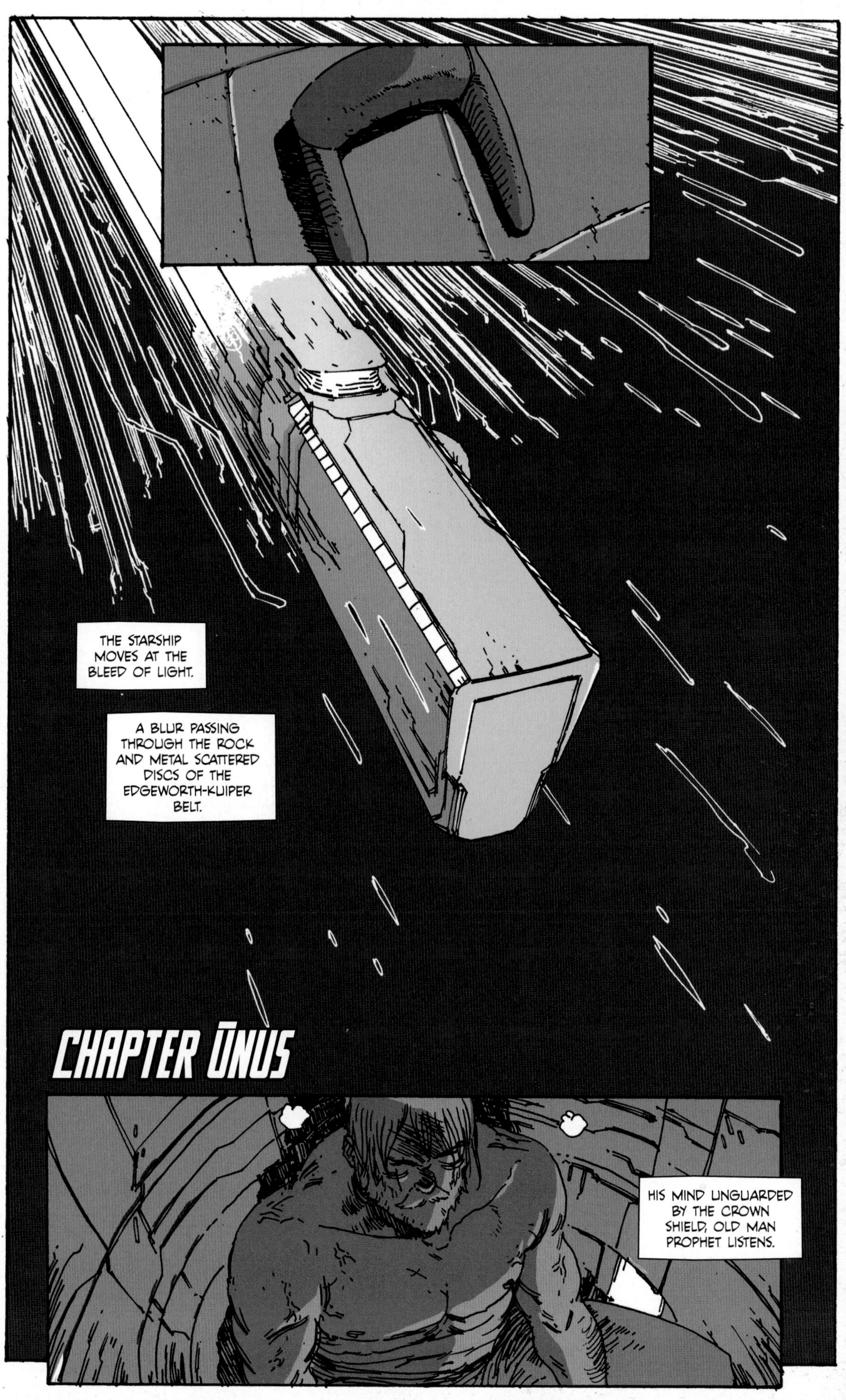
THE STARSHIP MOVES AT THE BLEED OF LIGHT.
A BLUR PASSING THROUGH THE ROCK AND METAL SCATTERED DISCS OF THE EDGEWORTH-KUIPER BELT.
CHAPTER ŪNUS
HIS MIND UNGUARDED BY THE CROWN SHIELD, OLD MAN PROPHET LISTENS.

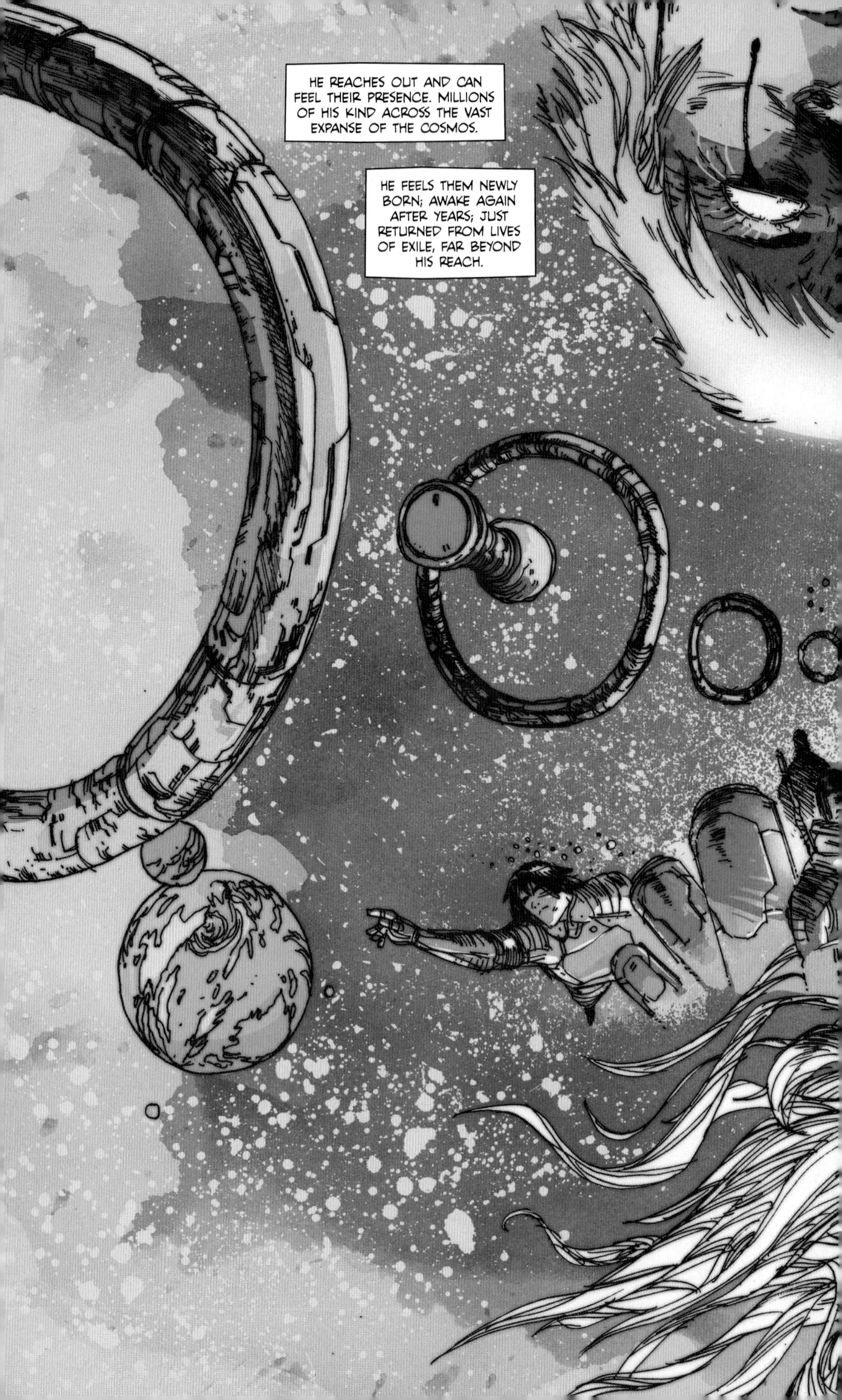
HE REACHES OUT AND CAN FEEL THEIR PRESENCE. MILLIONS OF HIS KIND ACROSS THE VAST EXPANSE OF THE COSMOS.
HE FEELS THEM NEWLY BORN; AWAKE AGAIN AFTER YEARS; JUST RETURNED FROM LIVES OF EXILE, FAR BEYOND HIS REACH.

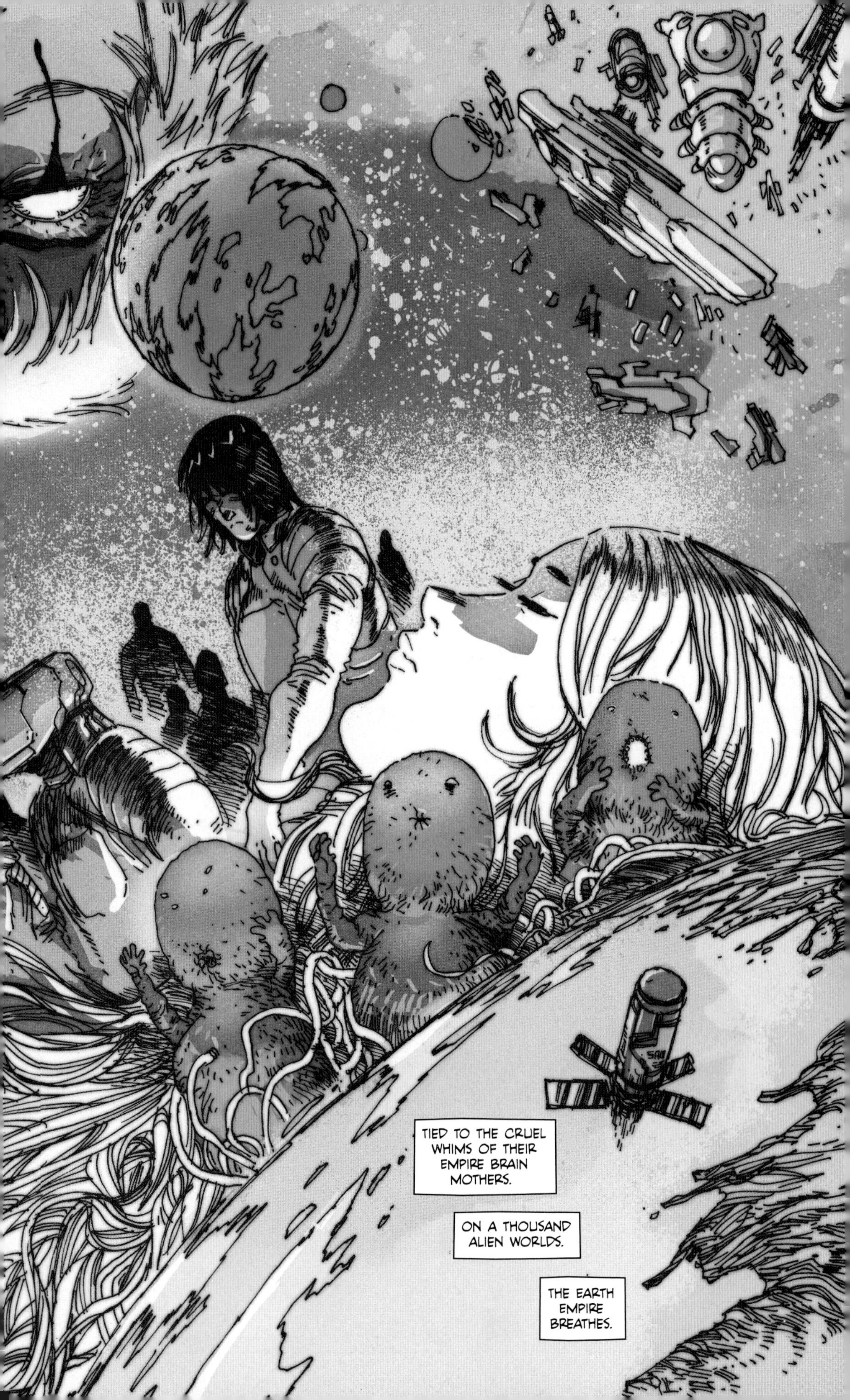
TIED TO THE CRUEL WHIMS OF THEIR EMPIRE BRAIN MOTHERS.
ON A THOUSAND ALIEN WORLDS.
THE EARTH EMPIRE BREATHES.

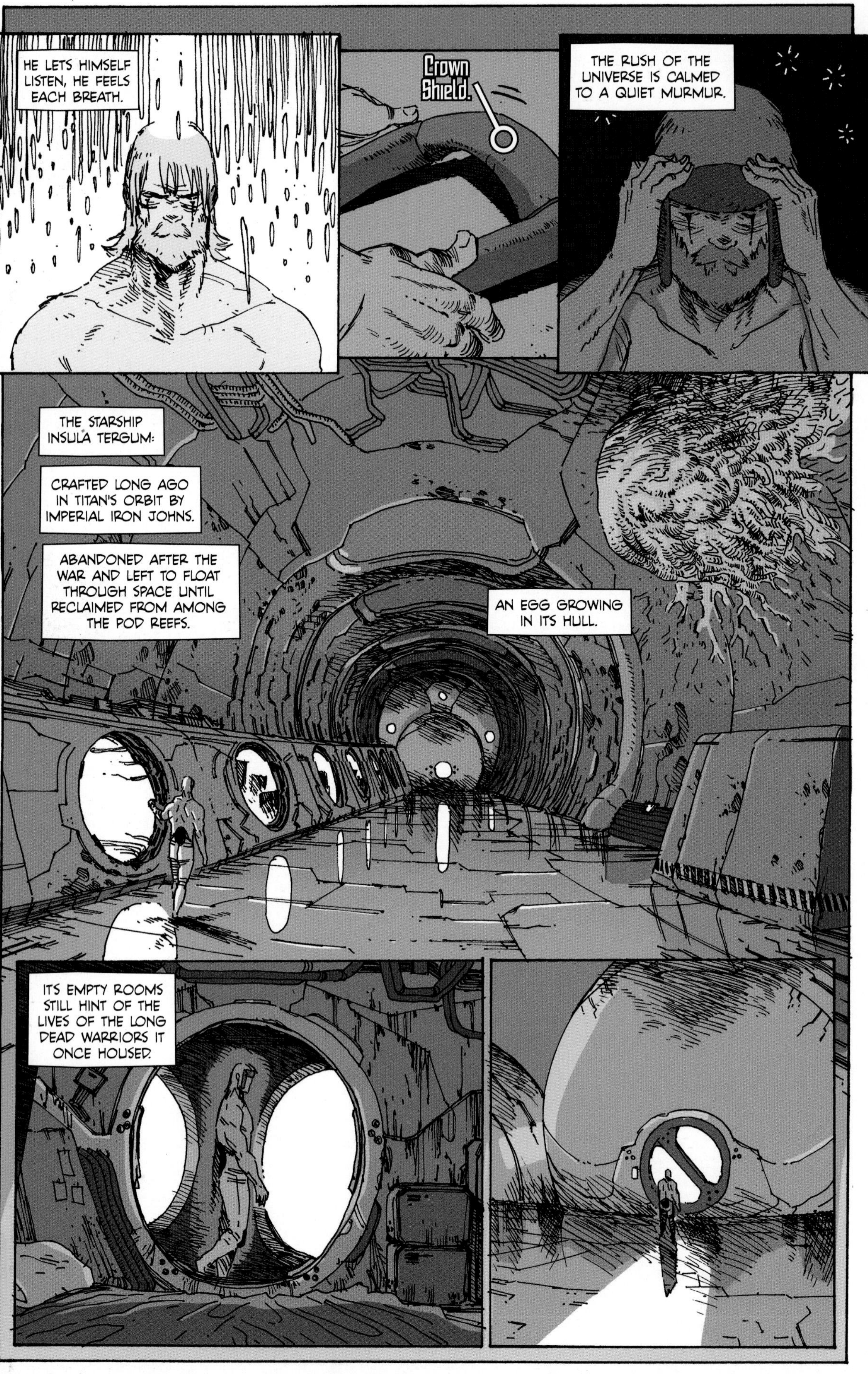
HE LETS HIMSELF LISTEN, HE FEELS EACH BREATH.
Crown Shield.
THE RUSH OF THE UNIVERSE IS CALMED TO A QUIET MURMUR.
THE STARSHIP INSULA TERGUM:
CRAFTED LONG AGO IN TITAN'S ORBIT BY IMPERIAL IRON JOHNS.
ABANDONED AFTER THE WAR AND LEFT TO FLOAT THROUGH SPACE UNTIL RECLAIMED FROM AMONG THE POD REEFS.
AN EGG GROWING IN ITS HULL.
ITS EMPTY ROOMS STILL HINT OF THE LIVES OF THE LONG DEAD WARRIORS IT ONCE HOUSED.

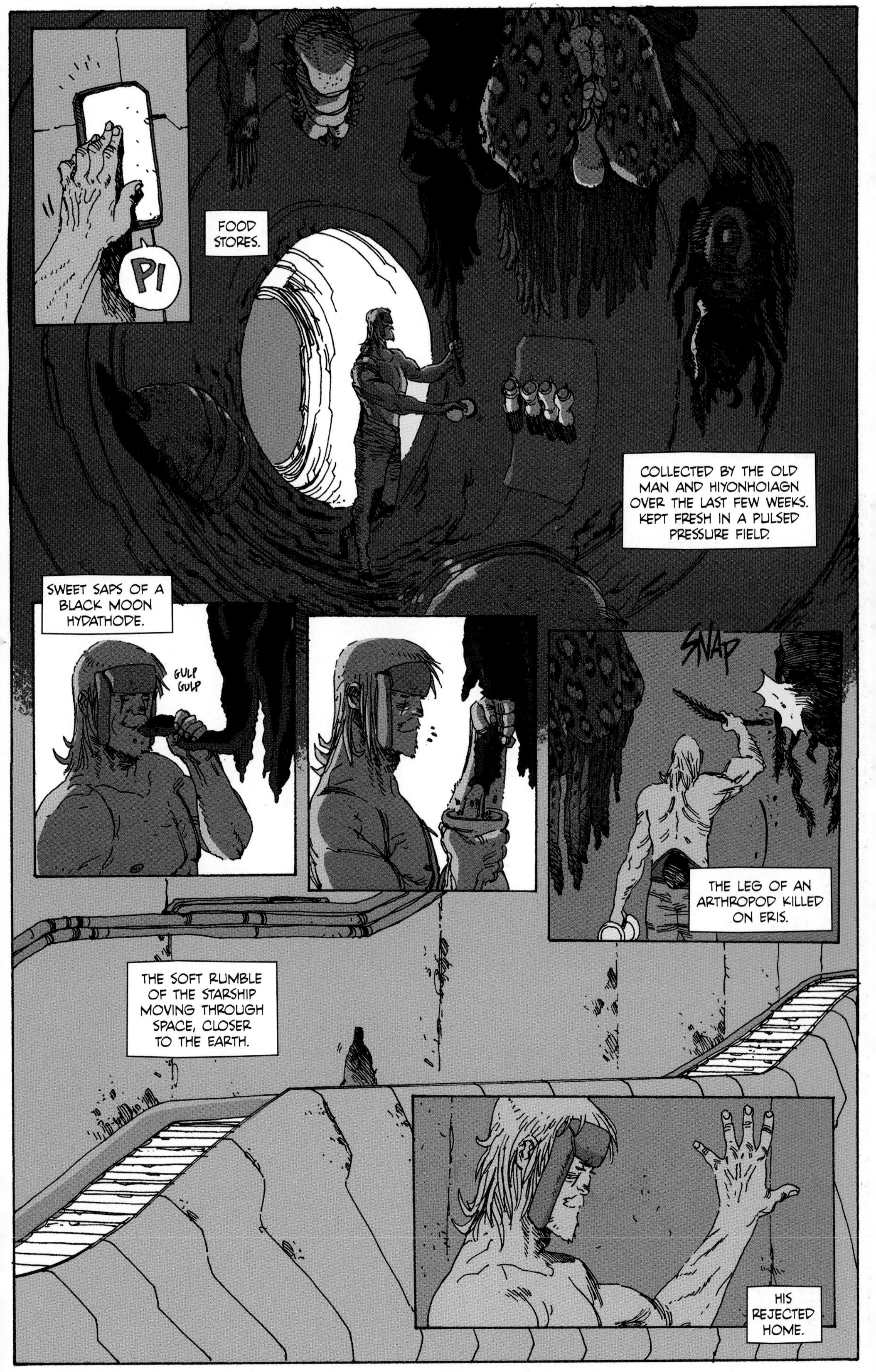
PI
FOOD STORES.
COLLECTED BY THE OLD MAN AND HIYONHOIAGN OVER THE LAST FEW WEEKS. KEPT FRESH IN A PULSED PRESSURE FIELD.
SWEET SAPS OF A BLACK MOON HYDATHODE.
GULP GULP
SNAP
THE LEG OF AN ARTHROPOD KILLED ON ERIS.
THE SOFT RUMBLE OF THE STARSHIP MOVING THROUGH SPACE, CLOSER TO THE EARTH.
HIS REJECTED HOME.

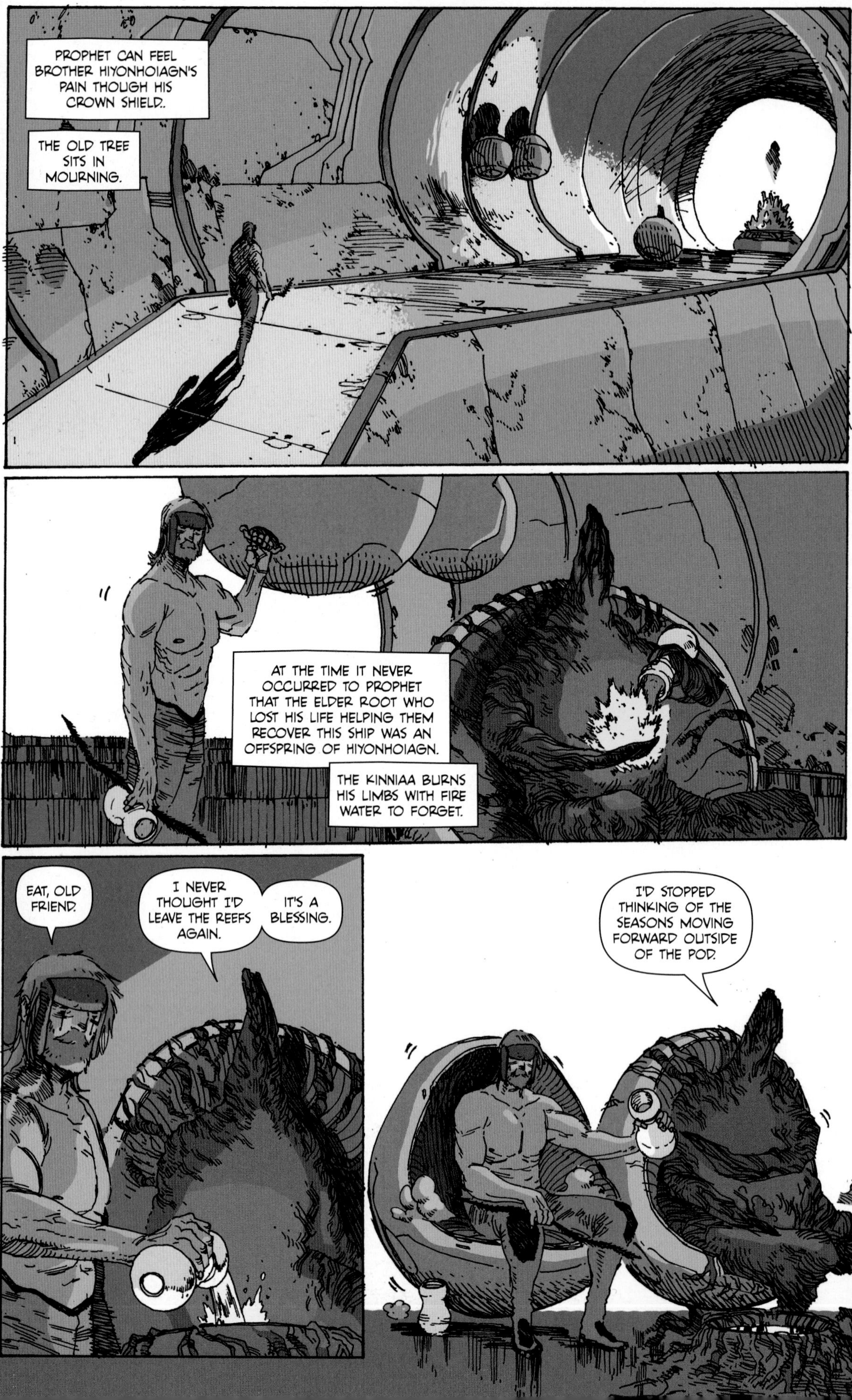

PROPHET CAN FEEL BROTHER HIYONHOIAGN'S PAIN THOUGH HIS CROWN SHIELD..
THE OLD TREE SITS IN MOURNING.
AT THE TIME IT NEVER OCCURRED TO PROPHET THAT THE ELDER ROOT WHO LOST HIS LIFE HELPING THEM RECOVER THIS SHIP WAS AN OFFSPRING OF HIYONHOIAGN.
THE KINNIAA BURNS HIS LIMBS WITH FIRE WATER TO FORGET.
EAT, OLD FRIEND.
I NEVER THOUGHT I'D LEAVE THE REEFS AGAIN.
IT'S A BLESSING.
I'D STOPPED THINKING OF THE SEASONS MOVING FORWARD OUTSIDE OF THE POD.

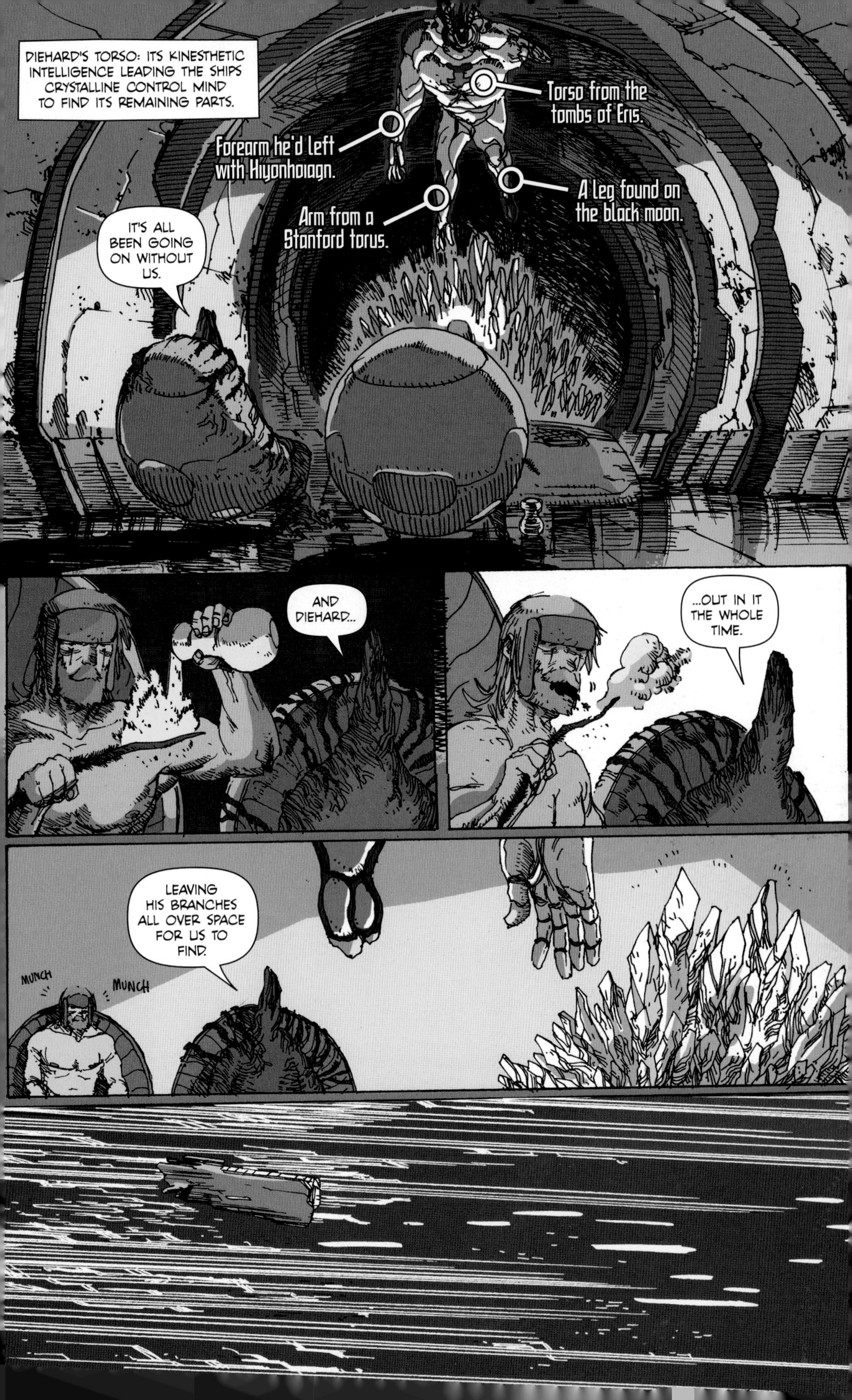
DIEHARD'S TORSO: ITS KINESTHETIC INTELLIGENCE LEADING THE SHIPS CRYSTALLINE CONTROL MIND TO FIND ITS REMAINING PARTS.
Torso from the tombs of Eris.
Forearm he'd left with Hiyonhoiagn.
A leg found on the black moon.
Arm from a Stanford torus.
IT'S ALL BEEN GOING ON WITHOUT US.
AND DIEHARD...
...OUT IN IT THE WHOLE TIME.
LEAVING HIS BRANCHES ALL OVER SPACE FOR US TO FIND.
MUNCH
MUNCH

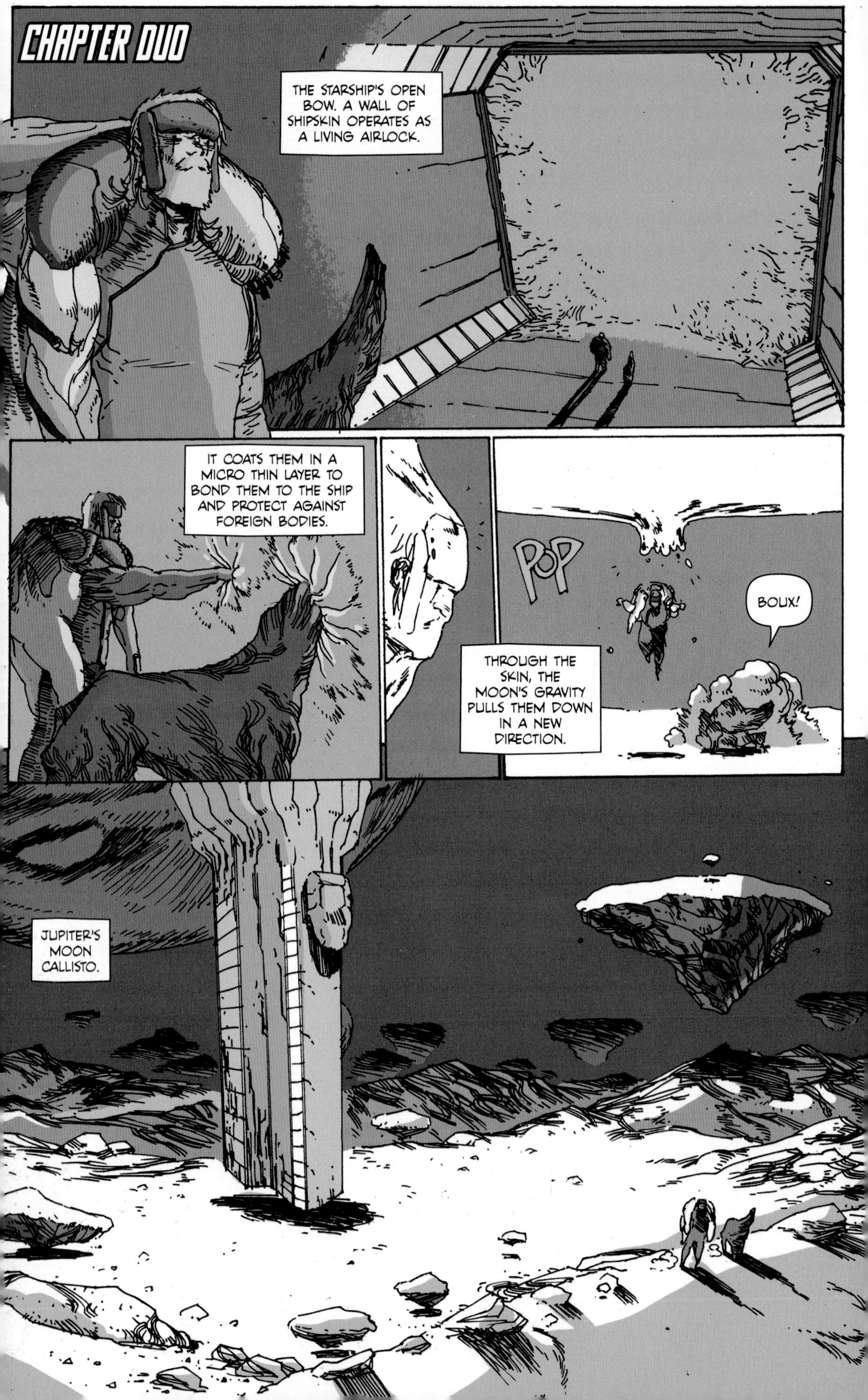
CHAPTER DUO
THE STARSHIP'S OPEN BOW. A WALL OF SHIPSKIN OPERATES AS A LIVING AIRLOCK.
IT COATS THEM IN A MICRO THIN LAYER TO BOND THEM TO THE SHIP AND PROTECT AGAINST FOREIGN BODIES.
POP
BOUX!
THROUGH THE SKIN, THE MOON'S GRAVITY PULLS THEM DOWN IN A NEW DIRECTION.
JUPITER'S MOON CALLISTO.

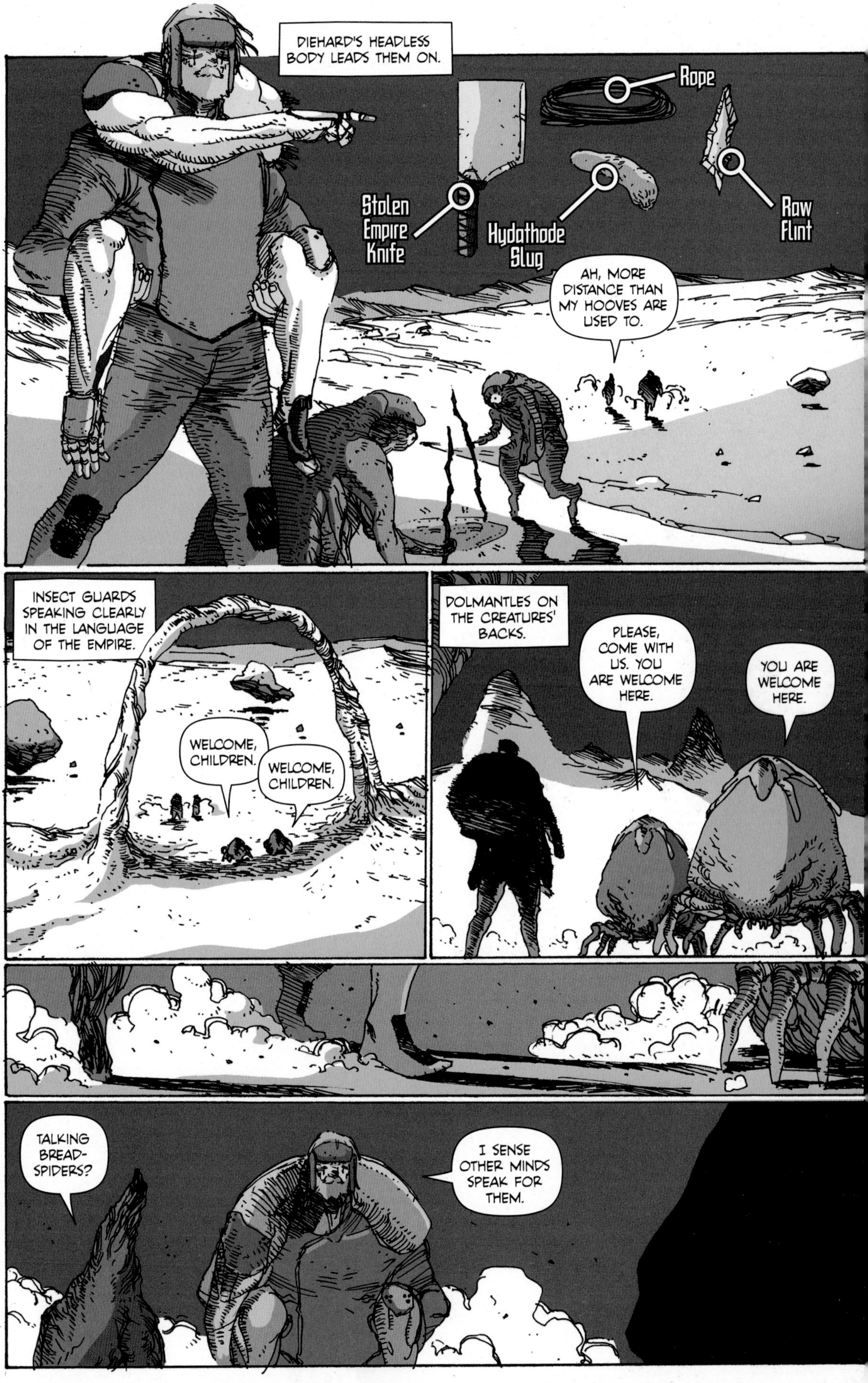
DIEHARD'S HEADLESS BODY LEADS THEM ON.
Rope
Stolen Empire Knife
Hydathode Slug
Raw Flint
AH, MORE DISTANCE THAN MY HOOVES ARE USED TO.
INSECT GUARDS SPEAKING CLEARLY IN THE LANGUAGE OF THE EMPIRE.
WELCOME, CHILDREN.
WELCOME, CHILDREN.
DOLMANTLES ON THE CREATURES' BACKS.
PLEASE, COME WITH US. YOU ARE WELCOME HERE.
YOU ARE WELCOME HERE.
TALKING BREAD-SPIDERS?
I SENSE OTHER MINDS SPEAK FOR THEM.

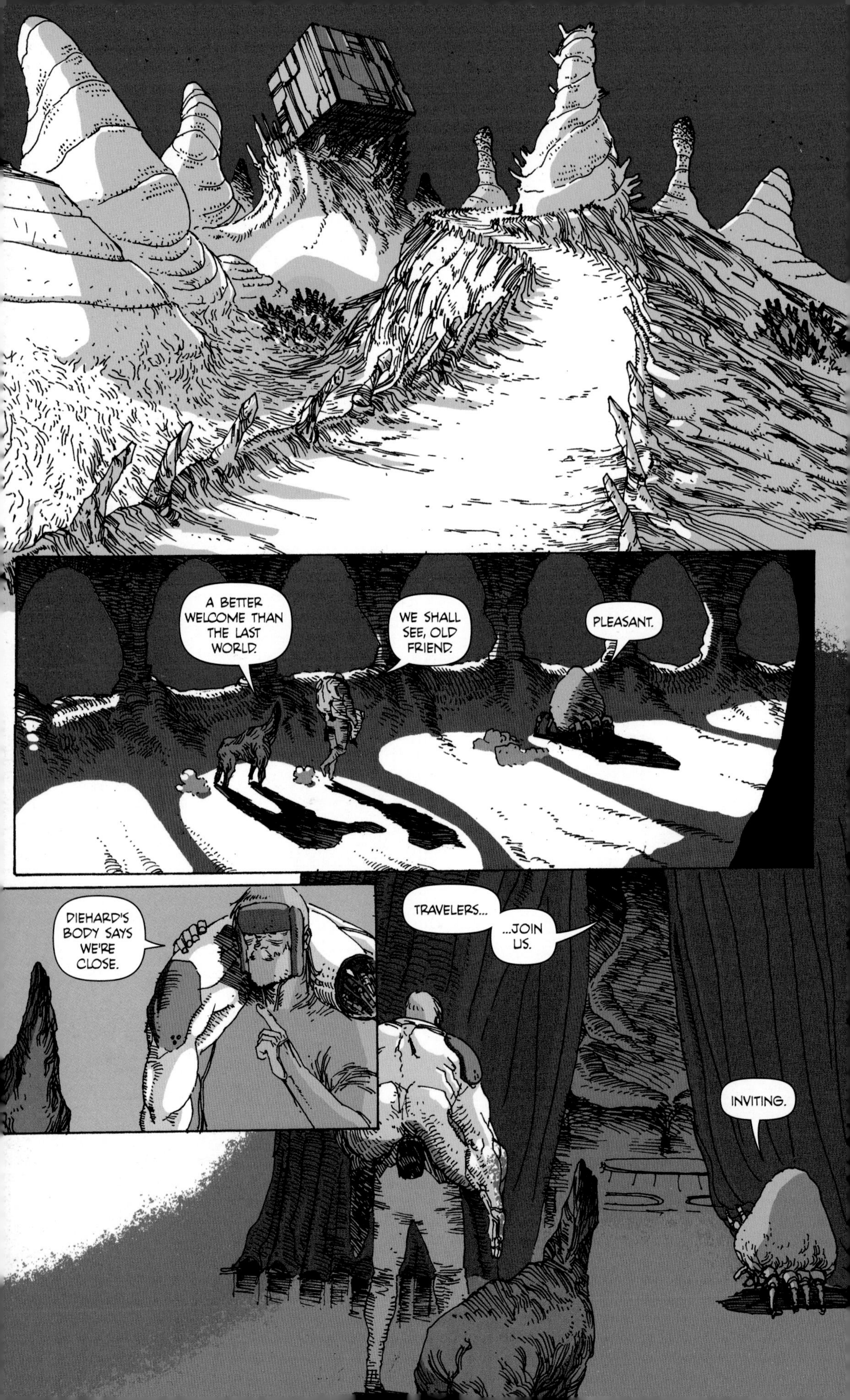
A BETTER WELCOME THAN THE LAST WORLD.
WE SHALL SEE, OLD FRIEND.
PLEASANT.
DIEHARD'S BODY SAYS WE'RE CLOSE.
TRAVELERS...
...JOIN US.
INVITING.

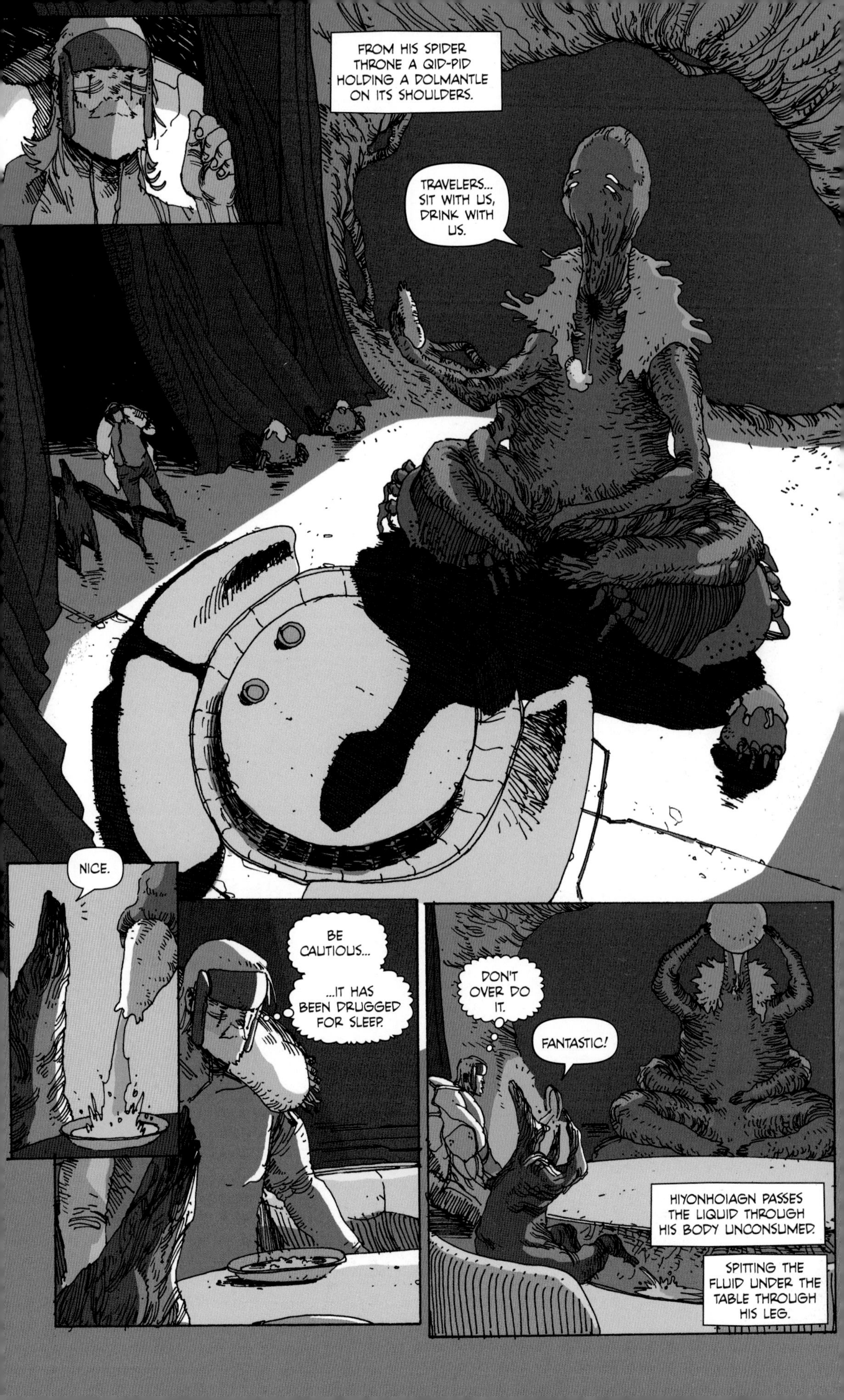
FROM HIS SPIDER THRONE A QID-PID HOLDING A DOLMANTLE ON ITS SHOULDERS.
TRAVELERS... SIT WITH US, DRINK WITH US.
NICE.
BE CAUTIOUS...
...IT HAS BEEN DRUGGED FOR SLEEP.
DON'T OVER DO IT.
FANTASTIC!
HIYONHOIAGN PASSES THE LIQUID THROUGH HIS BODY UNCONSUMED.
SPITTING THE FLUID UNDER THE TABLE THROUGH HIS LEG.

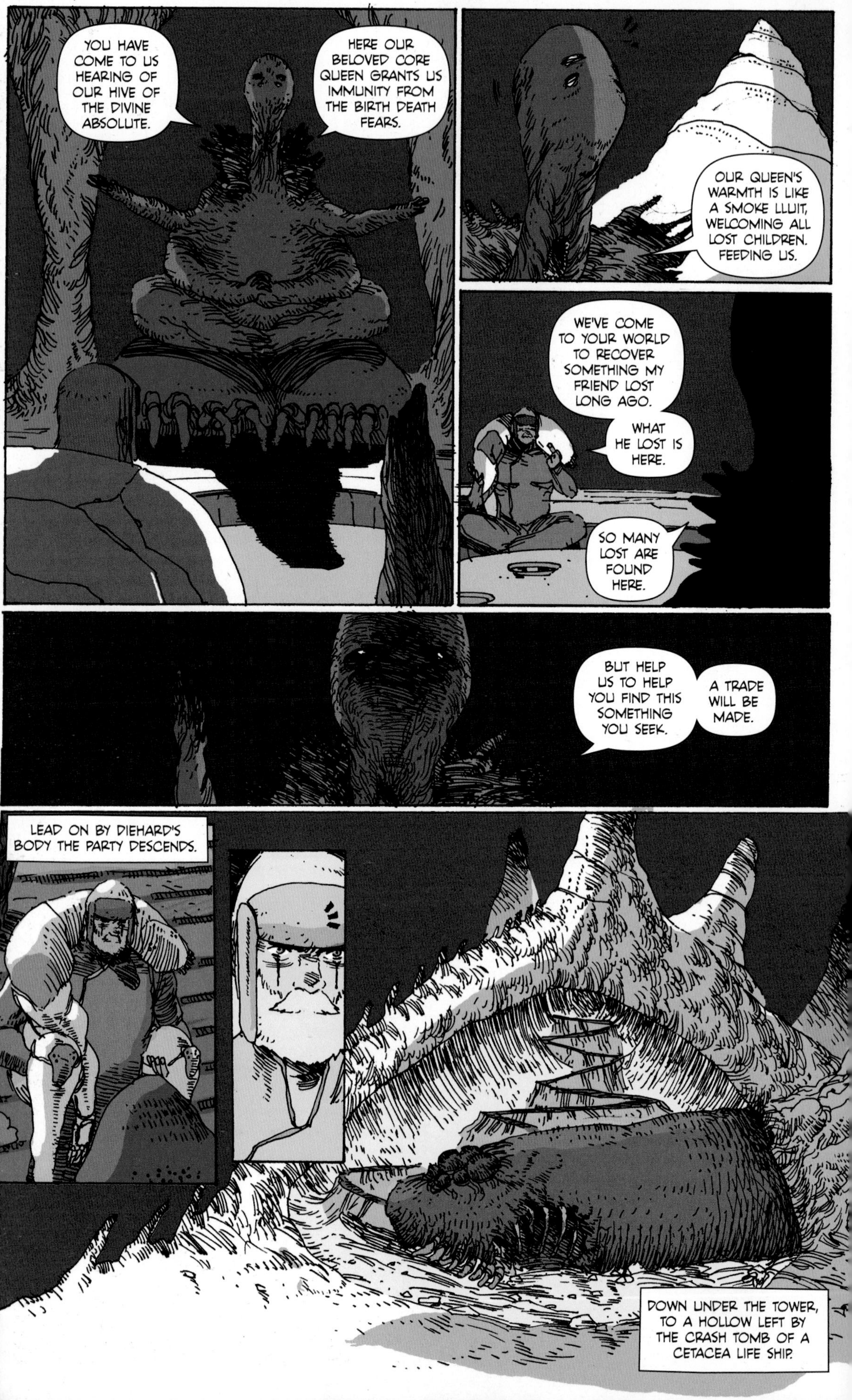

YOU HAVE COME TO US HEARING OF OUR HIVE OF THE DIVINE ABSOLUTE.
HERE OUR BELOVED CORE QUEEN GRANTS US IMMUNITY FROM THE BIRTH DEATH FEARS.
OUR QUEEN'S WARMTH IS LIKE A SMOKE LLUIT, WELCOMING ALL LOST CHILDREN. FEEDING US.
WE'VE COME TO YOUR WORLD TO RECOVER SOMETHING MY FRIEND LOST LONG AGO.
WHAT HE LOST IS HERE.
SO MANY LOST ARE FOUND HERE.
BUT HELP US TO HELP YOU FIND THIS SOMETHING YOU SEEK.
A TRADE WILL BE MADE.
LEAD ON BY DIEHARD'S BODY THE PARTY DESCENDS.
DOWN UNDER THE TOWER, TO A HOLLOW LEFT BY THE CRASH TOMB OF A CETACEA LIFE SHIP.

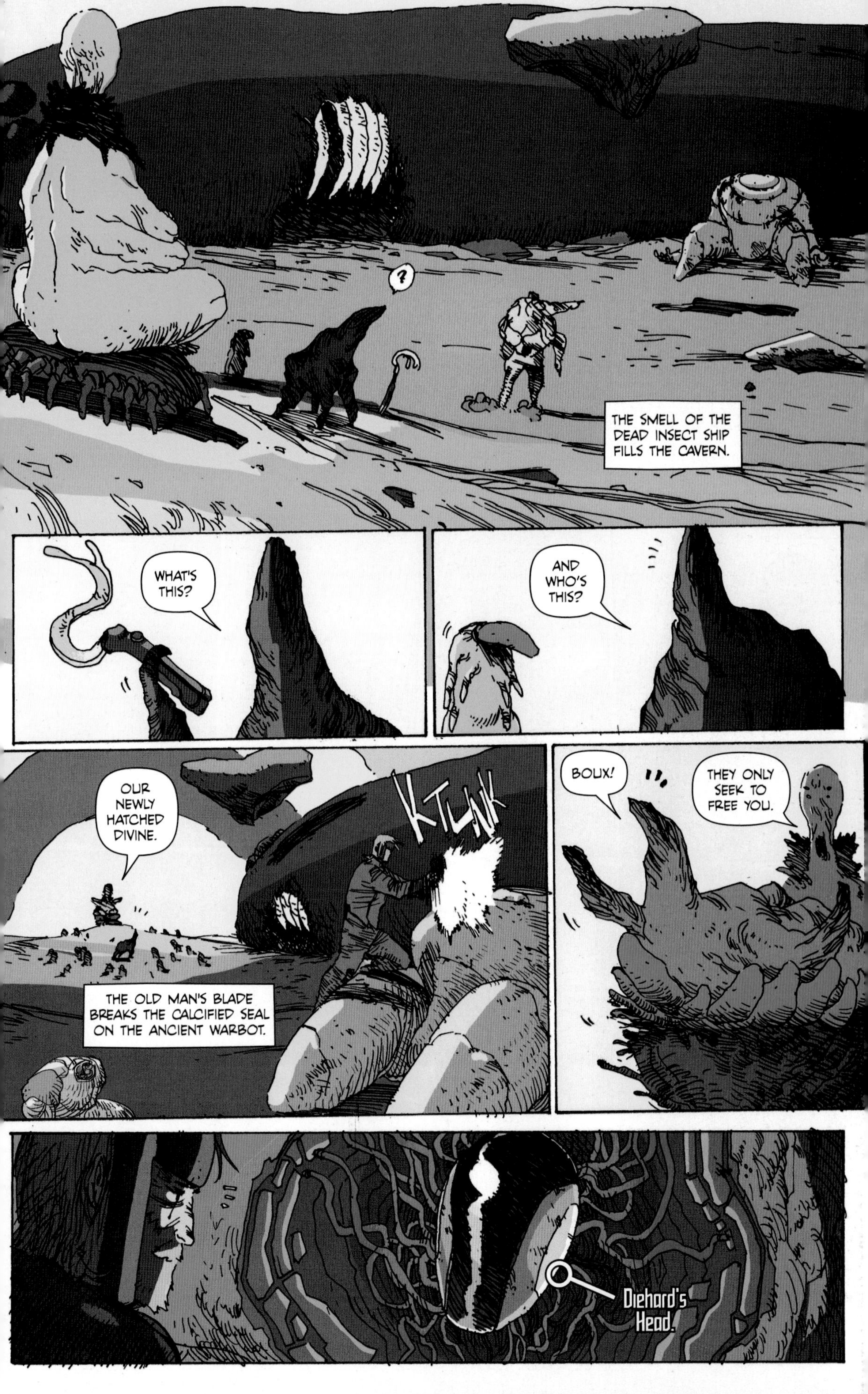
?
THE SMELL OF THE DEAD INSECT SHIP FILLS THE CAVERN.
WHAT'S THIS?
AND WHO'S THIS?
OUR NEWLY HATCHED DIVINE.
KTUNK
THE OLD MAN'S BLADE BREAKS THE CALCIFIED SEAL ON THE ANCIENT WARBOT.
BOUX!
THEY ONLY SEEK TO FREE YOU.
Diehard's Head.

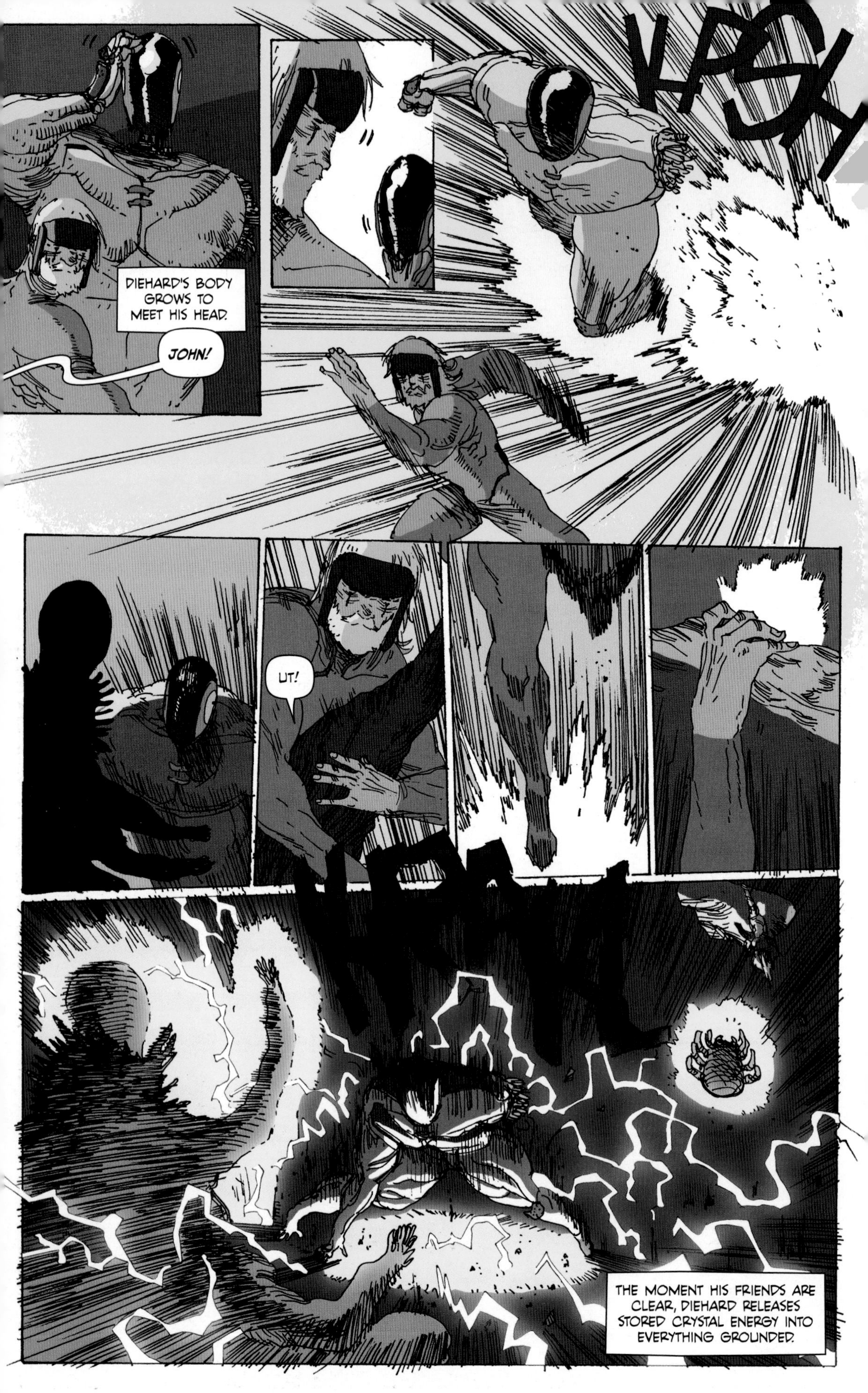
DIEHARD'S BODY GROWS TO MEET HIS HEAD.
JOHN!
KPSH
UT!
THE MOMENT HIS FRIENDS ARE CLEAR, DIEHARD RELEASES STORED CRYSTAL ENERGY INTO EVERYTHING GROUNDED.

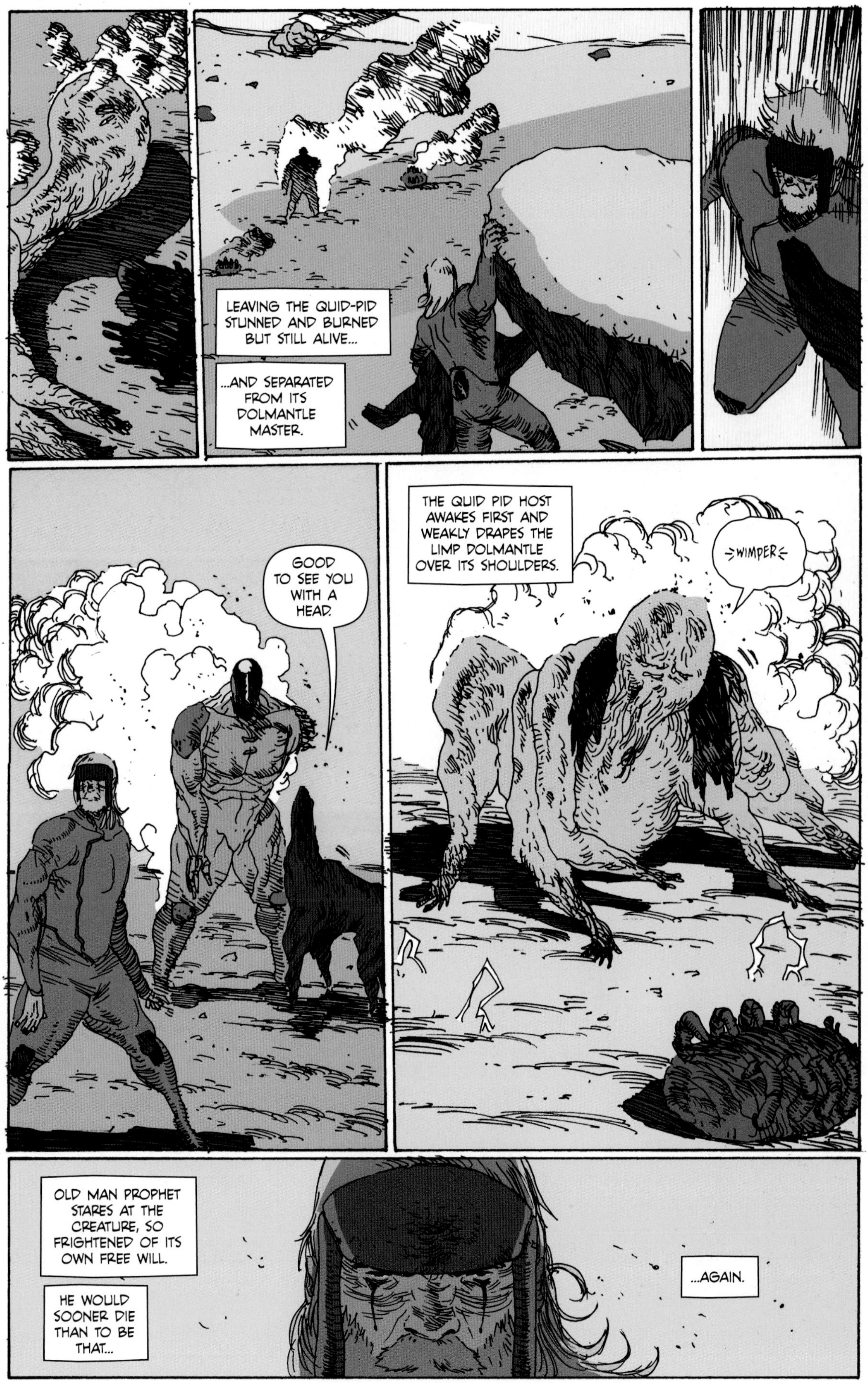
LEAVING THE QUID-PID STUNNED AND BURNED BUT STILL ALIVE...
...AND SEPARATED FROM ITS DOLMANTLE MASTER.
GOOD TO SEE YOU WITH A HEAD.
THE QUID PID HOST AWAKES FIRST AND WEAKLY DRAPES THE LIMP DOLMANTLE OVER ITS SHOULDERS.
WIMPER
OLD MAN PROPHET STARES AT THE CREATURE, SO FRIGHTENED OF ITS OWN FREE WILL.
HE WOULD SOONER DIE THAN TO BE THAT...
...AGAIN.

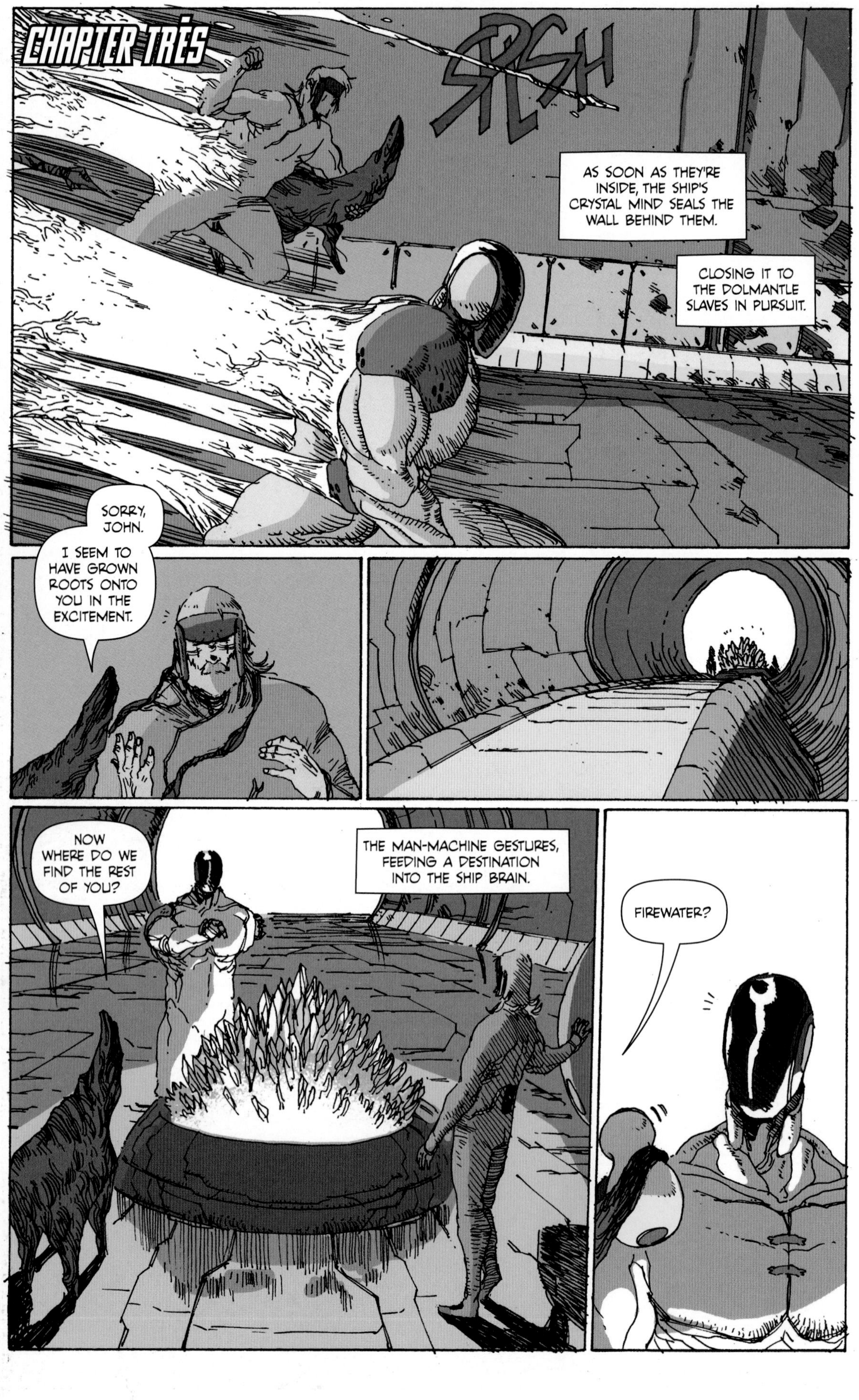
CHAPTER TRÉS
SPLSH
AS SOON AS THEY'RE INSIDE, THE SHIP'S CRYSTAL MIND SEALS THE WALL BEHIND THEM.
CLOSING IT TO THE DOLMANTLE SLAVES IN PURSUIT.
SORRY, JOHN.
I SEEM TO HAVE GROWN ROOTS ONTO YOU IN THE EXCITEMENT.
NOW WHERE DO WE FIND THE REST OF YOU?
THE MAN-MACHINE GESTURES, FEEDING A DESTINATION INTO THE SHIP BRAIN.
FIREWATER?

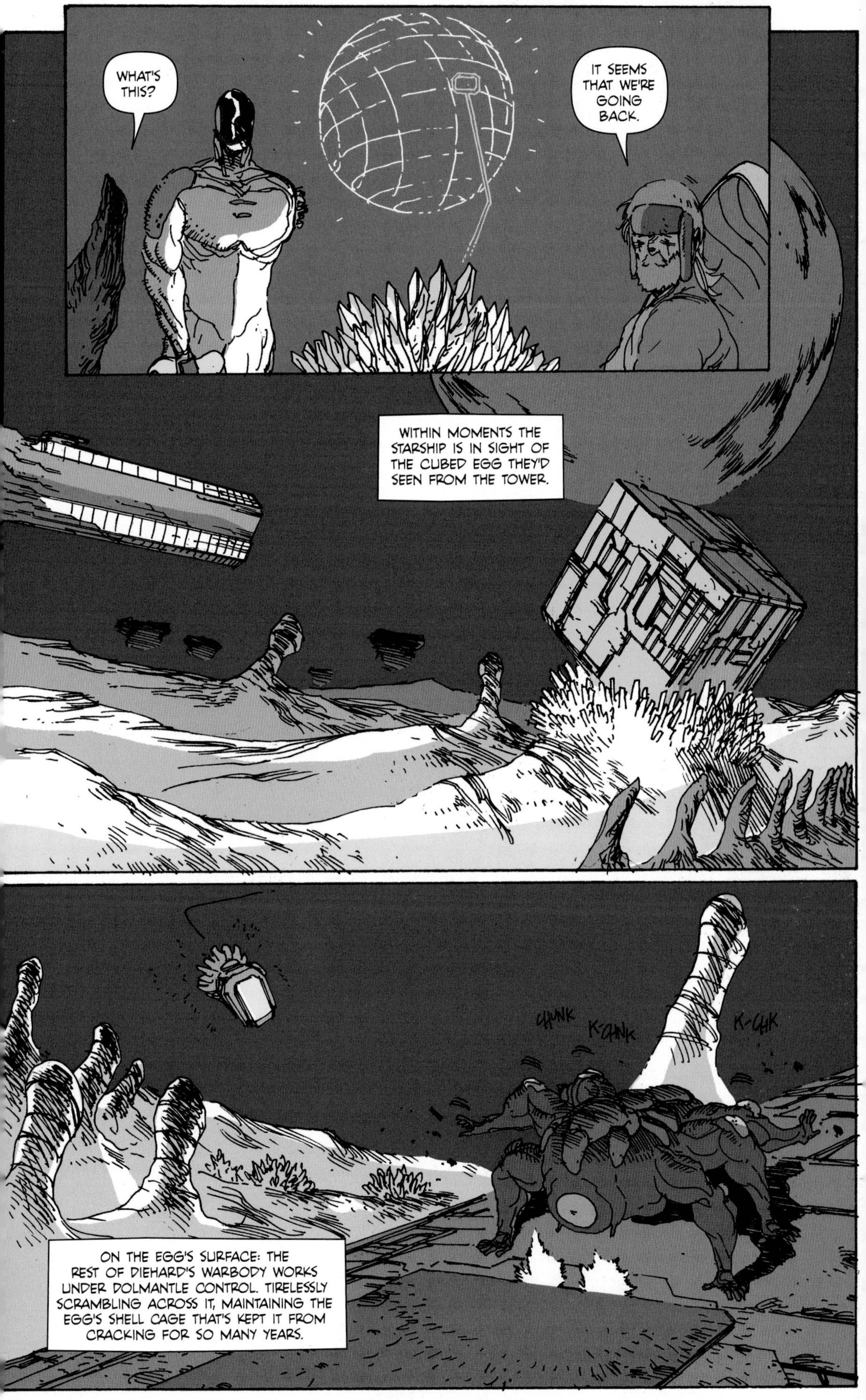
WHAT'S THIS?
IT SEEMS THAT WE'RE GOING BACK.
WITHIN MOMENTS THE STARSHIP IS IN SIGHT OF THE CUBED EGG THEY'D SEEN FROM THE TOWER.
CHUNK
K-CHANK
K-CHK
ON THE EGG'S SURFACE: THE REST OF DIEHARD'S WARBODY WORKS UNDER DOLMANTLE CONTROL. TIRELESSLY SCRAMBLING ACROSS IT, MAINTAINING THE EGG'S SHELL CAGE THAT'S KEPT IT FROM CRACKING FOR SO MANY YEARS.

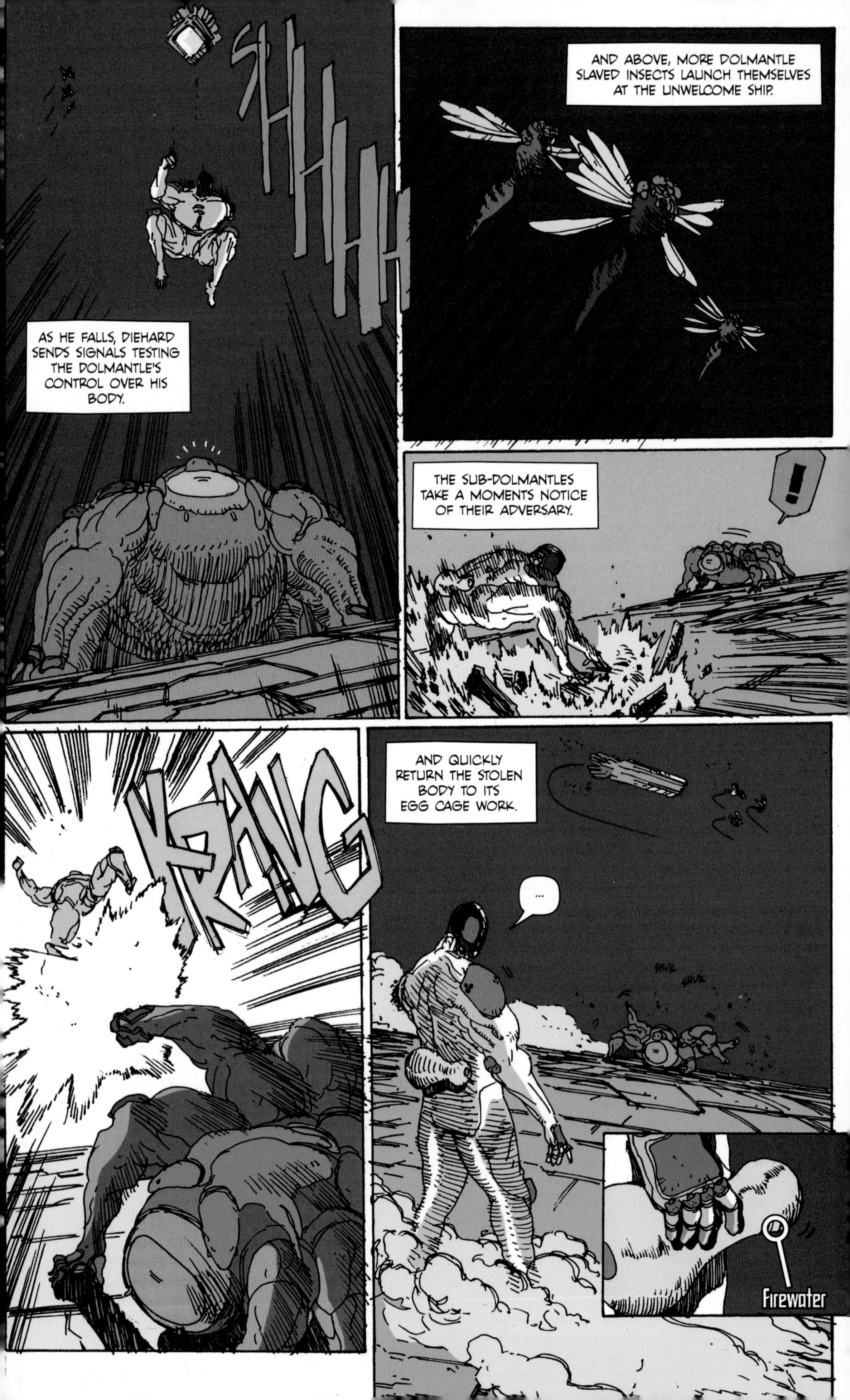
SHHHHHH
AS HE FALLS, DIEHARD SENDS SIGNALS TESTING THE DOLMANTLE'S CONTROL OVER HIS BODY.
AND ABOVE, MORE DOLMANTLE SLAVED INSECTS LAUNCH THEMSELVES AT THE UNWELCOME SHIP.
THE SUB-DOLMANTLES TAKE A MOMENTS NOTICE OF THEIR ADVERSARY.
!
KRANG
AND QUICKLY RETURN THE STOLEN BODY TO ITS EGG CAGE WORK.
...
SHUK
SHUK
Firewater

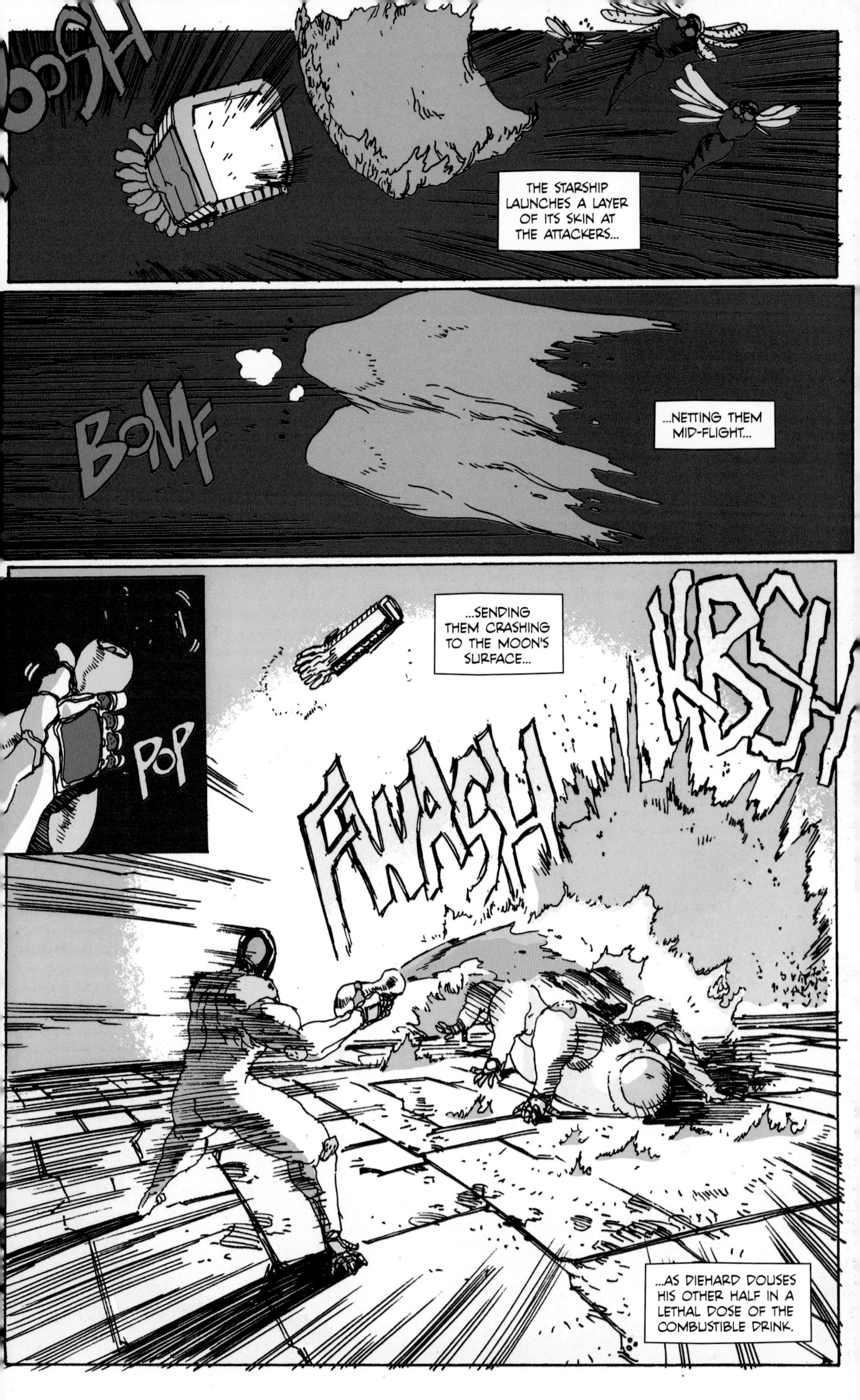
OOSH
THE STARSHIP LAUNCHES A LAYER OF ITS SKIN AT THE ATTACKERS...
BOMF
...NETTING THEM MID-FLIGHT...
POP
...SENDING THEM CRASHING TO THE MOON'S SURFACE...
FWASH
KBSH
...AS DIEHARD DOUSES HIS OTHER HALF IN A LETHAL DOSE OF THE COMBUSTIBLE DRINK.

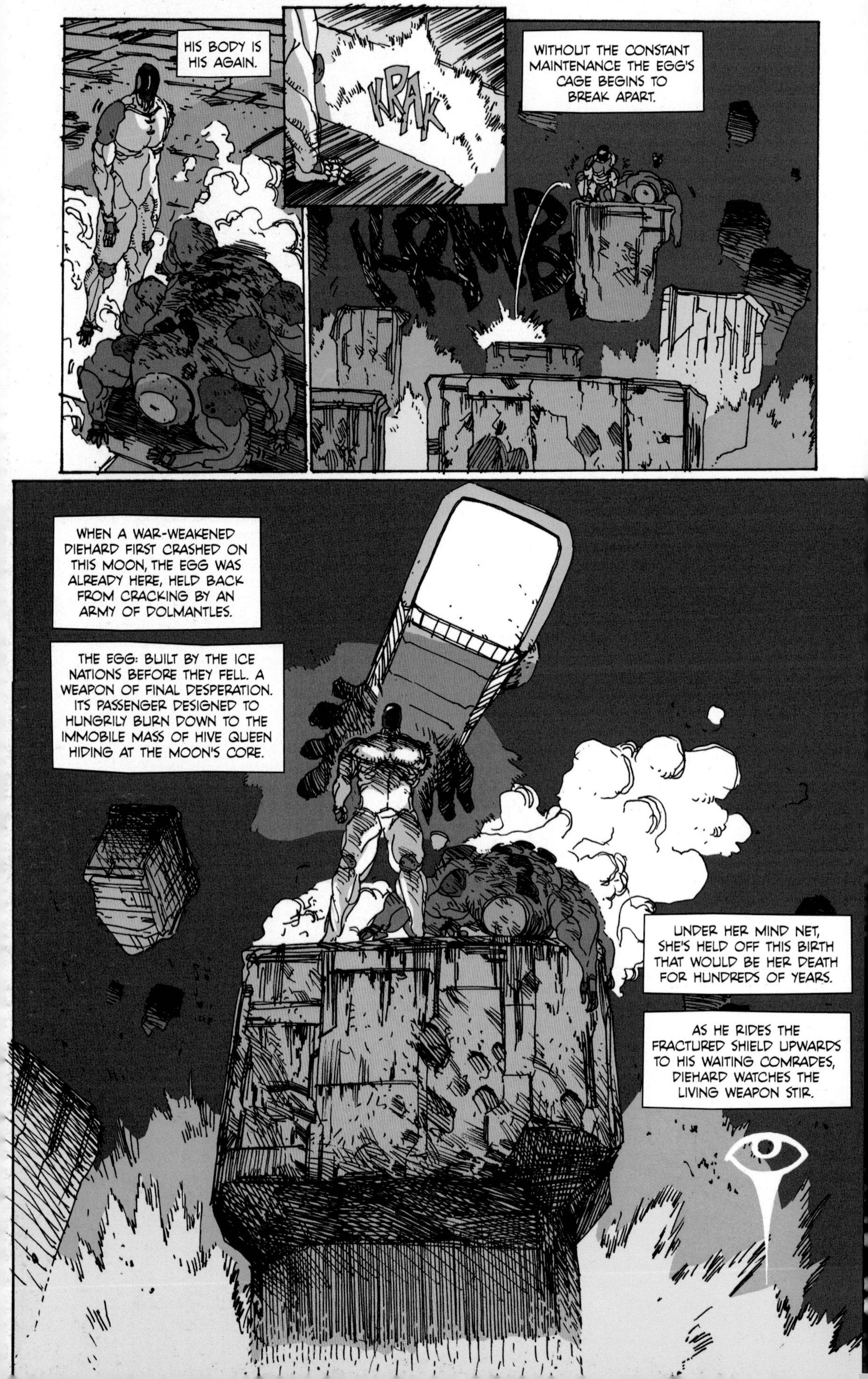
HIS BODY IS HIS AGAIN.
KRAK
WITHOUT THE CONSTANT MAINTENANCE THE EGG'S CAGE BEGINS TO BREAK APART.
KRMB
WHEN A WAR-WEAKENED DIEHARD FIRST CRASHED ON THIS MOON, THE EGG WAS ALREADY HERE, HELD BACK FROM CRACKING BY AN ARMY OF DOLMANTLES.
THE EGG: BUILT BY THE ICE NATIONS BEFORE THEY FELL. A WEAPON OF FINAL DESPERATION. ITS PASSENGER DESIGNED TO HUNGRILY BURN DOWN TO THE IMMOBILE MASS OF HIVE QUEEN HIDING AT THE MOON'S CORE.
UNDER HER MIND NET, SHE'S HELD OFF THIS BIRTH THAT WOULD BE HER DEATH FOR HUNDREDS OF YEARS.
AS HE RIDES THE FRACTURED SHIELD UPWARDS TO HIS WAITING COMRADES, DIEHARD WATCHES THE LIVING WEAPON STIR.

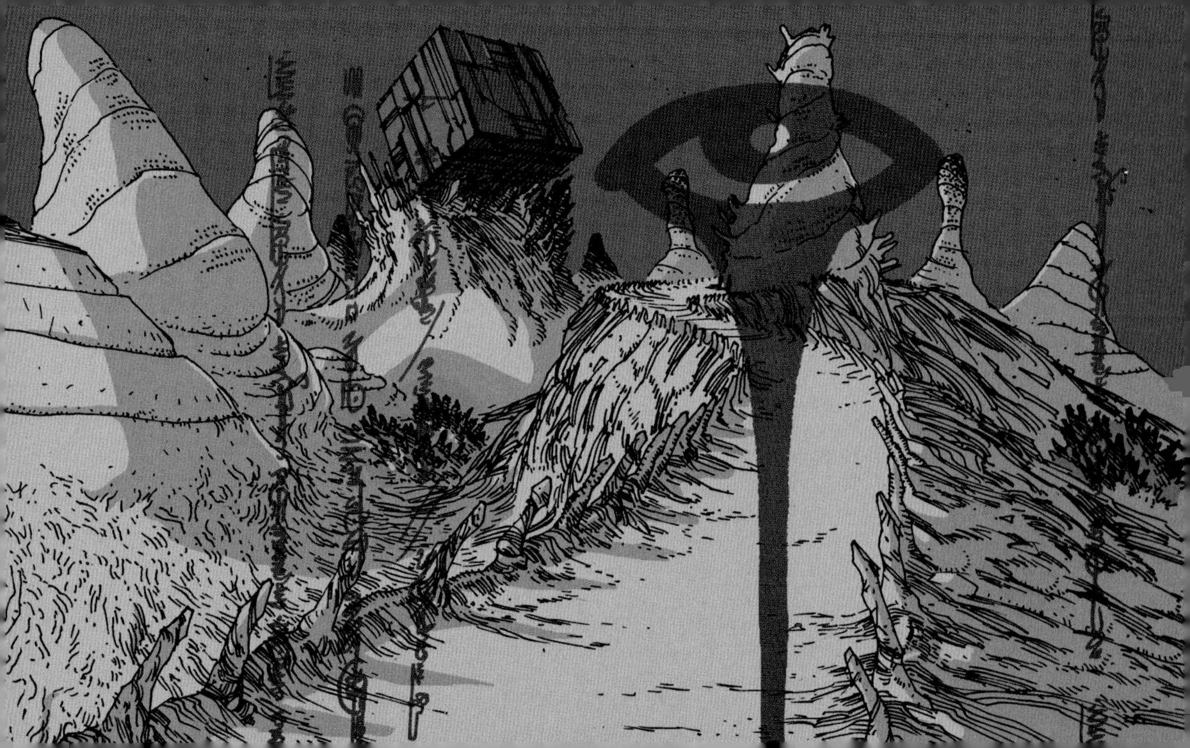

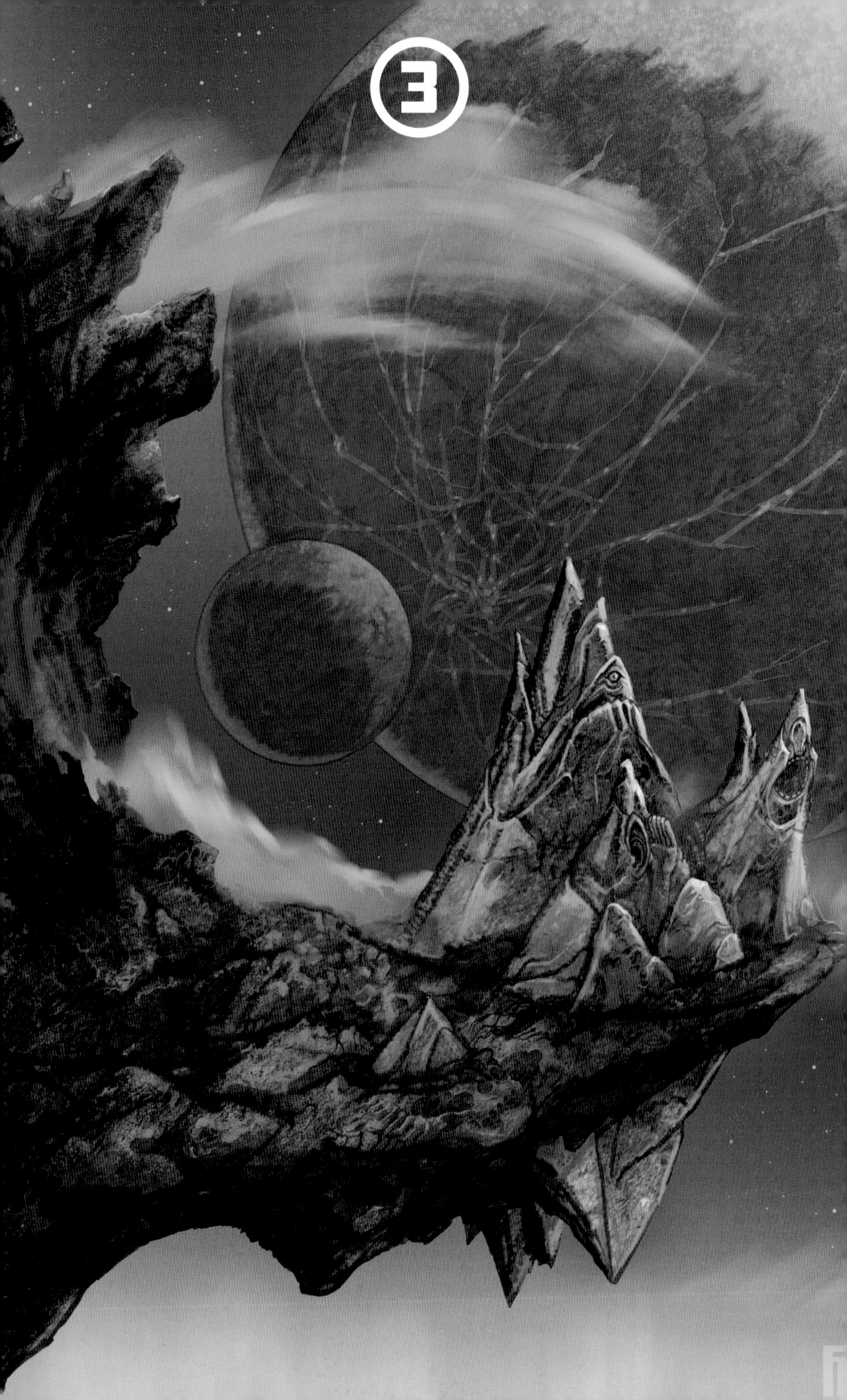
3

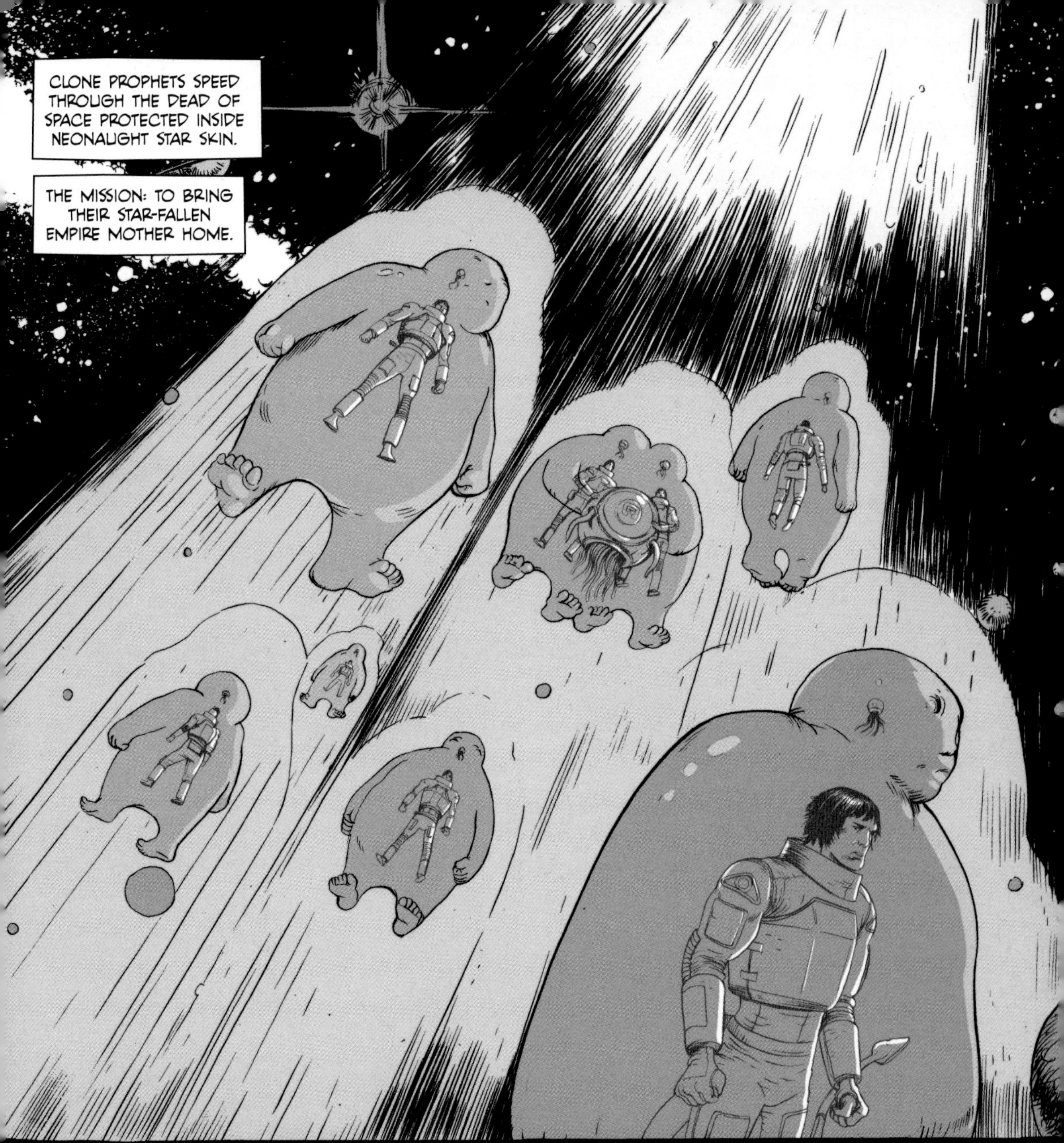
CLONE PROPHETS SPEED THROUGH THE DEAD OF SPACE PROTECTED INSIDE NEONAUGHT STAR SKIN.
THE MISSION: TO BRING THEIR STAR-FALLEN EMPIRE MOTHER HOME.

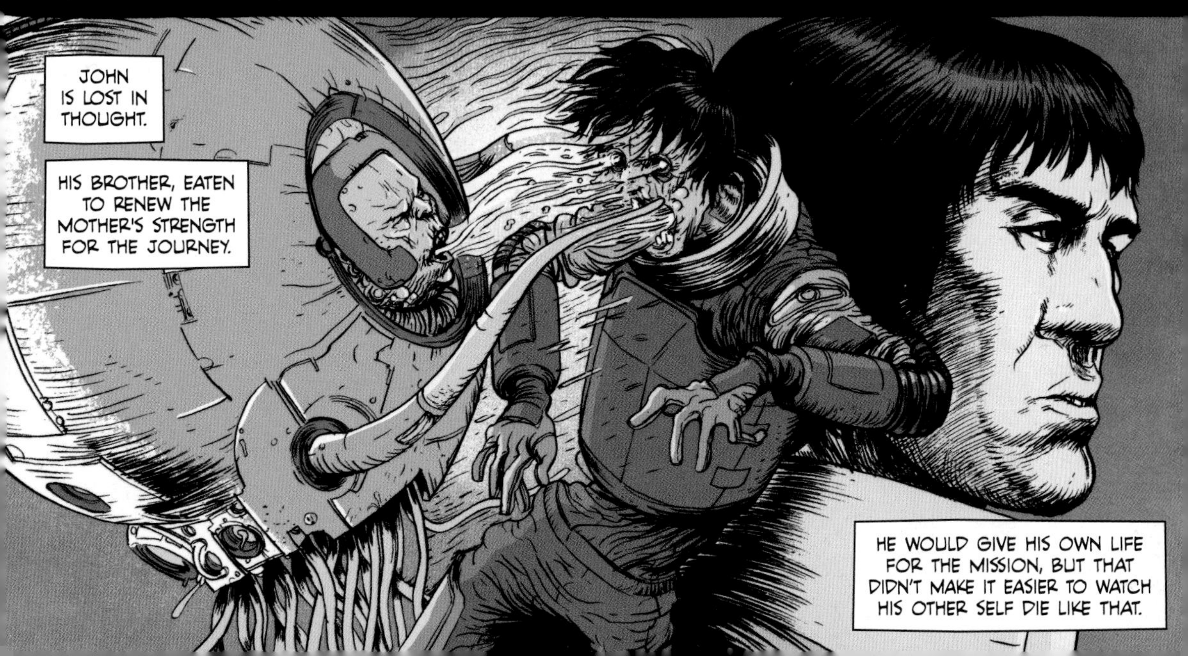
JOHN IS LOST IN THOUGHT.
HIS BROTHER, EATEN TO RENEW THE MOTHER'S STRENGTH FOR THE JOURNEY.
HE WOULD GIVE HIS OWN LIFE FOR THE MISSION, BUT THAT DIDN'T MAKE IT EASIER TO WATCH HIS OTHER SELF DIE LIKE THAT.

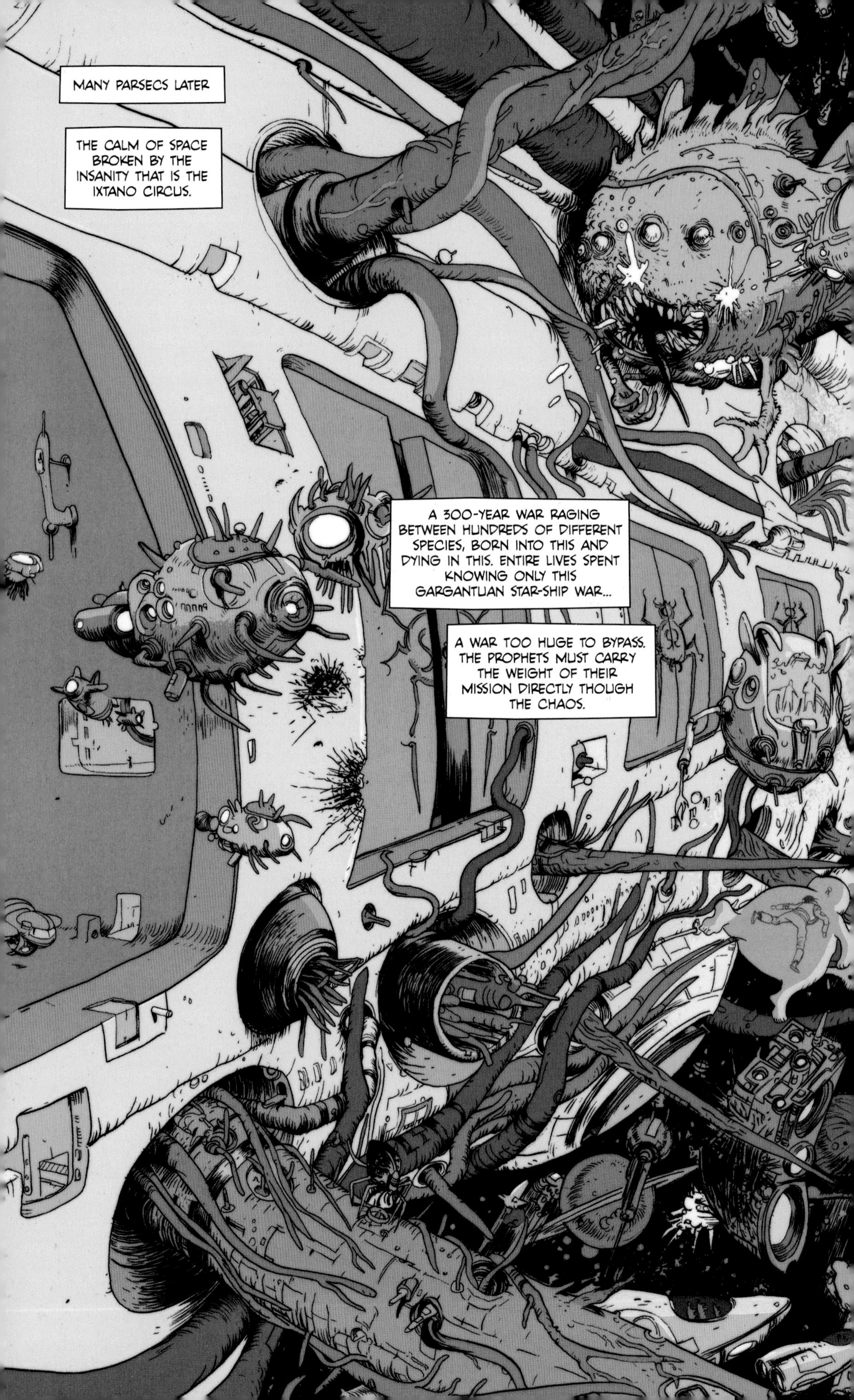
MANY PARSECS LATER
THE CALM OF SPACE BROKEN BY THE INSANITY THAT IS THE IXTANO CIRCUS.
A 300-YEAR WAR RAGING BETWEEN HUNDREDS OF DIFFERENT SPECIES, BORN INTO THIS AND DYING IN THIS. ENTIRE LIVES SPENT KNOWING ONLY THIS GARGANTUAN STAR-SHIP WAR...
A WAR TOO HUGE TO BYPASS. THE PROPHETS MUST CARRY THE WEIGHT OF THEIR MISSION DIRECTLY THOUGH THE CHAOS.

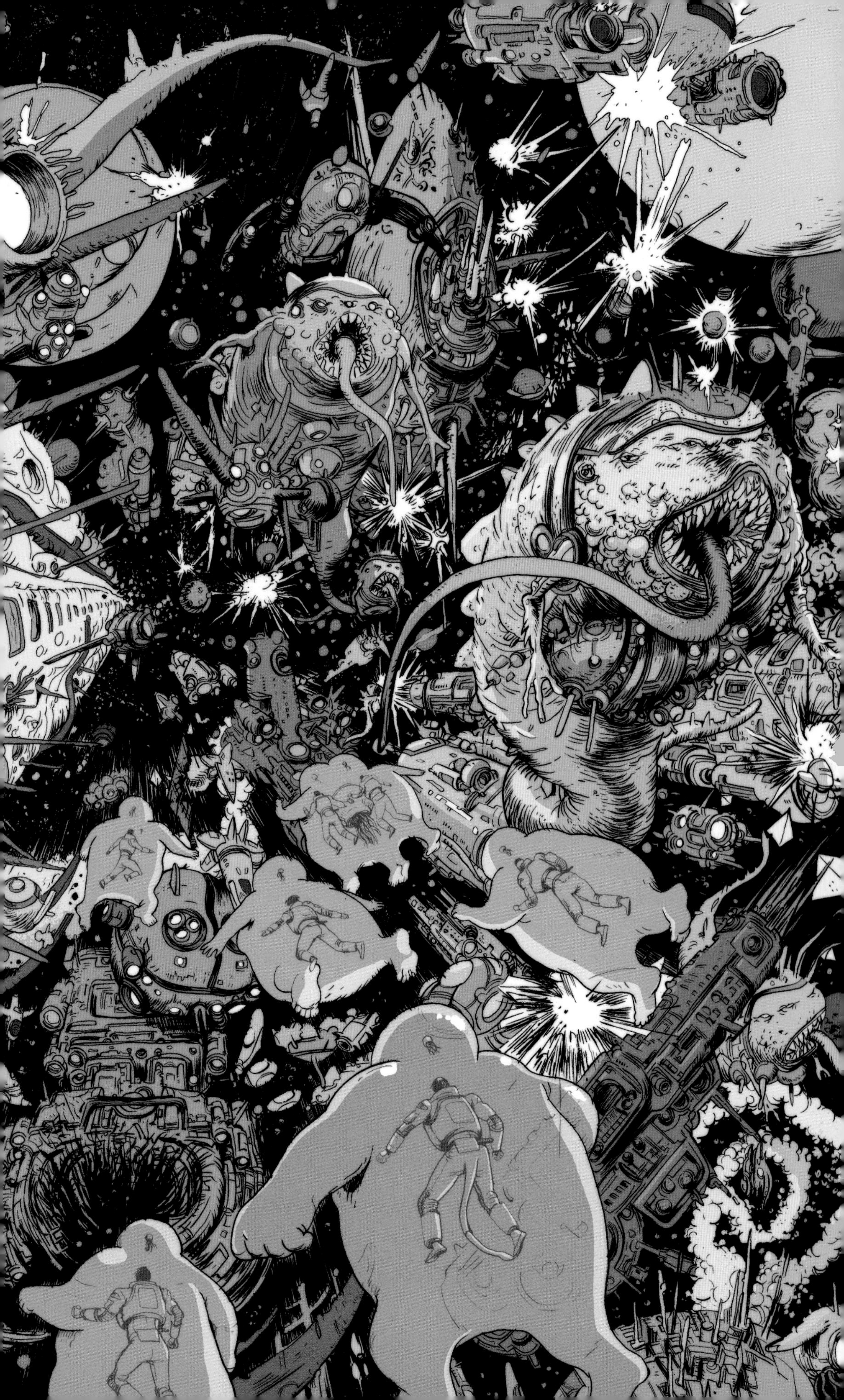

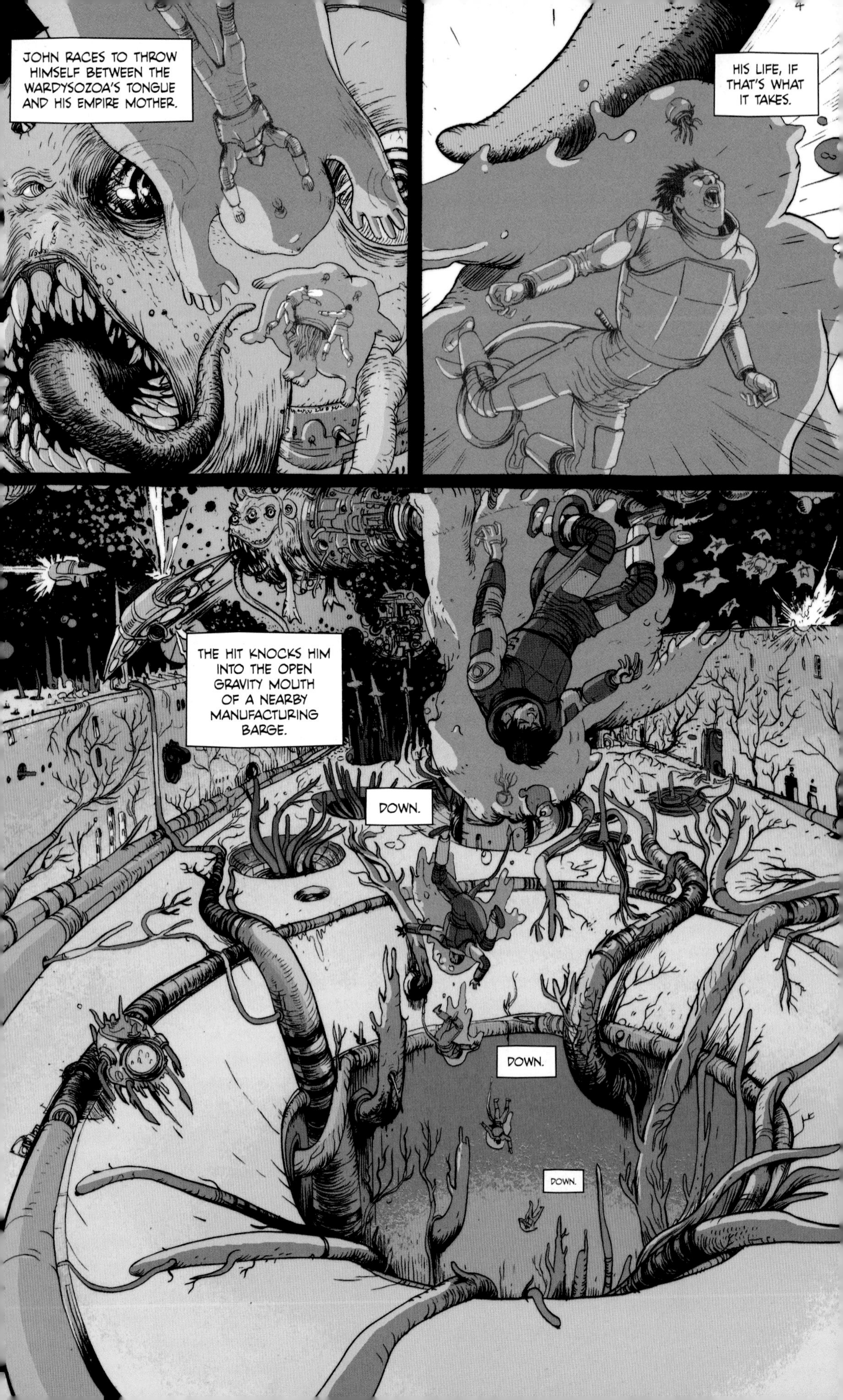
JOHN RACES TO THROW HIMSELF BETWEEN THE WARDYSOZOA'S TONGUE AND HIS EMPIRE MOTHER.
HIS LIFE, IF THAT'S WHAT IT TAKES.
THE HIT KNOCKS HIM INTO THE OPEN GRAVITY MOUTH OF A NEARBY MANUFACTURING BARGE.
DOWN.
DOWN.
DOWN.

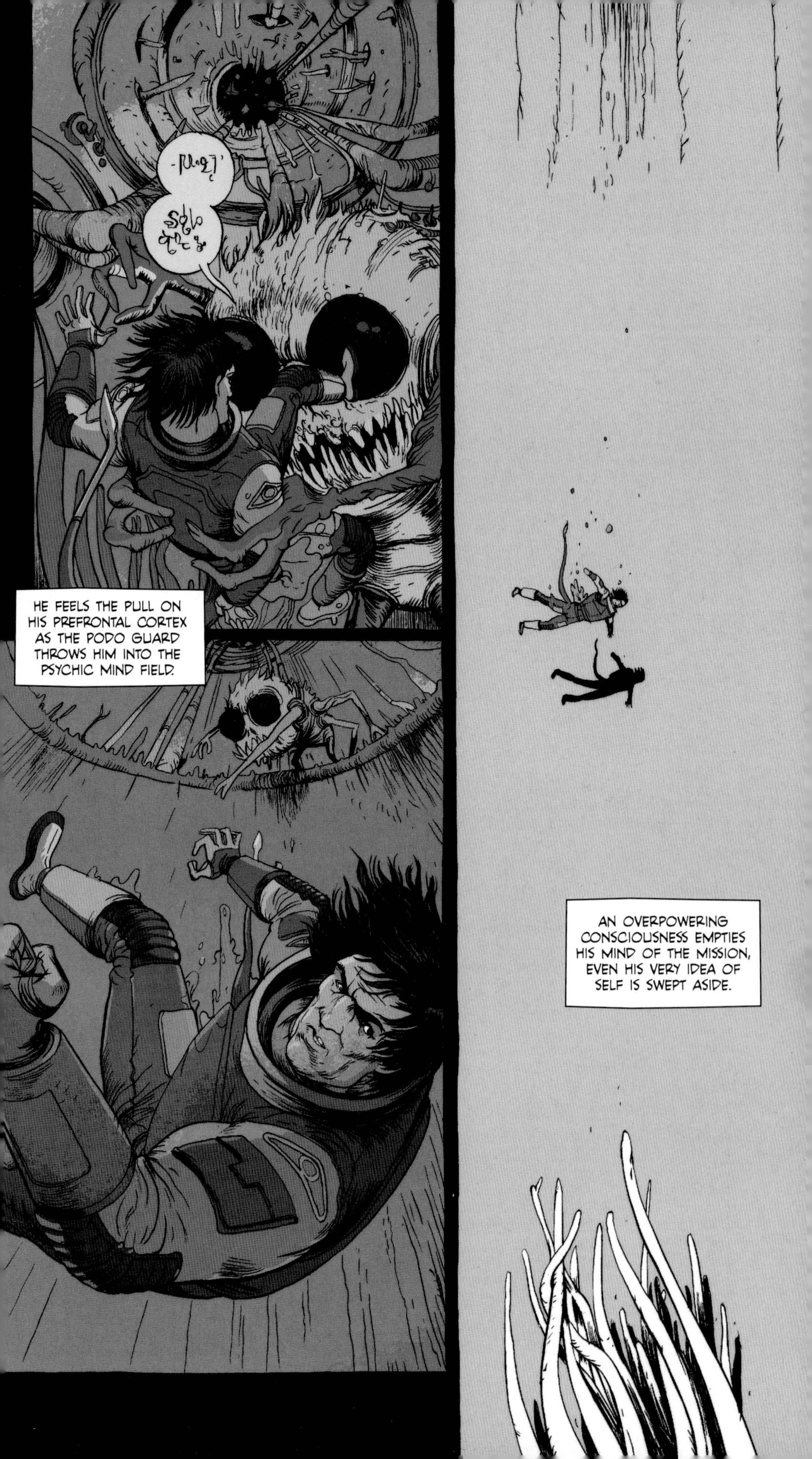
HE FEELS THE PULL ON HIS PREFRONTAL CORTEX AS THE PODO GUARD THROWS HIM INTO THE PSYCHIC MIND FIELD.
AN OVERPOWERING CONSCIOUSNESS EMPTIES HIS MIND OF THE MISSION, EVEN HIS VERY IDEA OF SELF IS SWEPT ASIDE.

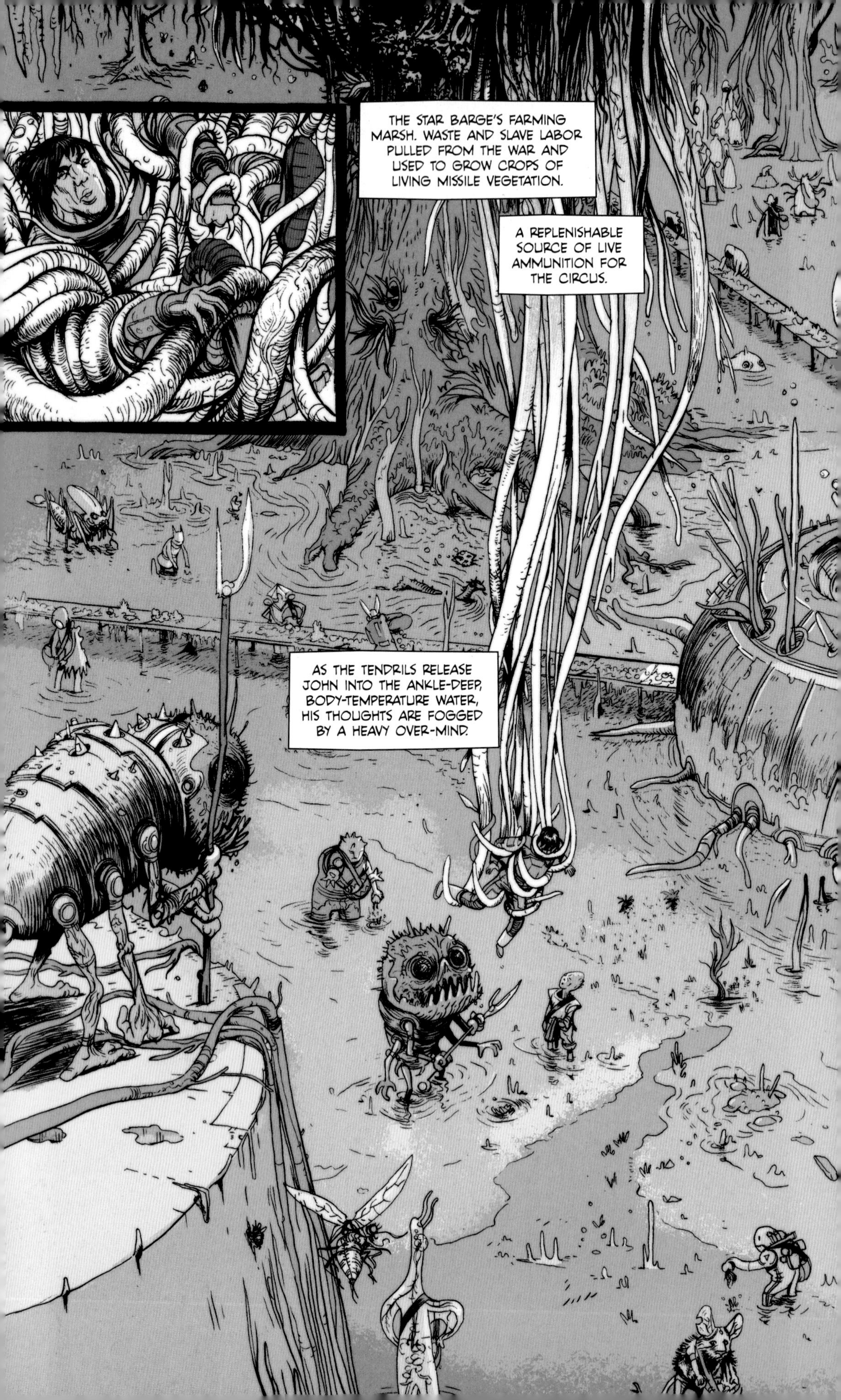
THE STAR BARGE'S FARMING MARSH. WASTE AND SLAVE LABOR PULLED FROM THE WAR AND USED TO GROW CROPS OF LIVING MISSILE VEGETATION.
A REPLENISHABLE SOURCE OF LIVE AMMUNITION FOR THE CIRCUS.
AS THE TENDRILS RELEASE JOHN INTO THE ANKLE-DEEP, BODY-TEMPERATURE WATER, HIS THOUGHTS ARE FOGGED BY A HEAVY OVER-MIND.

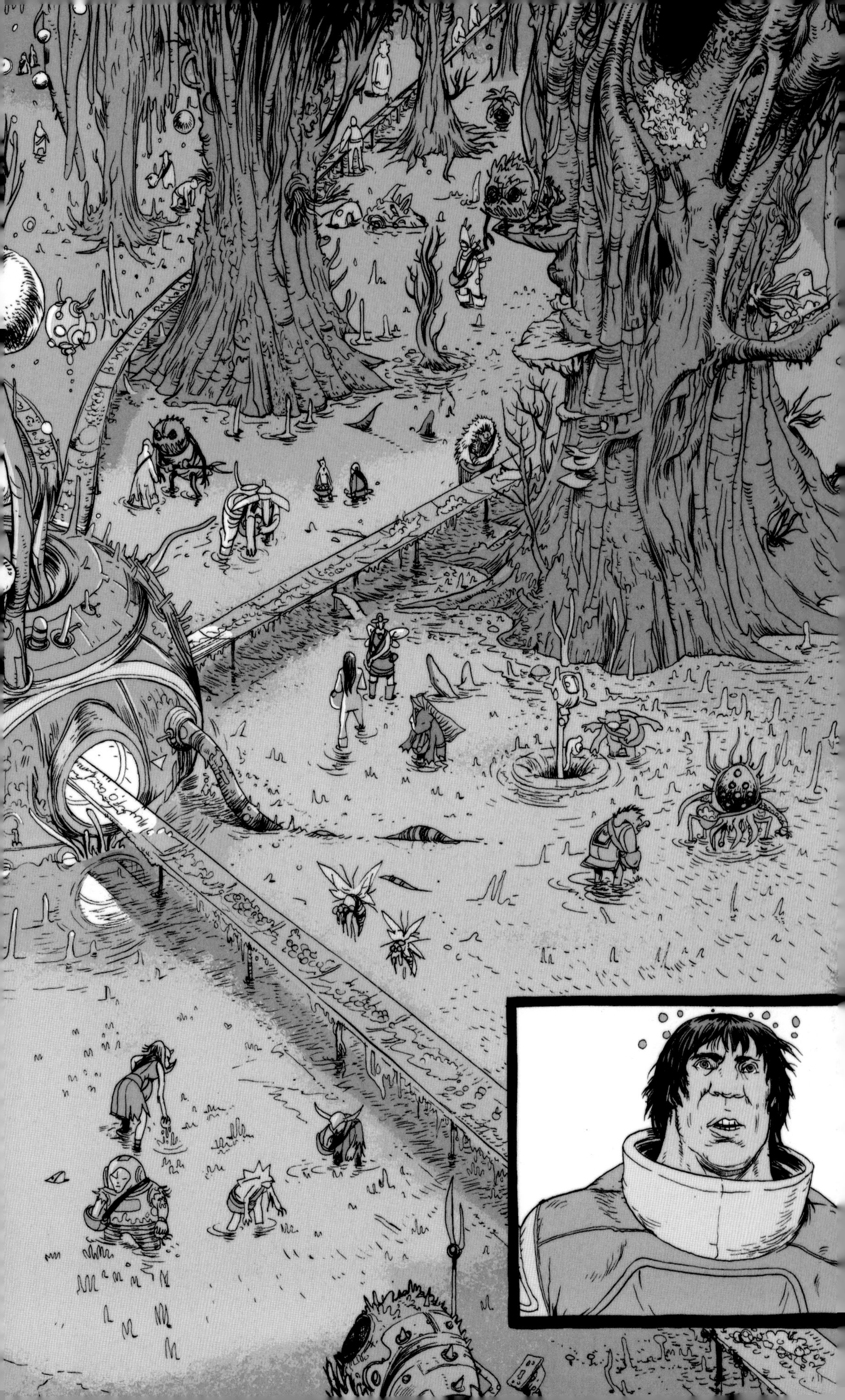

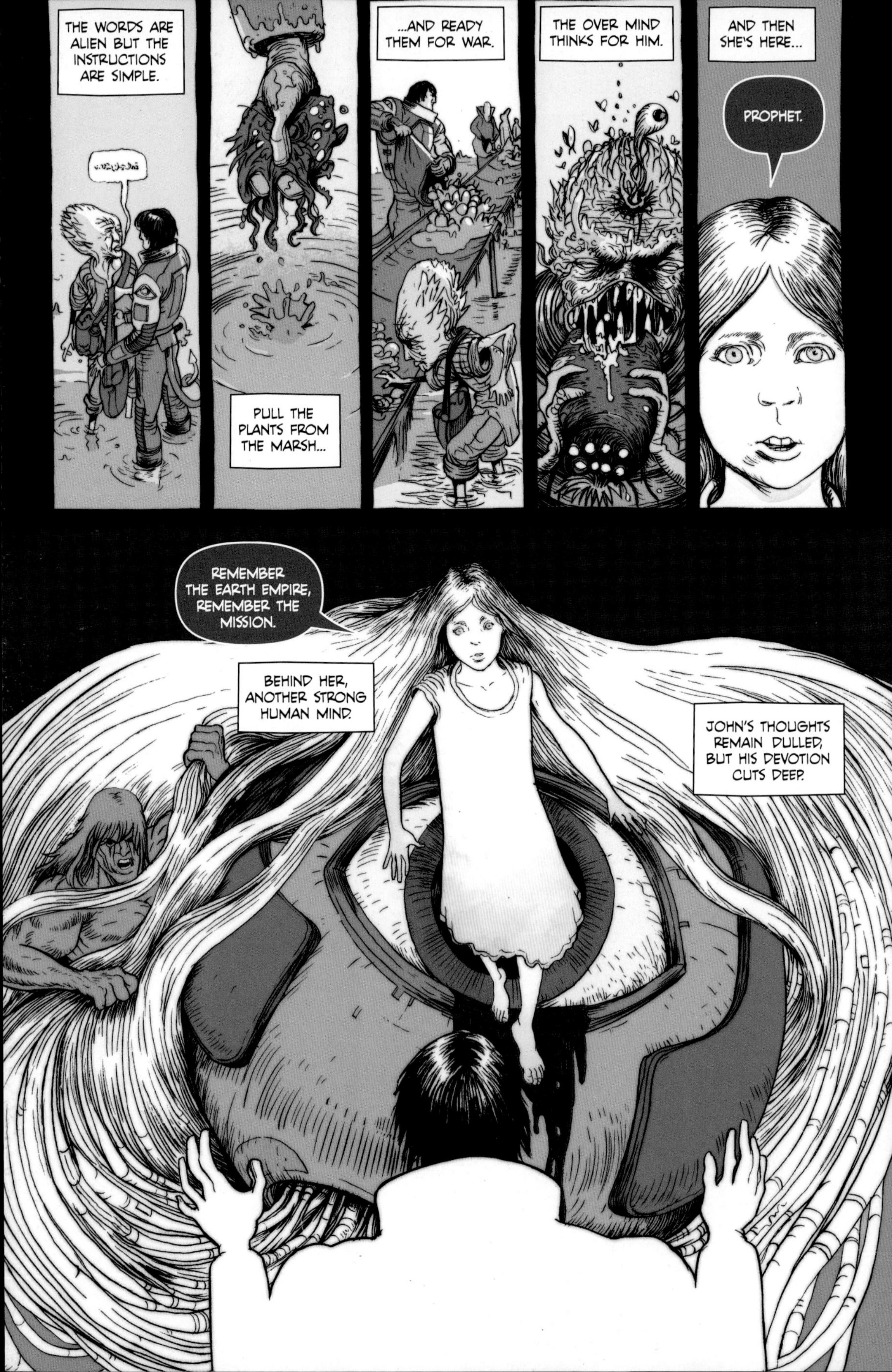
THE WORDS ARE ALIEN BUT THE INSTRUCTIONS ARE SIMPLE.
PULL THE PLANTS FROM THE MARSH...
...AND READY THEM FOR WAR.
THE OVER MIND THINKS FOR HIM.
AND THEN SHE'S HERE...
PROPHET.
REMEMBER THE EARTH EMPIRE, REMEMBER THE MISSION.
BEHIND HER, ANOTHER STRONG HUMAN MIND.
JOHN'S THOUGHTS REMAIN DULLED, BUT HIS DEVOTION CUTS DEEP.

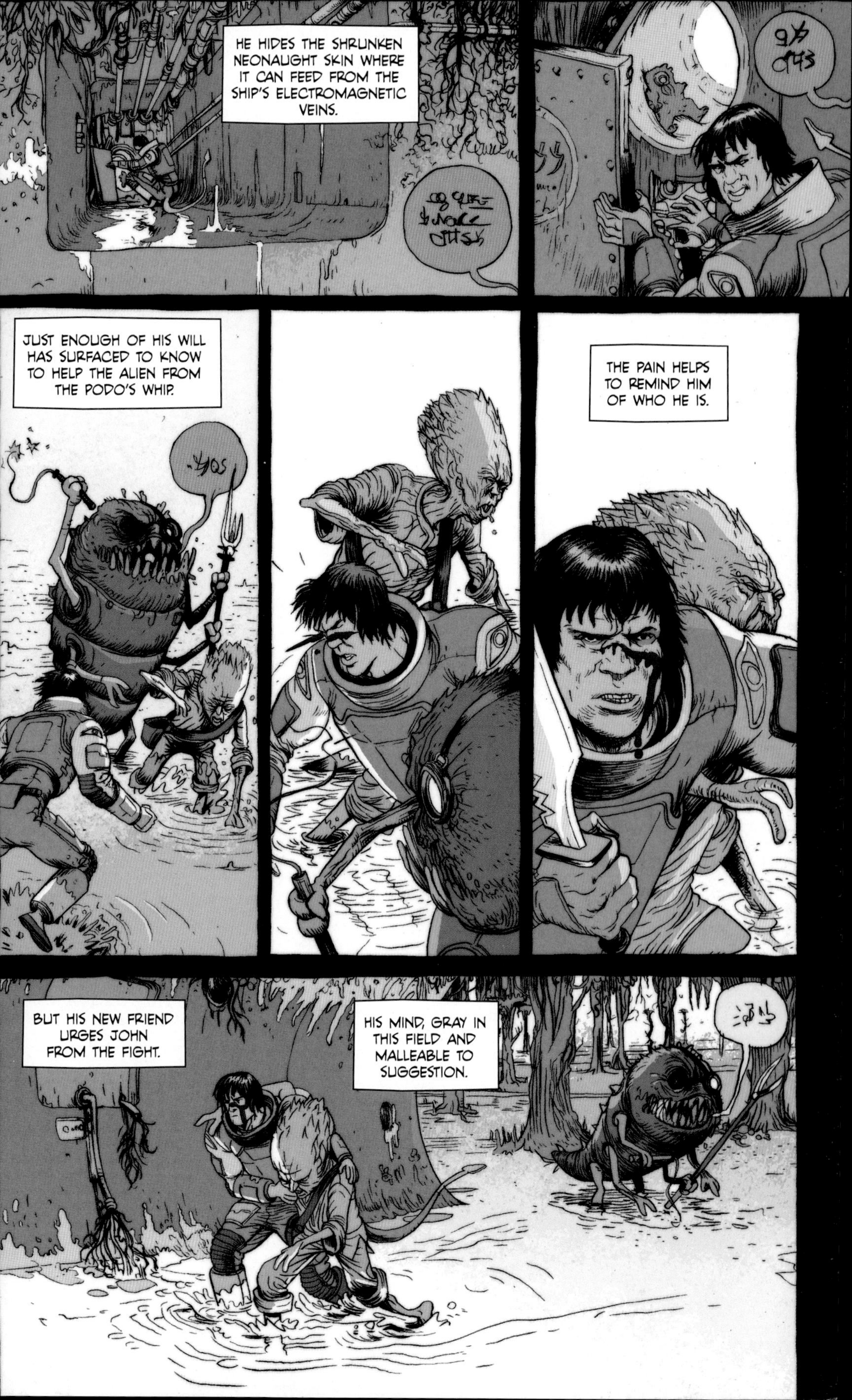
HE HIDES THE SHRUNKEN NEONAUGHT SKIN WHERE IT CAN FEED FROM THE SHIP'S ELECTROMAGNETIC VEINS.
JUST ENOUGH OF HIS WILL HAS SURFACED TO KNOW TO HELP THE ALIEN FROM THE PODO'S WHIP.
THE PAIN HELPS TO REMIND HIM OF WHO HE IS.
BUT HIS NEW FRIEND URGES JOHN FROM THE FIGHT.
HIS MIND, GRAY IN THIS FIELD AND MALLEABLE TO SUGGESTION.

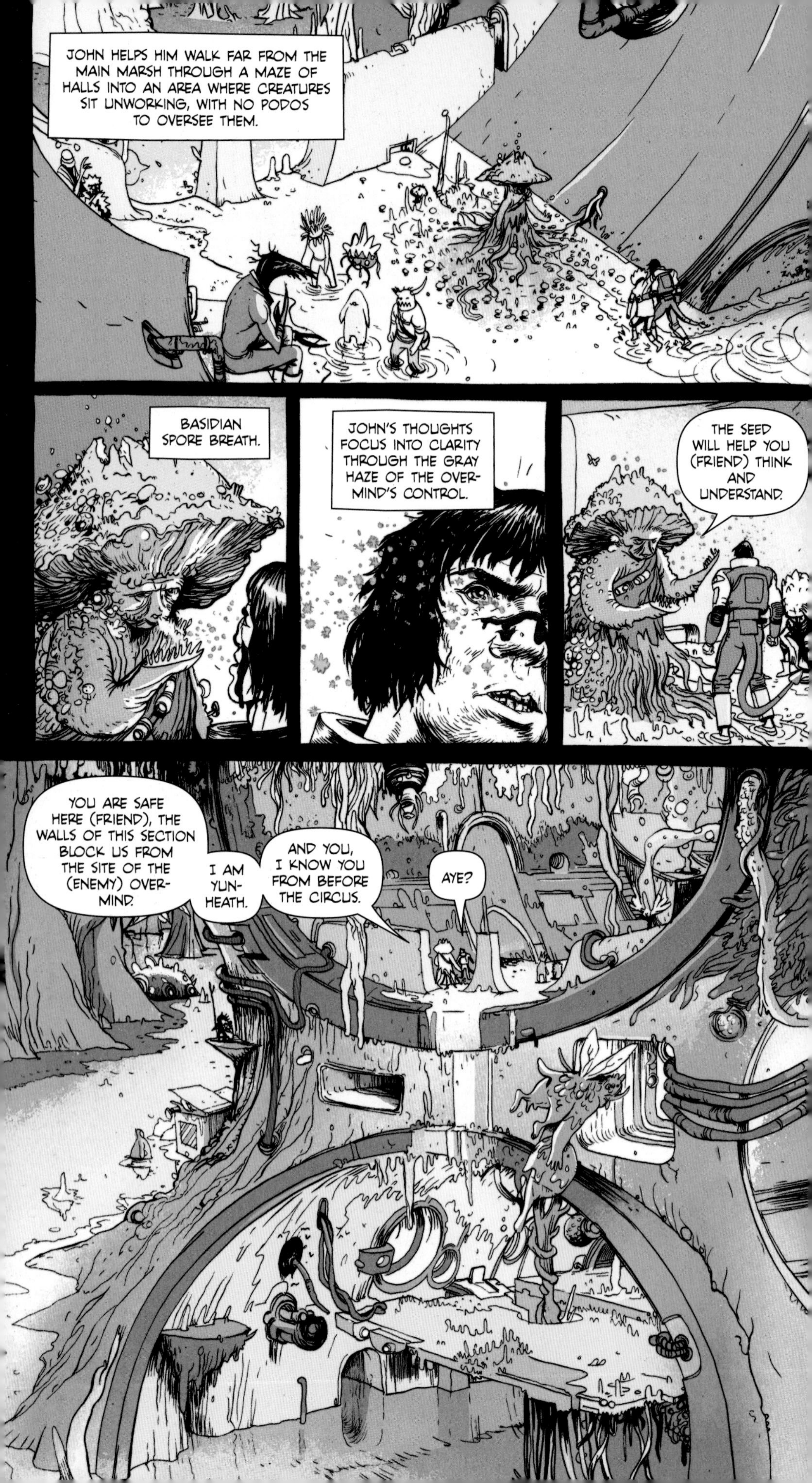
JOHN HELPS HIM WALK FAR FROM THE MAIN MARSH THROUGH A MAZE OF HALLS INTO AN AREA WHERE CREATURES SIT UNWORKING, WITH NO PODOS TO OVERSEE THEM.
BASIDIAN SPORE BREATH.
JOHN'S THOUGHTS FOCUS INTO CLARITY THROUGH THE GRAY HAZE OF THE OVER-MIND'S CONTROL.
THE SEED WILL HELP YOU (FRIEND) THINK AND UNDERSTAND.
YOU ARE SAFE HERE (FRIEND), THE WALLS OF THIS SECTION BLOCK US FROM THE SITE OF THE (ENEMY) OVER-MIND.
I AM YUN-HEATH.
AND YOU, I KNOW YOU FROM BEFORE THE CIRCUS.
AYE?

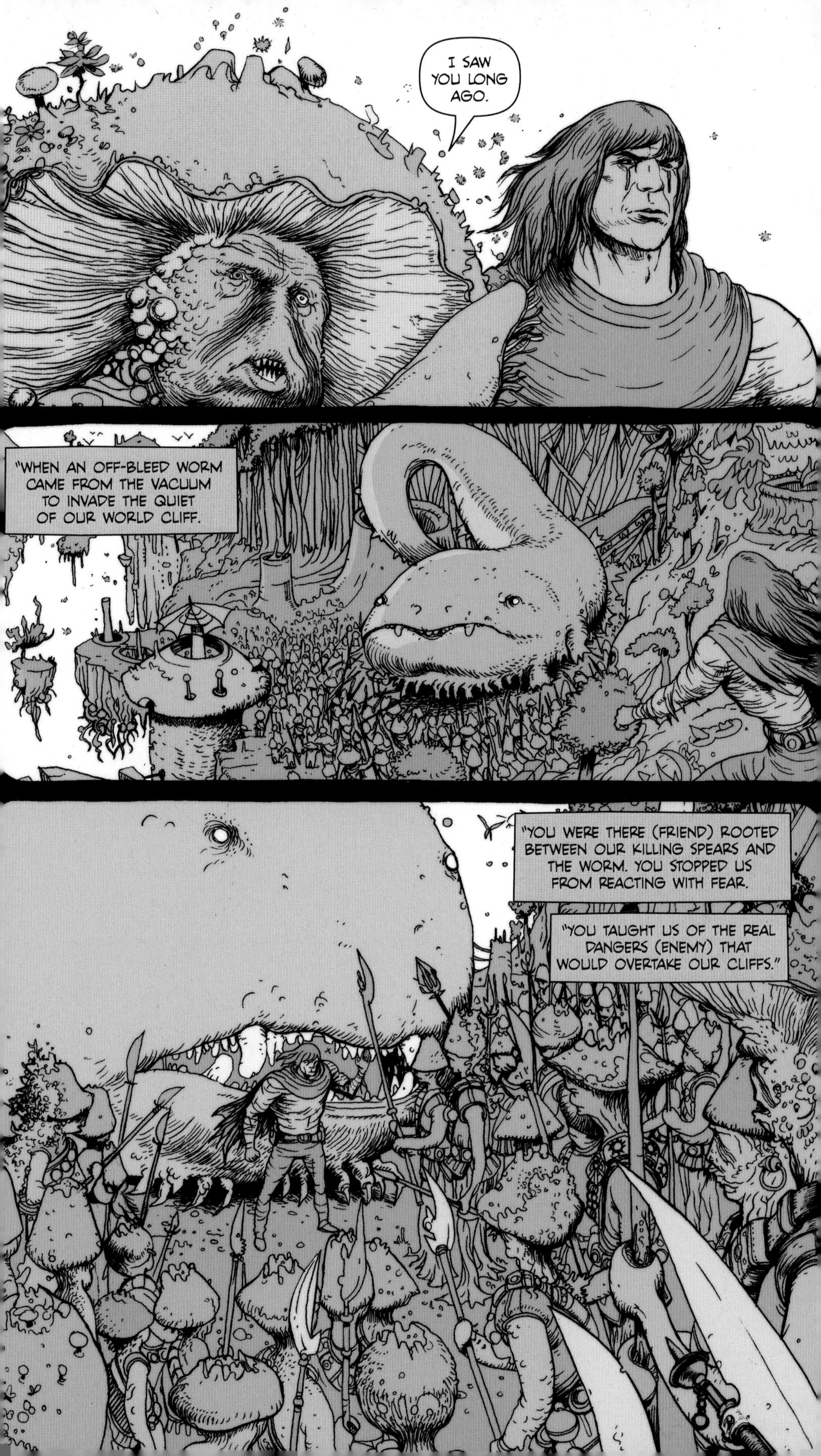
I SAW YOU LONG AGO.
"WHEN AN OFF-BLEED WORM CAME FROM THE VACUUM TO INVADE THE QUIET OF OUR WORLD CLIFF.
"YOU WERE THERE (FRIEND) ROOTED BETWEEN OUR KILLING SPEARS AND THE WORM. YOU STOPPED US FROM REACTING WITH FEAR.
"YOU TAUGHT US OF THE REAL DANGERS (ENEMY) THAT WOULD OVERTAKE OUR CLIFFS."

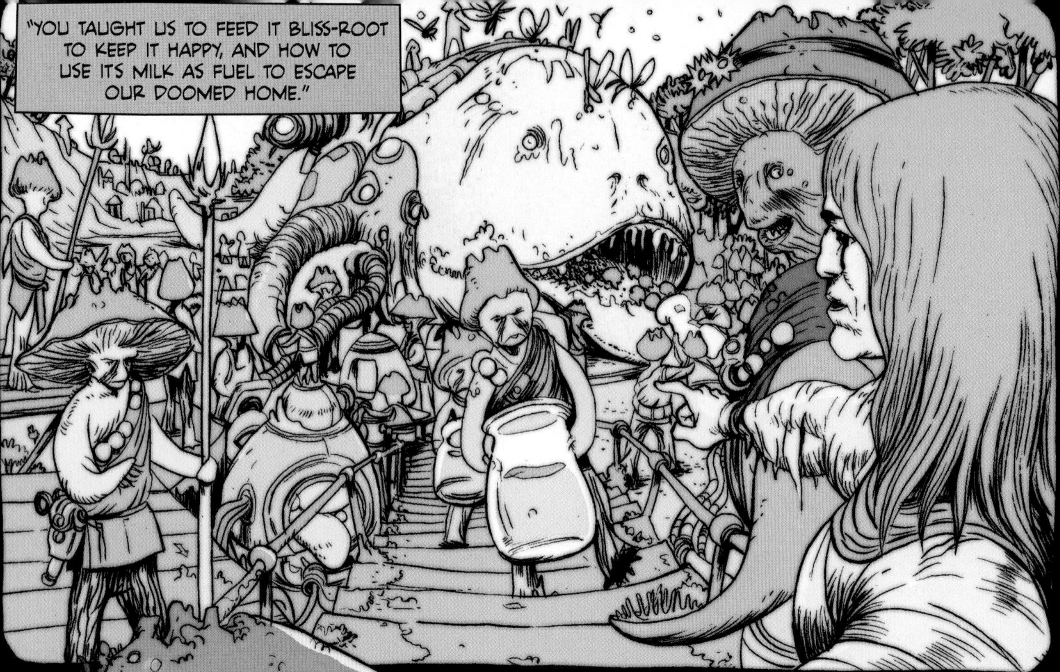
"YOU TAUGHT US TO FEED IT BLISS-ROOT TO KEEP IT HAPPY, AND HOW TO USE ITS MILK AS FUEL TO ESCAPE OUR DOOMED HOME."

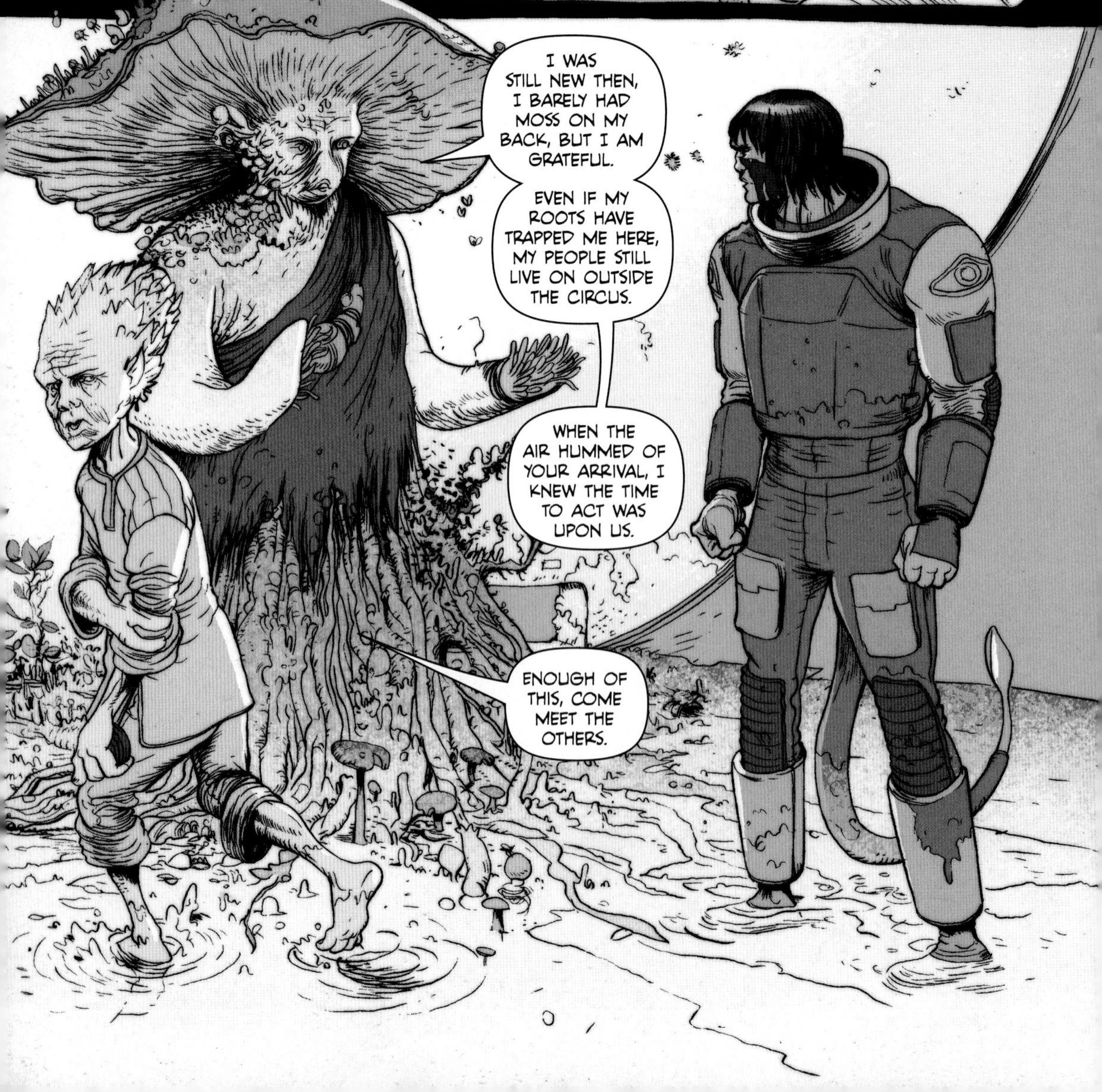
I WAS STILL NEW THEN, I BARELY HAD MOSS ON MY BACK, BUT I AM GRATEFUL.
EVEN IF MY ROOTS HAVE TRAPPED ME HERE, MY PEOPLE STILL LIVE ON OUTSIDE THE CIRCUS.
WHEN THE AIR HUMMED OF YOUR ARRIVAL, I KNEW THE TIME TO ACT WAS UPON US.
ENOUGH OF THIS, COME MEET THE OTHERS.

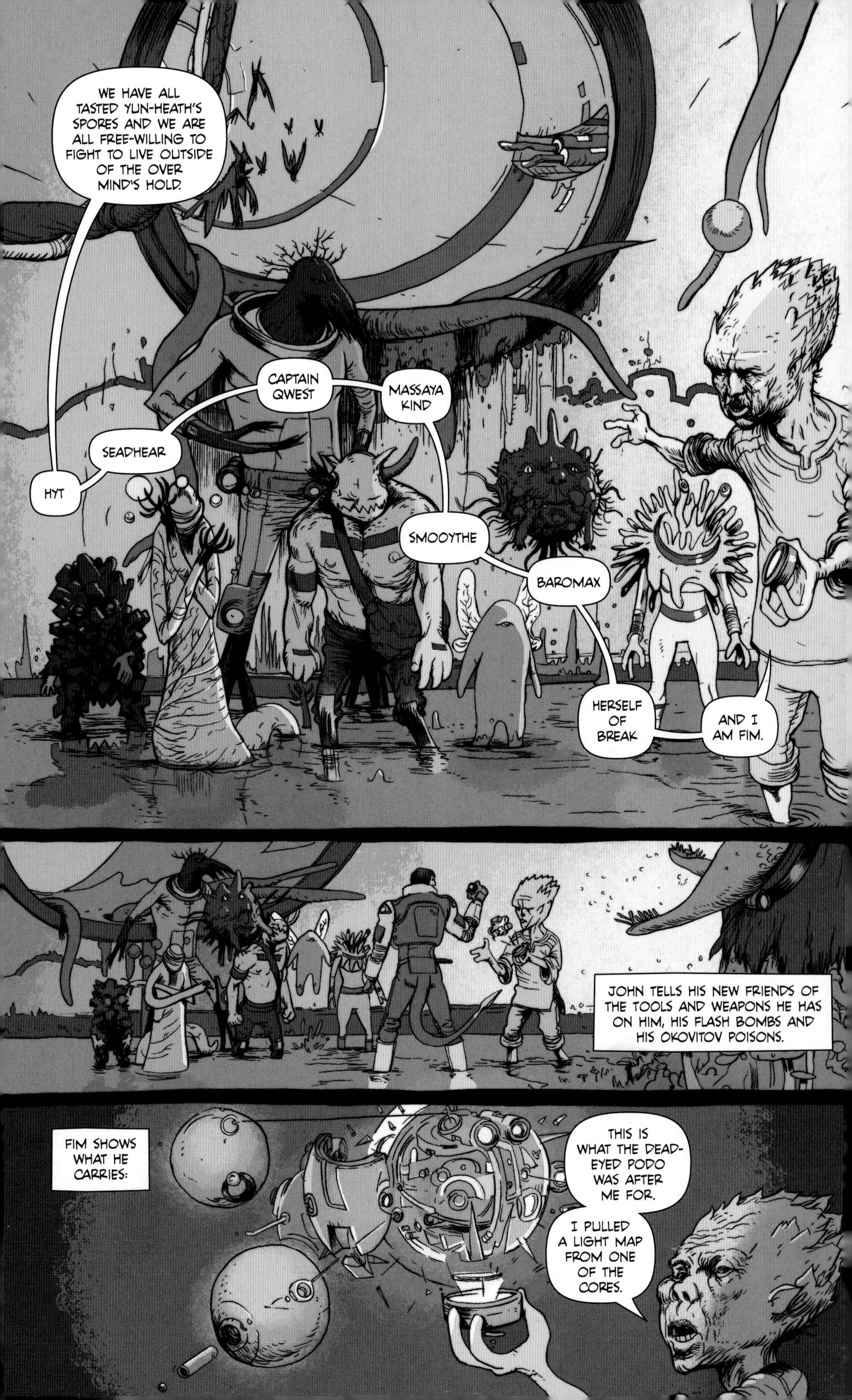
WE HAVE ALL TASTED YUN-HEATH'S SPORES AND WE ARE ALL FREE-WILLING TO FIGHT TO LIVE OUTSIDE OF THE OVER MIND'S HOLD.
HYT
SEADHEAR
CAPTAIN QWEST
MASSAYA KIND
SMOOYTHE
BAROMAX
HERSELF OF BREAK
AND I AM FIM.
JOHN TELLS HIS NEW FRIENDS OF THE TOOLS AND WEAPONS HE HAS ON HIM, HIS FLASH BOMBS AND HIS OKOVITOV POISONS.
FIM SHOWS WHAT HE CARRIES:
THIS IS WHAT THE DEAD-EYED PODO WAS AFTER ME FOR.
I PULLED A LIGHT MAP FROM ONE OF THE CORES.

WITH THE MAP THEY PLAN.

THE OVER-MIND IS DUG-IN, BUT VULNERABLE.

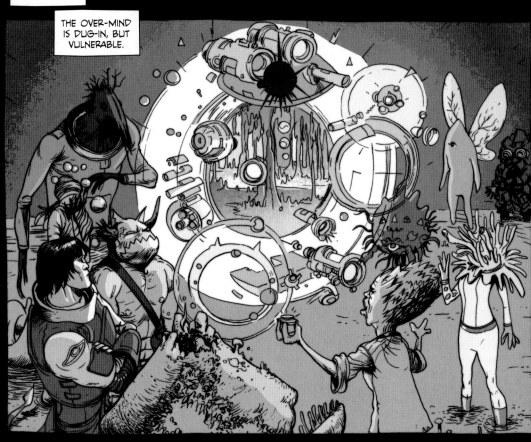

OVER THE NEXT DAYS THEY RETURN TO WORK.

WITH HIS MIND CLEARER THE WORK FEELS GRUELING AND INTERMINABLE.

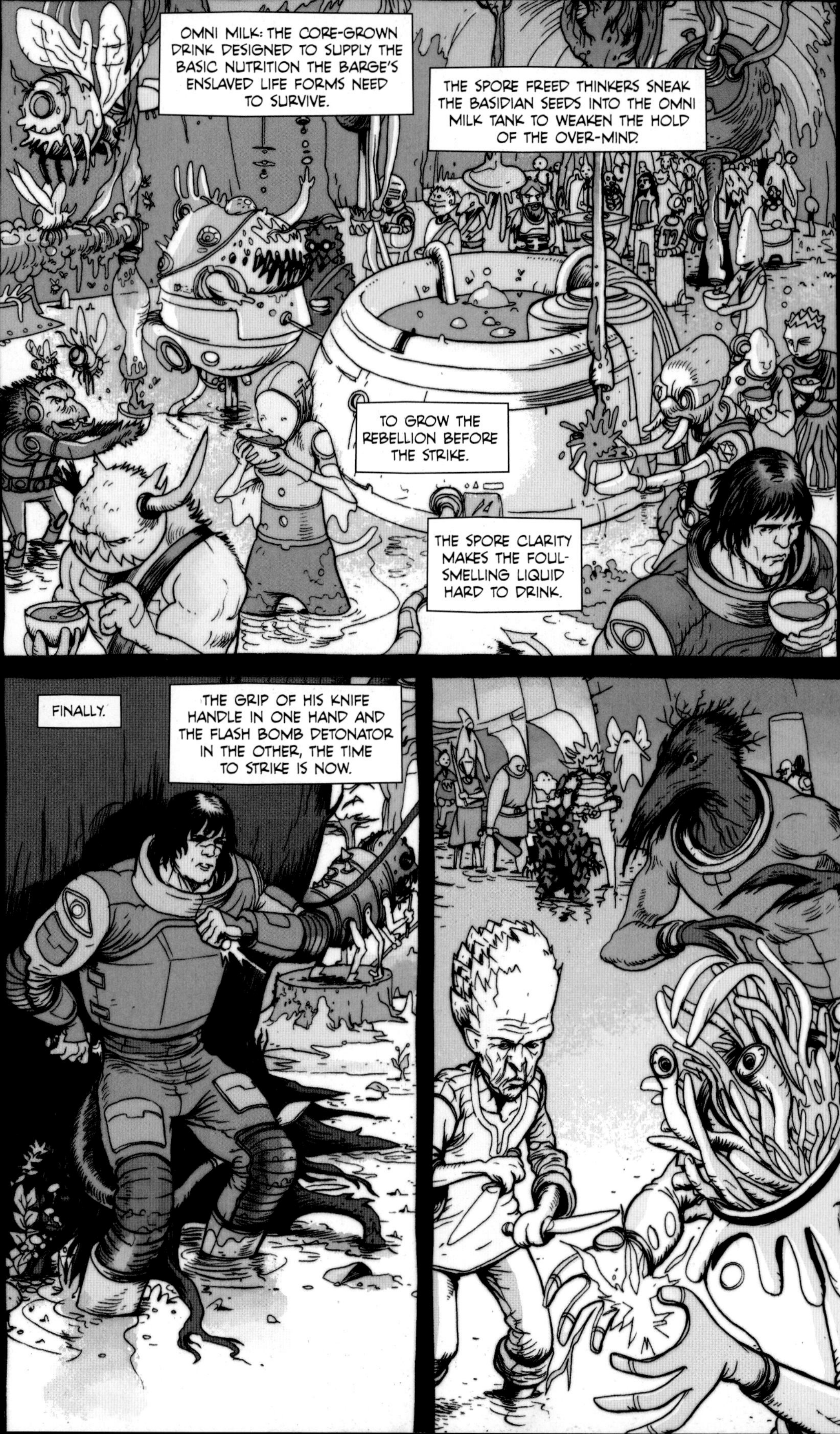
OMNI MILK: THE CORE-GROWN DRINK DESIGNED TO SUPPLY THE BASIC NUTRITION THE BARGE'S ENSLAVED LIFE FORMS NEED TO SURVIVE.
THE SPORE FREED THINKERS SNEAK THE BASIDIAN SEEDS INTO THE OMNI MILK TANK TO WEAKEN THE HOLD OF THE OVER-MIND.
TO GROW THE REBELLION BEFORE THE STRIKE.
THE SPORE CLARITY MAKES THE FOUL-SMELLING LIQUID HARD TO DRINK.
FINALLY.
THE GRIP OF HIS KNIFE HANDLE IN ONE HAND AND THE FLASH BOMB DETONATOR IN THE OTHER, THE TIME TO STRIKE IS NOW.

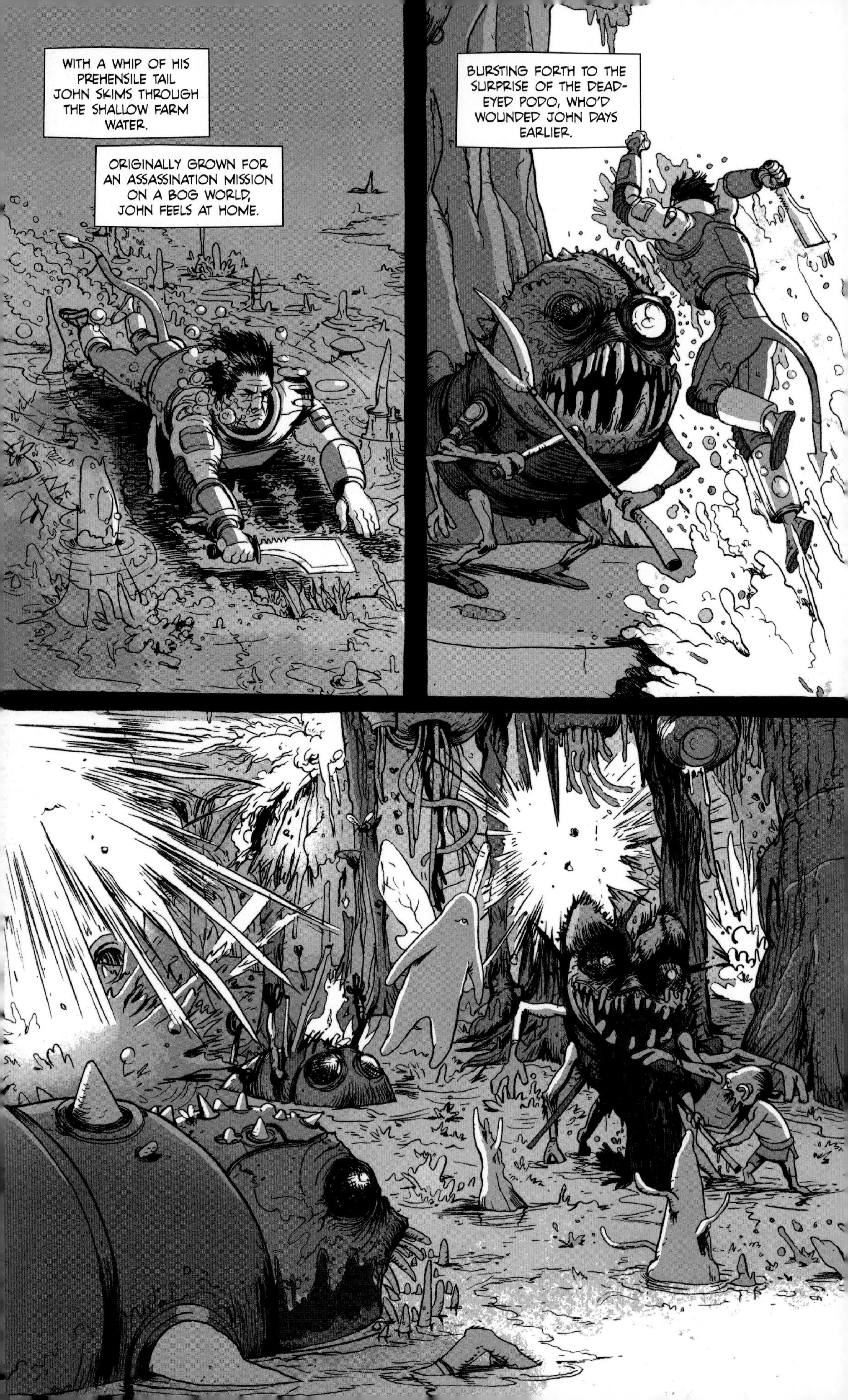
WITH A WHIP OF HIS PREHENSILE TAIL JOHN SKIMS THROUGH THE SHALLOW FARM WATER.
ORIGINALLY GROWN FOR AN ASSASSINATION MISSION ON A BOG WORLD, JOHN FEELS AT HOME.
BURSTING FORTH TO THE SURPRISE OF THE DEAD-EYED PODO, WHO'D WOUNDED JOHN DAYS EARLIER.

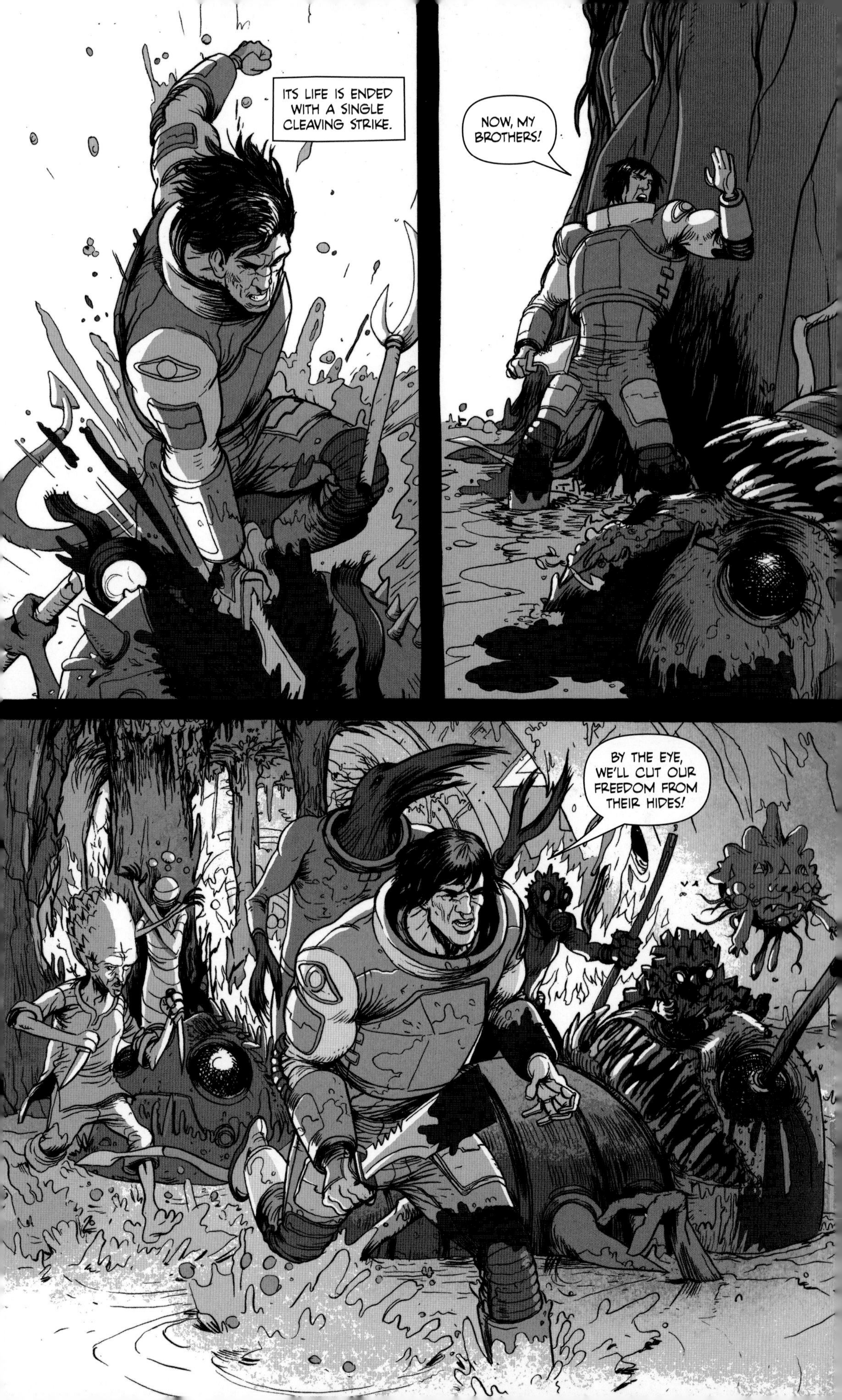
ITS LIFE IS ENDED WITH A SINGLE CLEAVING STRIKE.
NOW, MY BROTHERS!
BY THE EYE, WE'LL CUT OUR FREEDOM FROM THEIR HIDES!

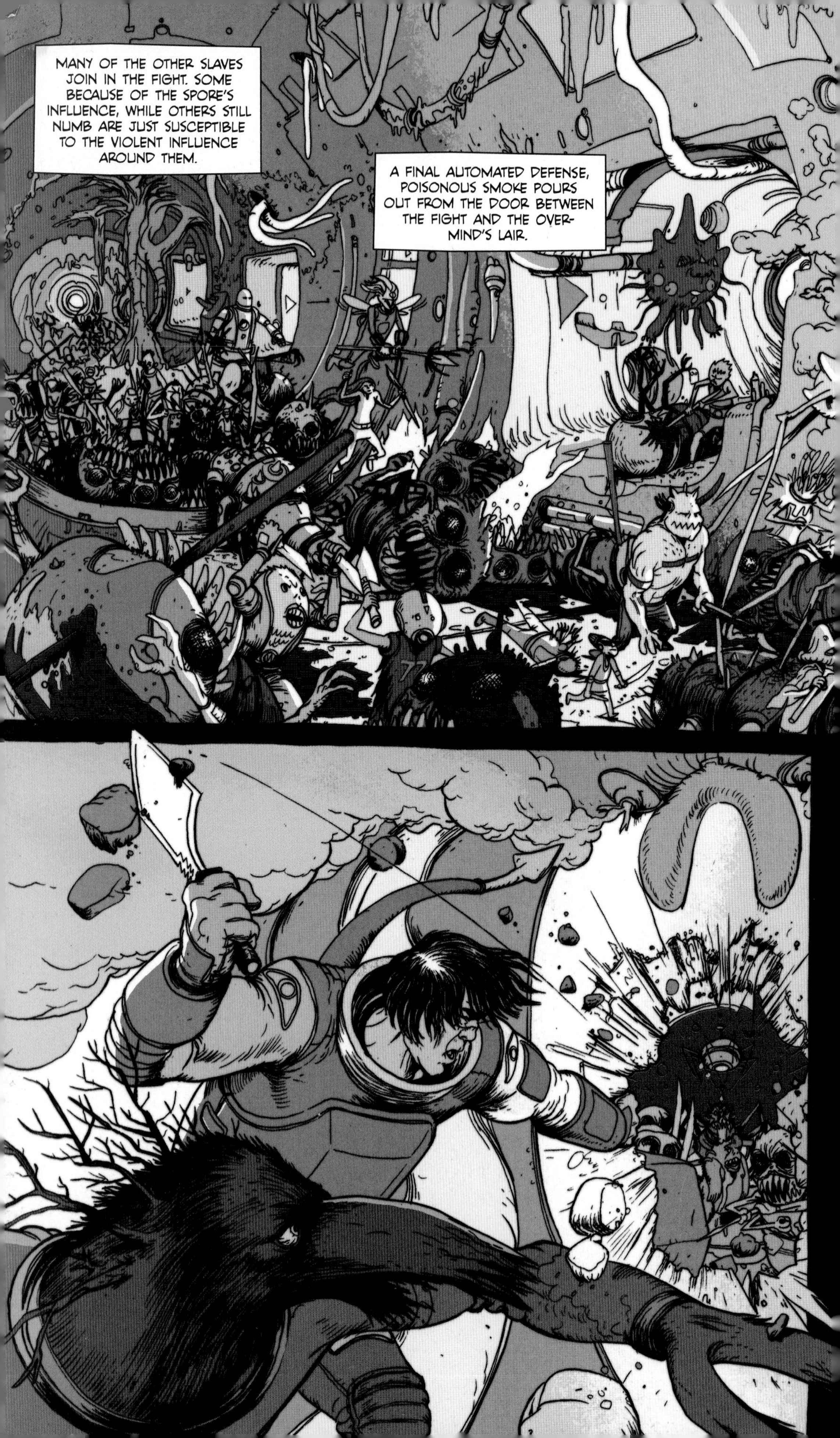
MANY OF THE OTHER SLAVES JOIN IN THE FIGHT. SOME BECAUSE OF THE SPORE'S INFLUENCE, WHILE OTHERS STILL NUMB ARE JUST SUSCEPTIBLE TO THE VIOLENT INFLUENCE AROUND THEM.
A FINAL AUTOMATED DEFENSE, POISONOUS SMOKE POURS OUT FROM THE DOOR BETWEEN THE FIGHT AND THE OVER-MIND'S LAIR.

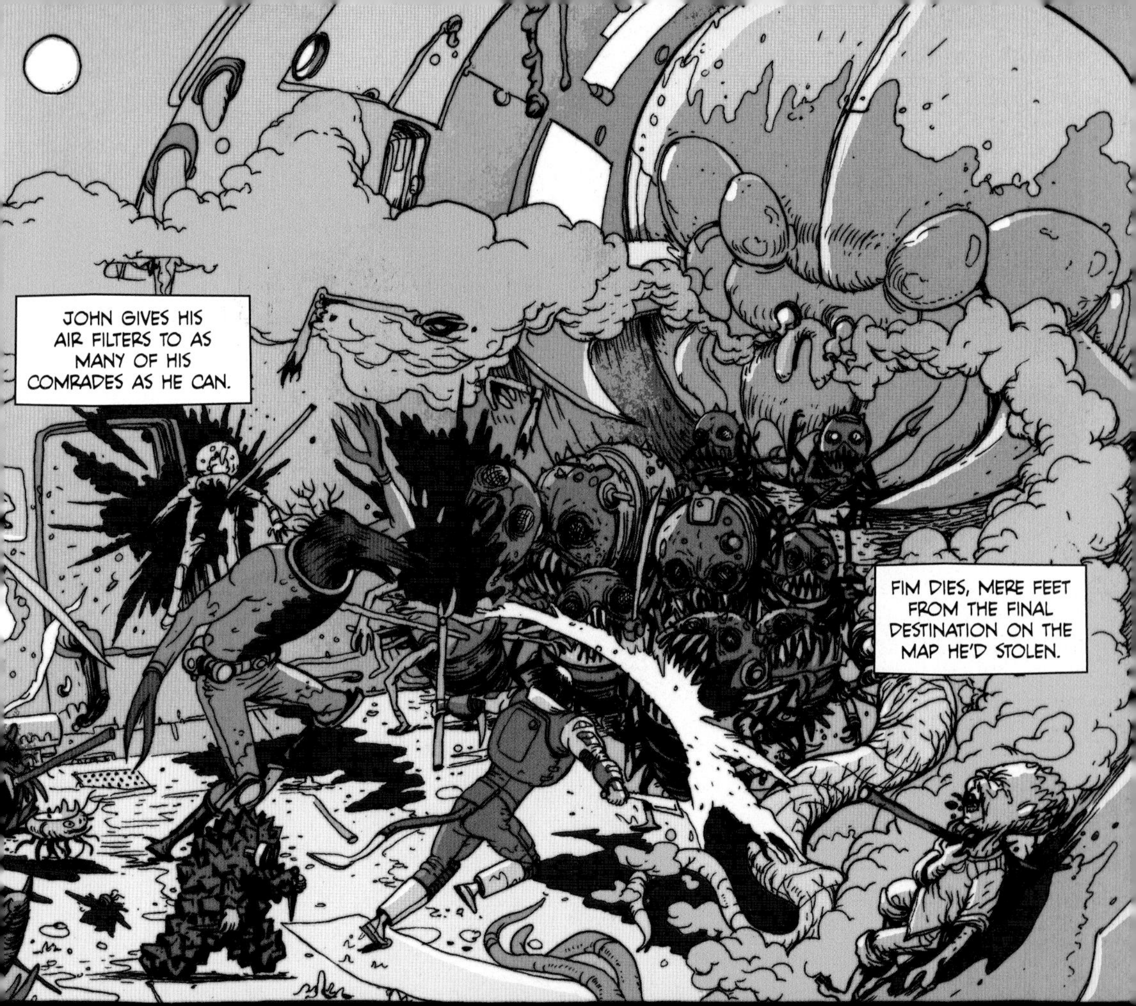
JOHN GIVES HIS AIR FILTERS TO AS MANY OF HIS COMRADES AS HE CAN.
FIM DIES, MERE FEET FROM THE FINAL DESTINATION ON THE MAP HE'D STOLEN.

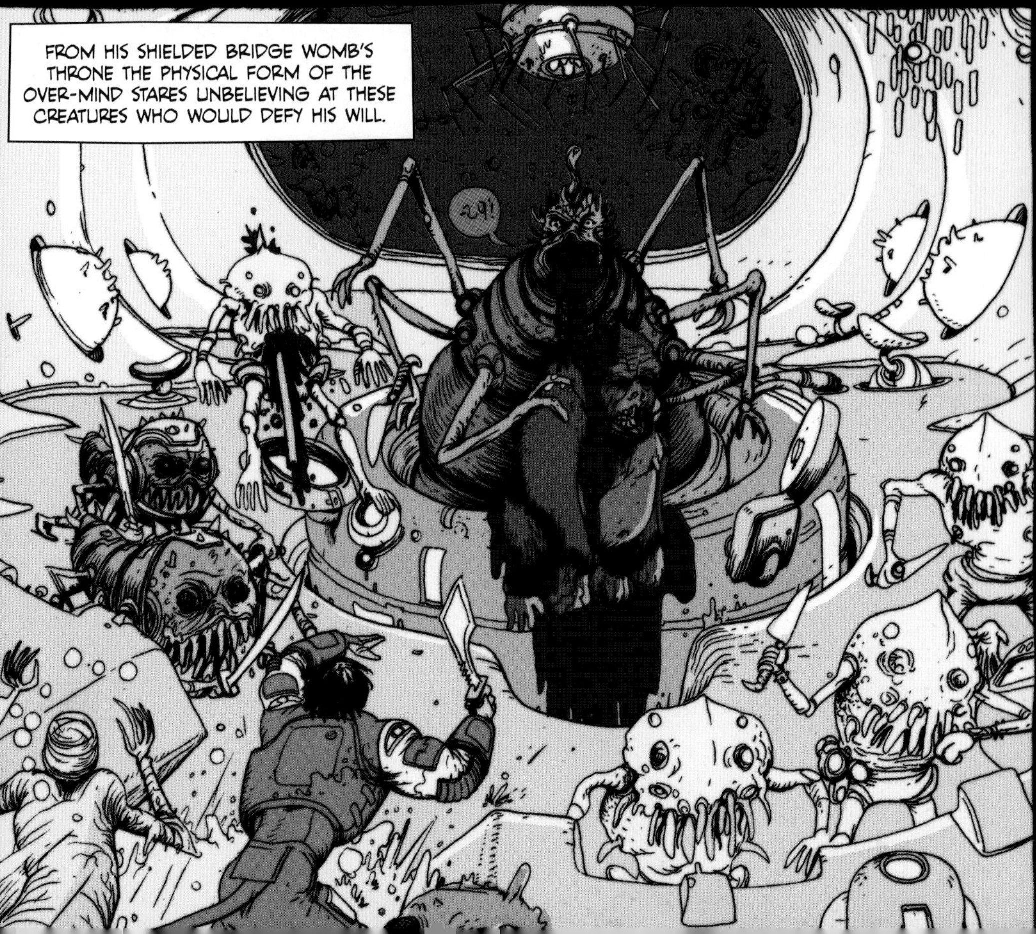
FROM HIS SHIELDED BRIDGE WOMB'S THRONE THE PHYSICAL FORM OF THE OVER-MIND STARES UNBELIEVING AT THESE CREATURES WHO WOULD DEFY HIS WILL.

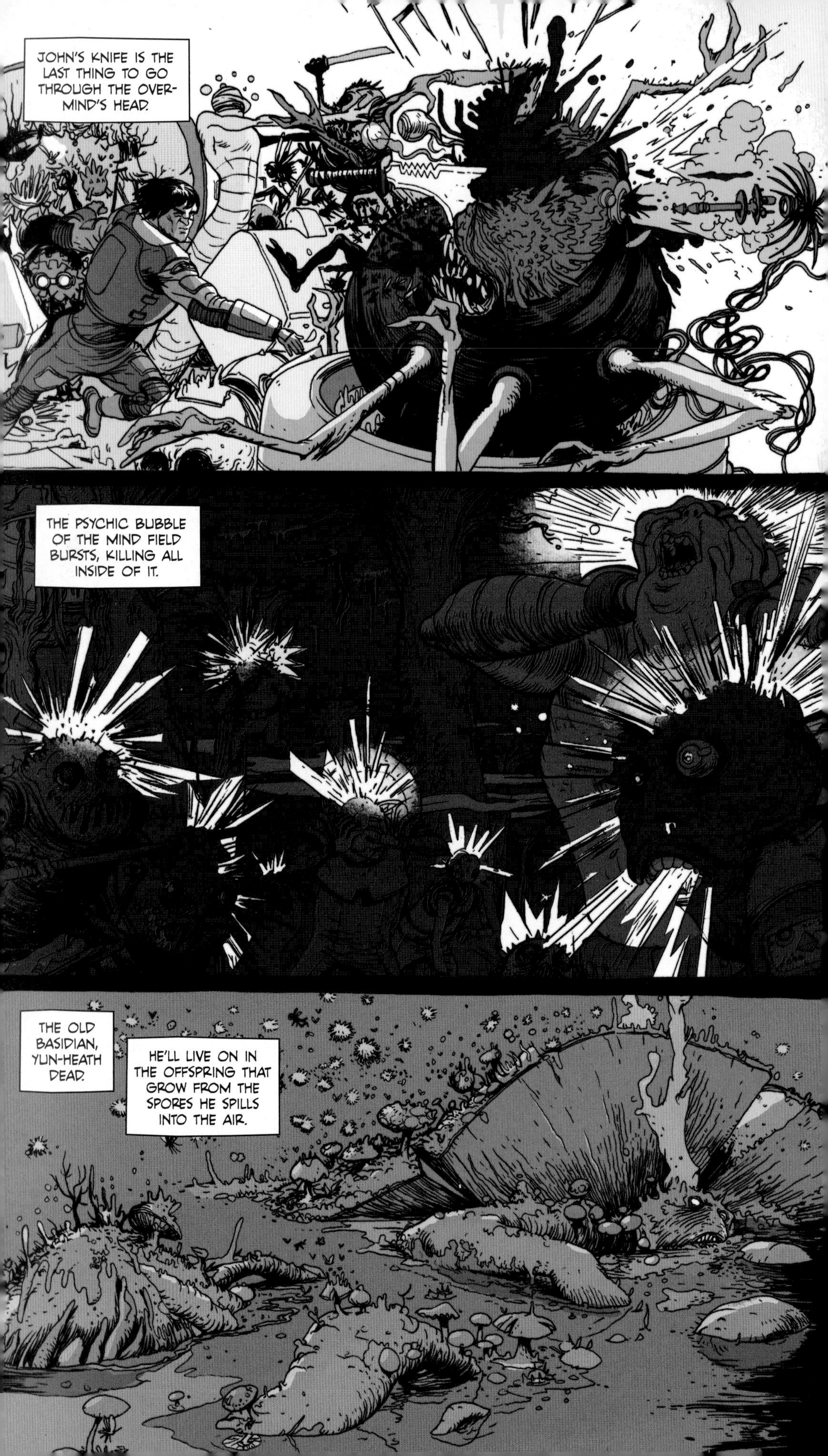
JOHN'S KNIFE IS THE LAST THING TO GO THROUGH THE OVER-MIND'S HEAD.
THE PSYCHIC BUBBLE OF THE MIND FIELD BURSTS, KILLING ALL INSIDE OF IT.
THE OLD BASIDIAN, YUN-HEATH DEAD.
HE'LL LIVE ON IN THE OFFSPRING THAT GROW FROM THE SPORES HE SPILLS INTO THE AIR.

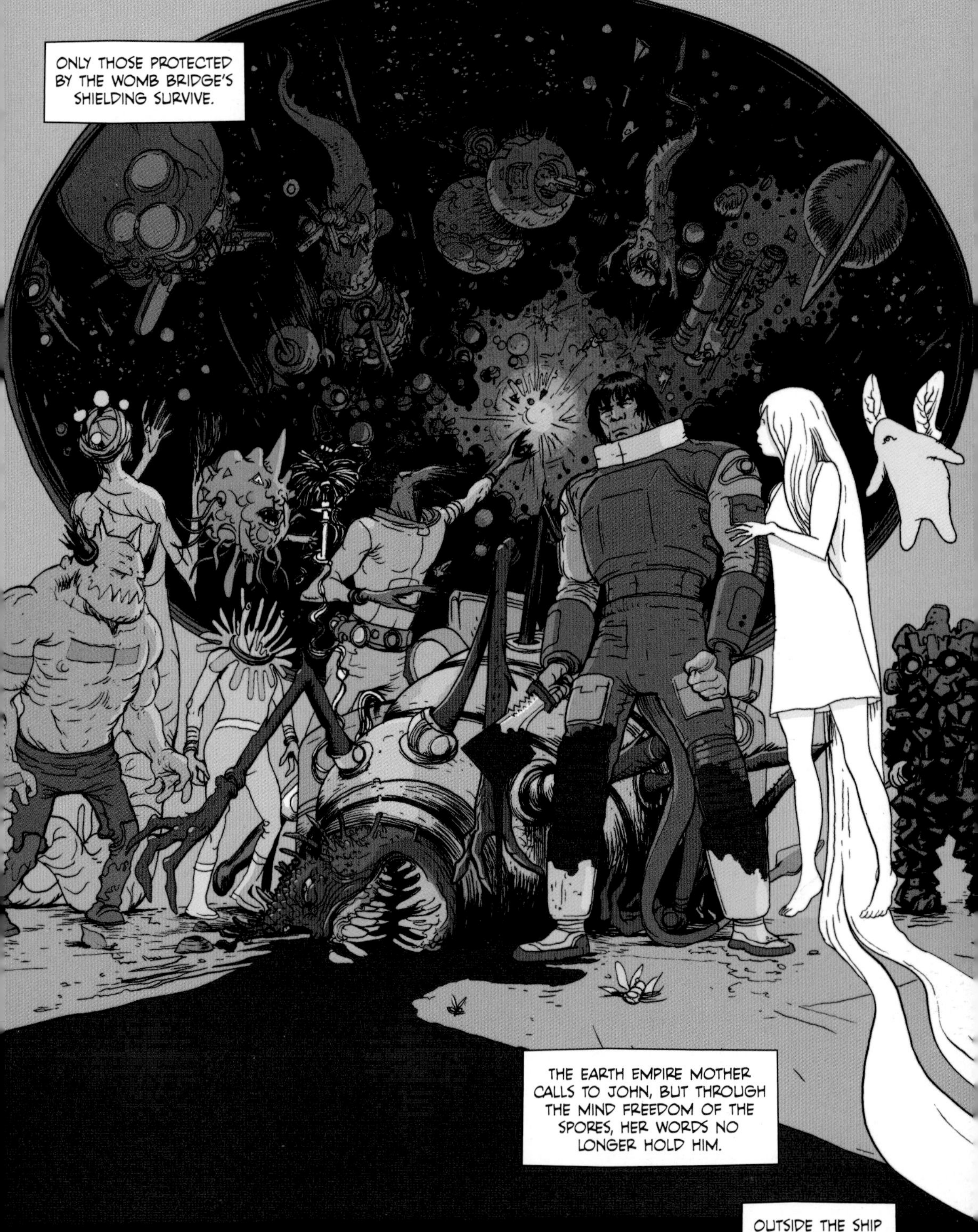
ONLY THOSE PROTECTED BY THE WOMB BRIDGE'S SHIELDING SURVIVE.
THE EARTH EMPIRE MOTHER CALLS TO JOHN, BUT THROUGH THE MIND FREEDOM OF THE SPORES, HER WORDS NO LONGER HOLD HIM.

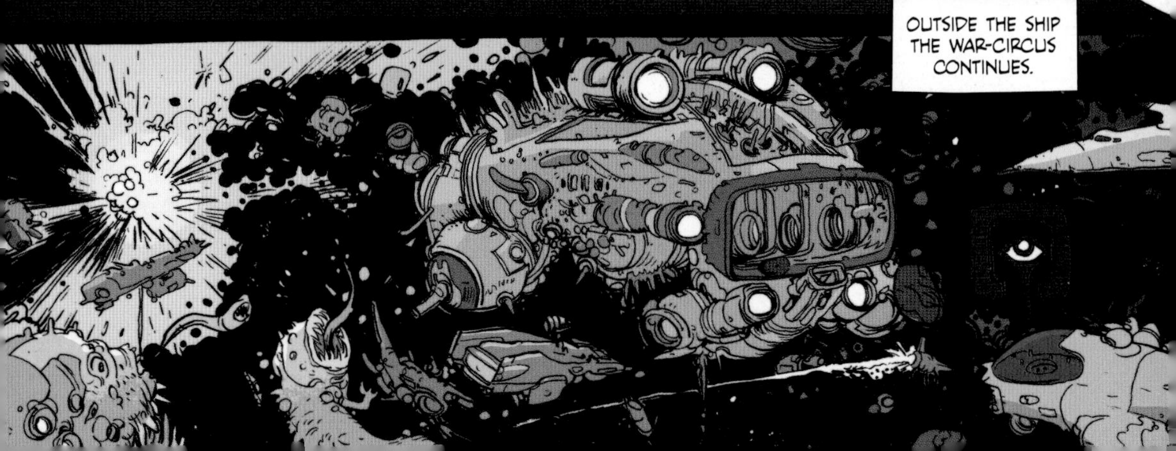
OUTSIDE THE SHIP THE WAR-CIRCUS CONTINUES.

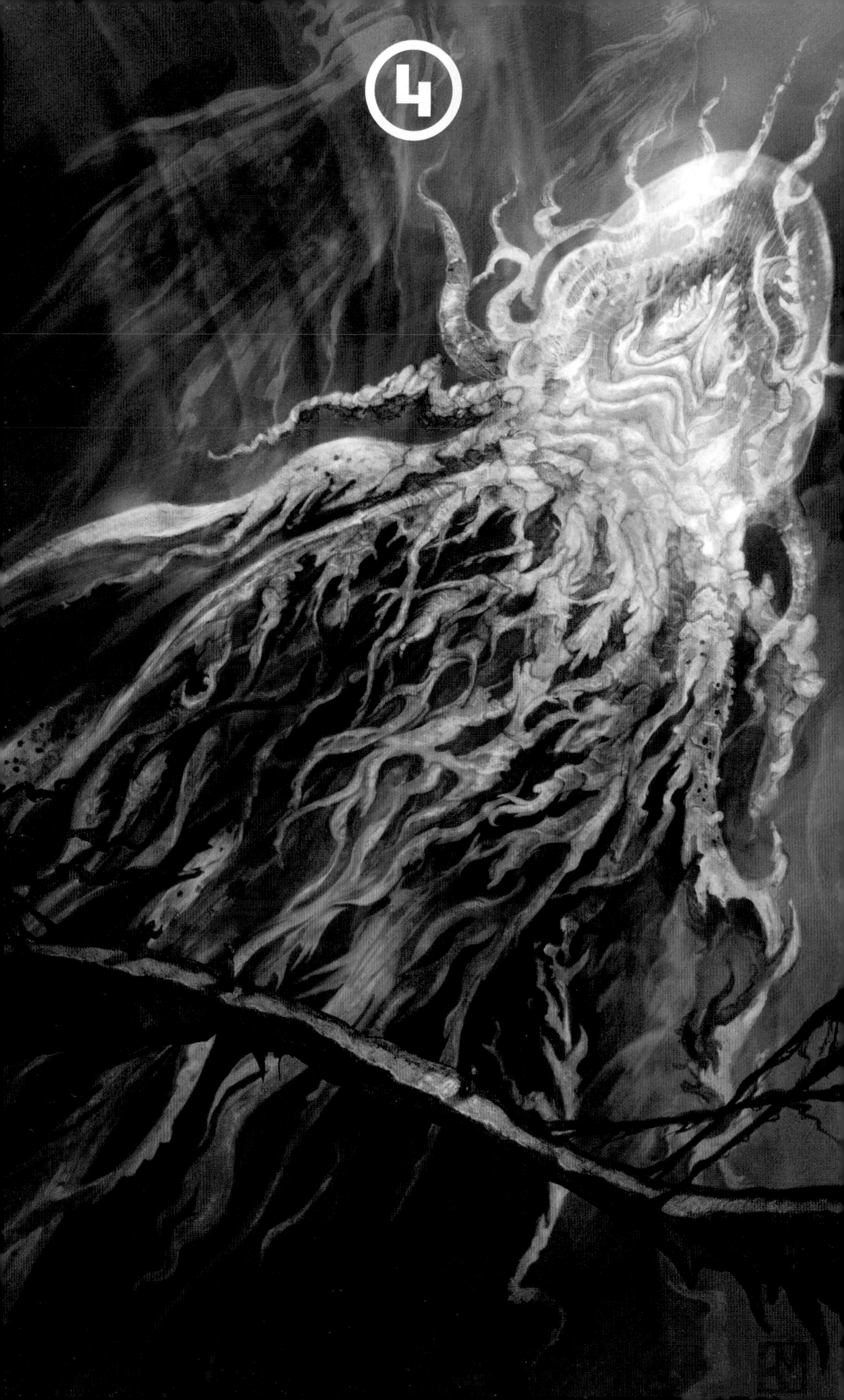
4

CHAPTER UNUS

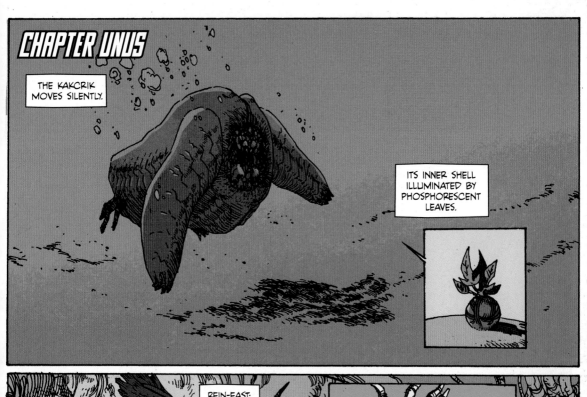

THE KAKCRIK MOVES SILENTLY.

ITS INNER SHELL ILLUMINATED BY PHOSPHORESCENT LEAVES.

REIN-EAST: ORPHANED ASSASSIN.

Igh Leaves: to conceal her scent.

Eye Stones.

SHE KNOWS THAT TONIGHT MAY BRING HER DEATH BUT ANY CHANCE TO KILL A MEMBER OF THE JINNAH IS WORTH THE RISK.

SHE WATCHES THE PALACE SWIM TOWARDS HER AND TRIES TO SLOW HER SHALLOW BREATHING.

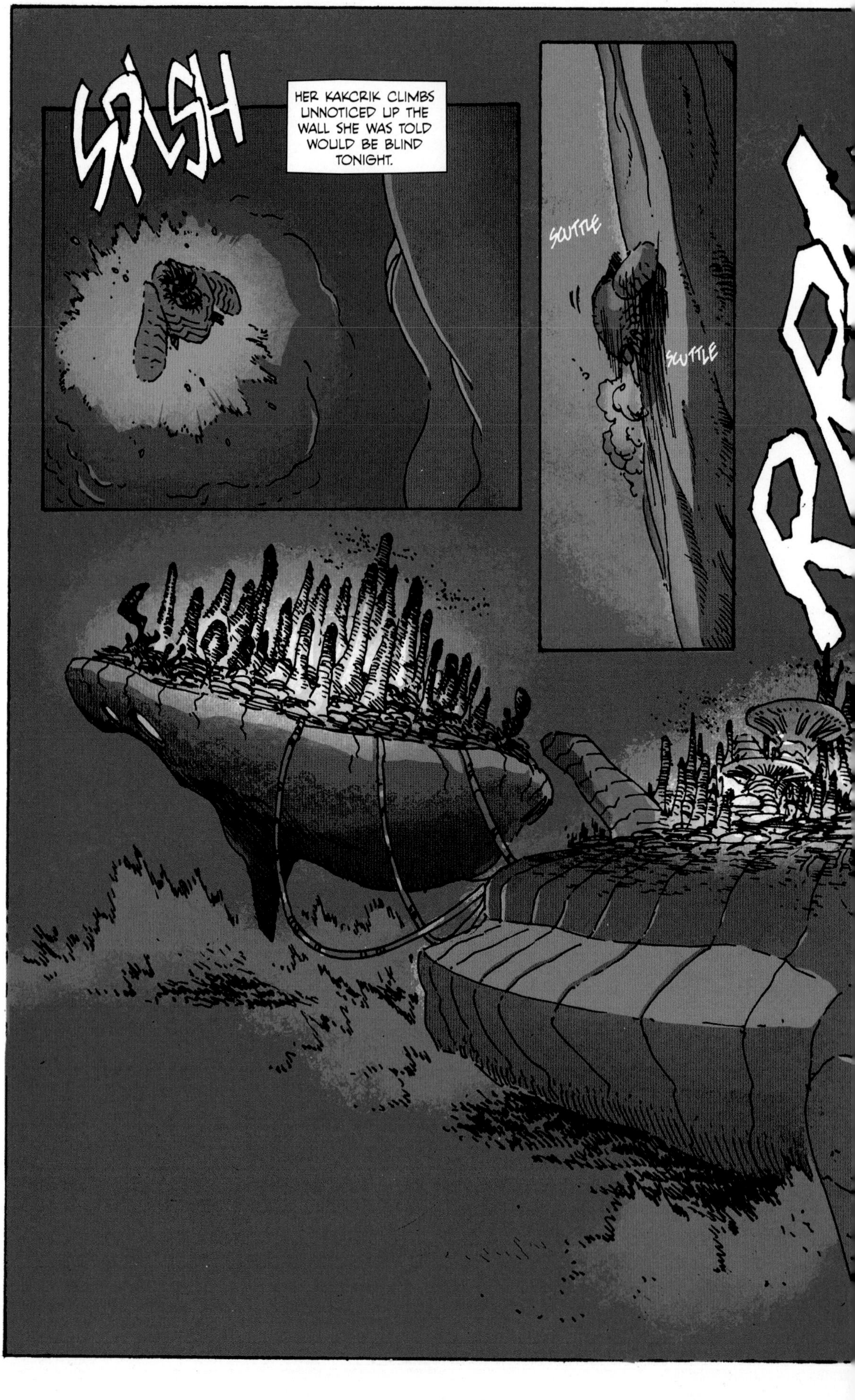
SPLSH
HER KAKCRIK CLIMBS UNNOTICED UP THE WALL SHE WAS TOLD WOULD BE BLIND TONIGHT.
SCUTTLE
SCUTTLE

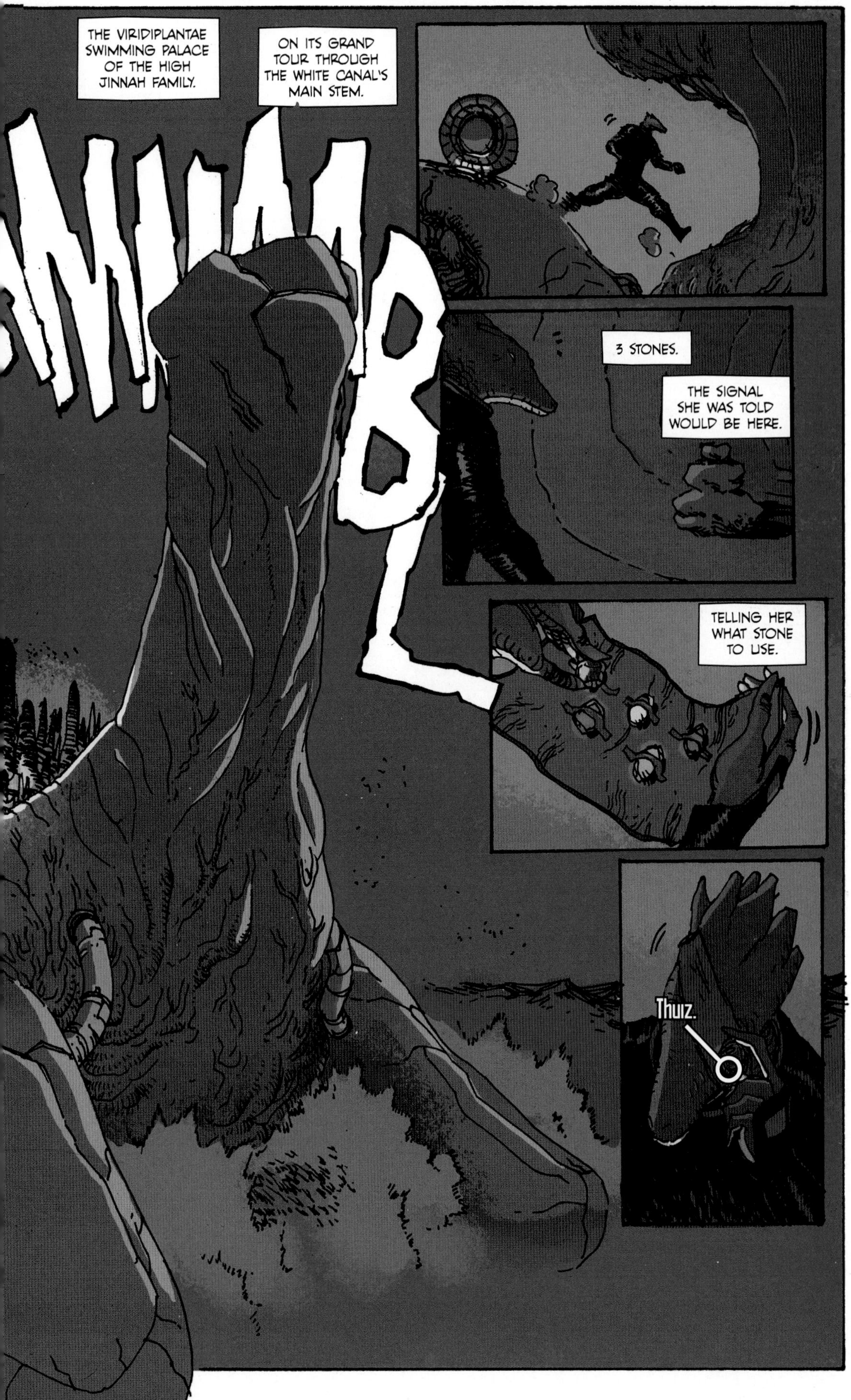
THE VIRIDIPLANTAE SWIMMING PALACE OF THE HIGH JINNAH FAMILY.
ON ITS GRAND TOUR THROUGH THE WHITE CANAL'S MAIN STEM.
3 STONES.
THE SIGNAL SHE WAS TOLD WOULD BE HERE.
TELLING HER WHAT STONE TO USE.
Thuiz.

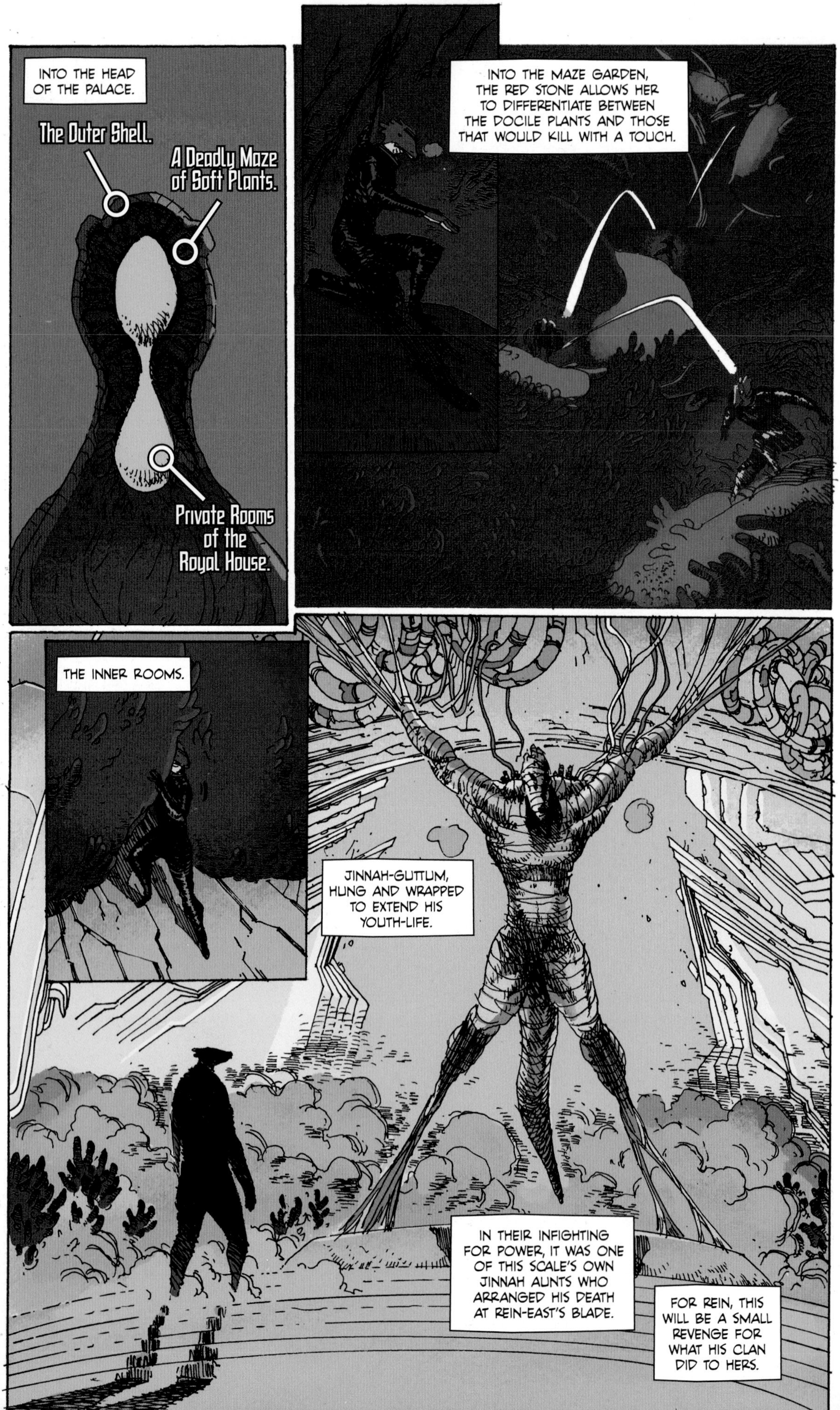

INTO THE HEAD OF THE PALACE.
The Outer Shell.
A Deadly Maze of Soft Plants.
Private Rooms of the Royal House.
INTO THE MAZE GARDEN, THE RED STONE ALLOWS HER TO DIFFERENTIATE BETWEEN THE DOCILE PLANTS AND THOSE THAT WOULD KILL WITH A TOUCH.
THE INNER ROOMS.
JINNAH-GUTTUM, HUNG AND WRAPPED TO EXTEND HIS YOUTH-LIFE.
IN THEIR INFIGHTING FOR POWER, IT WAS ONE OF THIS SCALE'S OWN JINNAH AUNTS WHO ARRANGED HIS DEATH AT REIN-EAST'S BLADE.
FOR REIN, THIS WILL BE A SMALL REVENGE FOR WHAT HIS CLAN DID TO HERS.

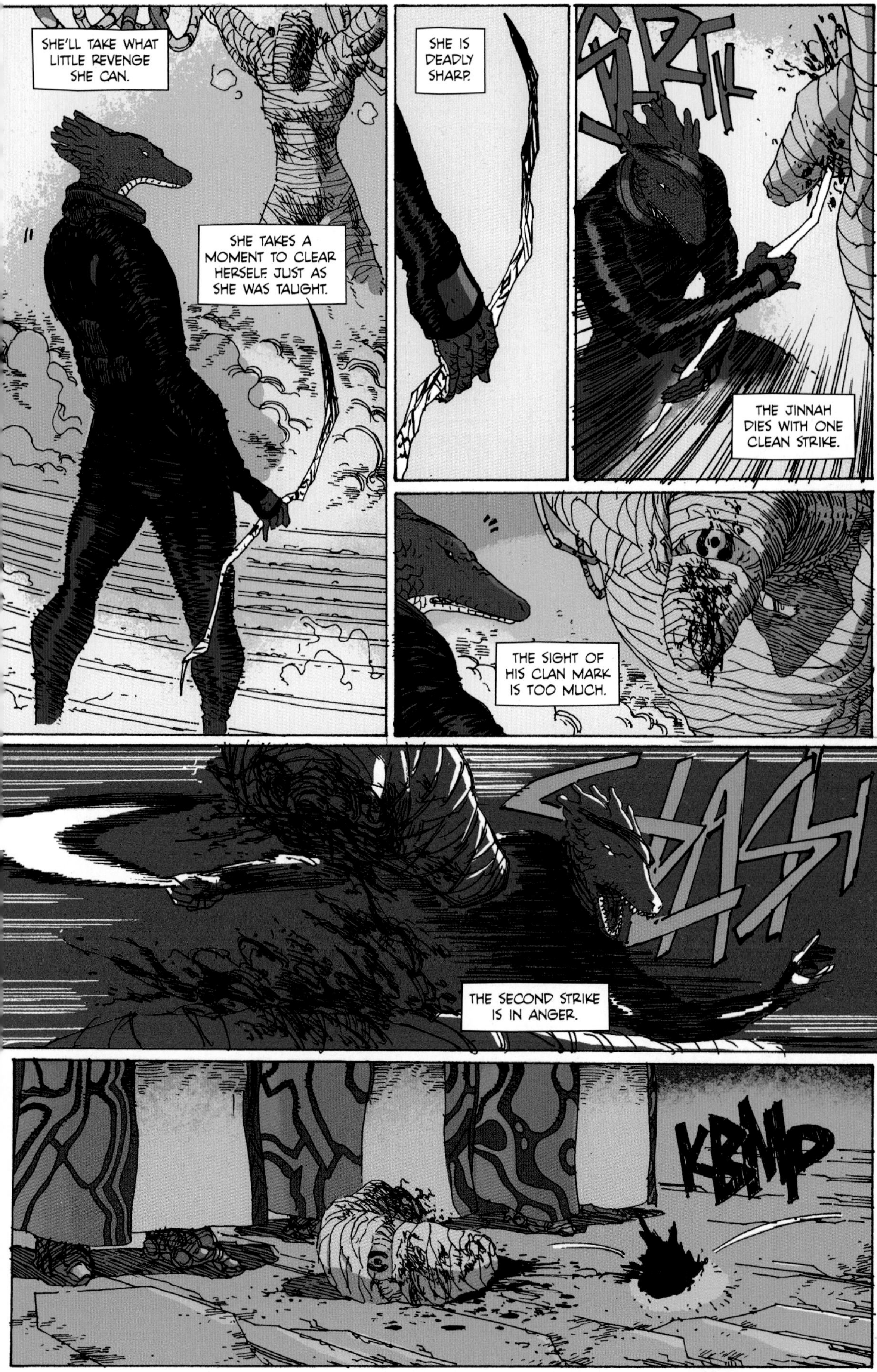
SHE'LL TAKE WHAT LITTLE REVENGE SHE CAN.
SHE TAKES A MOMENT TO CLEAR HERSELF. JUST AS SHE WAS TAUGHT.
SHE IS DEADLY SHARP.
THE JINNAH DIES WITH ONE CLEAN STRIKE.
THE SIGHT OF HIS CLAN MARK IS TOO MUCH.
THE SECOND STRIKE IS IN ANGER.

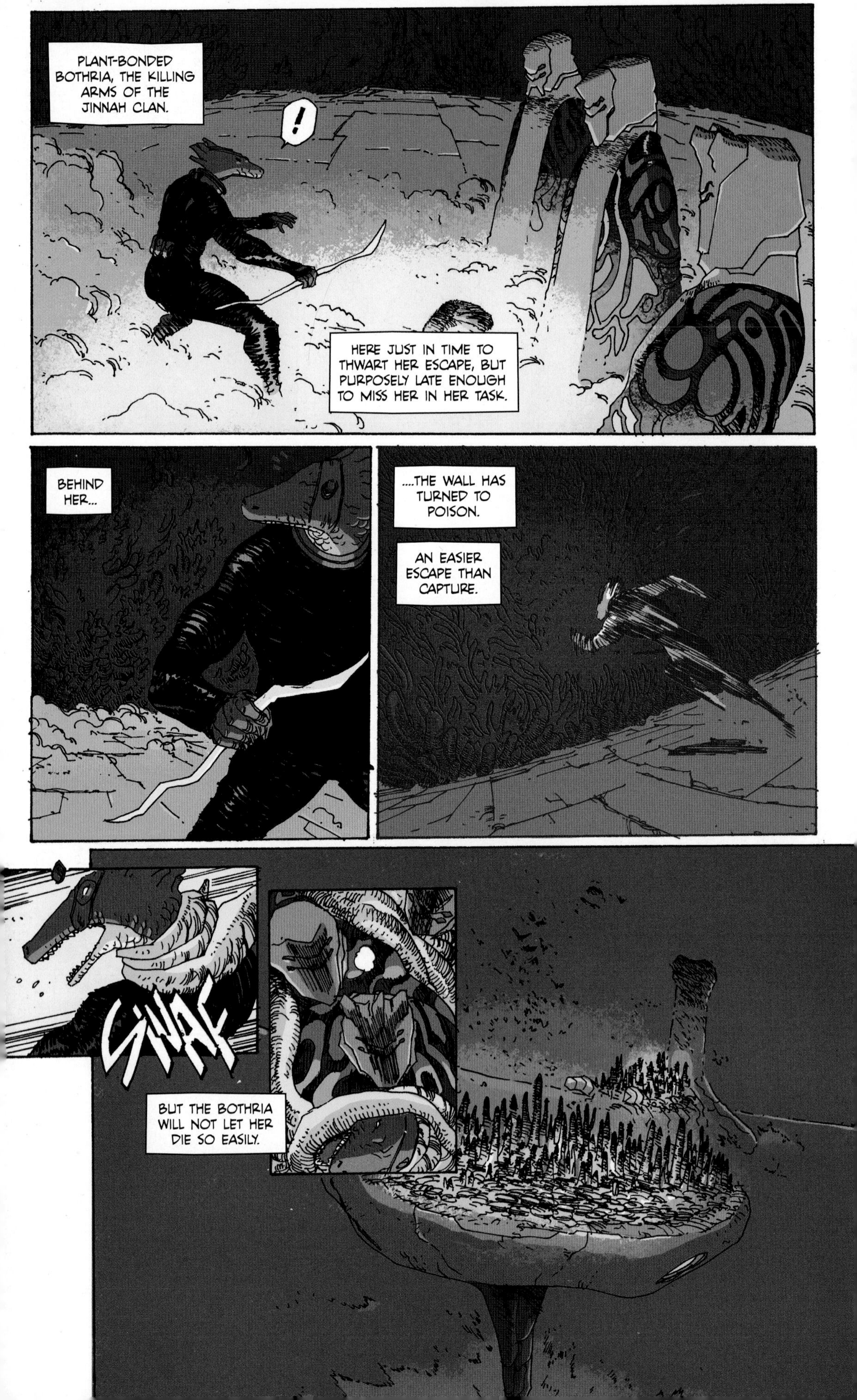
PLANT-BONDED BOTHRIA, THE KILLING ARMS OF THE JINNAH CLAN.
!
HERE JUST IN TIME TO THWART HER ESCAPE, BUT PURPOSELY LATE ENOUGH TO MISS HER IN HER TASK.
BEHIND HER...
....THE WALL HAS TURNED TO POISON.
AN EASIER ESCAPE THAN CAPTURE.
SNAP
BUT THE BOTHRIA WILL NOT LET HER DIE SO EASILY.

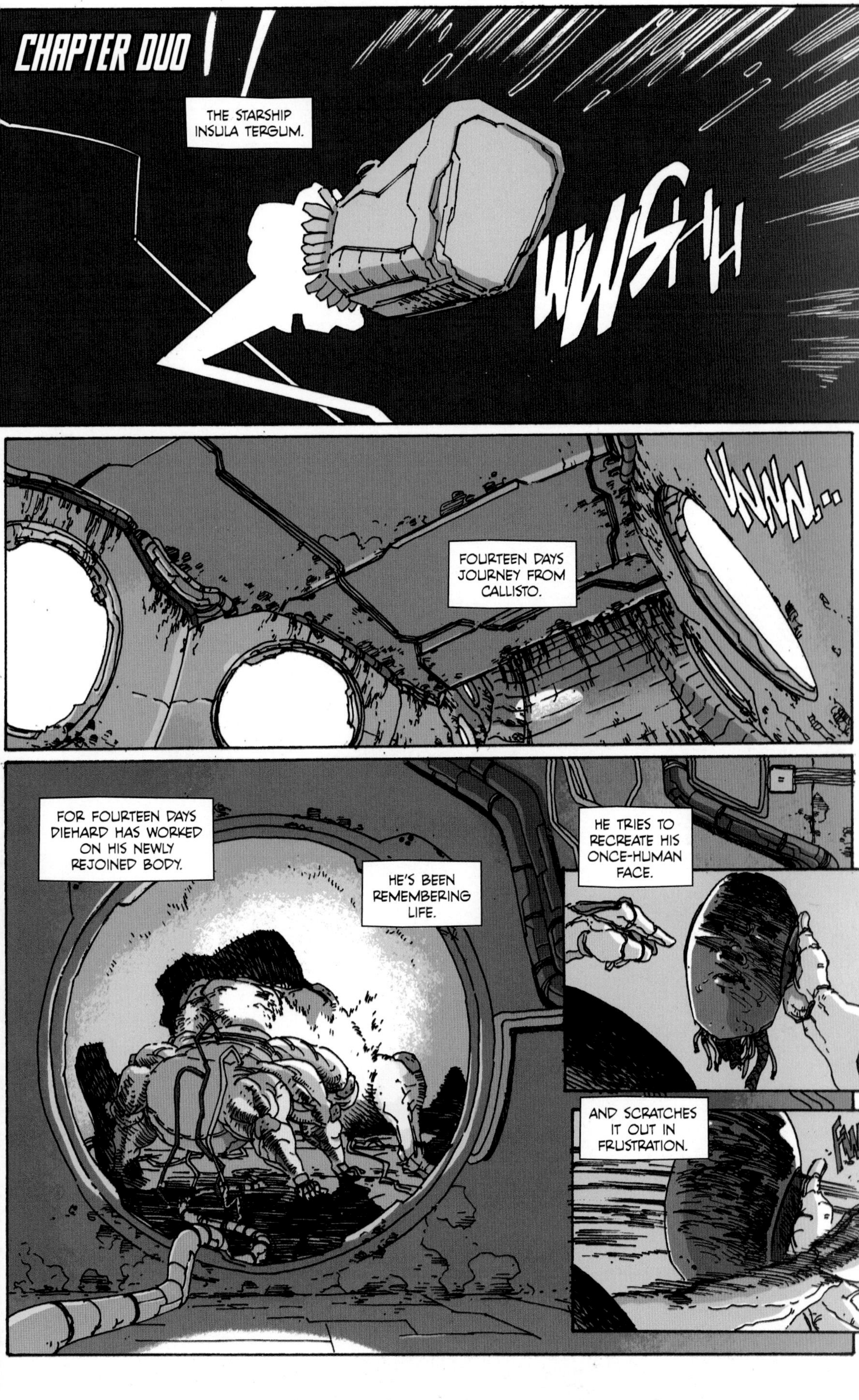CHAPTER DUO
THE STARSHIP INSULA TERGUM.
WWSHH
VNNN..
FOURTEEN DAYS JOURNEY FROM CALLISTO.
FOR FOURTEEN DAYS DIEHARD HAS WORKED ON HIS NEWLY REJOINED BODY.
HE'S BEEN REMEMBERING LIFE.
HE TRIES TO RECREATE HIS ONCE-HUMAN FACE.
AND SCRATCHES IT OUT IN FRUSTRATION.
FWP

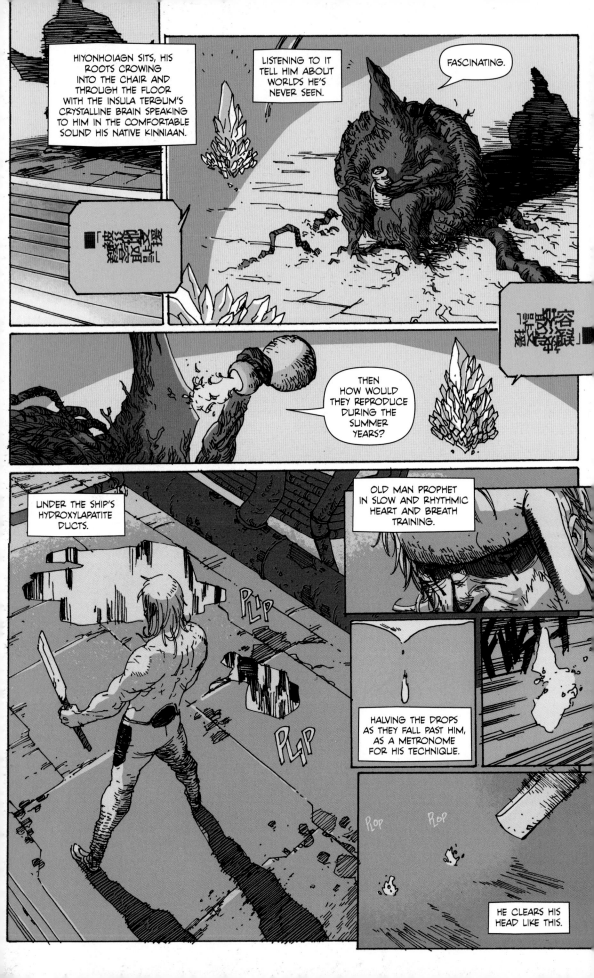

HIYONHOIAGN SITS, HIS ROOTS CROWING INTO THE CHAIR AND THROUGH THE FLOOR WITH THE INSULA TERGUM'S CRYSTALLINE BRAIN SPEAKING TO HIM IN THE COMFORTABLE SOUND HIS NATIVE KINNIAAN.

LISTENING TO IT TELL HIM ABOUT WORLDS HE'S NEVER SEEN.

FASCINATING.

THEN HOW WOULD THEY REPRODUCE DURING THE SUMMER YEARS?

UNDER THE SHIP'S HYDROXYLAPATITE DUCTS.

OLD MAN PROPHET IN SLOW AND RHYTHMIC HEART AND BREATH TRAINING.

PLIP

PLIP

HALVING THE DROPS AS THEY FALL PAST HIM, AS A METRONOME FOR HIS TECHNIQUE.

PLOP

PLOP

HE CLEARS HIS HEAD LIKE THIS.

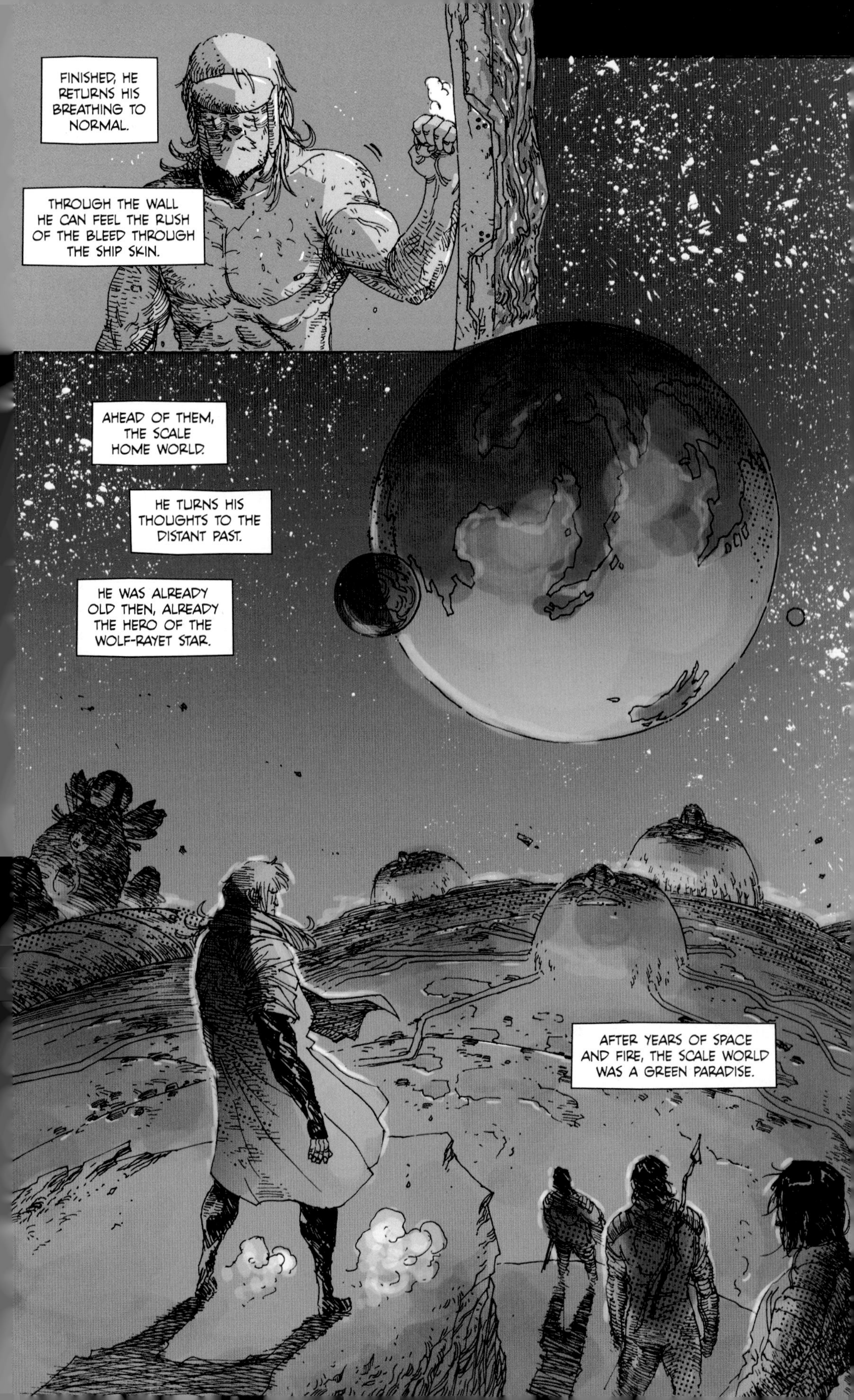
FINISHED, HE RETURNS HIS BREATHING TO NORMAL.
THROUGH THE WALL HE CAN FEEL THE RUSH OF THE BLEED THROUGH THE SHIP SKIN.
AHEAD OF THEM, THE SCALE HOME WORLD.
HE TURNS HIS THOUGHTS TO THE DISTANT PAST.
HE WAS ALREADY OLD THEN, ALREADY THE HERO OF THE WOLF-RAYET STAR.
AFTER YEARS OF SPACE AND FIRE, THE SCALE WORLD WAS A GREEN PARADISE.

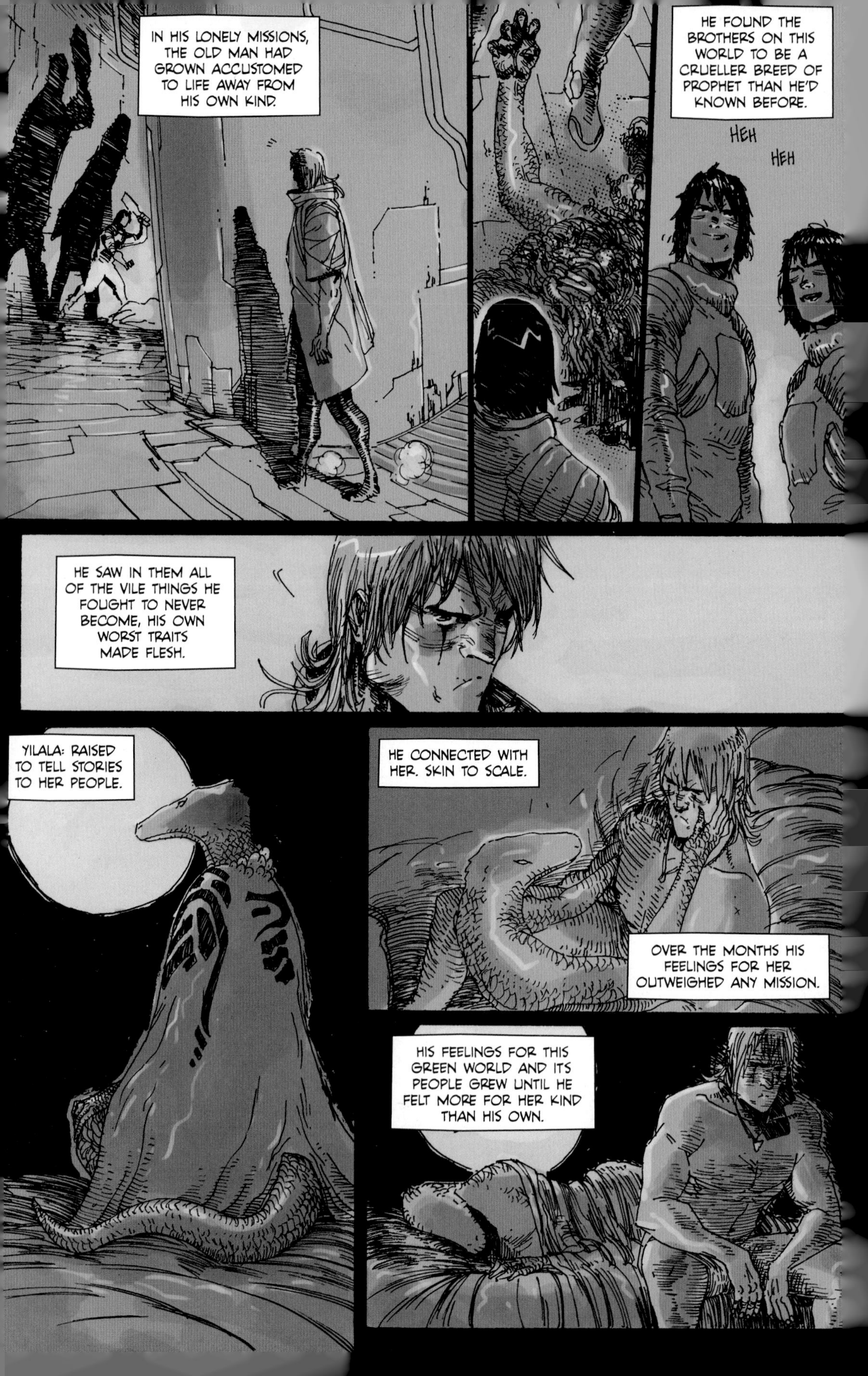
IN HIS LONELY MISSIONS, THE OLD MAN HAD GROWN ACCUSTOMED TO LIFE AWAY FROM HIS OWN KIND.
HE FOUND THE BROTHERS ON THIS WORLD TO BE A CRUELLER BREED OF PROPHET THAN HE'D KNOWN BEFORE.
HEH
HEH
HE SAW IN THEM ALL OF THE VILE THINGS HE FOUGHT TO NEVER BECOME, HIS OWN WORST TRAITS MADE FLESH.
YILALA: RAISED TO TELL STORIES TO HER PEOPLE.
HE CONNECTED WITH HER. SKIN TO SCALE.
OVER THE MONTHS HIS FEELINGS FOR HER OUTWEIGHED ANY MISSION.
HIS FEELINGS FOR THIS GREEN WORLD AND ITS PEOPLE GREW UNTIL HE FELT MORE FOR HER KIND THAN HIS OWN.

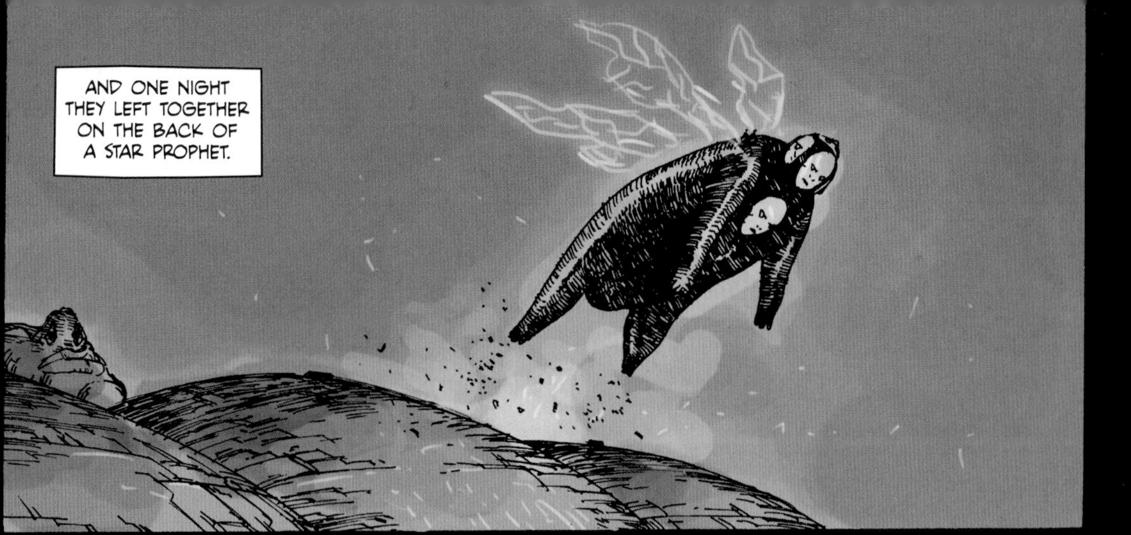
AND ONE NIGHT THEY LEFT TOGETHER ON THE BACK OF A STAR PROPHET.

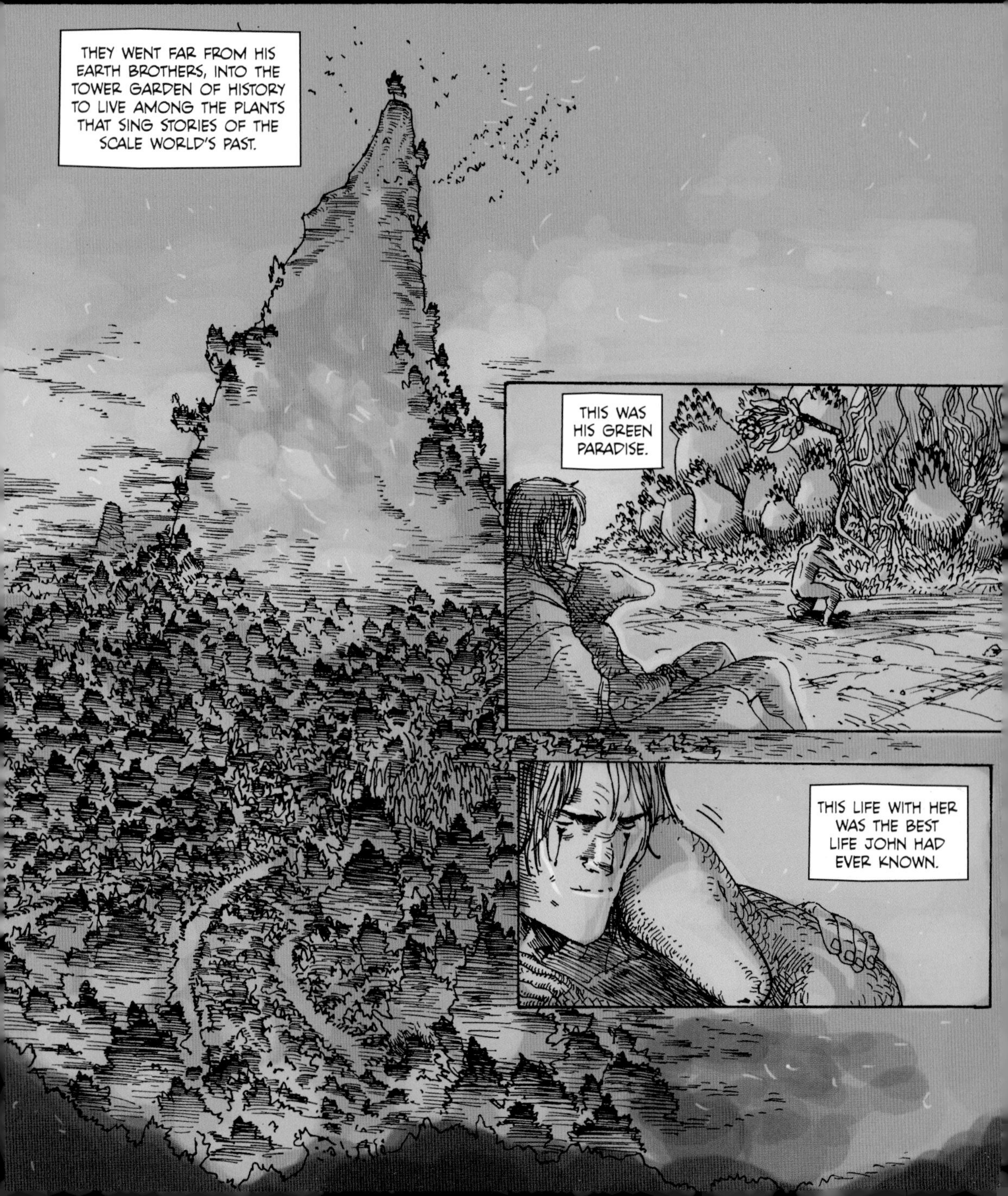
THEY WENT FAR FROM HIS EARTH BROTHERS, INTO THE TOWER GARDEN OF HISTORY TO LIVE AMONG THE PLANTS THAT SING STORIES OF THE SCALE WORLD'S PAST.
THIS WAS HIS GREEN PARADISE.
THIS LIFE WITH HER WAS THE BEST LIFE JOHN HAD EVER KNOWN.

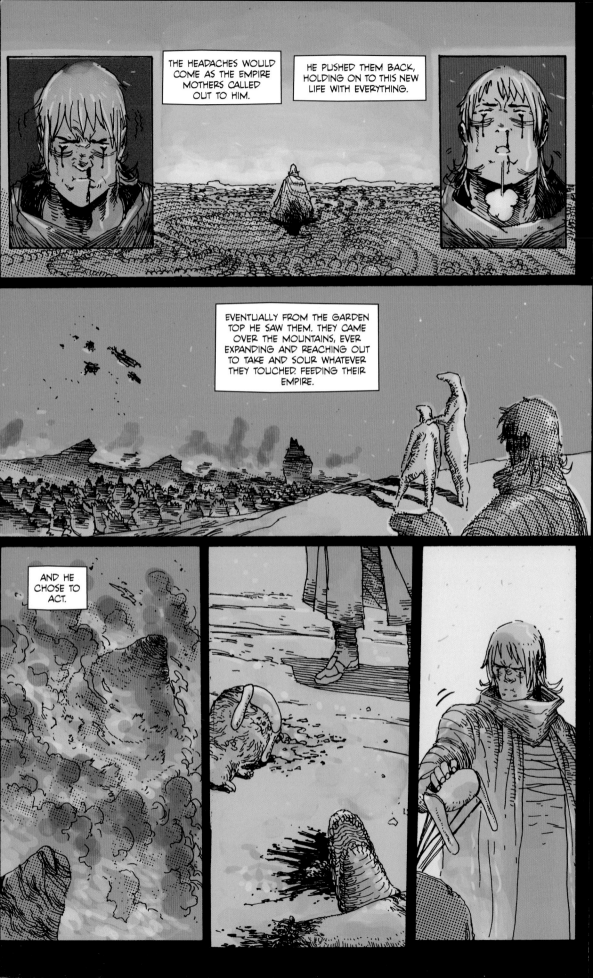

THE HEADACHES WOULD COME AS THE EMPIRE MOTHERS CALLED OUT TO HIM.

HE PUSHED THEM BACK, HOLDING ON TO THIS NEW LIFE WITH EVERYTHING.

EVENTUALLY FROM THE GARDEN TOP HE SAW THEM. THEY CAME OVER THE MOUNTAINS, EVER EXPANDING AND REACHING OUT TO TAKE AND SOUR WHATEVER THEY TOUCHED. FEEDING THEIR EMPIRE.

AND HE CHOSE TO ACT.

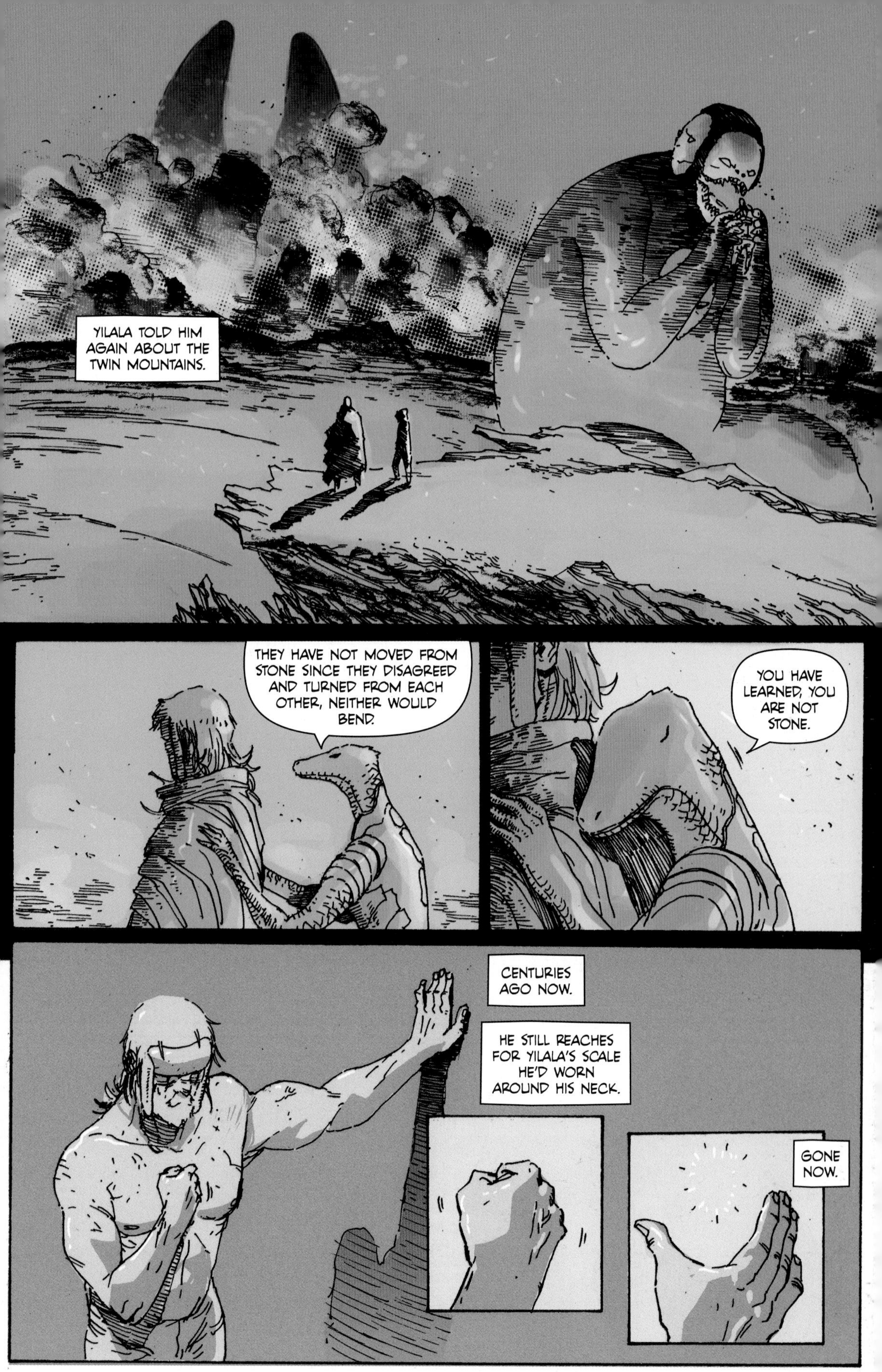
YILALA TOLD HIM AGAIN ABOUT THE TWIN MOUNTAINS.
THEY HAVE NOT MOVED FROM STONE SINCE THEY DISAGREED AND TURNED FROM EACH OTHER, NEITHER WOULD BEND.
YOU HAVE LEARNED, YOU ARE NOT STONE.
CENTURIES AGO NOW.
HE STILL REACHES FOR YILALA'S SCALE HE'D WORN AROUND HIS NECK.
GONE NOW.

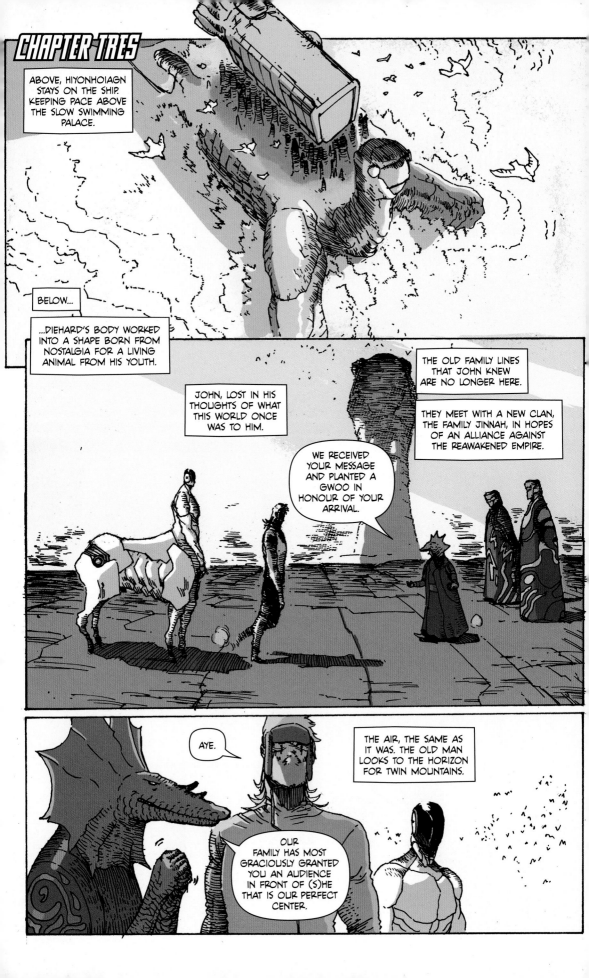

ABOVE, HIYONHOIAGN STAYS ON THE SHIP. KEEPING PACE ABOVE THE SLOW SWIMMING PALACE.

BELOW...

...DIEHARD'S BODY WORKED INTO A SHAPE BORN FROM NOSTALGIA FOR A LIVING ANIMAL FROM HIS YOUTH.

JOHN, LOST IN HIS THOUGHTS OF WHAT THIS WORLD ONCE WAS TO HIM.

THE OLD FAMILY LINES THAT JOHN KNEW ARE NO LONGER HERE.

THEY MEET WITH A NEW CLAN, THE FAMILY JINNAH, IN HOPES OF AN ALLIANCE AGAINST THE REAWAKENED EMPIRE.

WE RECEIVED YOUR MESSAGE AND PLANTED A GWOO IN HONOUR OF YOUR ARRIVAL.

AYE.

THE AIR, THE SAME AS IT WAS. THE OLD MAN LOOKS TO THE HORIZON FOR TWIN MOUNTAINS.

OUR FAMILY HAS MOST GRACIOUSLY GRANTED YOU AN AUDIENCE IN FRONT OF (S)HE THAT IS OUR PERFECT CENTER.

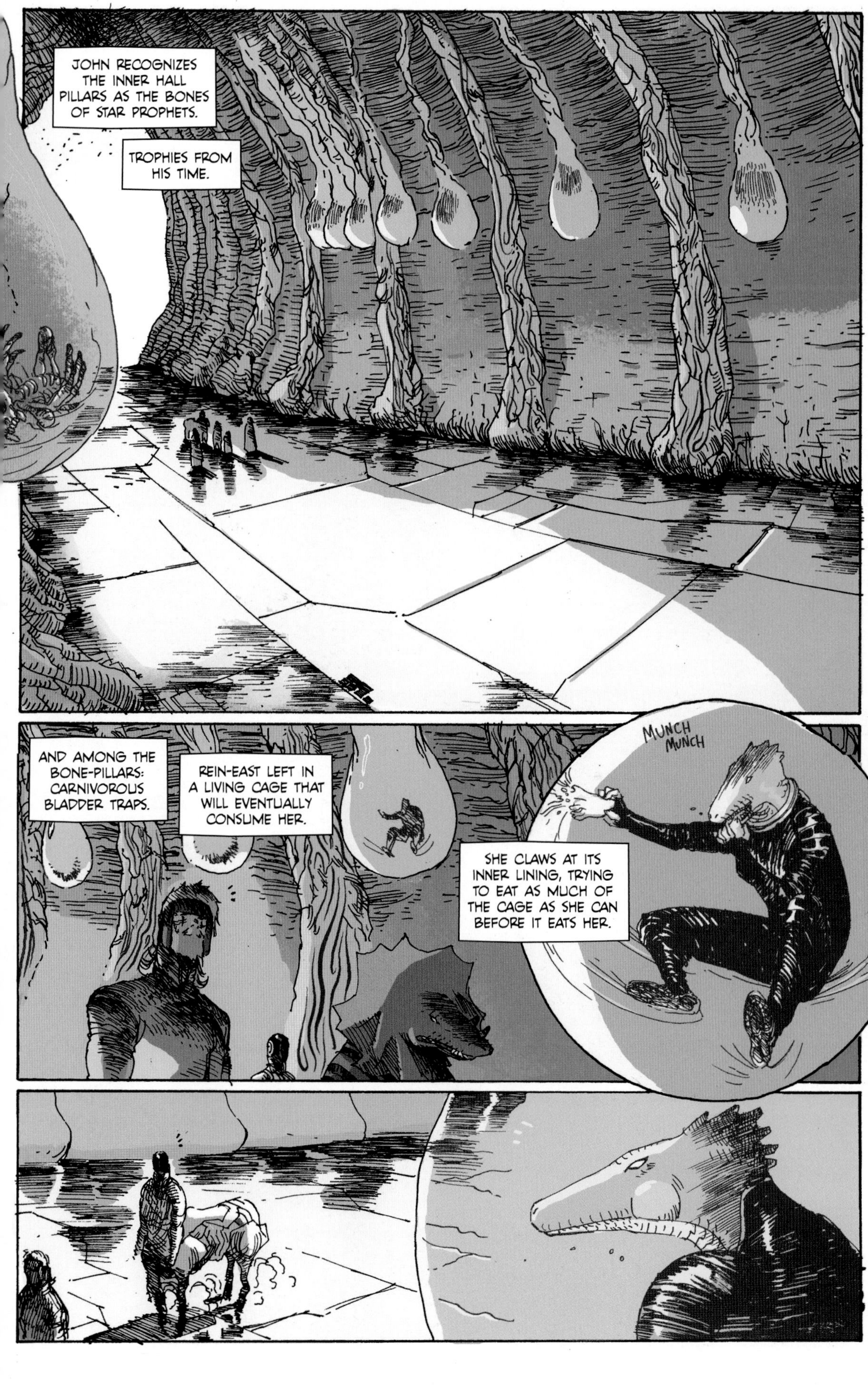
JOHN RECOGNIZES THE INNER HALL PILLARS AS THE BONES OF STAR PROPHETS.
TROPHIES FROM HIS TIME.
AND AMONG THE BONE-PILLARS: CARNIVOROUS BLADDER TRAPS.
REIN-EAST LEFT IN A LIVING CAGE THAT WILL EVENTUALLY CONSUME HER.
MUNCH MUNCH
SHE CLAWS AT ITS INNER LINING, TRYING TO EAT AS MUCH OF THE CAGE AS SHE CAN BEFORE IT EATS HER.

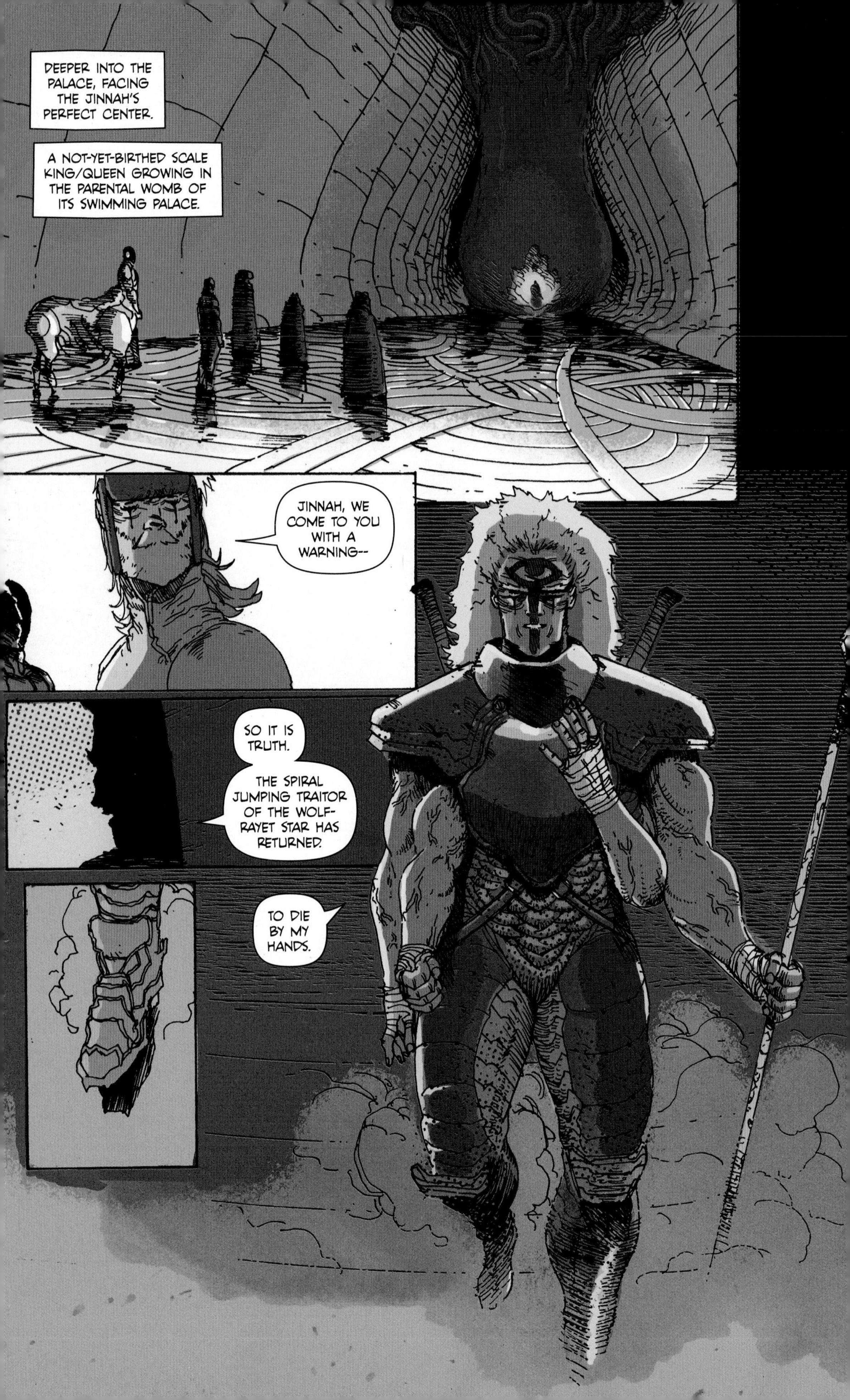
DEEPER INTO THE PALACE, FACING THE JINNAH'S PERFECT CENTER.
A NOT-YET-BIRTHED SCALE KING/QUEEN GROWING IN THE PARENTAL WOMB OF ITS SWIMMING PALACE.
JINNAH, WE COME TO YOU WITH A WARNING--
SO IT IS TRUTH.
THE SPIRAL JUMPING TRAITOR OF THE WOLF-RAYET STAR HAS RETURNED.
TO DIE BY MY HANDS.

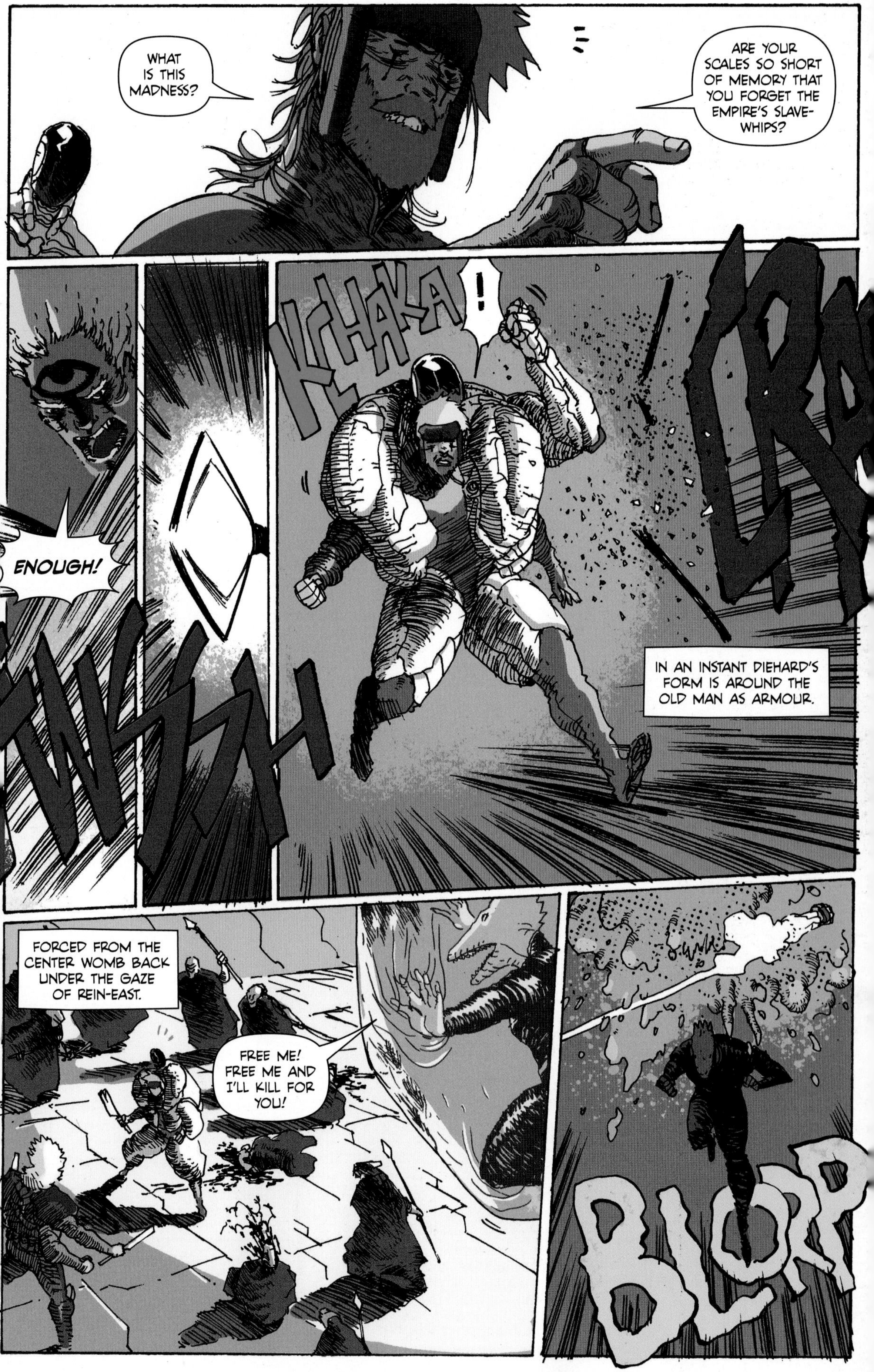
WHAT IS THIS MADNESS?
ARE YOUR SCALES SO SHORT OF MEMORY THAT YOU FORGET THE EMPIRE'S SLAVE-WHIPS?
ENOUGH!
KCHAKA
!
IN AN INSTANT DIEHARD'S FORM IS AROUND THE OLD MAN AS ARMOUR.
FORCED FROM THE CENTER WOMB BACK UNDER THE GAZE OF REIN-EAST.
FREE ME! FREE ME AND I'LL KILL FOR YOU!
BLORP

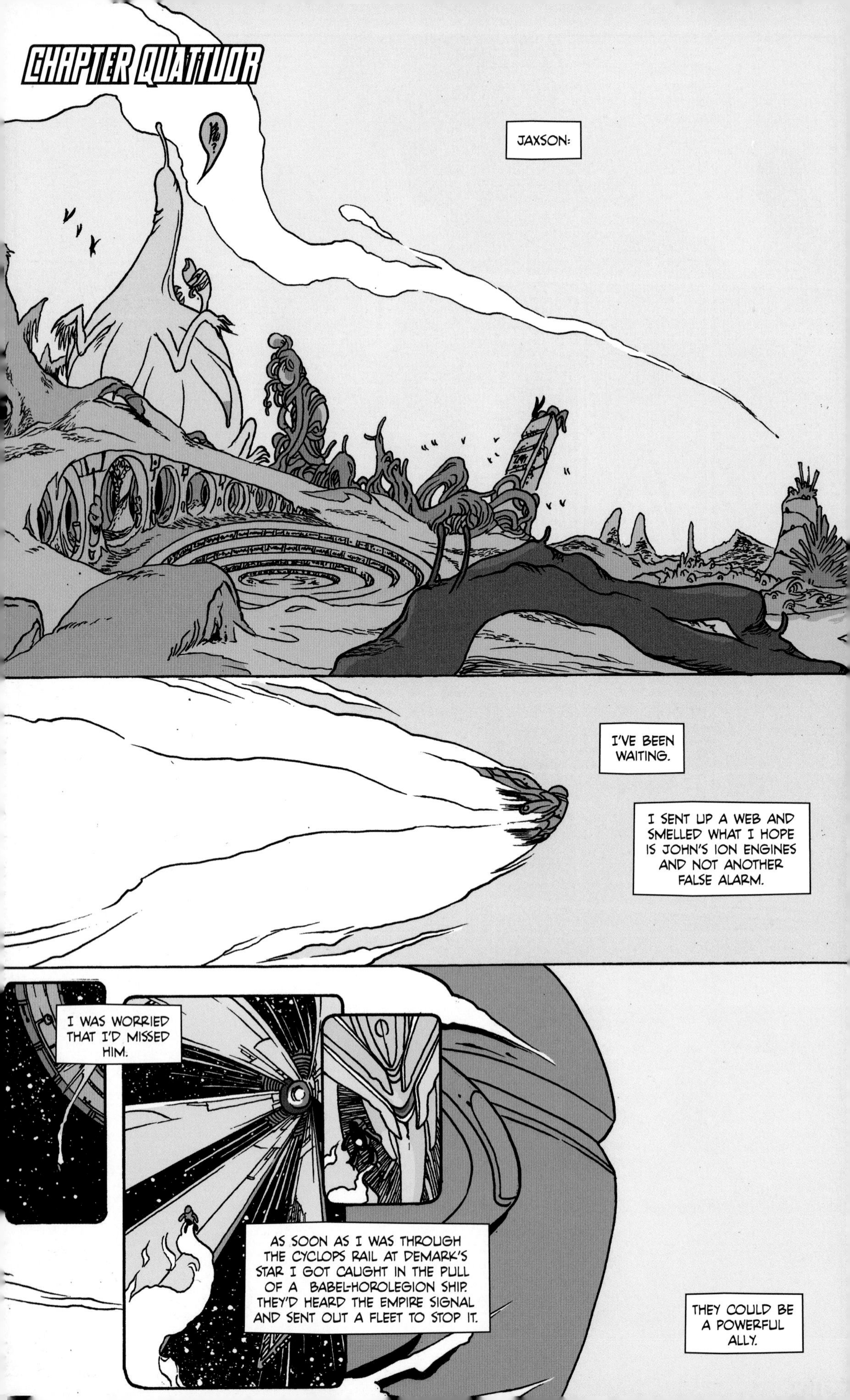
CHAPTER QUATTUOR
JAXSON:
I'VE BEEN WAITING.
I SENT UP A WEB AND SMELLED WHAT I HOPE IS JOHN'S ION ENGINES AND NOT ANOTHER FALSE ALARM.
I WAS WORRIED THAT I'D MISSED HIM.
AS SOON AS I WAS THROUGH THE CYCLOPS RAIL AT DEMARK'S STAR I GOT CAUGHT IN THE PULL OF A BABEL-HOROLEGION SHIP. THEY'D HEARD THE EMPIRE SIGNAL AND SENT OUT A FLEET TO STOP IT.
THEY COULD BE A POWERFUL ALLY.

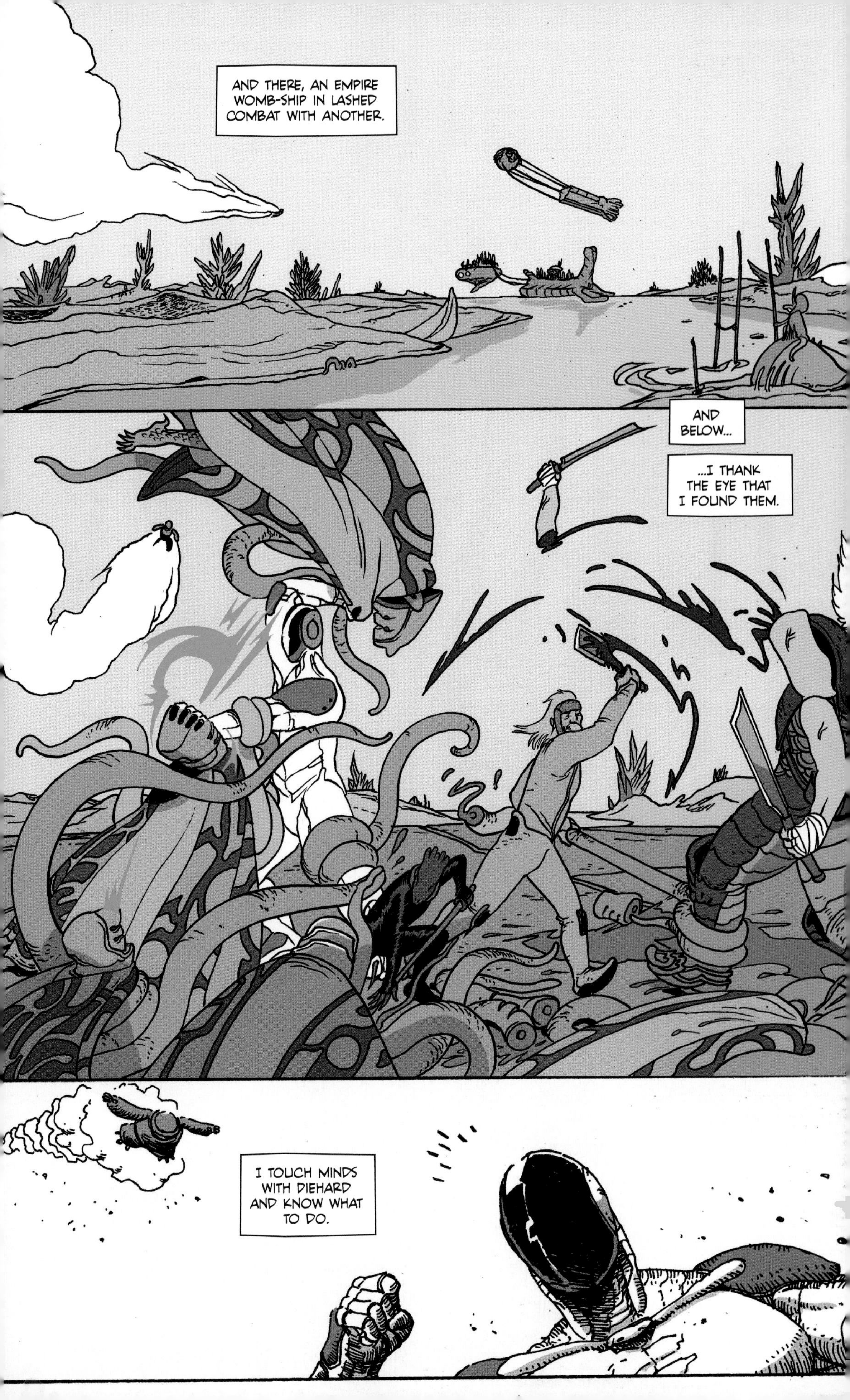
AND THERE, AN EMPIRE WOMB-SHIP IN LASHED COMBAT WITH ANOTHER.
AND BELOW...
...I THANK THE EYE THAT I FOUND THEM.
I TOUCH MINDS WITH DIEHARD AND KNOW WHAT TO DO.

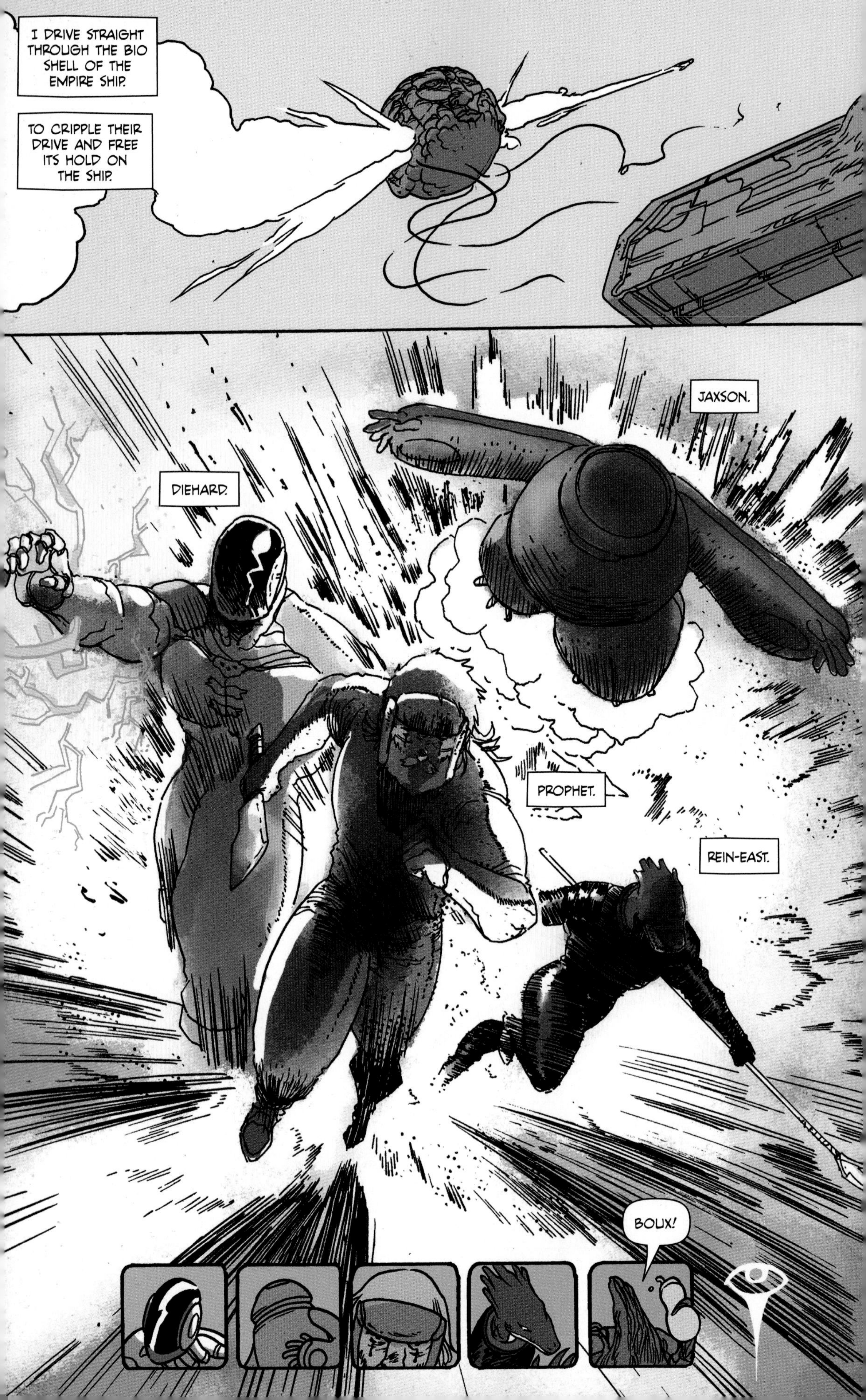
I DRIVE STRAIGHT THROUGH THE BIO SHELL OF THE EMPIRE SHIP.
TO CRIPPLE THEIR DRIVE AND FREE ITS HOLD ON THE SHIP.
JAXSON.
DIEHARD.
PROPHET.
REIN-EAST.
BOUX!

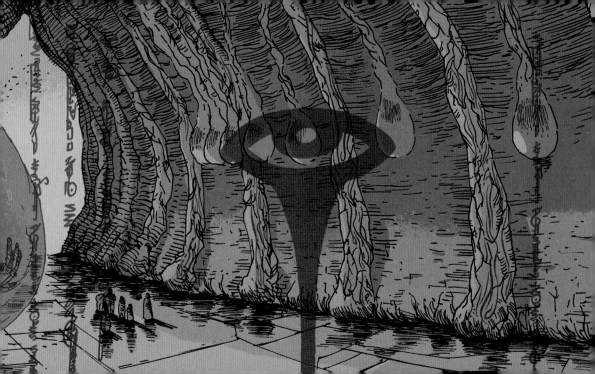

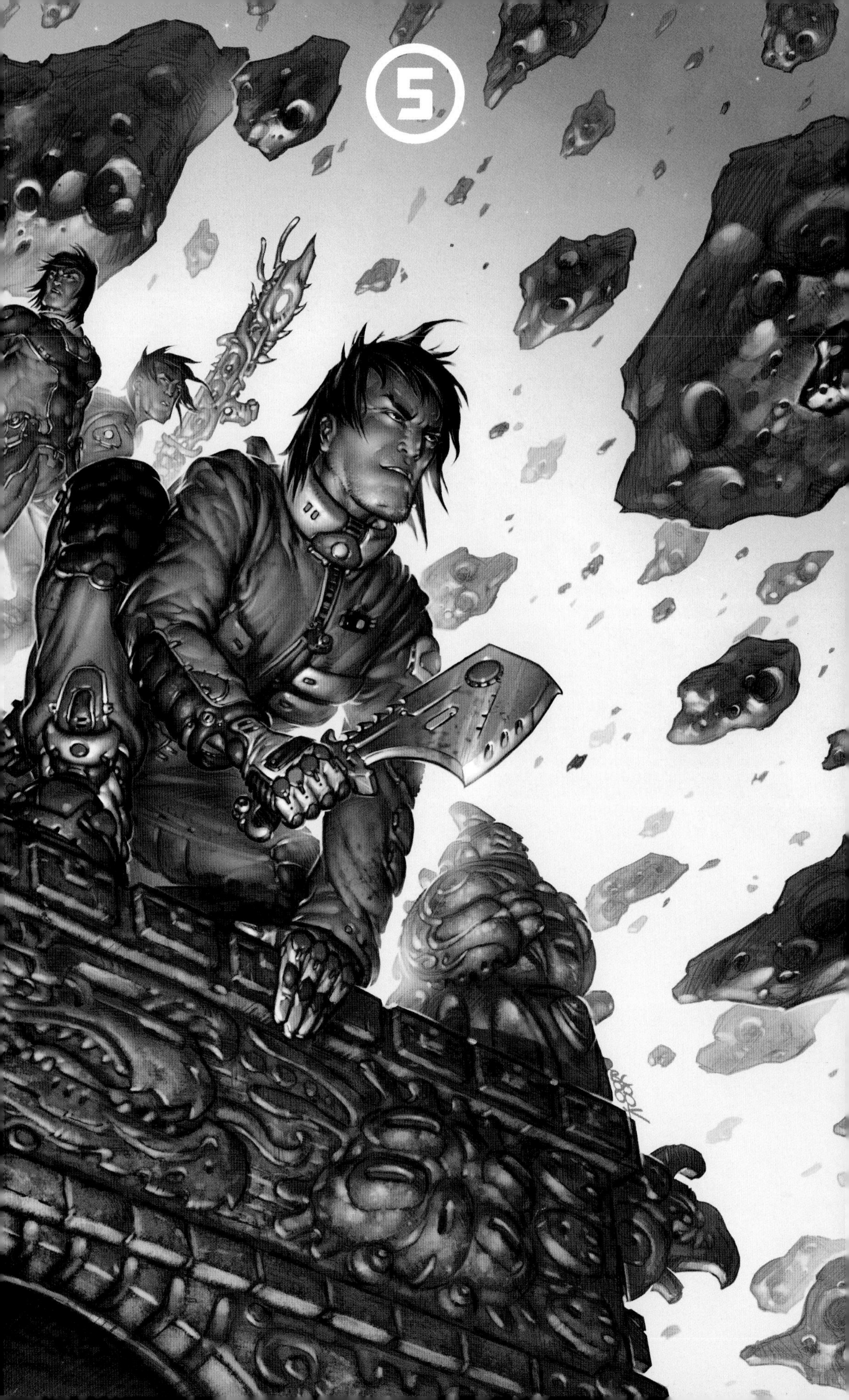
5

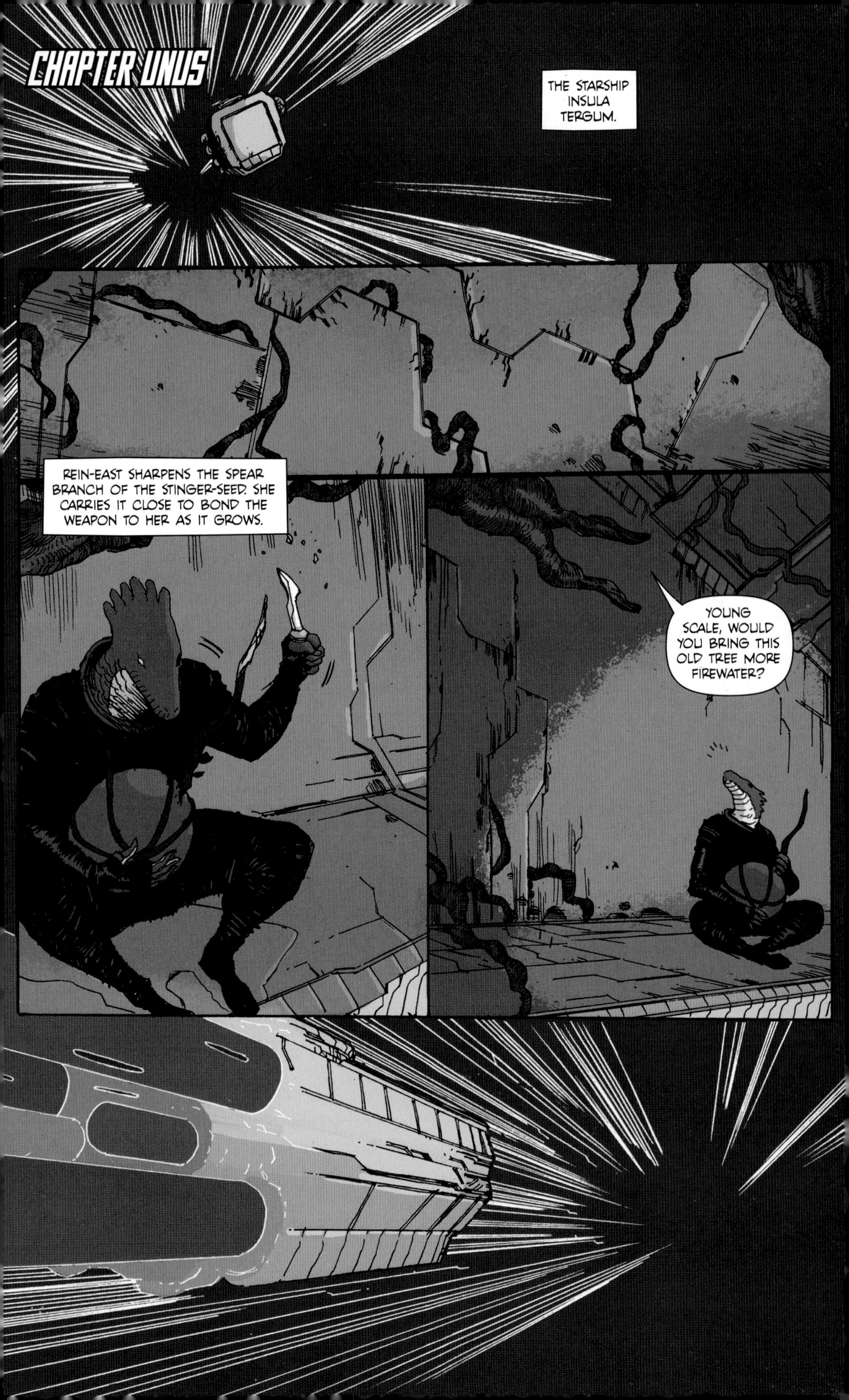
CHAPTER UNUS
THE STARSHIP INSULA TERGUM.
REIN-EAST SHARPENS THE SPEAR BRANCH OF THE STINGER-SEED. SHE CARRIES IT CLOSE TO BOND THE WEAPON TO HER AS IT GROWS.
YOUNG SCALE, WOULD YOU BRING THIS OLD TREE MORE FIREWATER?

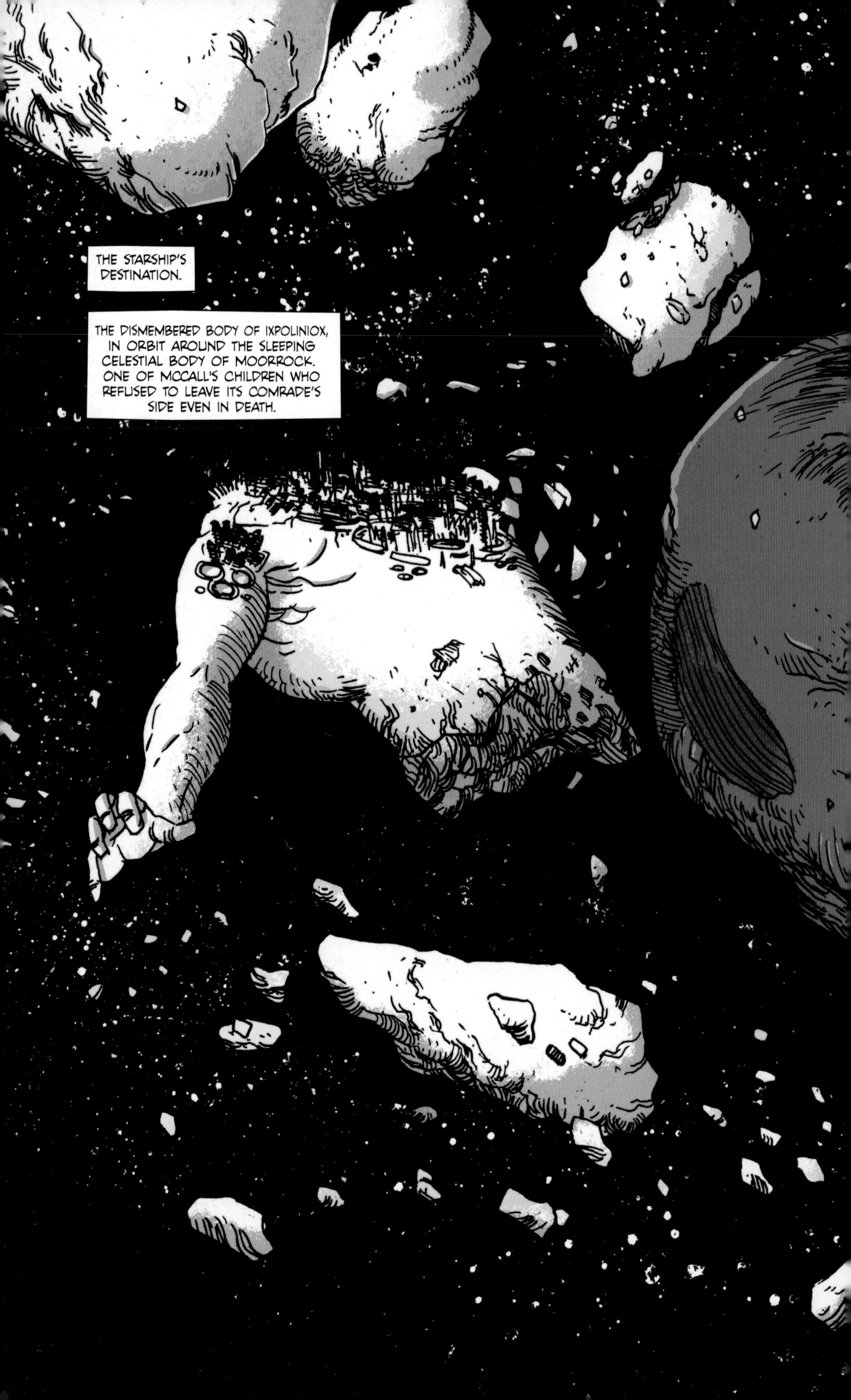
THE STARSHIP'S DESTINATION.
THE DISMEMBERED BODY OF IXPOLINIOX, IN ORBIT AROUND THE SLEEPING CELESTIAL BODY OF MOORROCK. ONE OF MCCALL'S CHILDREN WHO REFUSED TO LEAVE ITS COMRADE'S SIDE EVEN IN DEATH.

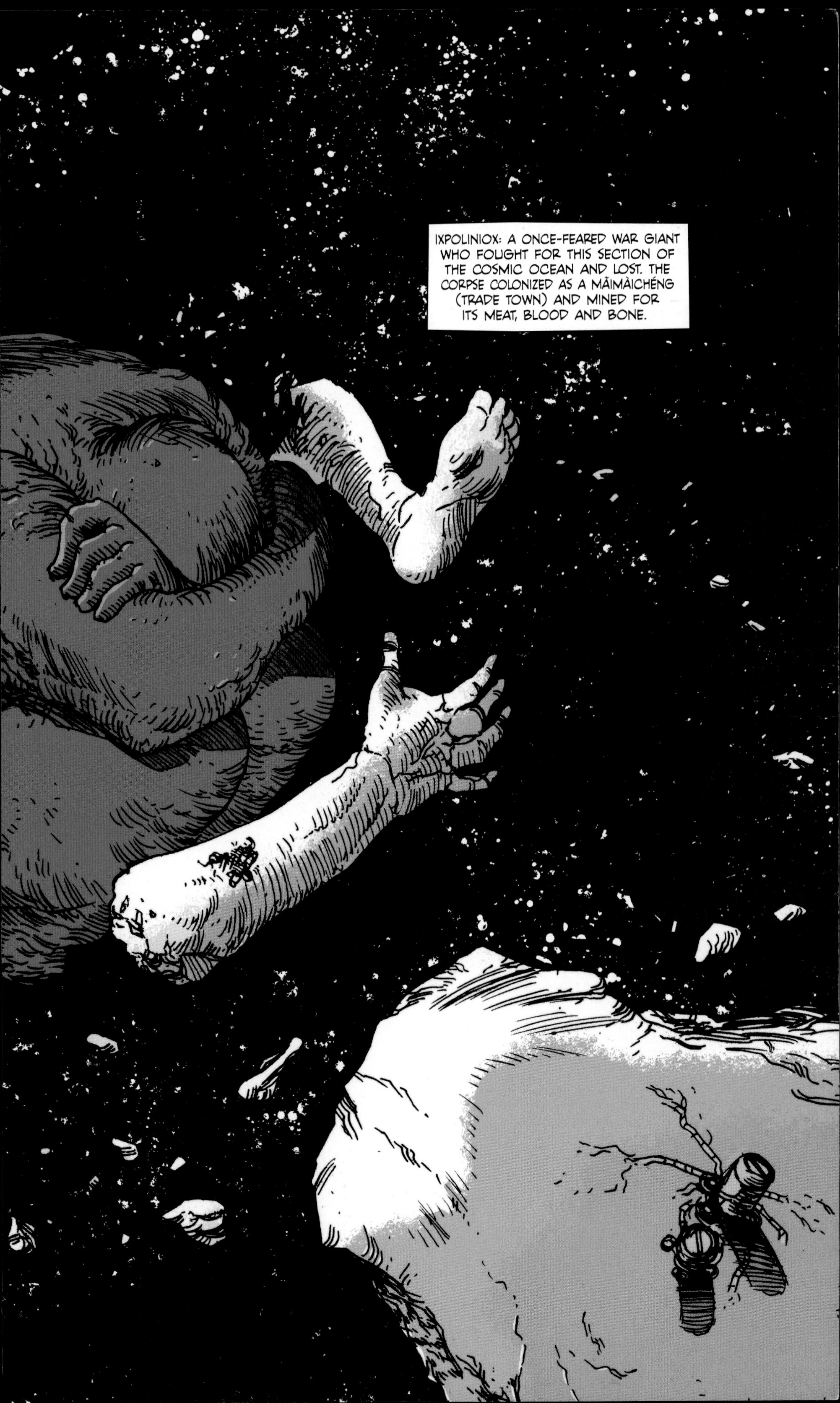
IXPOLINIOX: A ONCE-FEARED WAR GIANT WHO FOUGHT FOR THIS SECTION OF THE COSMIC OCEAN AND LOST. THE CORPSE COLONIZED AS A MĂIMÀICHÉNG (TRADE TOWN) AND MINED FOR ITS MEAT, BLOOD AND BONE.

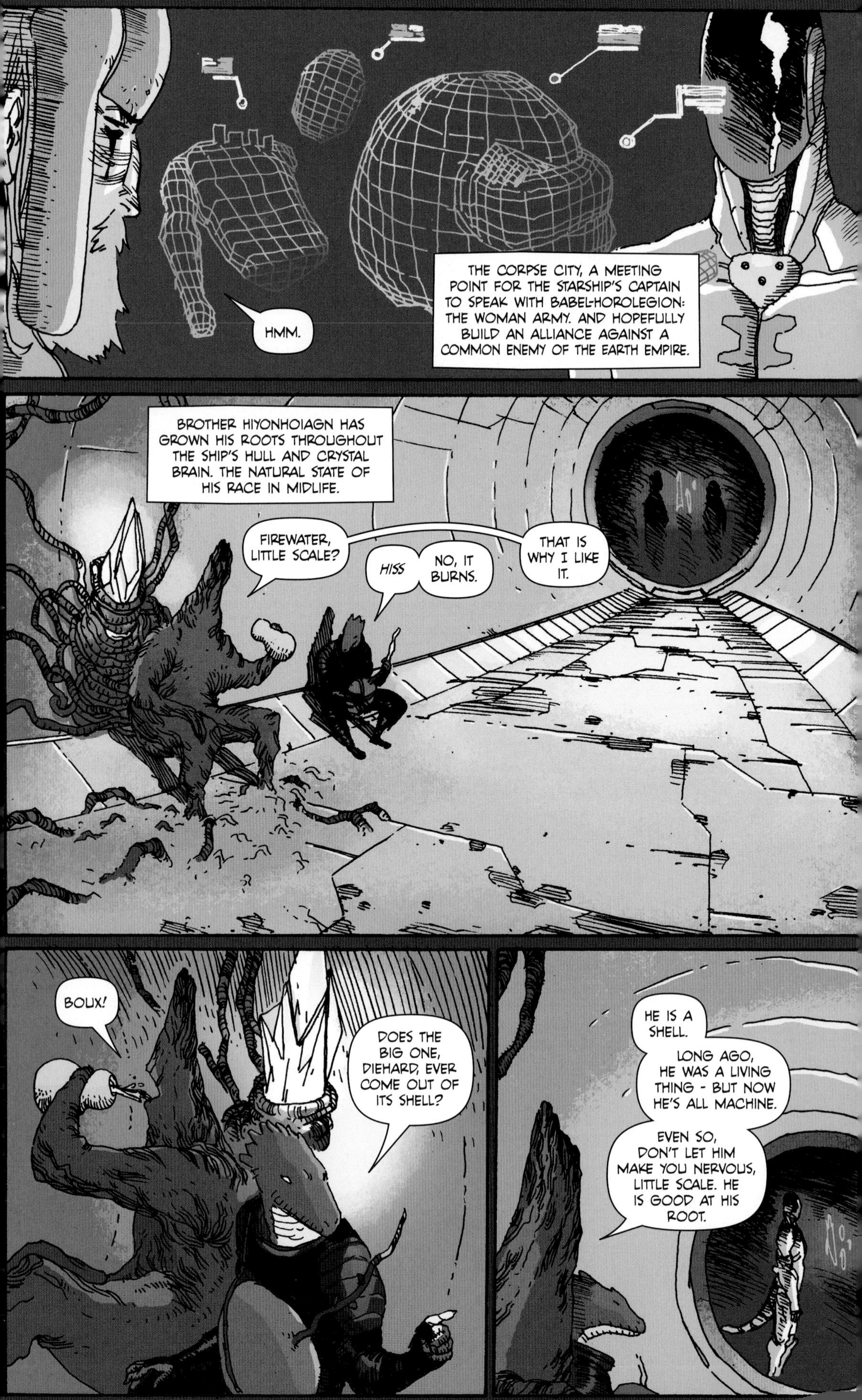

HMM.
THE CORPSE CITY, A MEETING POINT FOR THE STARSHIP'S CAPTAIN TO SPEAK WITH BABEL-HOROLEGION: THE WOMAN ARMY. AND HOPEFULLY BUILD AN ALLIANCE AGAINST A COMMON ENEMY OF THE EARTH EMPIRE.
BROTHER HIYONHOIAGN HAS GROWN HIS ROOTS THROUGHOUT THE SHIP'S HULL AND CRYSTAL BRAIN. THE NATURAL STATE OF HIS RACE IN MIDLIFE.
FIREWATER, LITTLE SCALE?
HISS
NO, IT BURNS.
THAT IS WHY I LIKE IT.
BOUX!
DOES THE BIG ONE, DIEHARD, EVER COME OUT OF ITS SHELL?
HE IS A SHELL.
LONG AGO, HE WAS A LIVING THING - BUT NOW HE'S ALL MACHINE.
EVEN SO, DON'T LET HIM MAKE YOU NERVOUS, LITTLE SCALE. HE IS GOOD AT HIS ROOT.

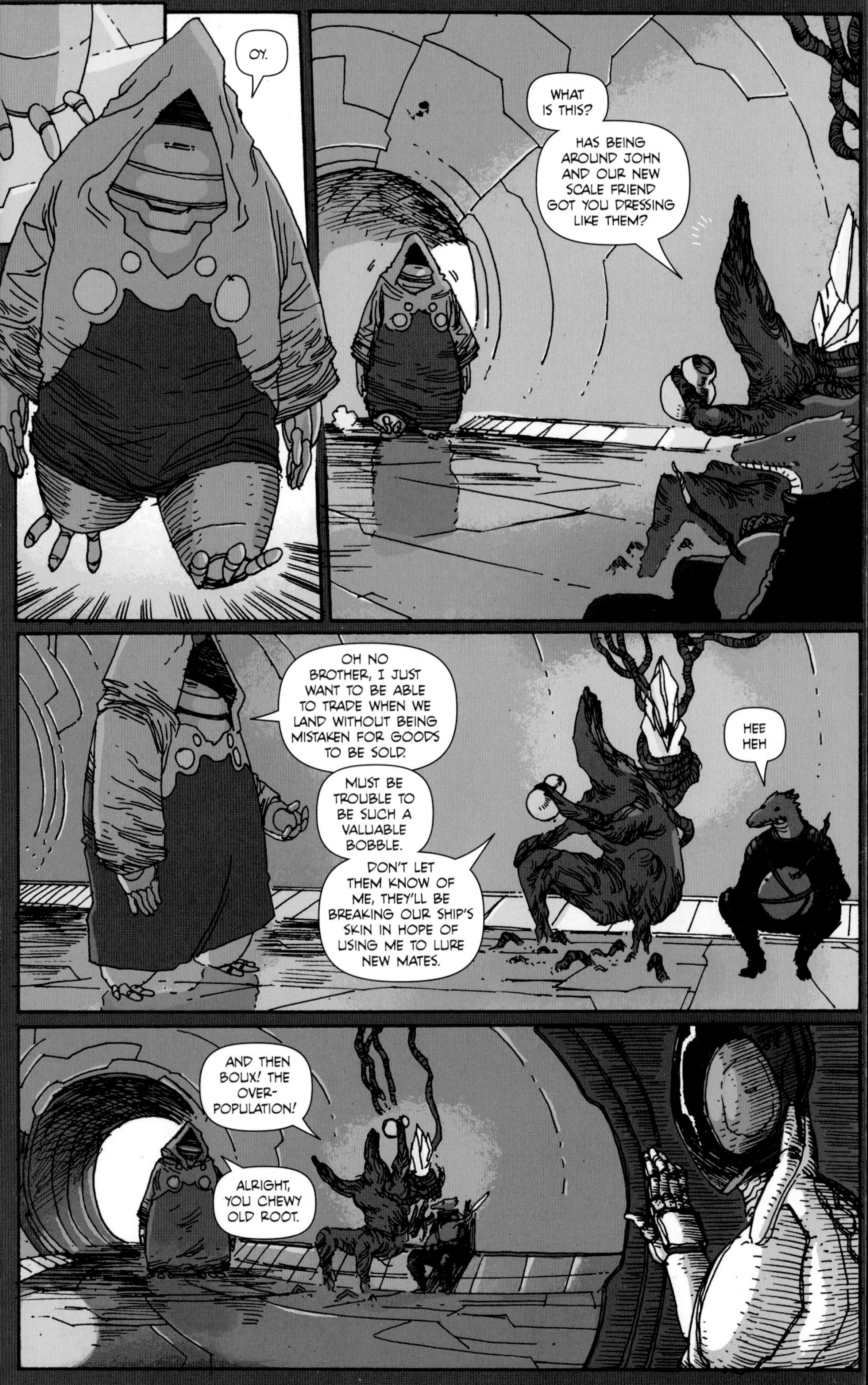
OY.
WHAT IS THIS?
HAS BEING AROUND JOHN AND OUR NEW SCALE FRIEND GOT YOU DRESSING LIKE THEM?
OH NO BROTHER, I JUST WANT TO BE ABLE TO TRADE WHEN WE LAND WITHOUT BEING MISTAKEN FOR GOODS TO BE SOLD.
HEE HEH
MUST BE TROUBLE TO BE SUCH A VALUABLE BOBBLE.
DON'T LET THEM KNOW OF ME, THEY'LL BE BREAKING OUR SHIP'S SKIN IN HOPE OF USING ME TO LURE NEW MATES.
AND THEN BOUX! THE OVER-POPULATION!
ALRIGHT, YOU CHEWY OLD ROOT.

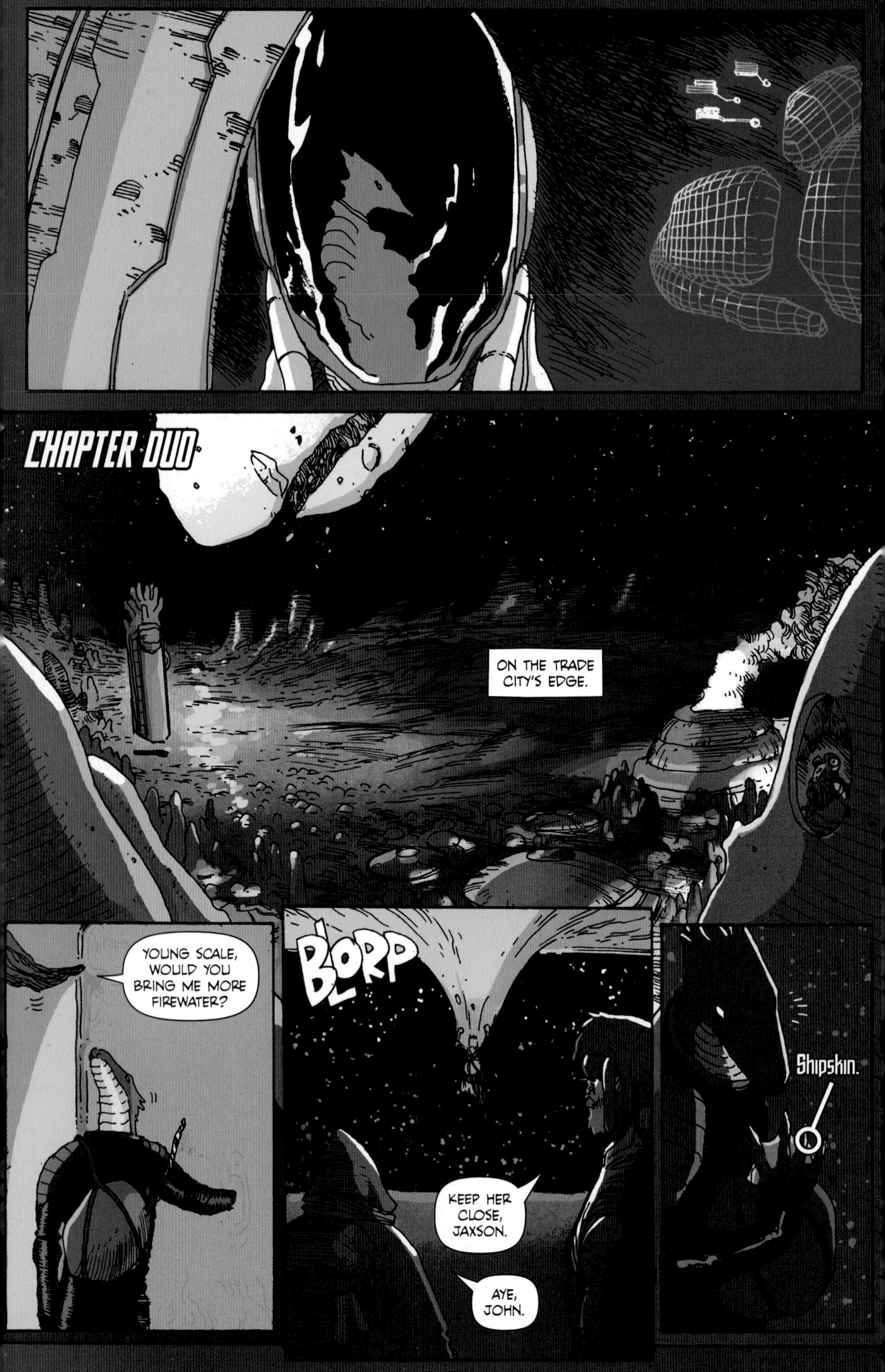
CHAPTER DUO
ON THE TRADE CITY'S EDGE.
YOUNG SCALE, WOULD YOU BRING ME MORE FIREWATER?
BLORP
KEEP HER CLOSE, JAXSON.
AYE, JOHN.
Shipskin.

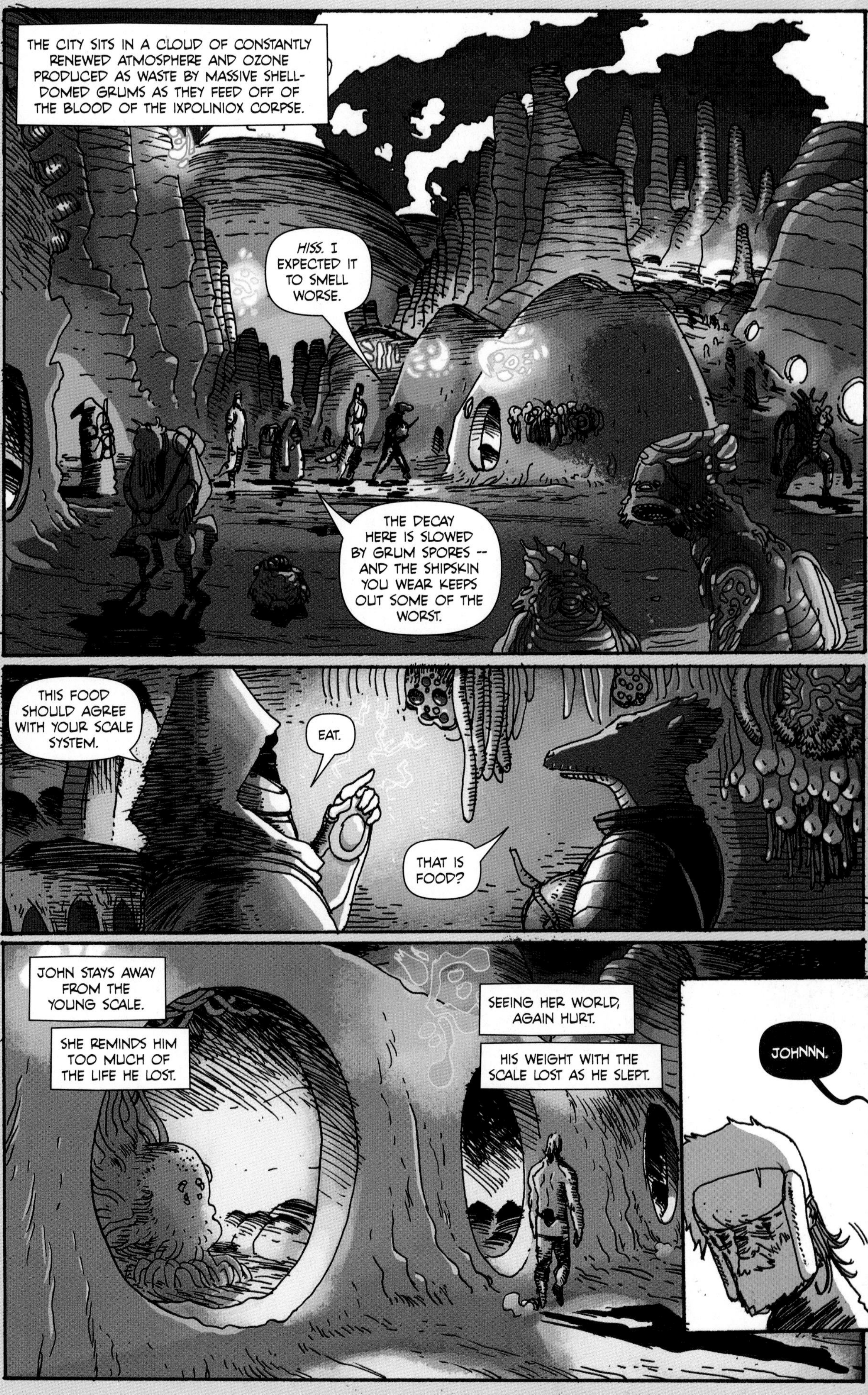
THE CITY SITS IN A CLOUD OF CONSTANTLY RENEWED ATMOSPHERE AND OZONE PRODUCED AS WASTE BY MASSIVE SHELL-DOMED GRUMS AS THEY FEED OFF OF THE BLOOD OF THE IXPOLINIOX CORPSE.
HISS. I EXPECTED IT TO SMELL WORSE.
THE DECAY HERE IS SLOWED BY GRUM SPORES -- AND THE SHIPSKIN YOU WEAR KEEPS OUT SOME OF THE WORST.
THIS FOOD SHOULD AGREE WITH YOUR SCALE SYSTEM.
EAT.
THAT IS FOOD?
JOHN STAYS AWAY FROM THE YOUNG SCALE.
SHE REMINDS HIM TOO MUCH OF THE LIFE HE LOST.
SEEING HER WORLD, AGAIN HURT.
HIS WEIGHT WITH THE SCALE LOST AS HE SLEPT.
JOHNNN.

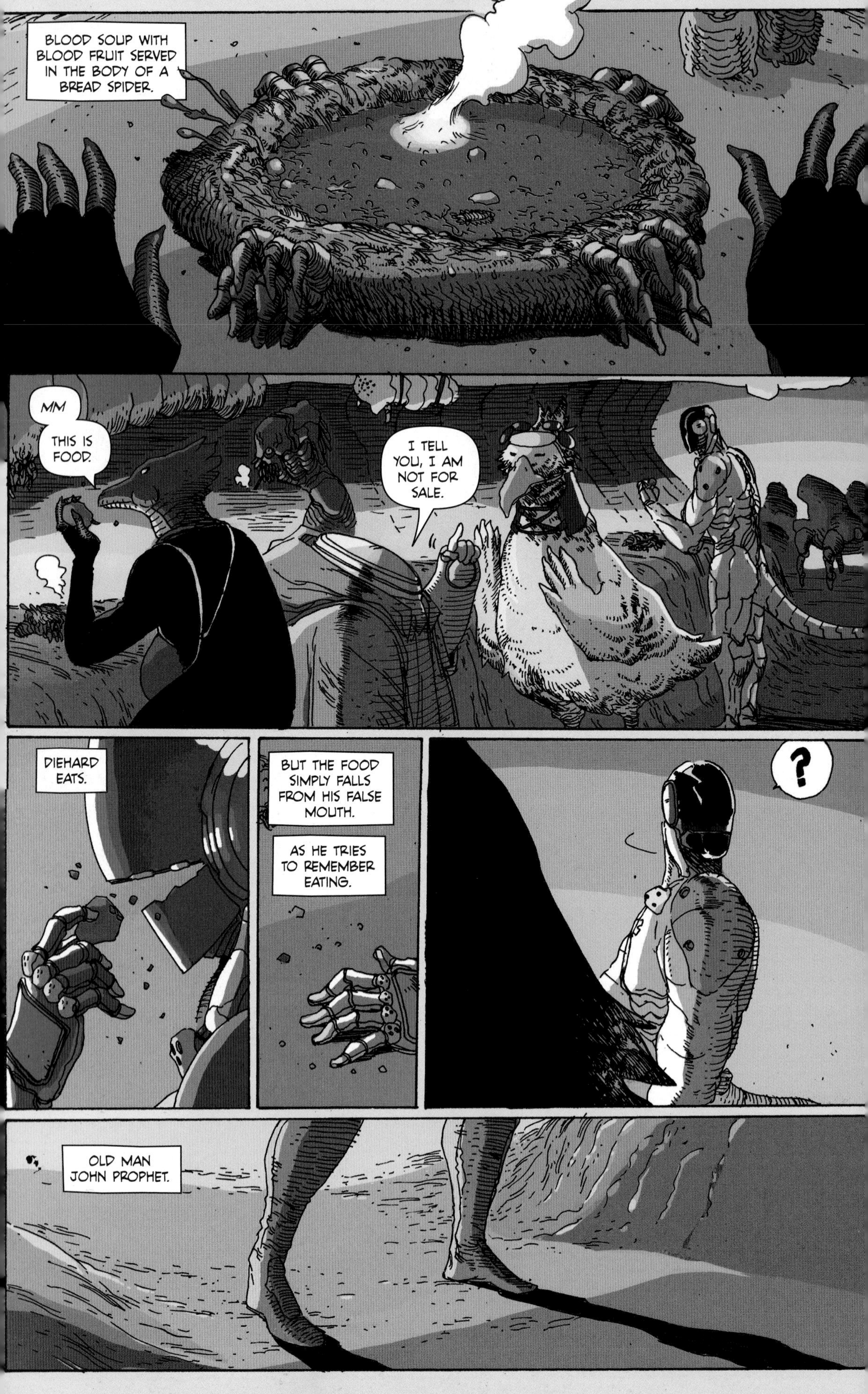
BLOOD SOUP WITH BLOOD FRUIT SERVED IN THE BODY OF A BREAD SPIDER.
MM
THIS IS FOOD.
I TELL YOU, I AM NOT FOR SALE.
DIEHARD EATS.
BUT THE FOOD SIMPLY FALLS FROM HIS FALSE MOUTH.
AS HE TRIES TO REMEMBER EATING.
?
OLD MAN JOHN PROPHET.

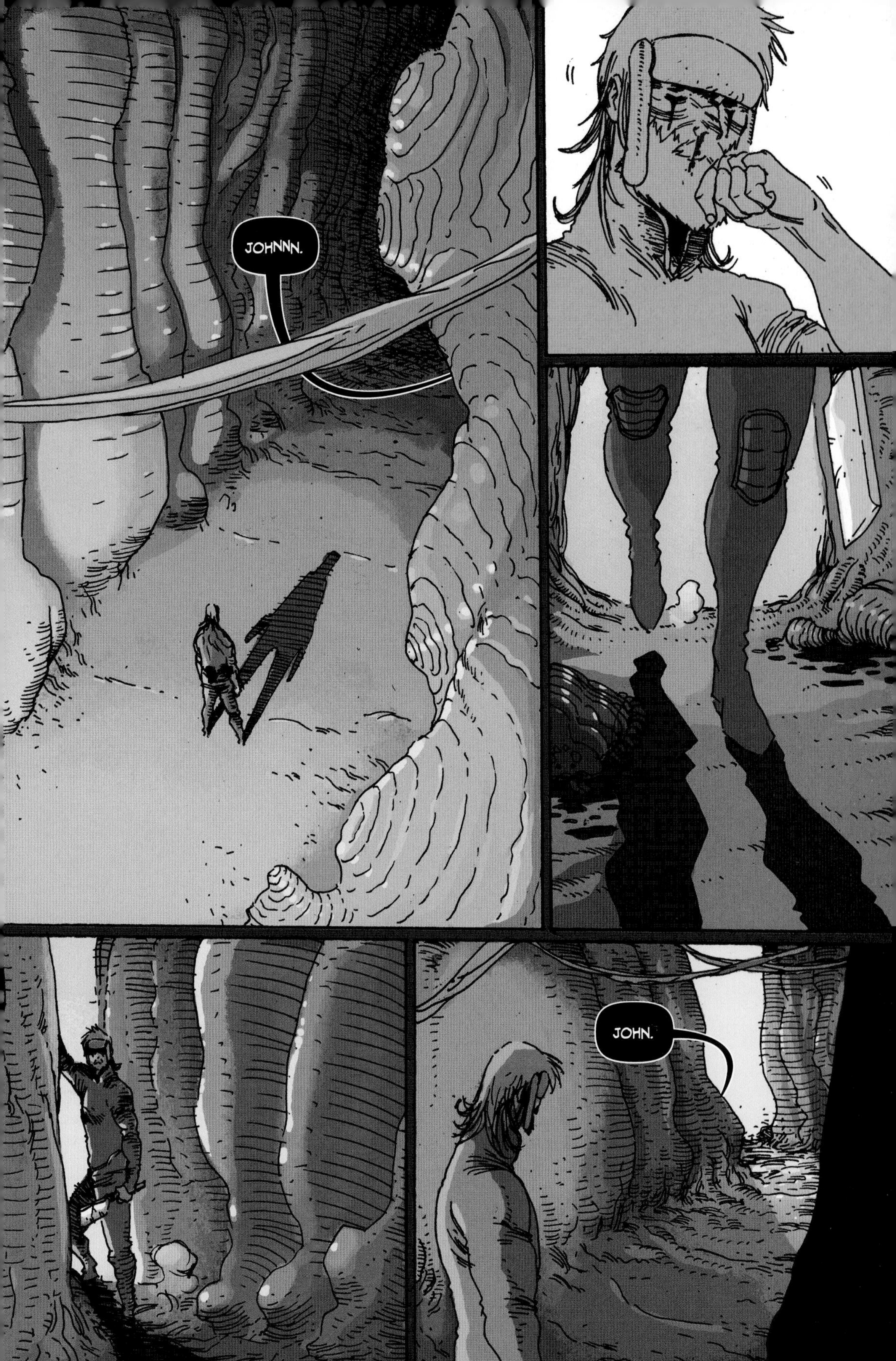
JOHNNN.
JOHN.

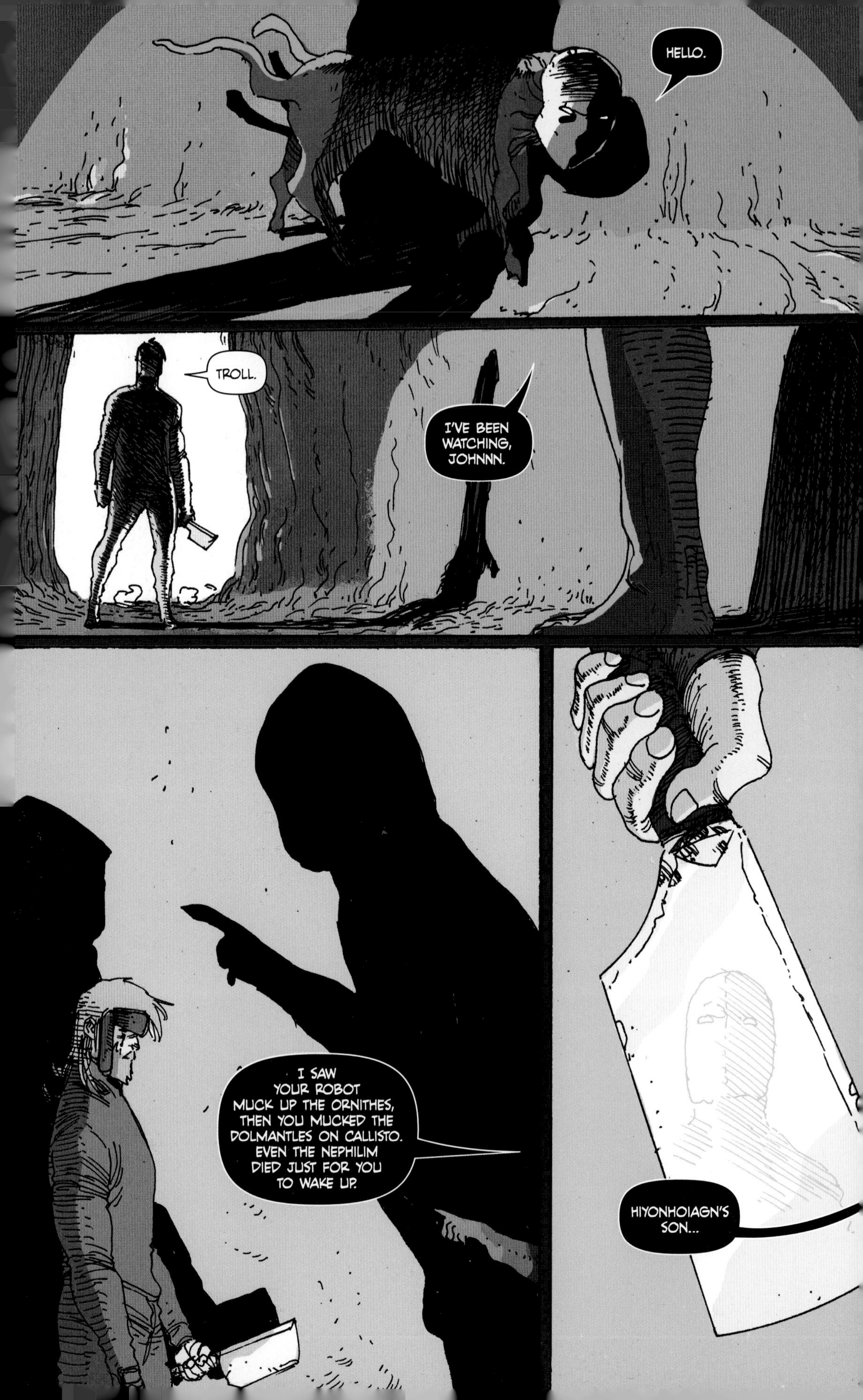
HELLO.
TROLL.
I'VE BEEN WATCHING, JOHNNN.
I SAW YOUR ROBOT MUCK UP THE ORNITHES, THEN YOU MUCKED THE DOLMANTLES ON CALLISTO. EVEN THE NEPHILIM DIED JUST FOR YOU TO WAKE UP.
HIYONHOIAGN'S SON...

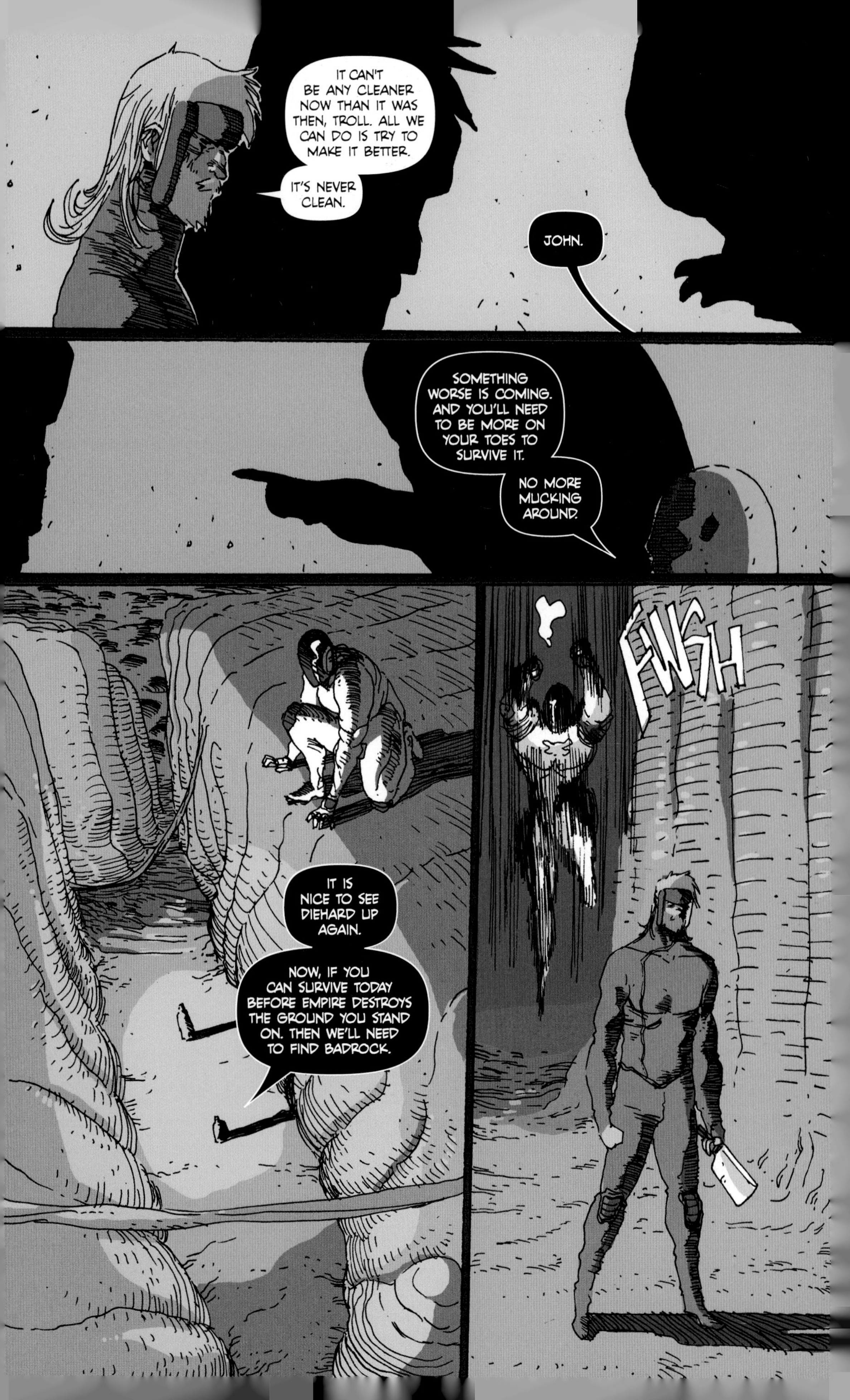
IT CAN'T BE ANY CLEANER NOW THAN IT WAS THEN, TROLL. ALL WE CAN DO IS TRY TO MAKE IT BETTER.
IT'S NEVER CLEAN.
JOHN.
SOMETHING WORSE IS COMING. AND YOU'LL NEED TO BE MORE ON YOUR TOES TO SURVIVE IT.
NO MORE MUCKING AROUND.
IT IS NICE TO SEE DIEHARD UP AGAIN.
NOW, IF YOU CAN SURVIVE TODAY BEFORE EMPIRE DESTROYS THE GROUND YOU STAND ON. THEN WE'LL NEED TO FIND BADROCK.
FWSH

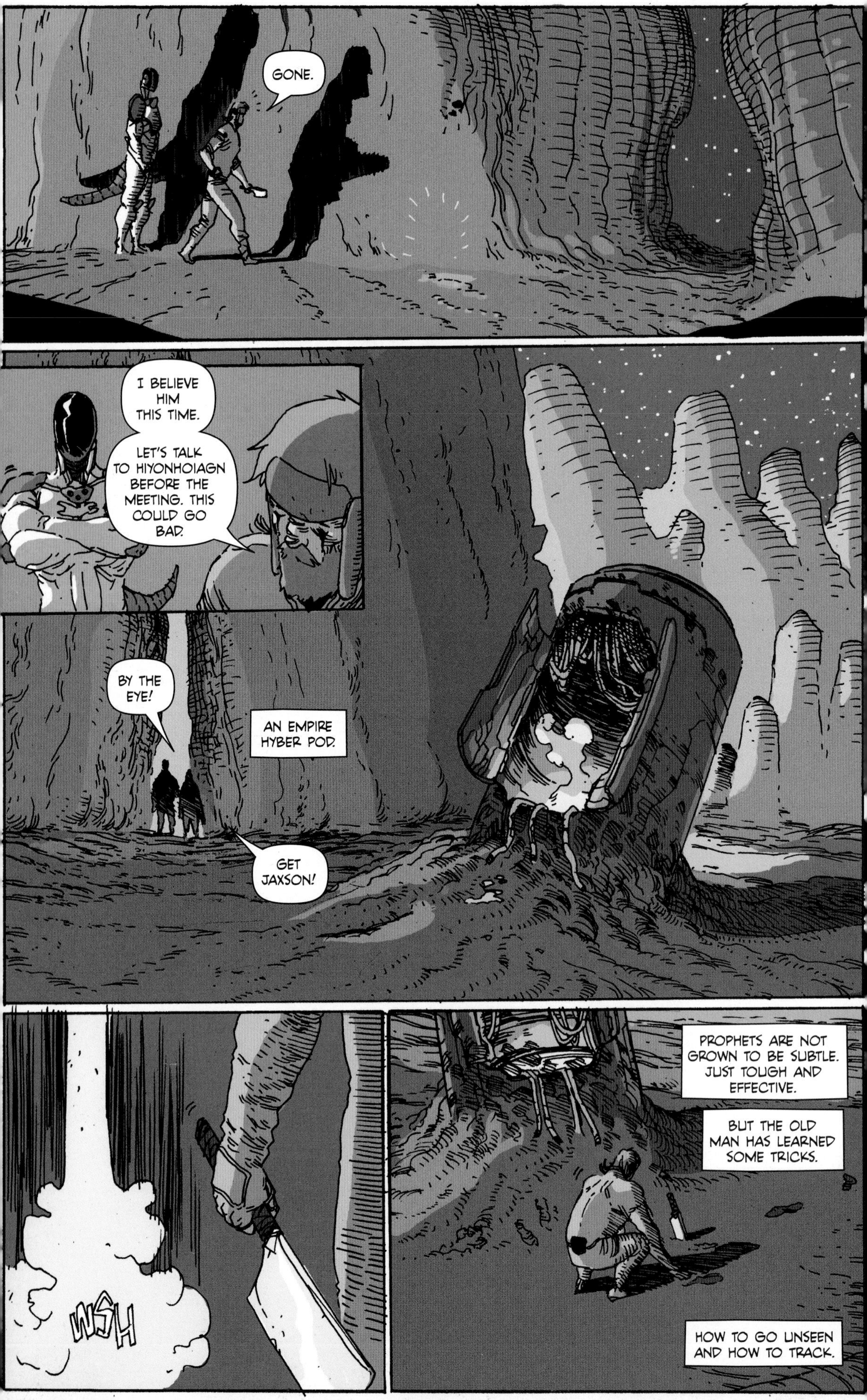
GONE.
I BELIEVE HIM THIS TIME.
LET'S TALK TO HIYONHOIAGN BEFORE THE MEETING. THIS COULD GO BAD.
BY THE EYE!
AN EMPIRE HYBER POD.
GET JAXSON!
WSH
PROPHETS ARE NOT GROWN TO BE SUBTLE. JUST TOUGH AND EFFECTIVE.
BUT THE OLD MAN HAS LEARNED SOME TRICKS.
HOW TO GO UNSEEN AND HOW TO TRACK.

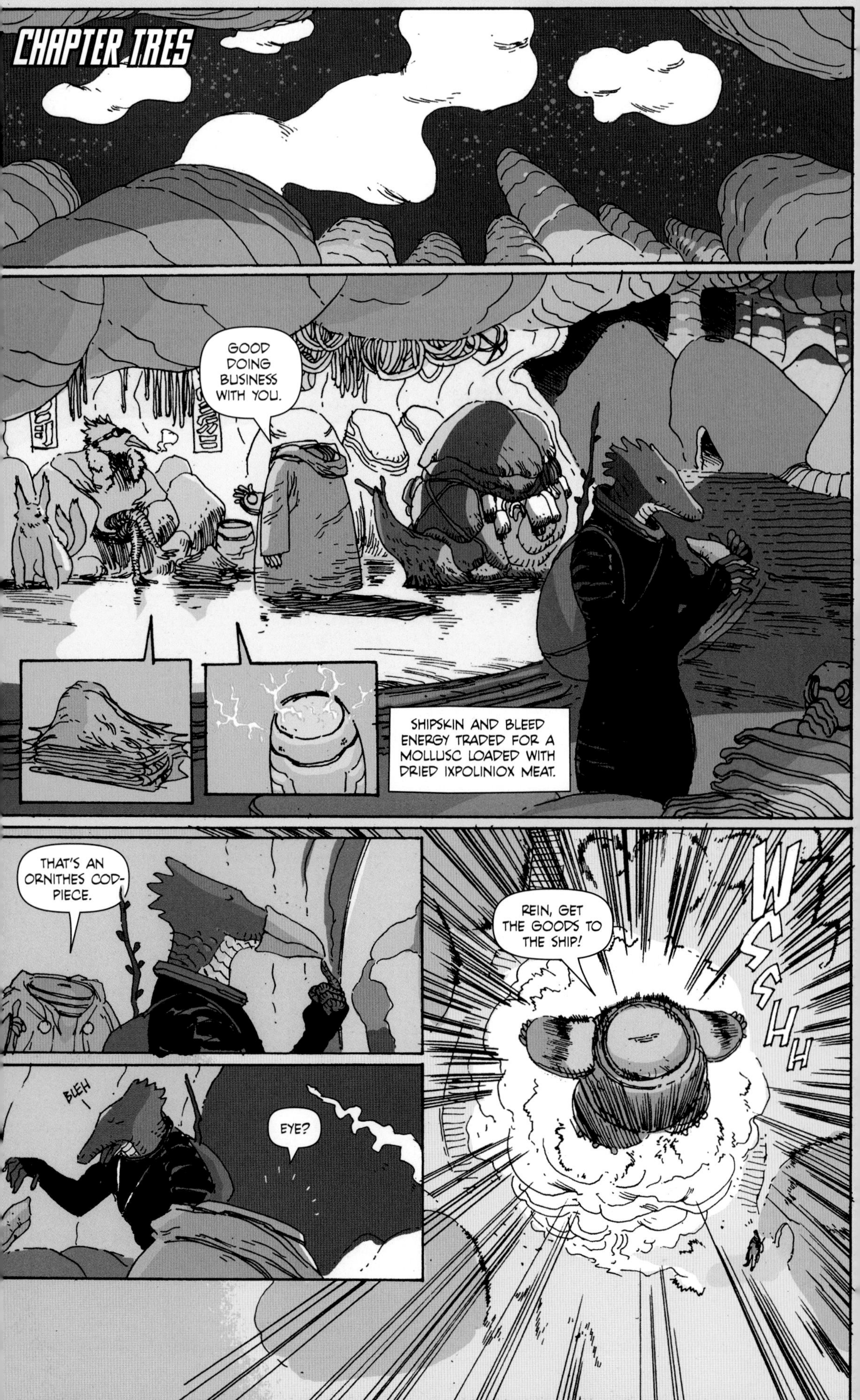
CHAPTER TRES
GOOD DOING BUSINESS WITH YOU.
SHIPSKIN AND BLEED ENERGY TRADED FOR A MOLLUSC LOADED WITH DRIED IXPOLINIOX MEAT.
THAT'S AN ORNITHES COD-PIECE.
REIN, GET THE GOODS TO THE SHIP!
WSSHH
BLEH
EYE?

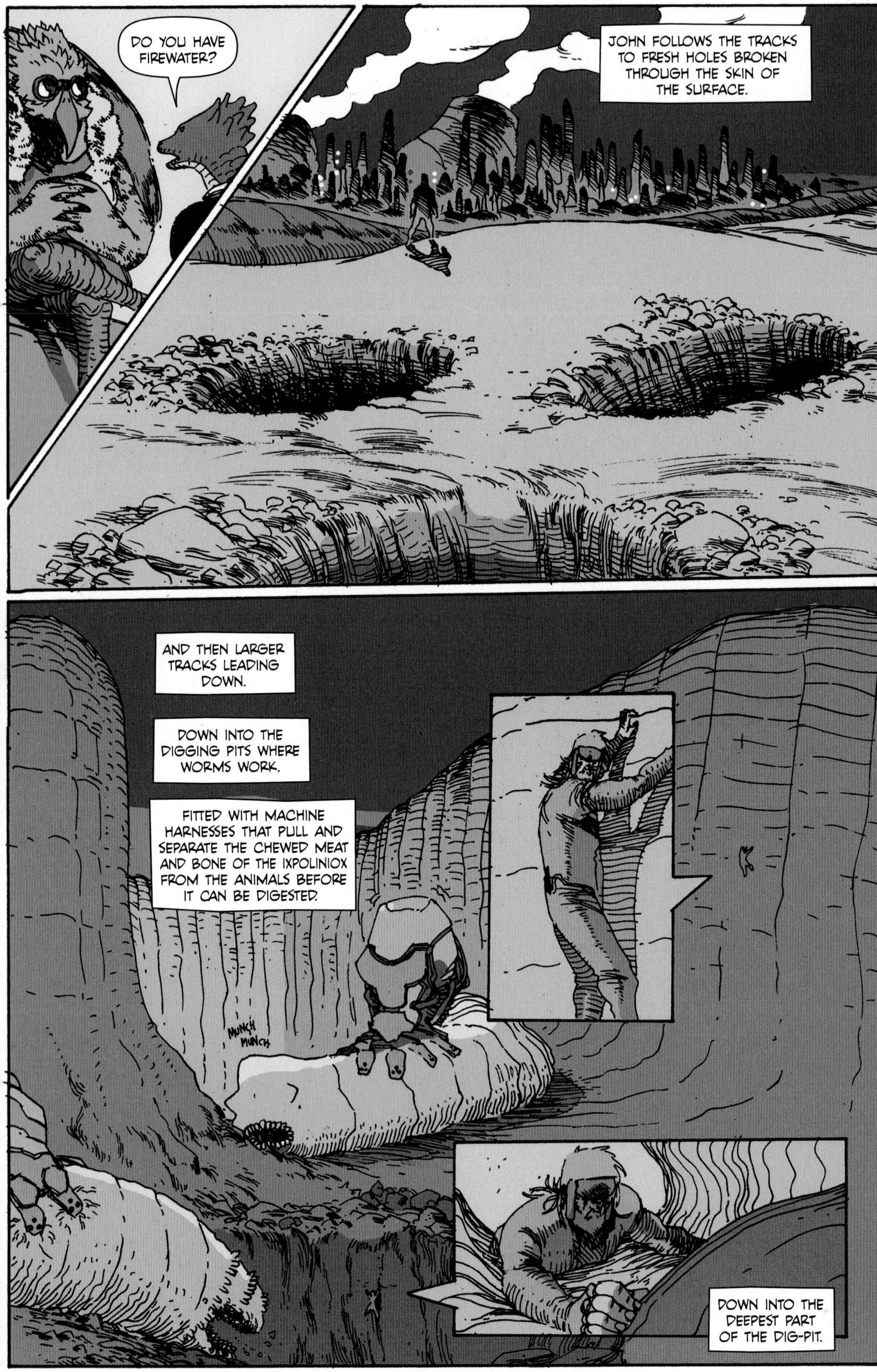
DO YOU HAVE FIREWATER?
JOHN FOLLOWS THE TRACKS TO FRESH HOLES BROKEN THROUGH THE SKIN OF THE SURFACE.
AND THEN LARGER TRACKS LEADING DOWN.
DOWN INTO THE DIGGING PITS WHERE WORMS WORK.
FITTED WITH MACHINE HARNESSES THAT PULL AND SEPARATE THE CHEWED MEAT AND BONE OF THE IXPOLINIOX FROM THE ANIMALS BEFORE IT CAN BE DIGESTED.
MUNCH MUNCH
DOWN INTO THE DEEPEST PART OF THE DIG-PIT.

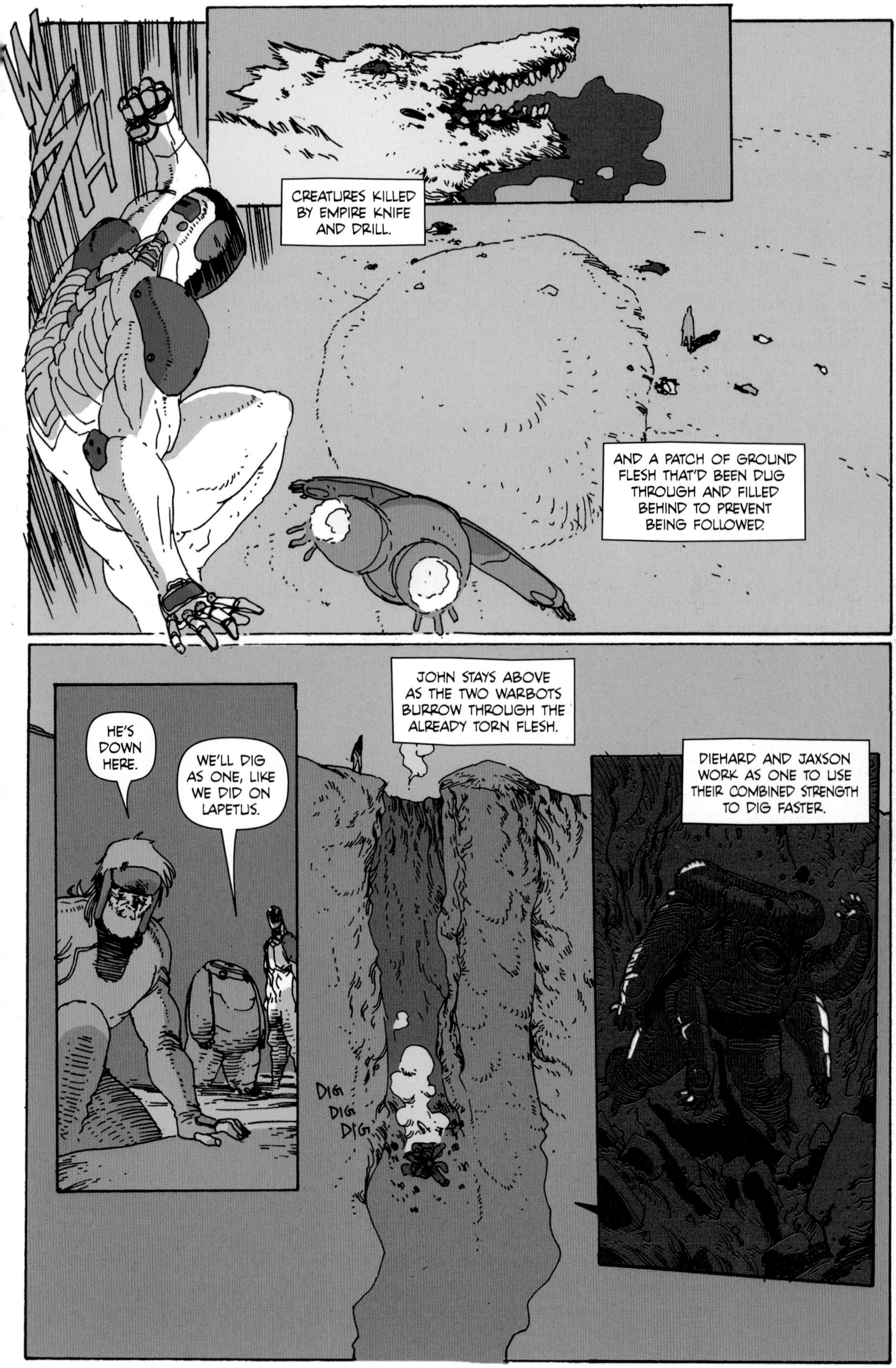
WSSTH
CREATURES KILLED BY EMPIRE KNIFE AND DRILL.
AND A PATCH OF GROUND FLESH THAT'D BEEN DUG THROUGH AND FILLED BEHIND TO PREVENT BEING FOLLOWED.
JOHN STAYS ABOVE AS THE TWO WARBOTS BURROW THROUGH THE ALREADY TORN FLESH.
HE'S DOWN HERE.
WE'LL DIG AS ONE, LIKE WE DID ON LAPETUS.
DIG DIG DIG
DIEHARD AND JAXSON WORK AS ONE TO USE THEIR COMBINED STRENGTH TO DIG FASTER.

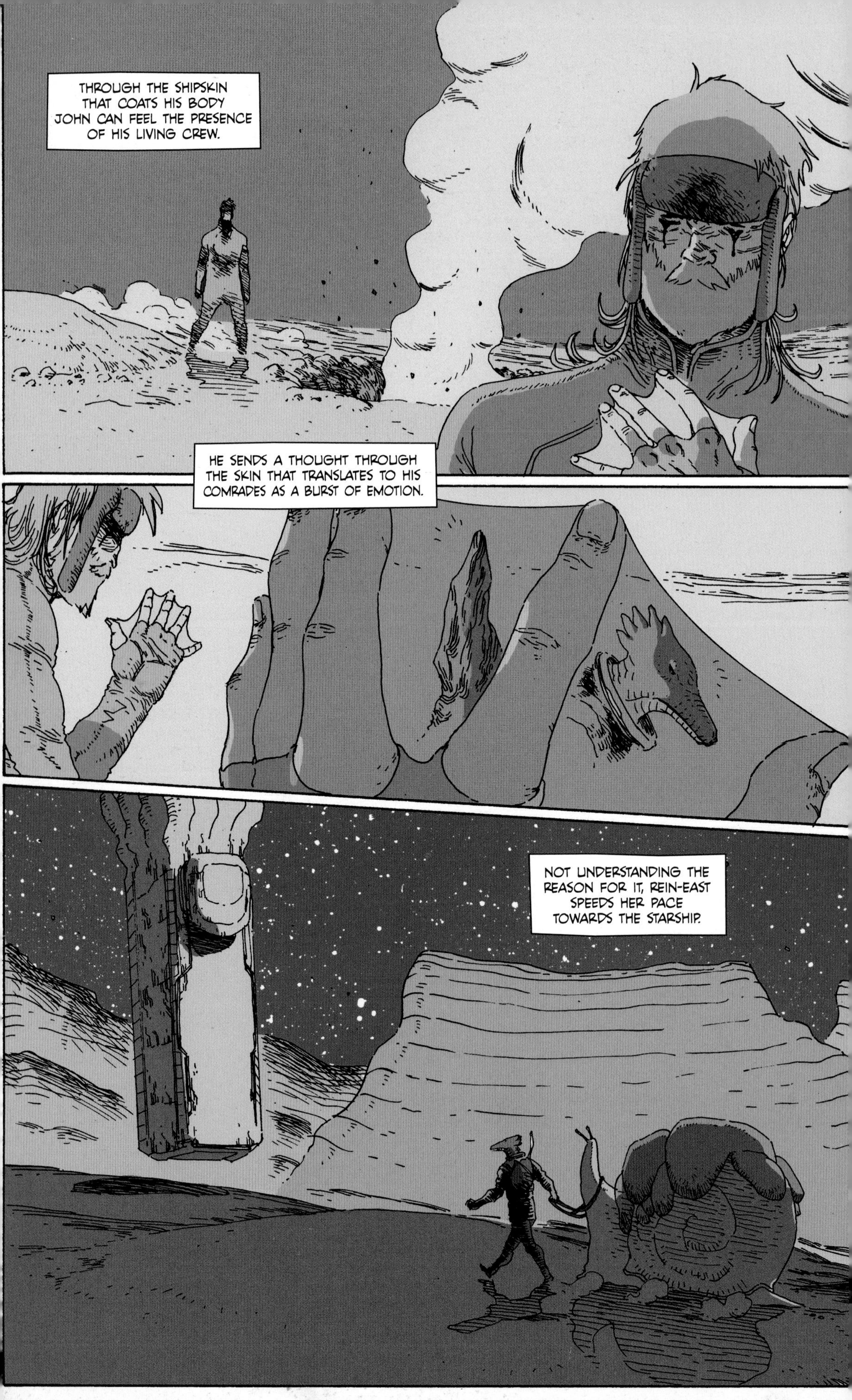
THROUGH THE SHIPSKIN THAT COATS HIS BODY JOHN CAN FEEL THE PRESENCE OF HIS LIVING CREW.
HE SENDS A THOUGHT THROUGH THE SKIN THAT TRANSLATES TO HIS COMRADES AS A BURST OF EMOTION.
NOT UNDERSTANDING THE REASON FOR IT, REIN-EAST SPEEDS HER PACE TOWARDS THE STARSHIP.

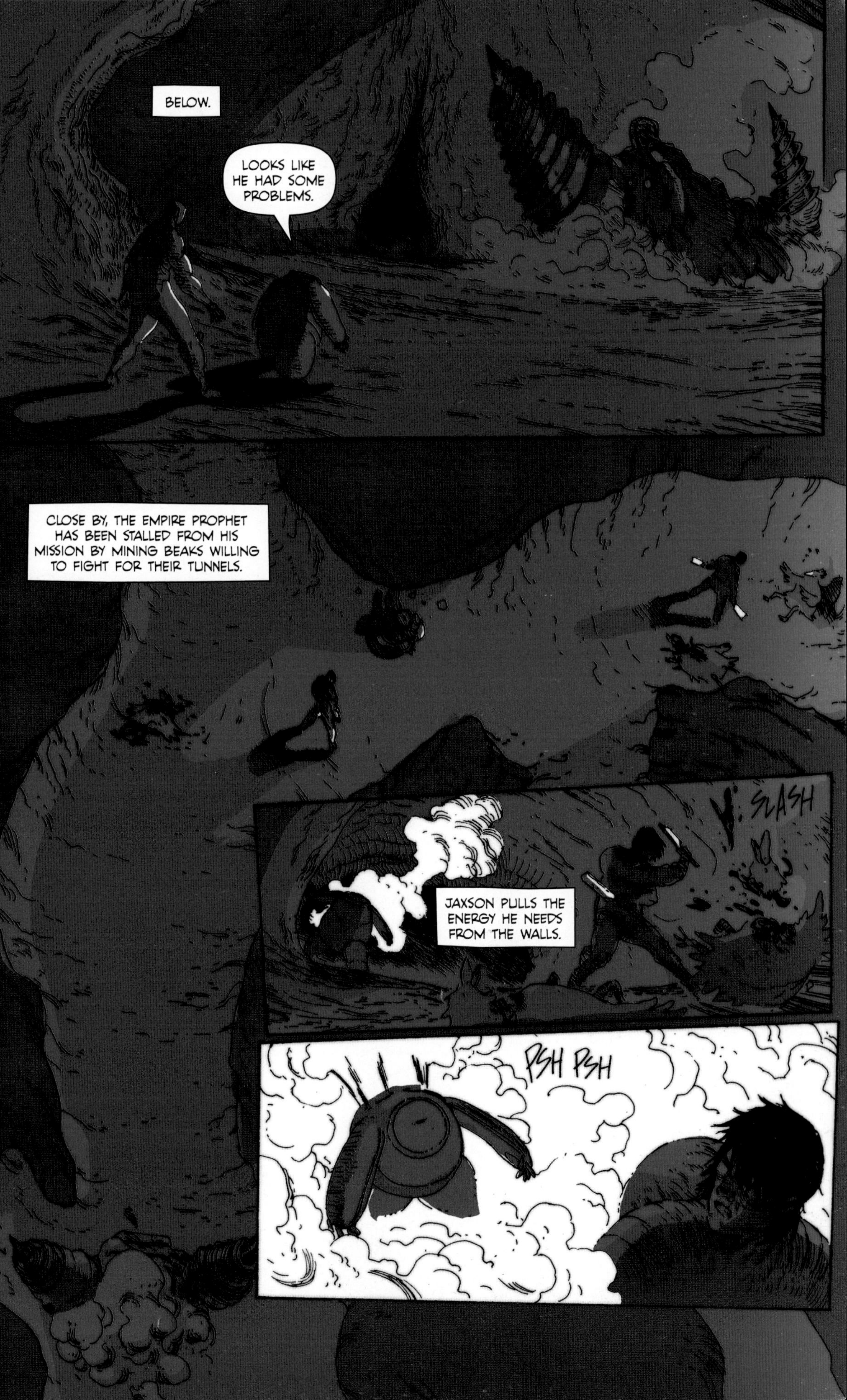
BELOW.
LOOKS LIKE HE HAD SOME PROBLEMS.
CLOSE BY, THE EMPIRE PROPHET HAS BEEN STALLED FROM HIS MISSION BY MINING BEAKS WILLING TO FIGHT FOR THEIR TUNNELS.
SLASH
JAXSON PULLS THE ENERGY HE NEEDS FROM THE WALLS.
PSH PSH

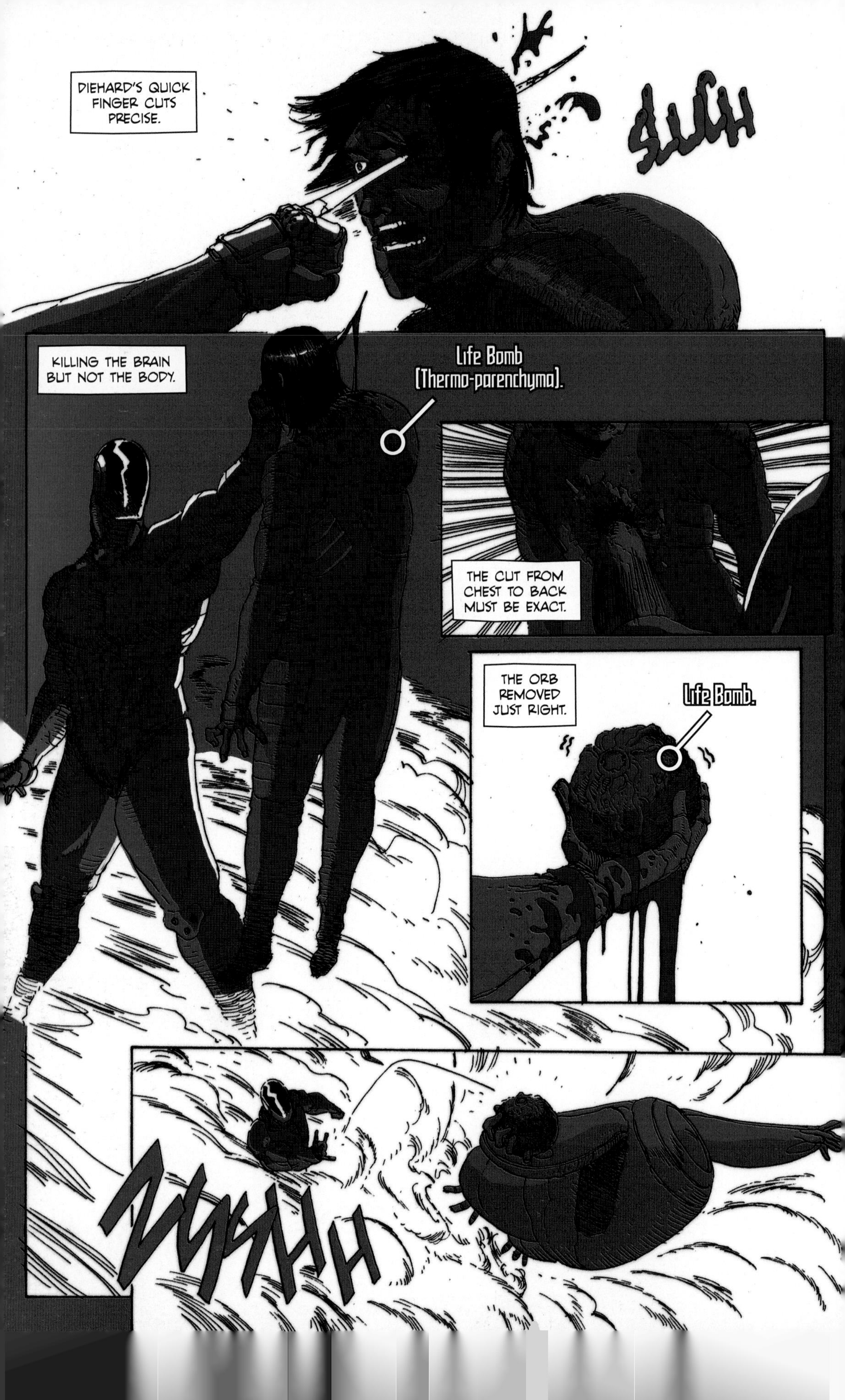
DIEHARD'S QUICK FINGER CUTS PRECISE.
SLICH
KILLING THE BRAIN BUT NOT THE BODY.
Life Bomb (Thermo-parenchyma).
THE CUT FROM CHEST TO BACK MUST BE EXACT.
THE ORB REMOVED JUST RIGHT.
Life Bomb.
ZWHH

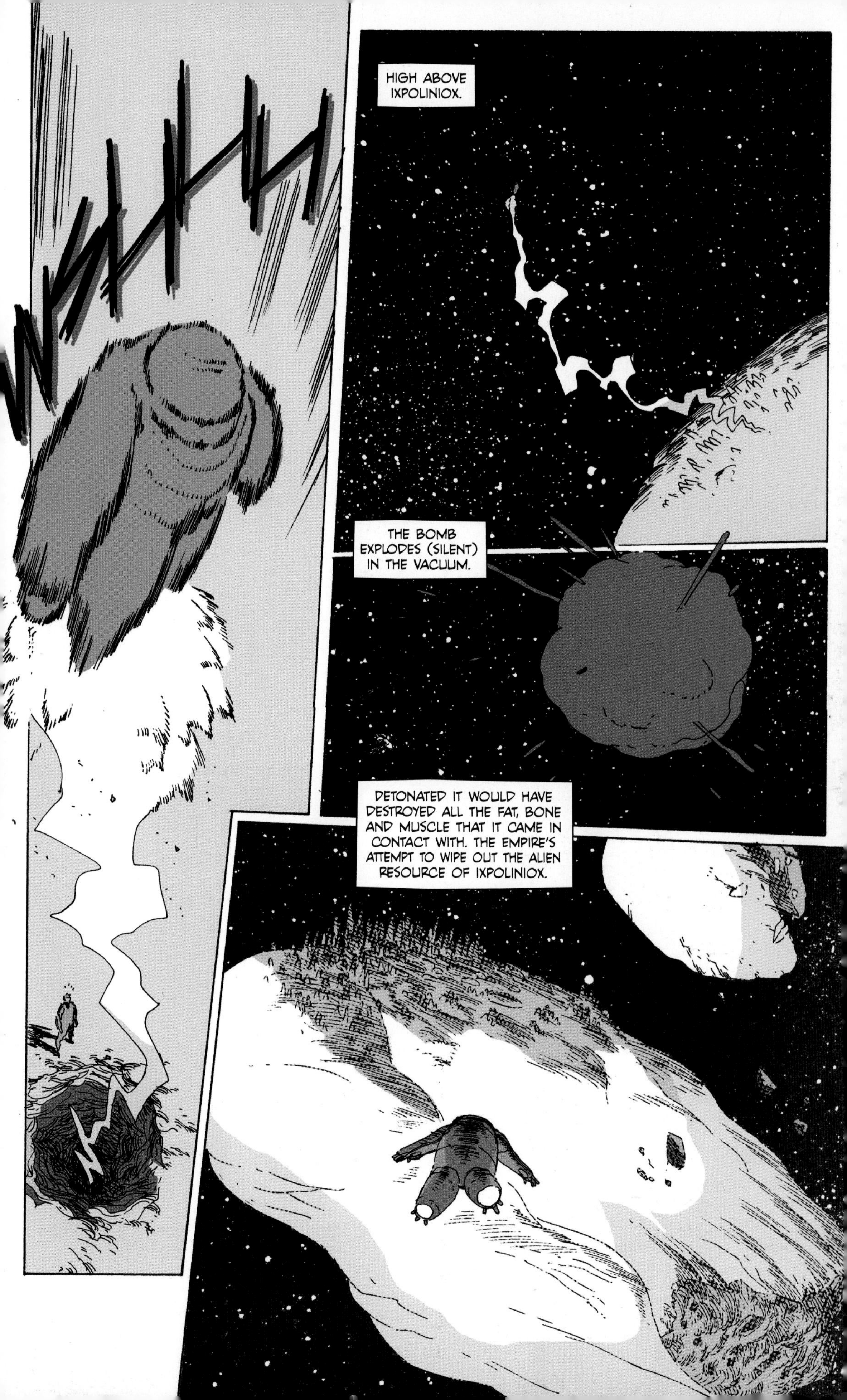
HIGH ABOVE IXPOLINIOX.
THE BOMB EXPLODES (SILENT) IN THE VACUUM.
DETONATED IT WOULD HAVE DESTROYED ALL THE FAT, BONE AND MUSCLE THAT IT CAME IN CONTACT WITH. THE EMPIRE'S ATTEMPT TO WIPE OUT THE ALIEN RESOURCE OF IXPOLINIOX.

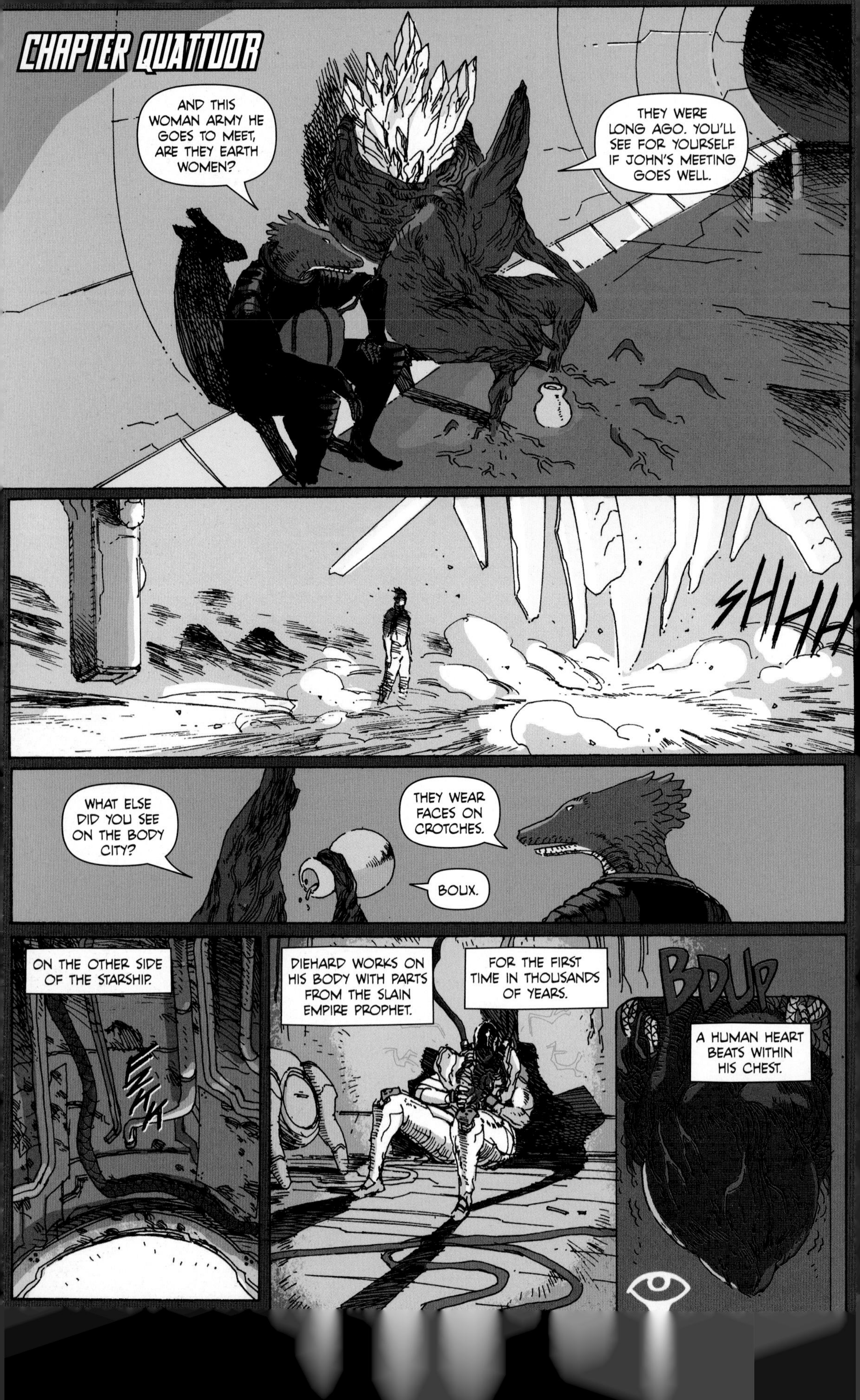
CHAPTER QUATTUOR
AND THIS WOMAN ARMY HE GOES TO MEET, ARE THEY EARTH WOMEN?
THEY WERE LONG AGO. YOU'LL SEE FOR YOURSELF IF JOHN'S MEETING GOES WELL.
SHHH
WHAT ELSE DID YOU SEE ON THE BODY CITY?
THEY WEAR FACES ON CROTCHES.
BOUX.
ON THE OTHER SIDE OF THE STARSHIP.
DIEHARD WORKS ON HIS BODY WITH PARTS FROM THE SLAIN EMPIRE PROPHET.
FOR THE FIRST TIME IN THOUSANDS OF YEARS.
BDUP
A HUMAN HEART BEATS WITHIN HIS CHEST.

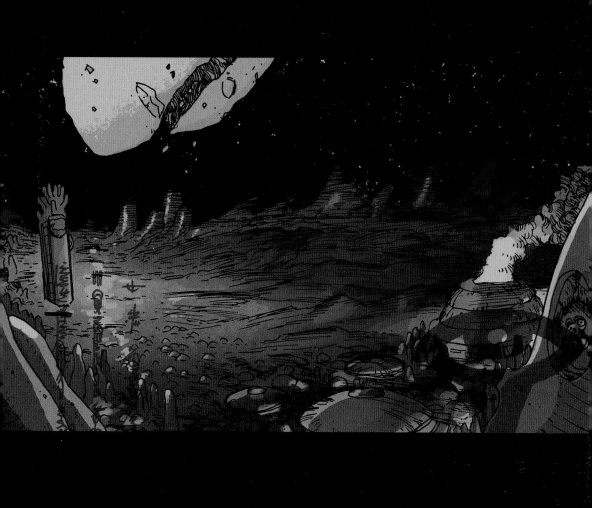

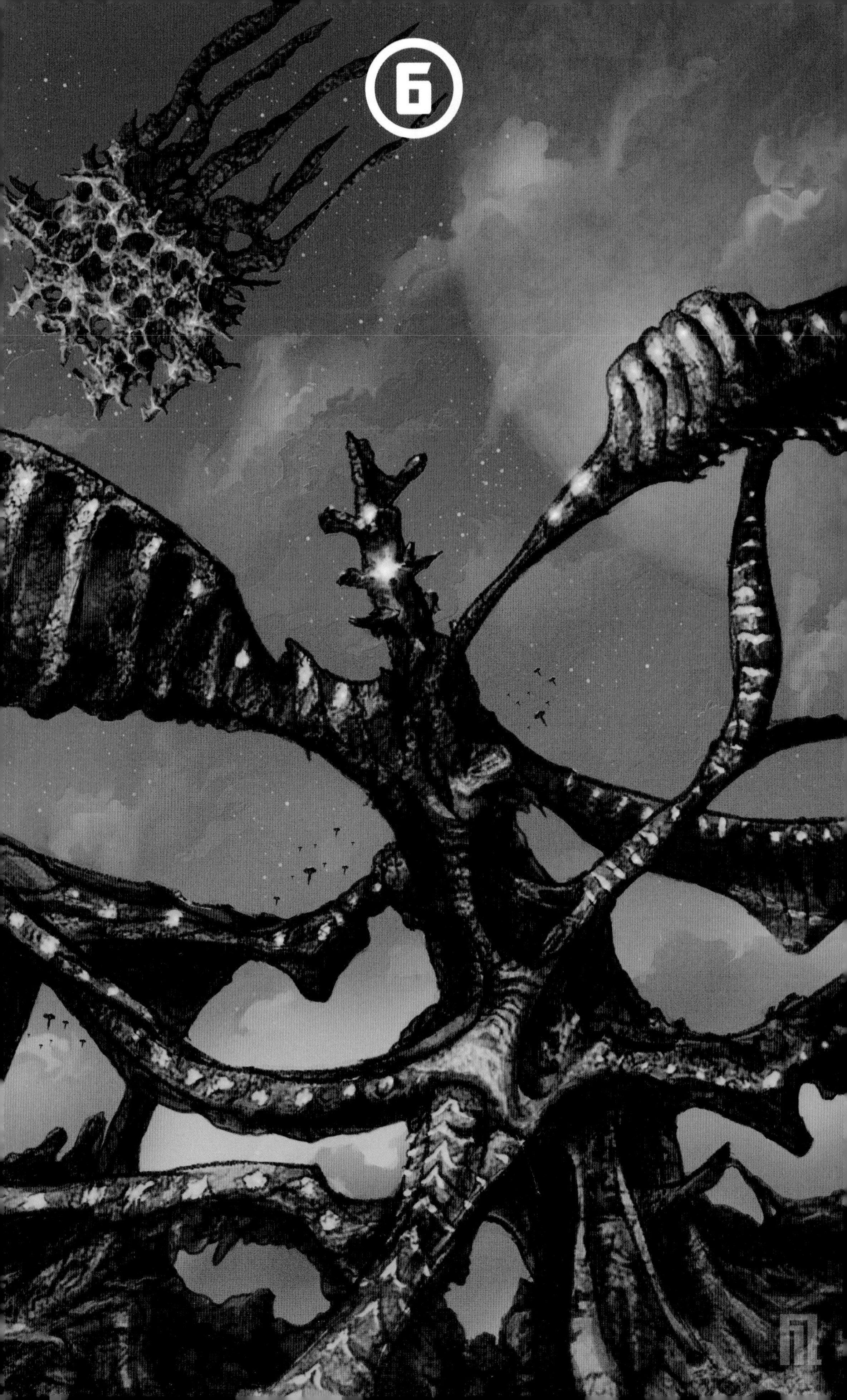
6

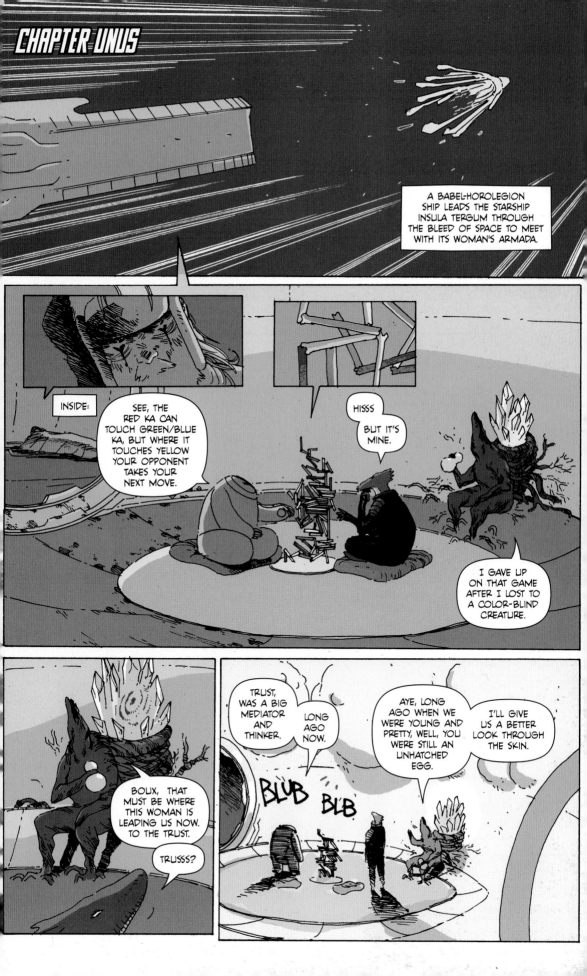

A BABEL-HOROLEGION SHIP LEADS THE STARSHIP INSULA TERGUM THROUGH THE BLEED OF SPACE TO MEET WITH ITS WOMAN'S ARMADA.

INSIDE:

SEE, THE RED KA CAN TOUCH GREEN/BLUE KA, BUT WHERE IT TOUCHES YELLOW YOUR OPPONENT TAKES YOUR NEXT MOVE.

HISSS

BUT IT'S MINE.

I GAVE UP ON THAT GAME AFTER I LOST TO A COLOR-BLIND CREATURE.

BOUX, THAT MUST BE WHERE THIS WOMAN IS LEADING US NOW. TO THE TRUST.

TRUSSS?

TRUST, WAS A BIG MEDIATOR AND THINKER.

LONG AGO NOW.

AYE, LONG AGO WHEN WE WERE YOUNG AND PRETTY, WELL, YOU WERE STILL AN UNHATCHED EGG.

I'LL GIVE US A BETTER LOOK THROUGH THE SKIN.

BLUB BLB

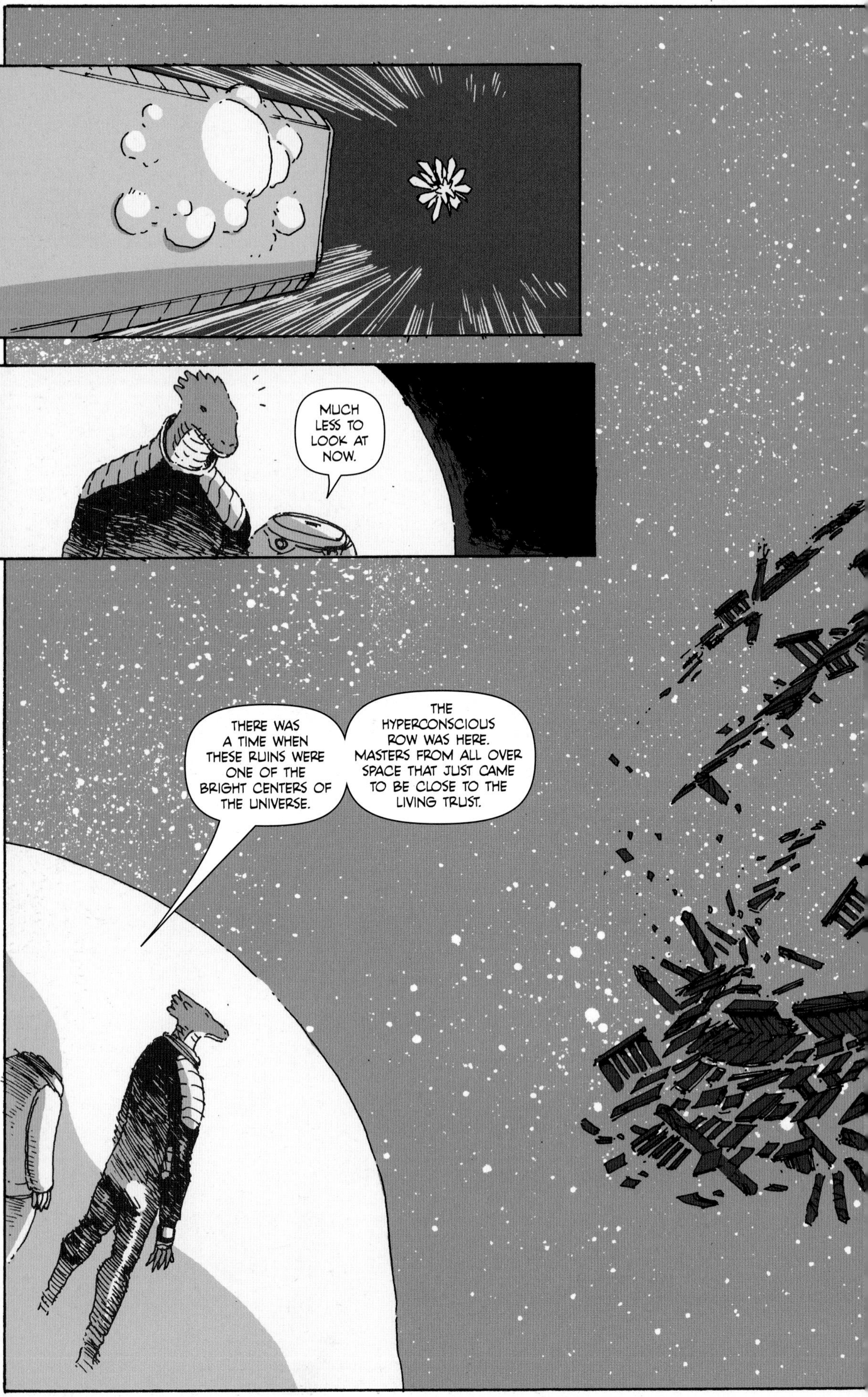
MUCH LESS TO LOOK AT NOW.
THERE WAS A TIME WHEN THESE RUINS WERE ONE OF THE BRIGHT CENTERS OF THE UNIVERSE.
THE HYPERCONSCIOUS ROW WAS HERE. MASTERS FROM ALL OVER SPACE THAT JUST CAME TO BE CLOSE TO THE LIVING TRUST.

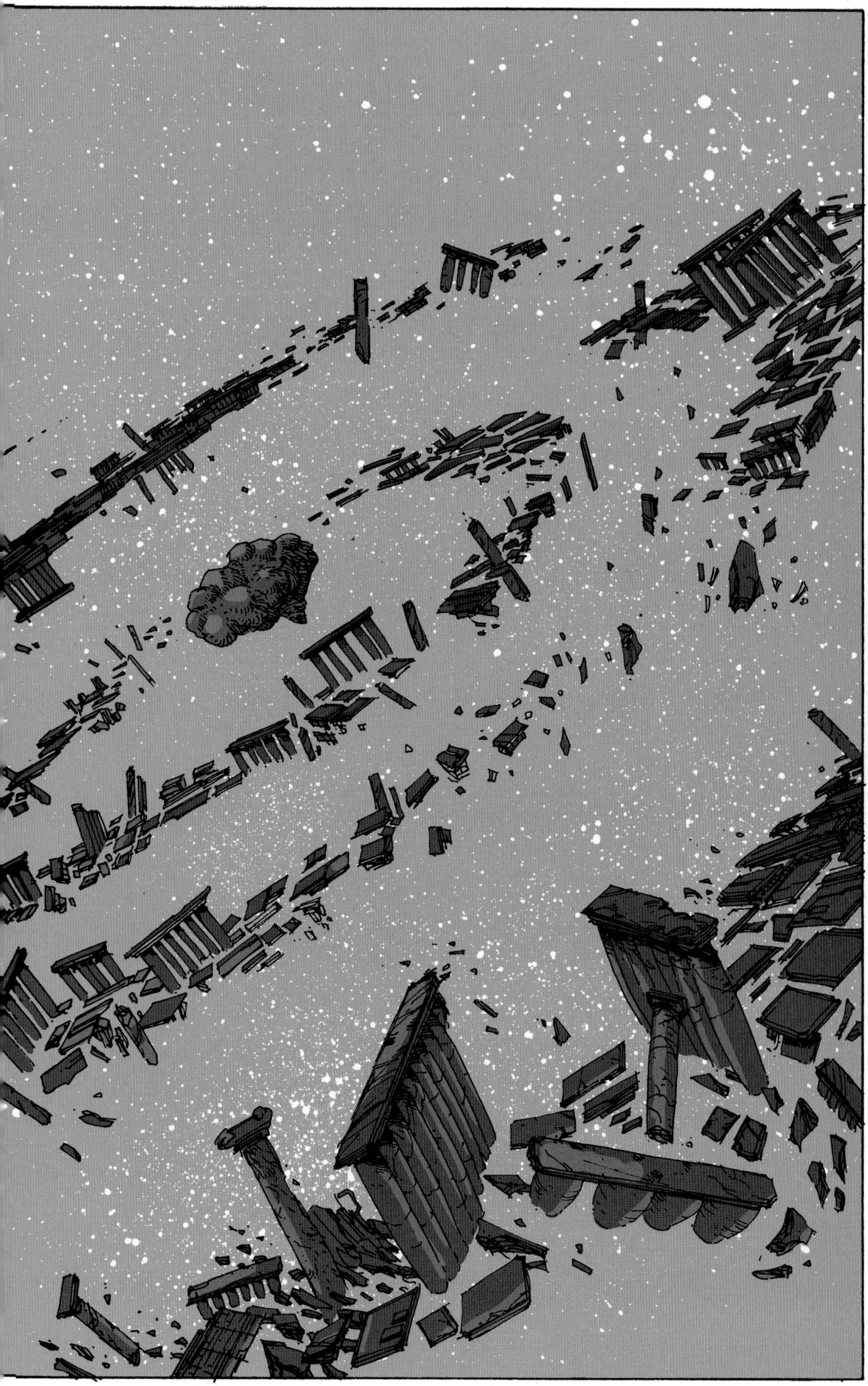

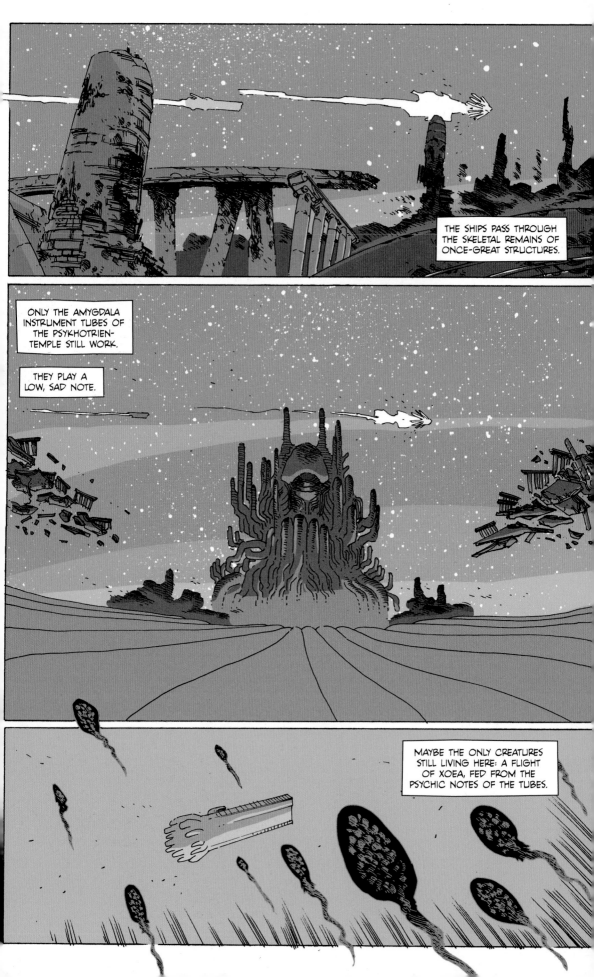

THE SHIPS PASS THROUGH THE SKELETAL REMAINS OF ONCE-GREAT STRUCTURES.

ONLY THE AMYGDALA INSTRUMENT TUBES OF THE PSYKHOTRIEN-TEMPLE STILL WORK.

THEY PLAY A LOW, SAD NOTE.

MAYBE THE ONLY CREATURES STILL LIVING HERE: A FLIGHT OF XOEA, FED FROM THE PSYCHIC NOTES OF THE TUBES.

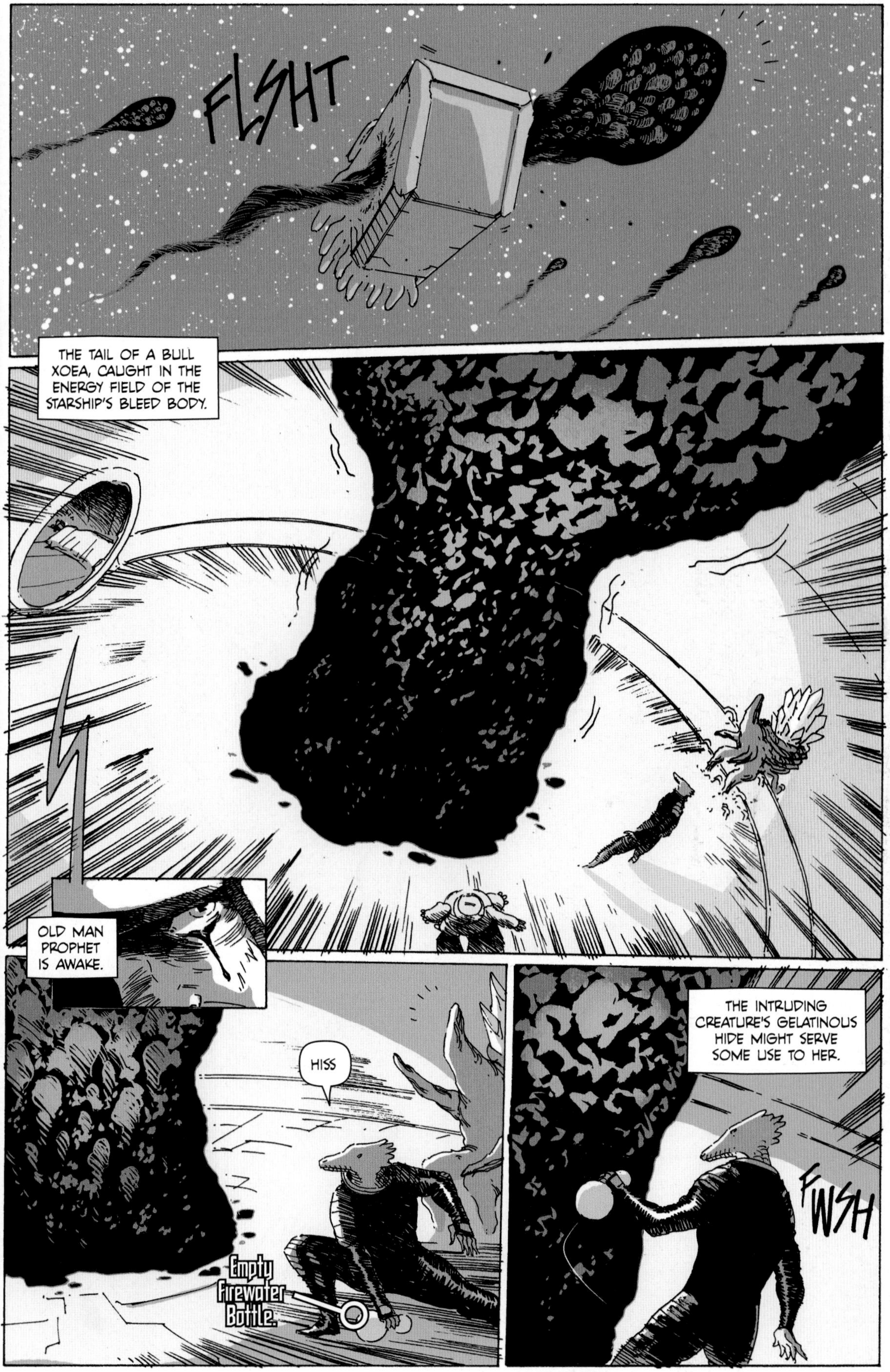
FLSHT
THE TAIL OF A BULL XOEA, CAUGHT IN THE ENERGY FIELD OF THE STARSHIP'S BLEED BODY.
OLD MAN PROPHET IS AWAKE.
HISS
Empty Firewater Bottle.
THE INTRUDING CREATURE'S GELATINOUS HIDE MIGHT SERVE SOME USE TO HER.
FWSH

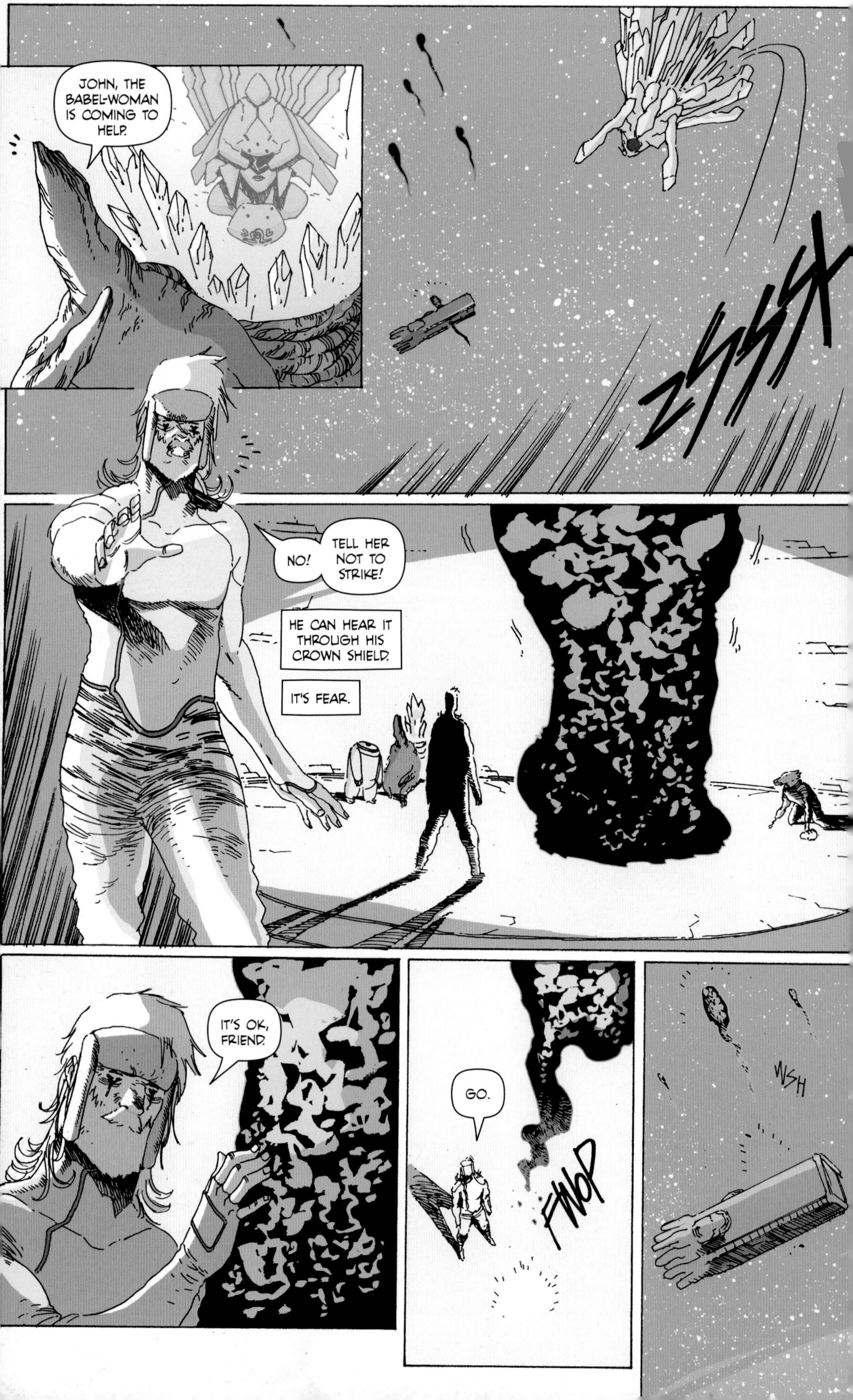
JOHN, THE BABEL-WOMAN IS COMING TO HELP.
ZSSSSK
NO!
TELL HER NOT TO STRIKE!
HE CAN HEAR IT THROUGH HIS CROWN SHIELD.
IT'S FEAR.
IT'S OK, FRIEND.
GO.
FWOP
WSH

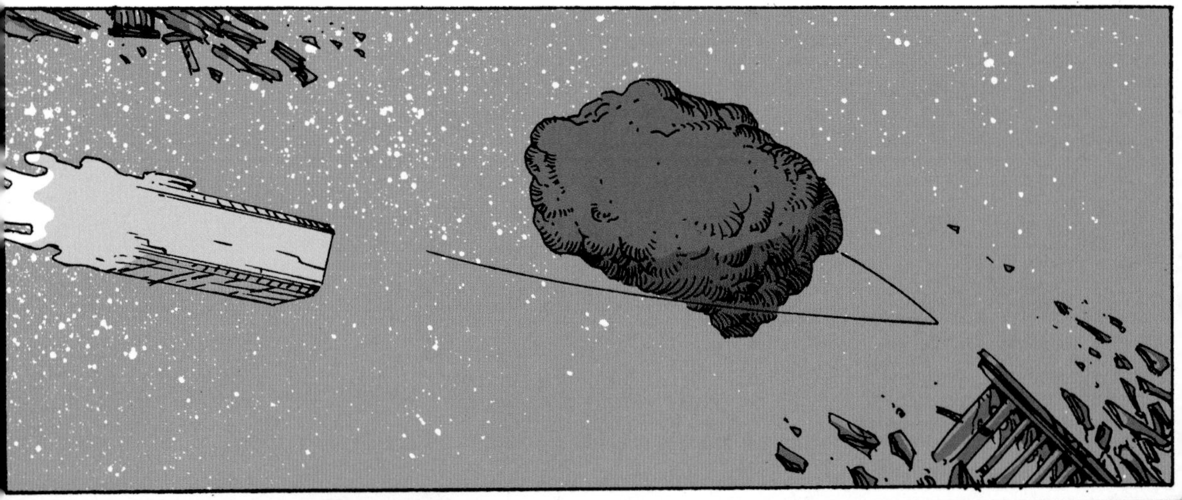

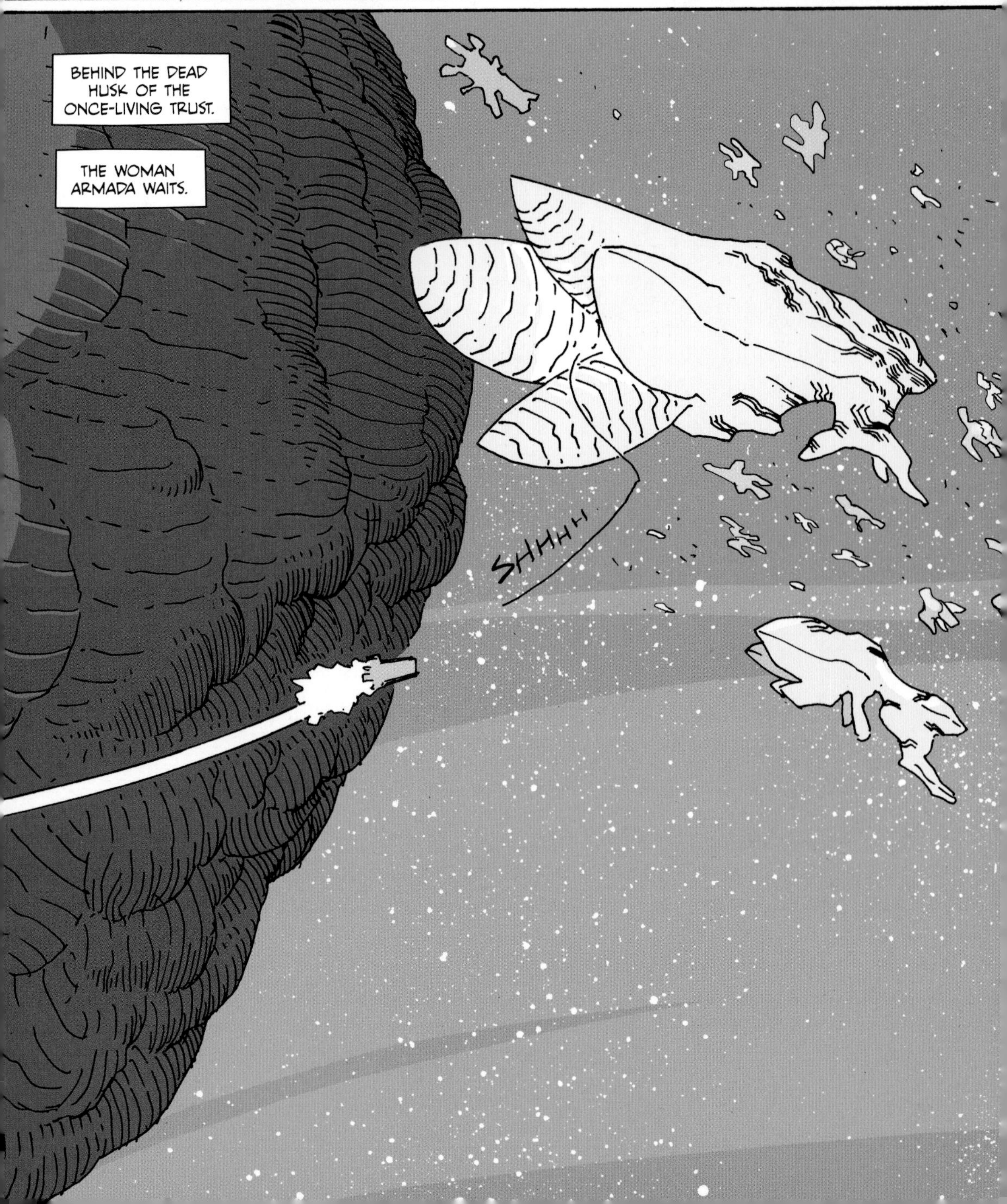
BEHIND THE DEAD HUSK OF THE ONCE-LIVING TRUST.
THE WOMAN ARMADA WAITS.
SHHHH

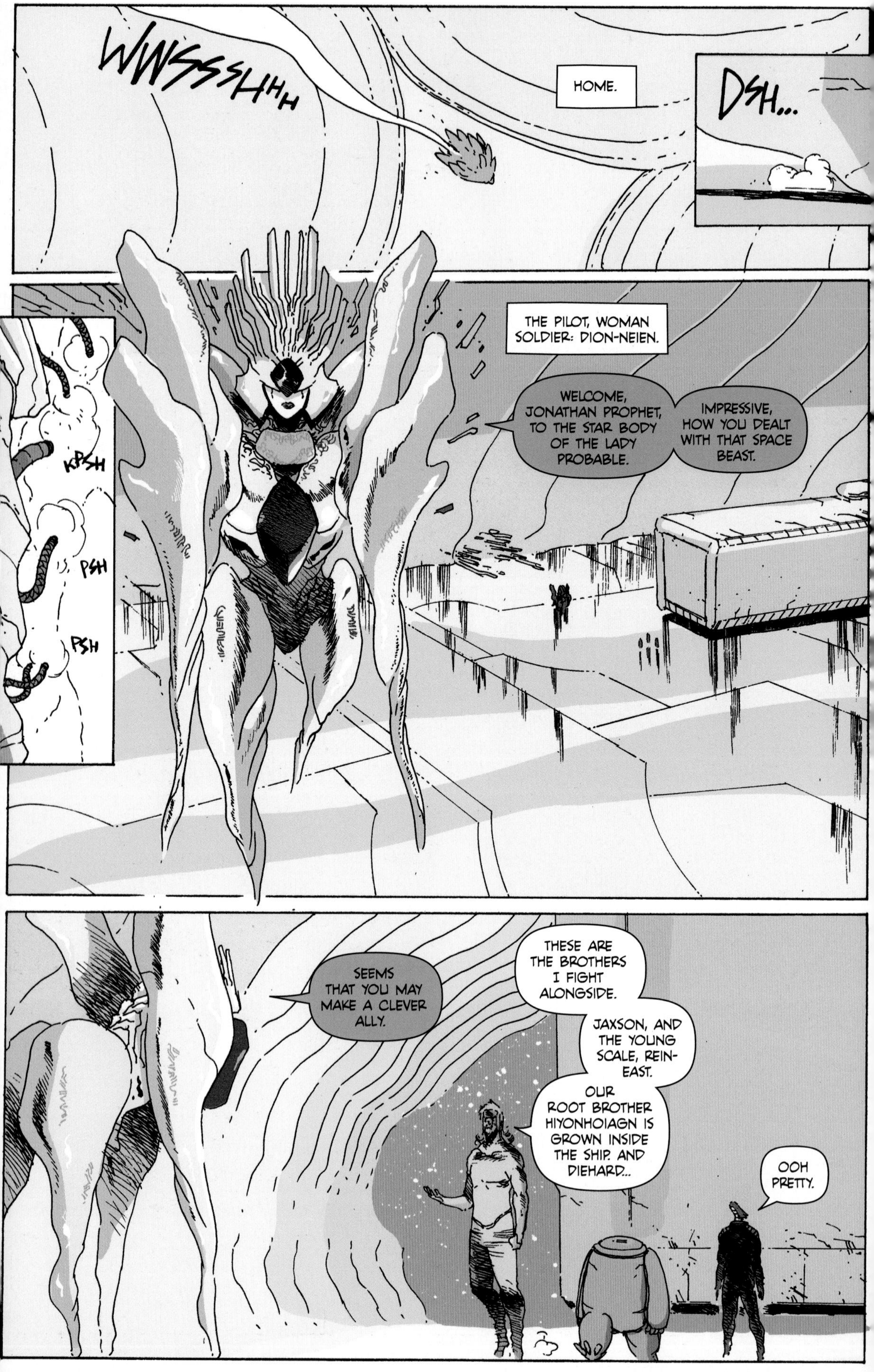
WWSSSSHHH
HOME.
DSH...
THE PILOT, WOMAN SOLDIER: DION-NEIEN.
KPSH
PSH
PSH
WELCOME, JONATHAN PROPHET, TO THE STAR BODY OF THE LADY PROBABLE.
IMPRESSIVE, HOW YOU DEALT WITH THAT SPACE BEAST.
SEEMS THAT YOU MAY MAKE A CLEVER ALLY.
THESE ARE THE BROTHERS I FIGHT ALONGSIDE.
JAXSON, AND THE YOUNG SCALE, REIN-EAST.
OUR ROOT BROTHER HIYONHOIAGN IS GROWN INSIDE THE SHIP. AND DIEHARD...
OOH PRETTY.

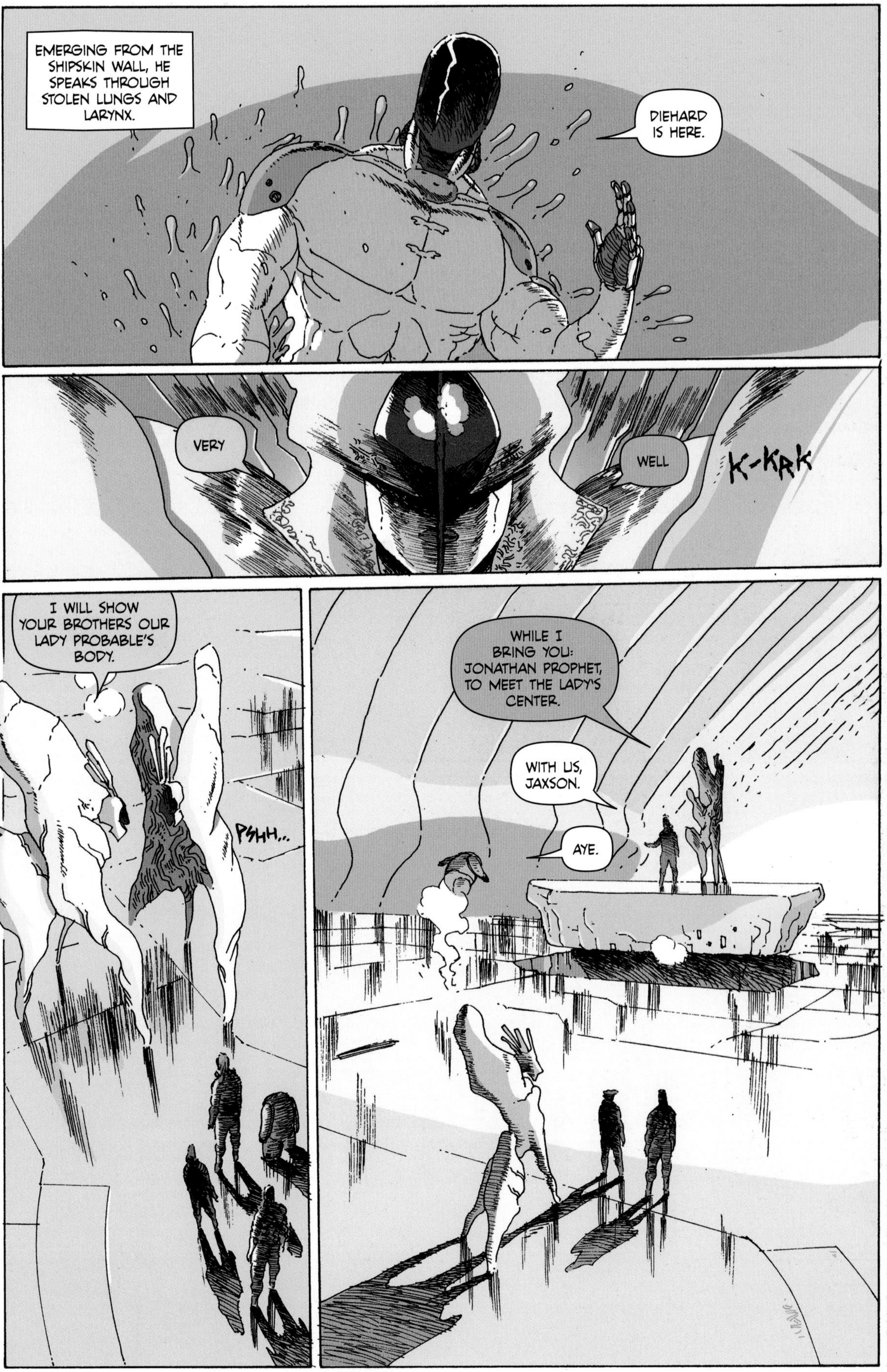
EMERGING FROM THE SHIPSKIN WALL, HE SPEAKS THROUGH STOLEN LUNGS AND LARYNX.
DIEHARD IS HERE.
VERY
WELL
K-KRK
I WILL SHOW YOUR BROTHERS OUR LADY PROBABLE'S BODY.
PSHH...
WHILE I BRING YOU: JONATHAN PROPHET, TO MEET THE LADY'S CENTER.
WITH US, JAXSON.
AYE.

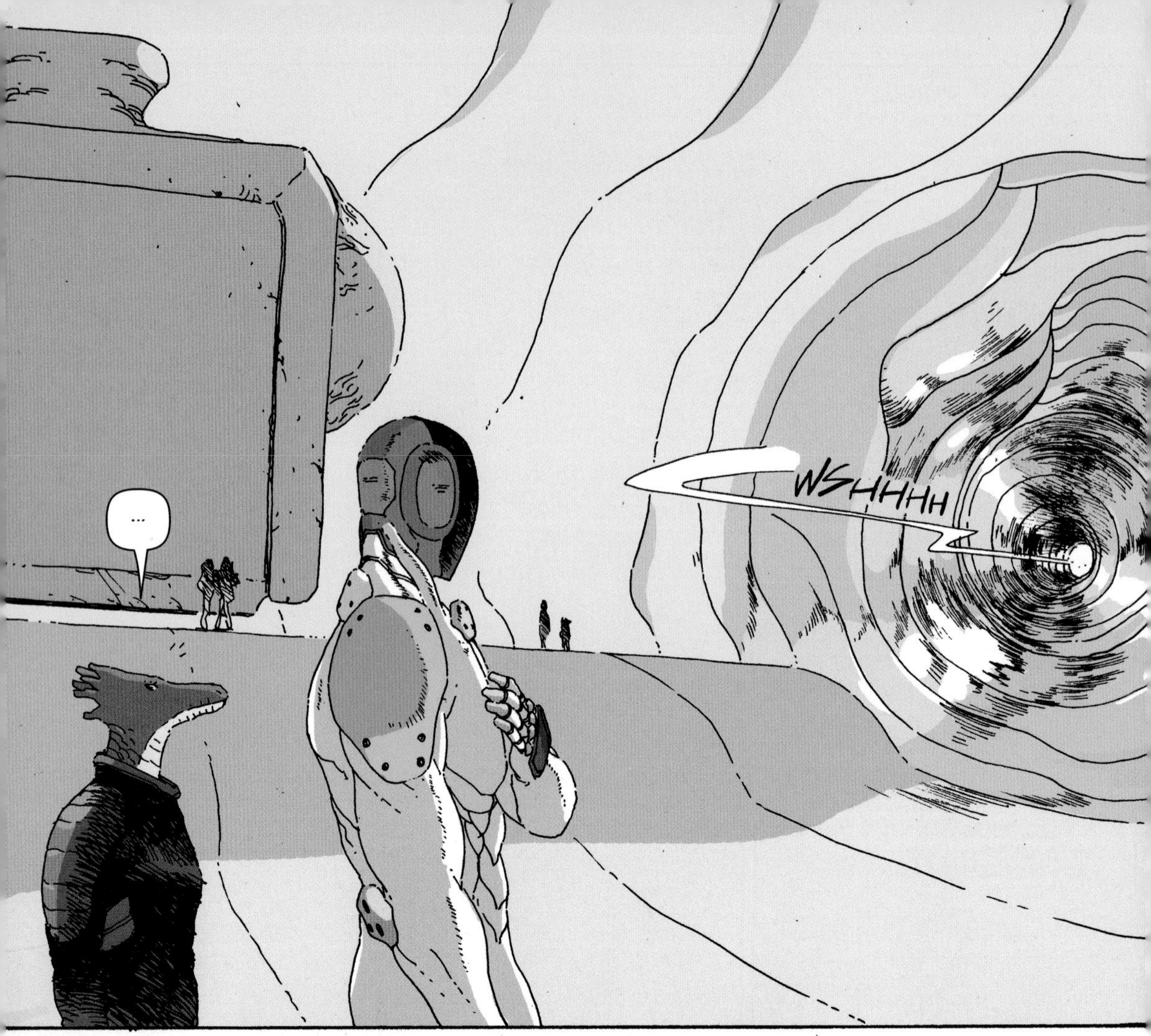
...
WSHHHH

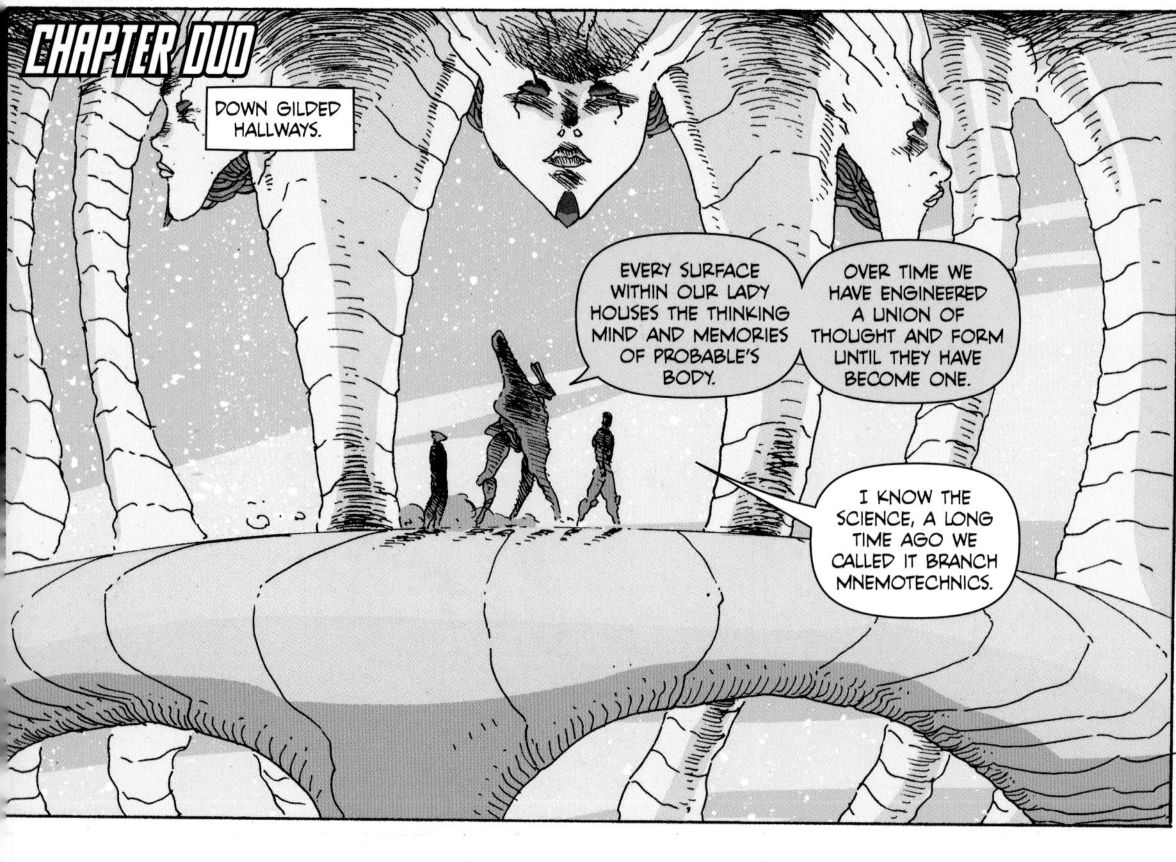
CHAPTER DUO
DOWN GILDED HALLWAYS.
EVERY SURFACE WITHIN OUR LADY HOUSES THE THINKING MIND AND MEMORIES OF PROBABLE'S BODY.
OVER TIME WE HAVE ENGINEERED A UNION OF THOUGHT AND FORM UNTIL THEY HAVE BECOME ONE.
I KNOW THE SCIENCE, A LONG TIME AGO WE CALLED IT BRANCH MNEMOTECHNICS.

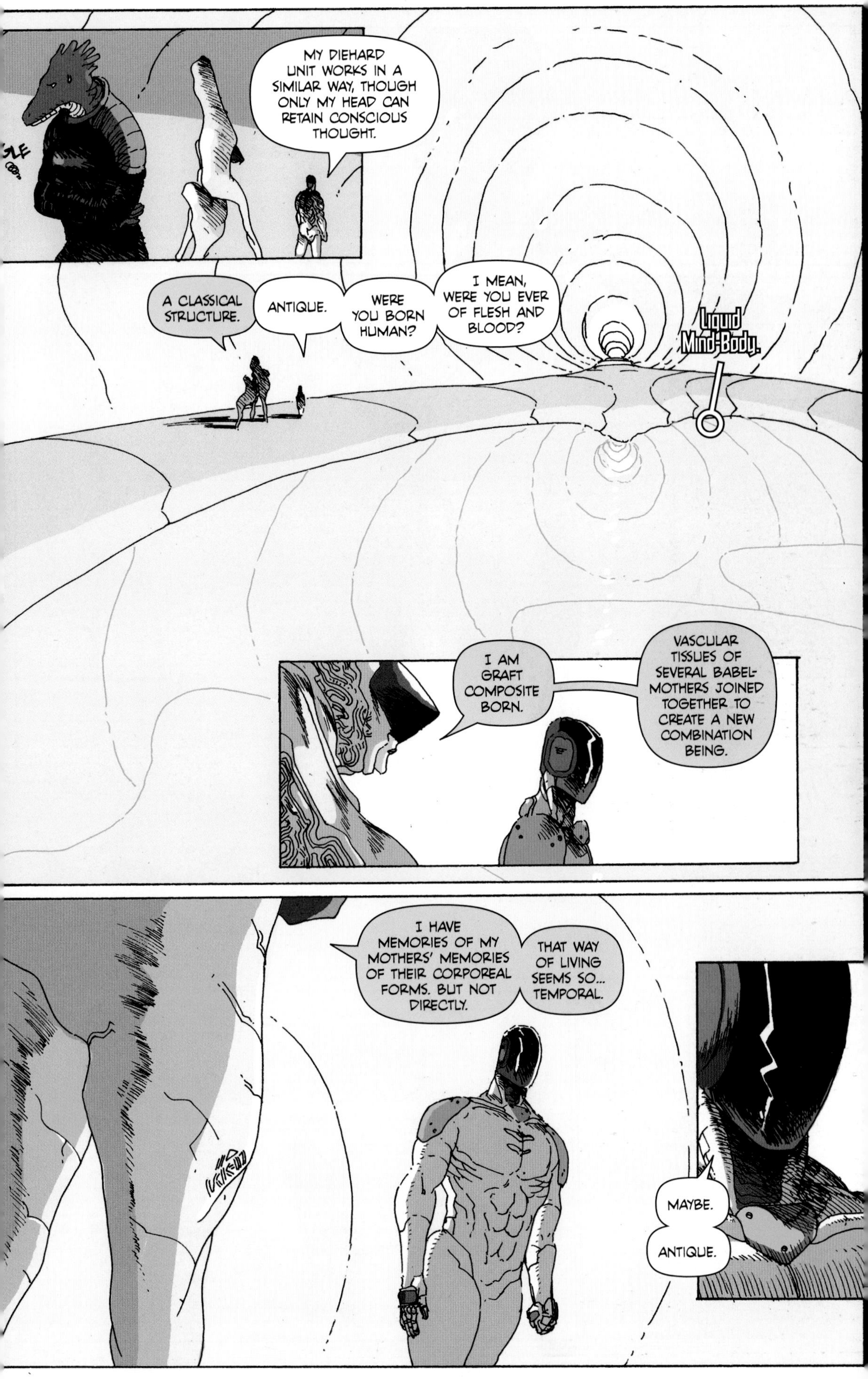
MY DIEHARD UNIT WORKS IN A SIMILAR WAY, THOUGH ONLY MY HEAD CAN RETAIN CONSCIOUS THOUGHT.
A CLASSICAL STRUCTURE.
ANTIQUE.
WERE YOU BORN HUMAN?
I MEAN, WERE YOU EVER OF FLESH AND BLOOD?
Liquid Mind-Body.
I AM GRAFT COMPOSITE BORN.
VASCULAR TISSUES OF SEVERAL BABEL-MOTHERS JOINED TOGETHER TO CREATE A NEW COMBINATION BEING.
I HAVE MEMORIES OF MY MOTHERS' MEMORIES OF THEIR CORPOREAL FORMS. BUT NOT DIRECTLY.
THAT WAY OF LIVING SEEMS SO... TEMPORAL.
MAYBE.
ANTIQUE.

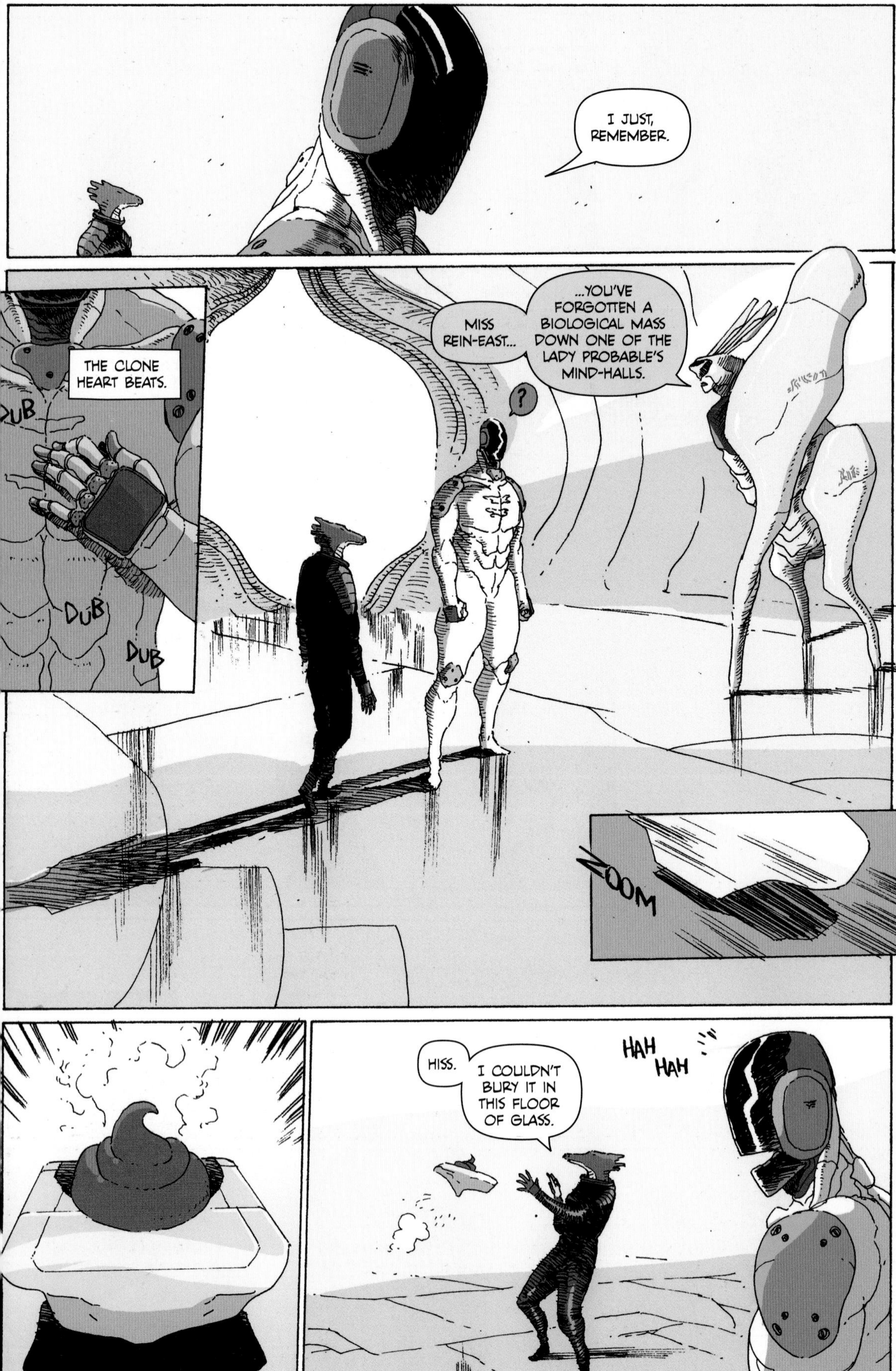
I JUST, REMEMBER.
THE CLONE HEART BEATS.
DUB
DUB
DUB
MISS REIN-EAST...
...YOU'VE FORGOTTEN A BIOLOGICAL MASS DOWN ONE OF THE LADY PROBABLE'S MIND-HALLS.
?
ZOOM
HISS.
I COULDN'T BURY IT IN THIS FLOOR OF GLASS.
HAH HAH

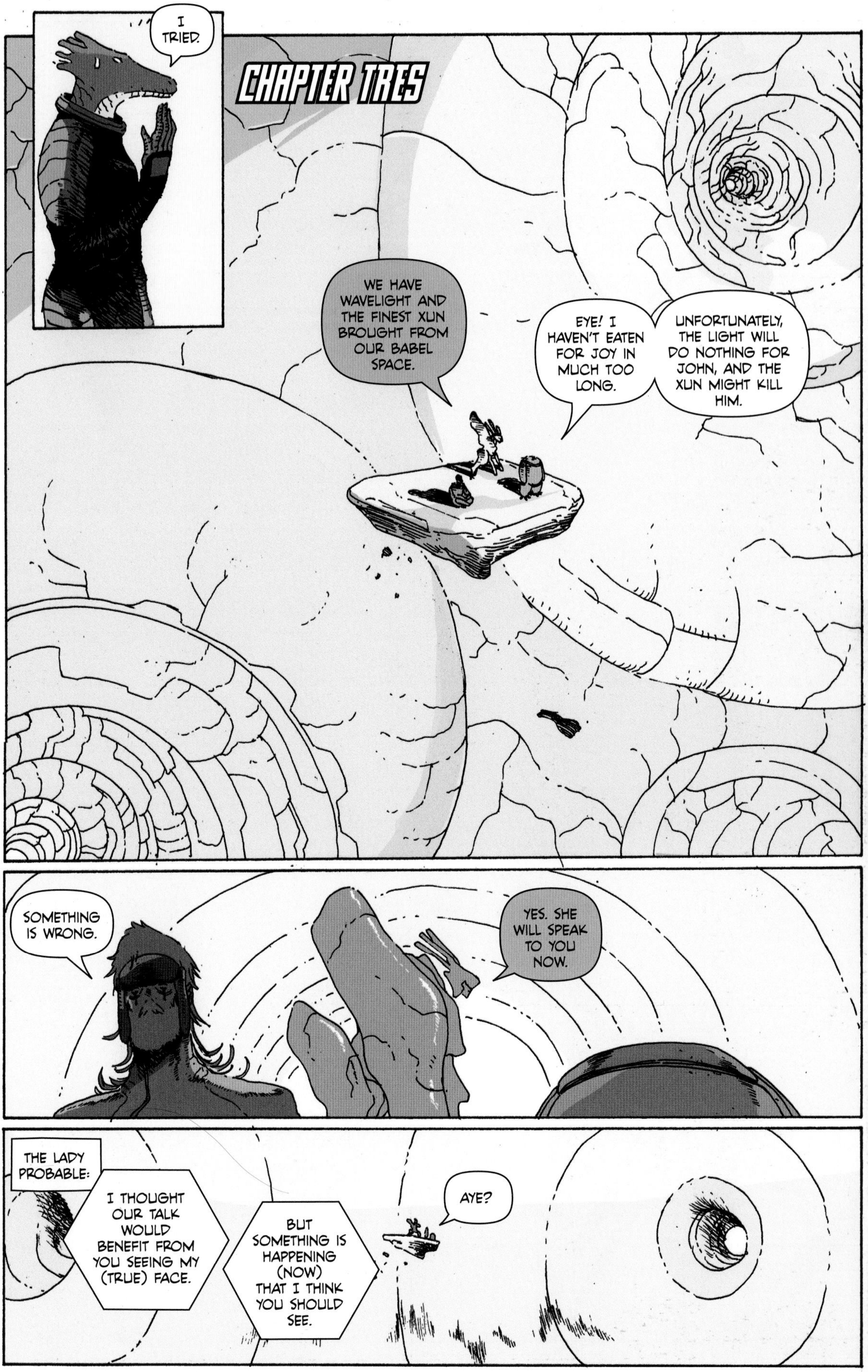
I TRIED.
CHAPTER TRES
WE HAVE WAVELIGHT AND THE FINEST XUN BROUGHT FROM OUR BABEL SPACE.
EYE! I HAVEN'T EATEN FOR JOY IN MUCH TOO LONG.
UNFORTUNATELY, THE LIGHT WILL DO NOTHING FOR JOHN, AND THE XUN MIGHT KILL HIM.
SOMETHING IS WRONG.
YES. SHE WILL SPEAK TO YOU NOW.
THE LADY PROBABLE:
I THOUGHT OUR TALK WOULD BENEFIT FROM YOU SEEING MY (TRUE) FACE.
BUT SOMETHING IS HAPPENING (NOW) THAT I THINK YOU SHOULD SEE.
AYE?

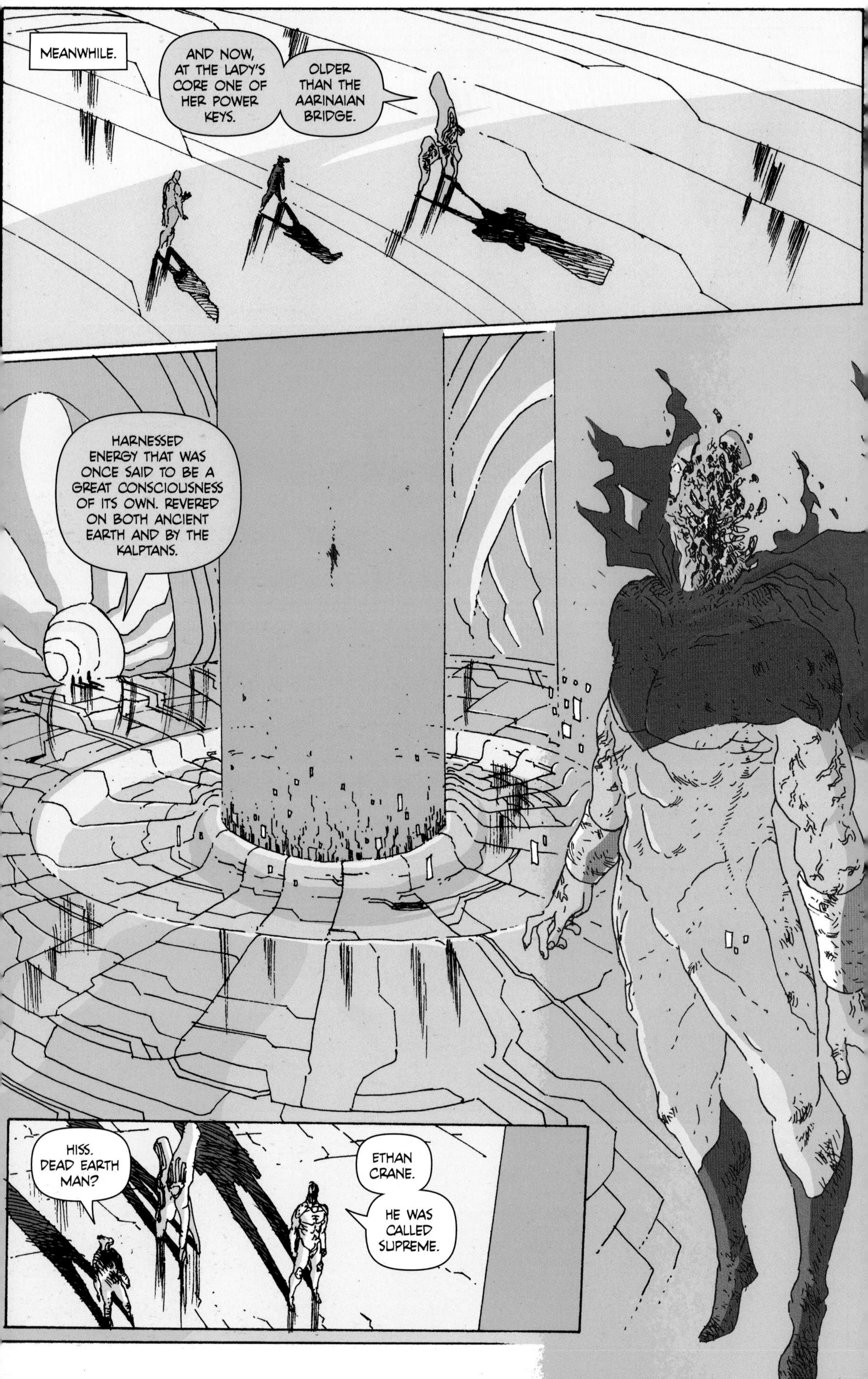
MEANWHILE.
AND NOW, AT THE LADY'S CORE ONE OF HER POWER KEYS.
OLDER THAN THE AARINAIAN BRIDGE.
HARNESSED ENERGY THAT WAS ONCE SAID TO BE A GREAT CONSCIOUSNESS OF ITS OWN. REVERED ON BOTH ANCIENT EARTH AND BY THE KALPTANS.
HISS. DEAD EARTH MAN?
ETHAN CRANE.
HE WAS CALLED SUPREME.

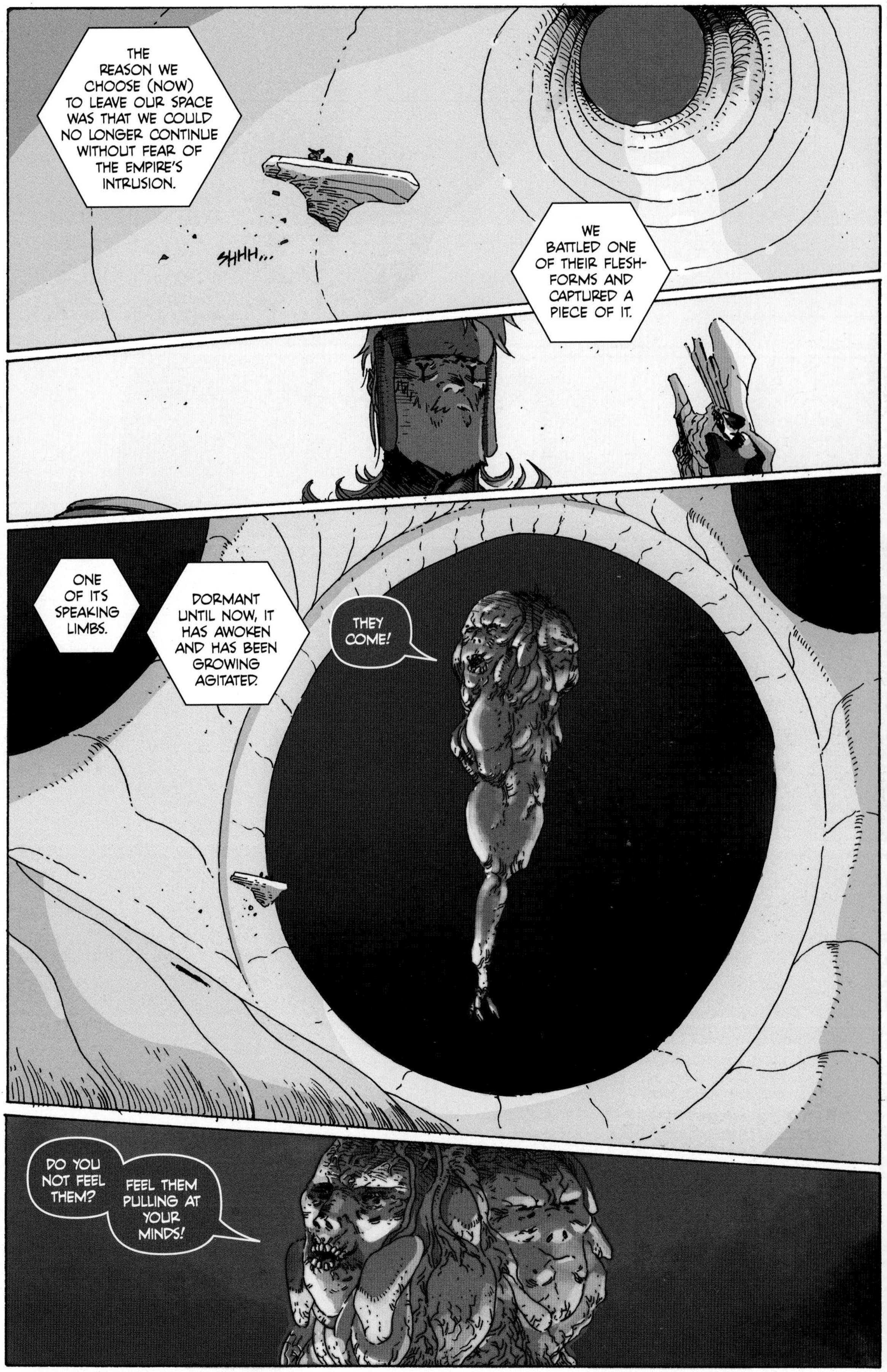
THE REASON WE CHOOSE (NOW) TO LEAVE OUR SPACE WAS THAT WE COULD NO LONGER CONTINUE WITHOUT FEAR OF THE EMPIRE'S INTRUSION.
SHHH...
WE BATTLED ONE OF THEIR FLESH-FORMS AND CAPTURED A PIECE OF IT.
ONE OF ITS SPEAKING LIMBS.
DORMANT UNTIL NOW, IT HAS AWOKEN AND HAS BEEN GROWING AGITATED.
THEY COME!
DO YOU NOT FEEL THEM?
FEEL THEM PULLING AT YOUR MINDS!

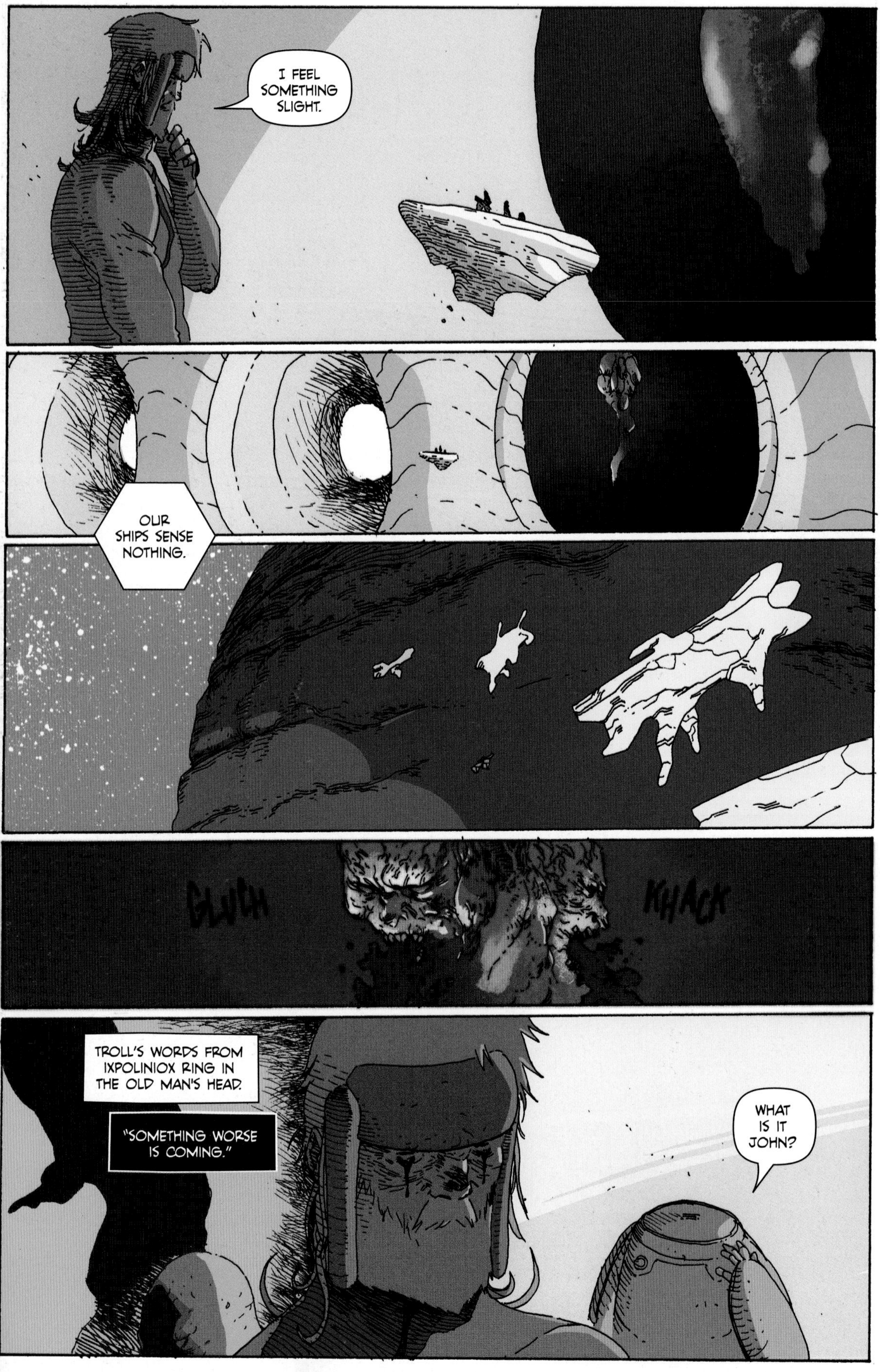

I FEEL SOMETHING SLIGHT.
OUR SHIPS SENSE NOTHING.
GLUCH
KHACK
TROLL'S WORDS FROM IXPOLINIOX RING IN THE OLD MAN'S HEAD.
"SOMETHING WORSE IS COMING."
WHAT IS IT JOHN?

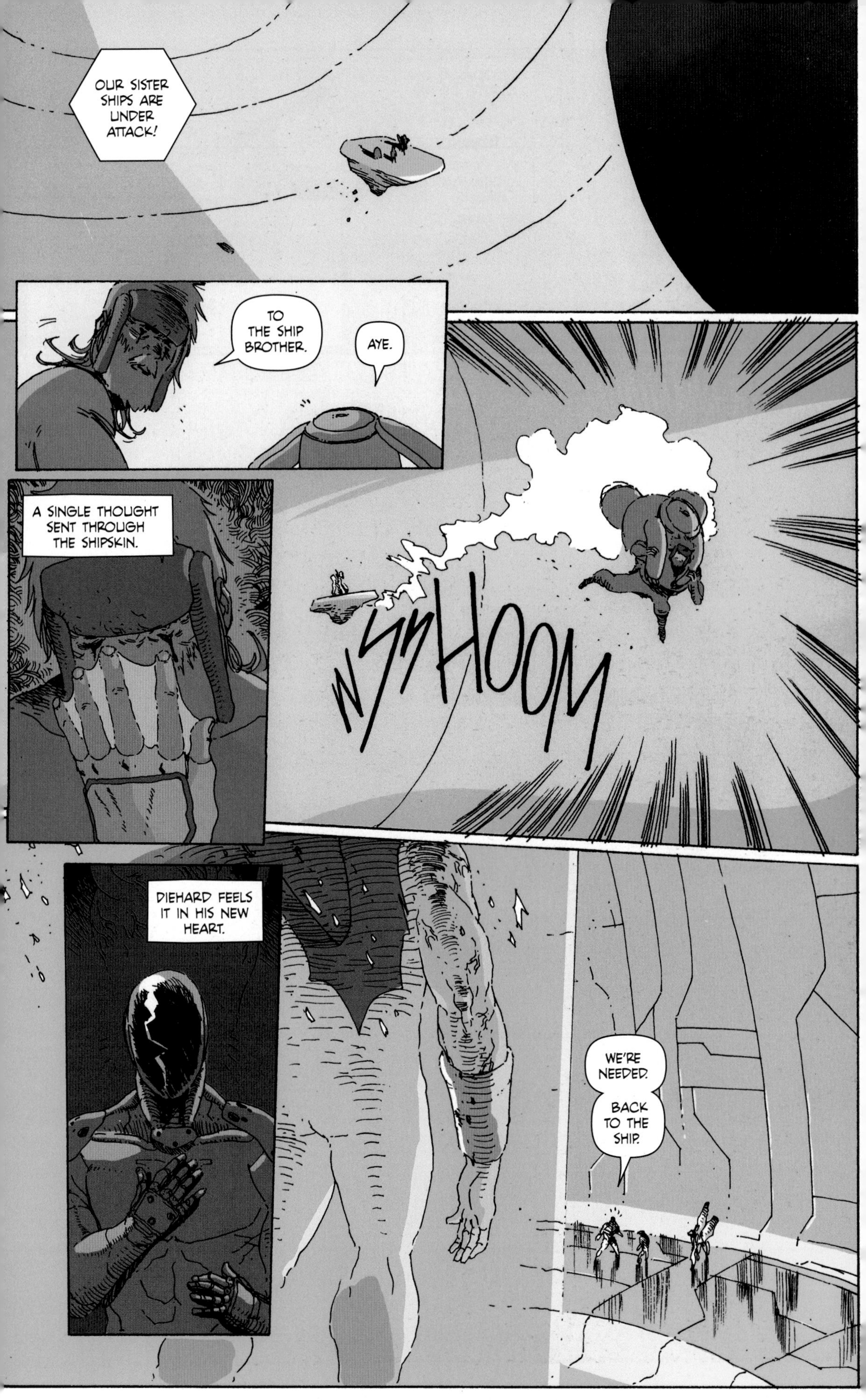
OUR SISTER SHIPS ARE UNDER ATTACK!
TO THE SHIP BROTHER.
AYE.
A SINGLE THOUGHT SENT THROUGH THE SHIPSKIN.
WSSHOOM
DIEHARD FEELS IT IN HIS NEW HEART.
WE'RE NEEDED.
BACK TO THE SHIP.

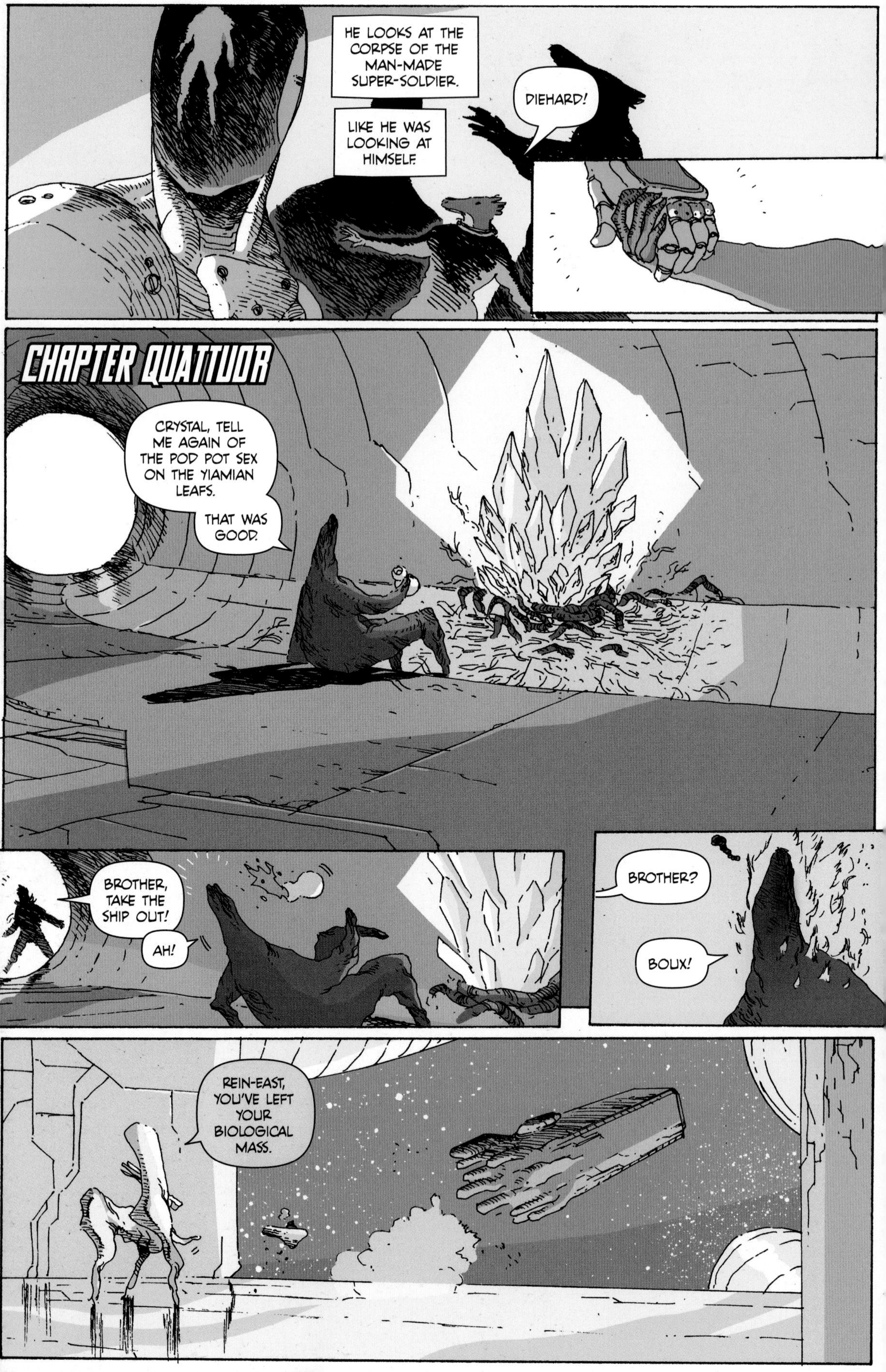
HE LOOKS AT THE CORPSE OF THE MAN-MADE SUPER-SOLDIER.
LIKE HE WAS LOOKING AT HIMSELF.
DIEHARD!
CHAPTER QUATTUOR
CRYSTAL, TELL ME AGAIN OF THE POD POT SEX ON THE YIAMIAN LEAFS.
THAT WAS GOOD.
BROTHER, TAKE THE SHIP OUT!
AH!
BROTHER?
BOUX!
REIN-EAST, YOU'VE LEFT YOUR BIOLOGICAL MASS.

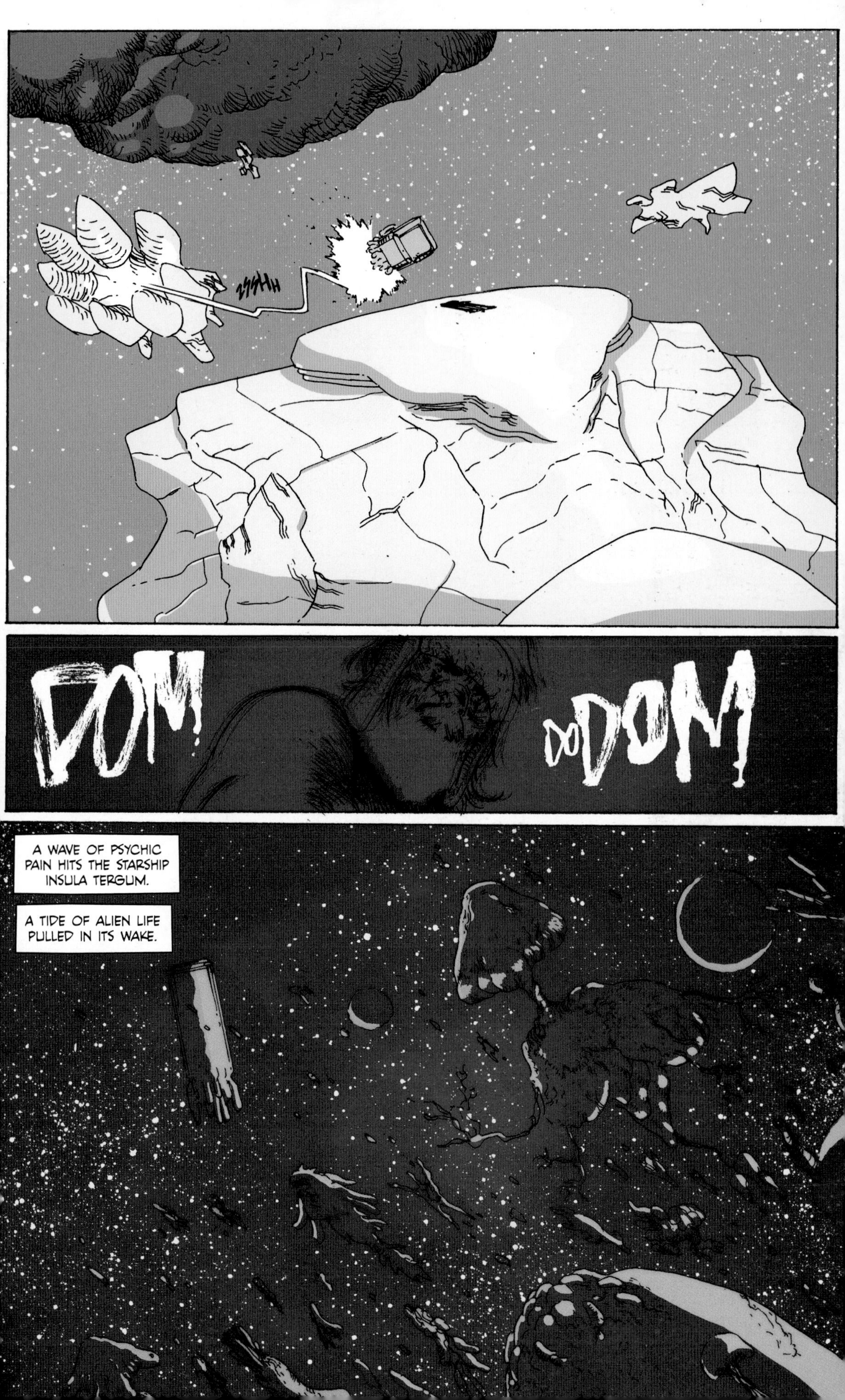
ZSSHH
DOM
DODOM
A WAVE OF PSYCHIC PAIN HITS THE STARSHIP INSULA TERGUM.
A TIDE OF ALIEN LIFE PULLED IN ITS WAKE.

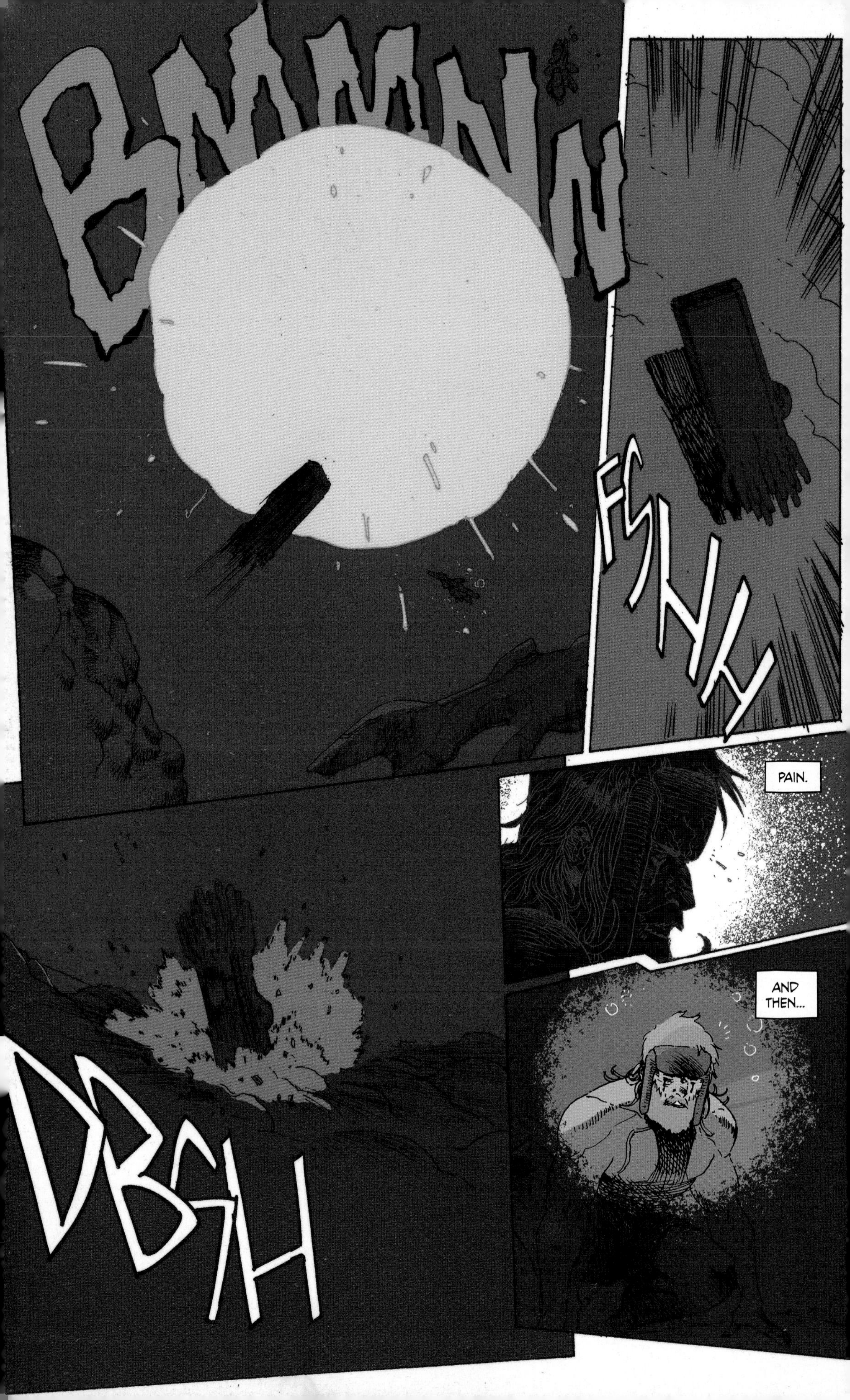
BMMMN
FSHHY
PAIN.
AND THEN...
DBGSH

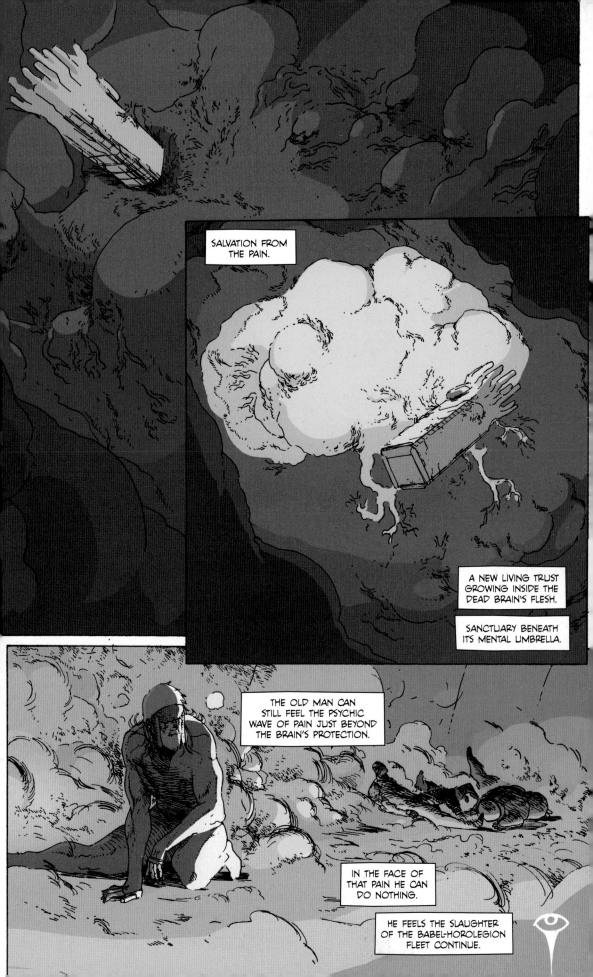

SALVATION FROM THE PAIN.

A NEW LIVING TRUST GROWING INSIDE THE DEAD BRAIN'S FLESH.

SANCTUARY BENEATH ITS MENTAL UMBRELLA.

THE OLD MAN CAN STILL FEEL THE PSYCHIC WAVE OF PAIN JUST BEYOND THE BRAIN'S PROTECTION.

IN THE FACE OF THAT PAIN HE CAN DO NOTHING.

HE FEELS THE SLAUGHTER OF THE BABEL-HOROLEGION FLEET CONTINUE.

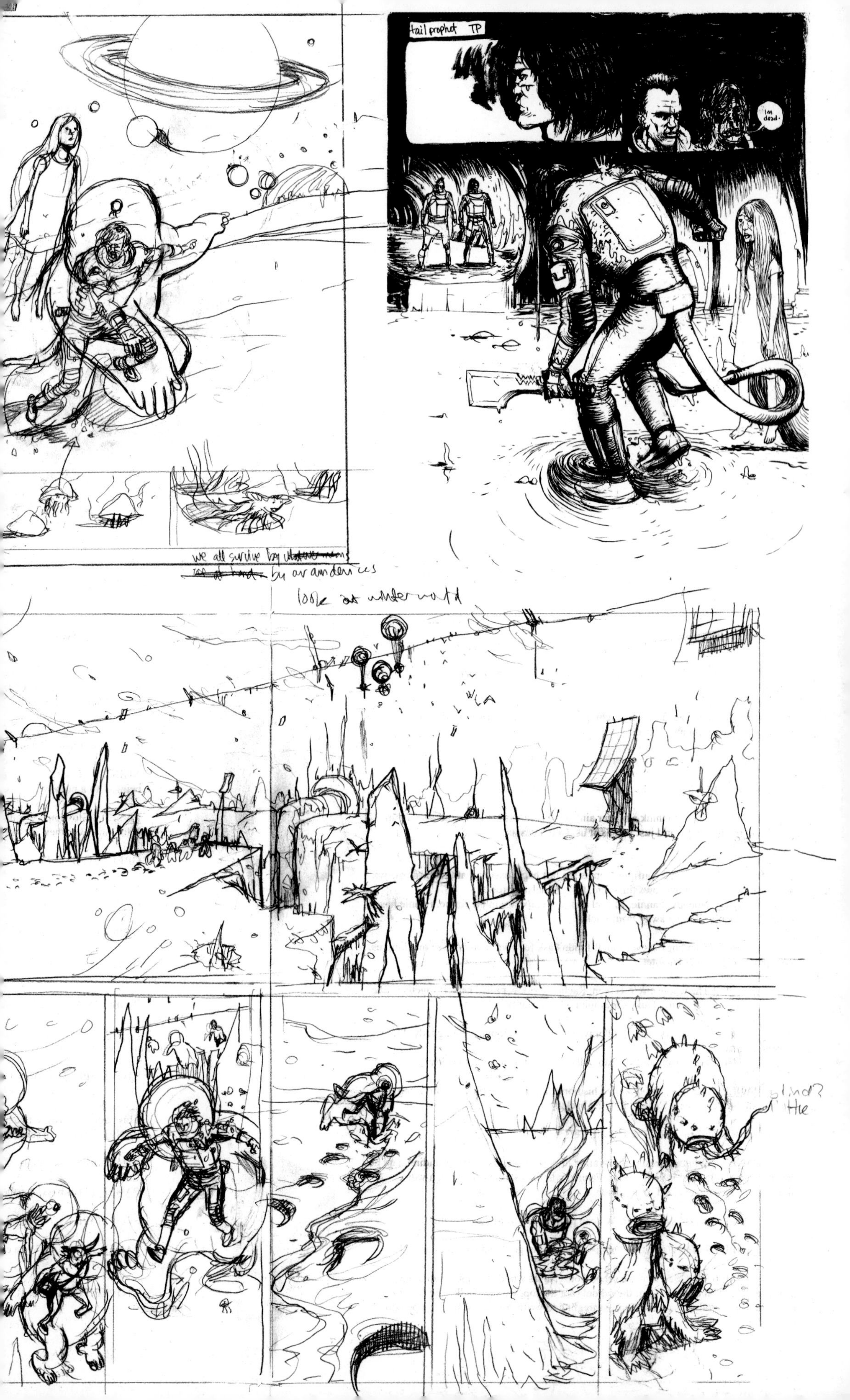
tail prophet TP
Im dead.
we all survive by
look at underworld

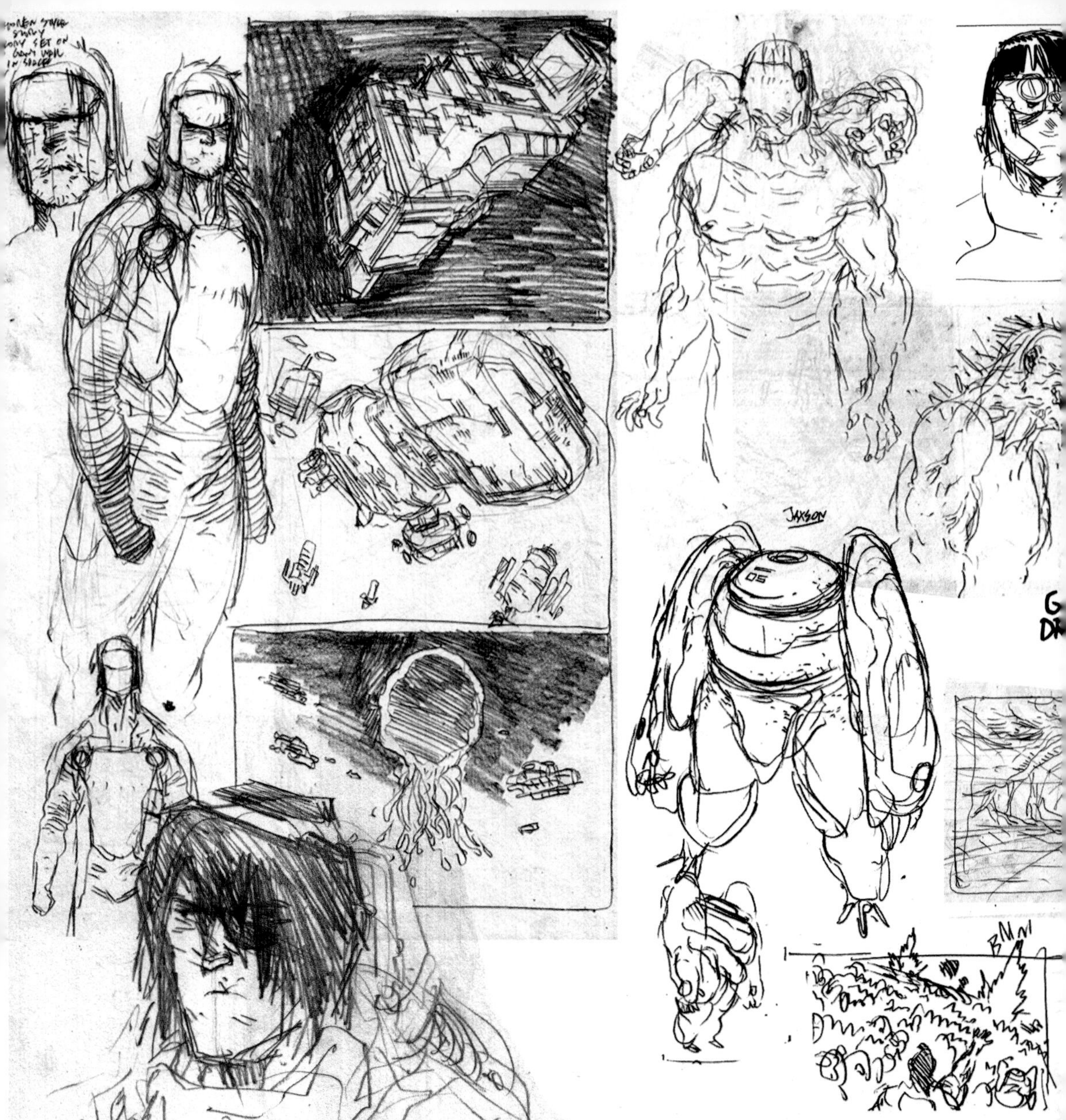
JAXSON

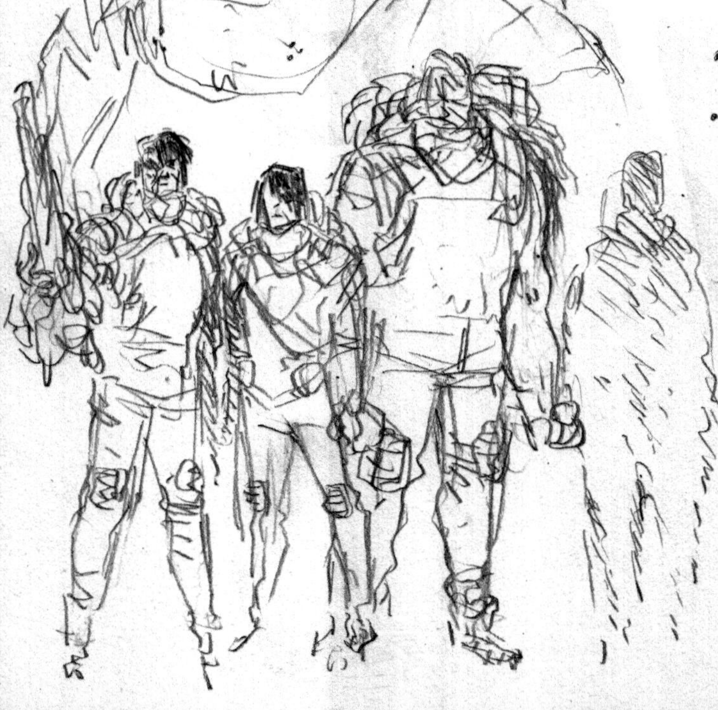

- MAIN LEADER PROPHET
  - LADY WITH EYEPATCH
- BIG "THING" PROPHET
  CARRIES ALL THE LIVING
  WEAPON CREATURES, MAYBE
  HE ENDS UP GETTING EATEN
  BY THOSE?
- PSYCHIC/GHOST PROPHET (?)
  HE WAS KILLED SOMETIME
  IN THE PAST AND HIS
  PROJECTION TAGS ALONG
  WITH THE REST OF THE
  TEAM?
- "TWO-FACE" PROPHET
  LOST HALF HIS FACE
  WHEN HIS ACID SPITTING
  ORGANIC WEAPON
  BACKFIRED
  (ALSO IT'S A PARASITE
  HE CAN'T GET
  RID OF?)

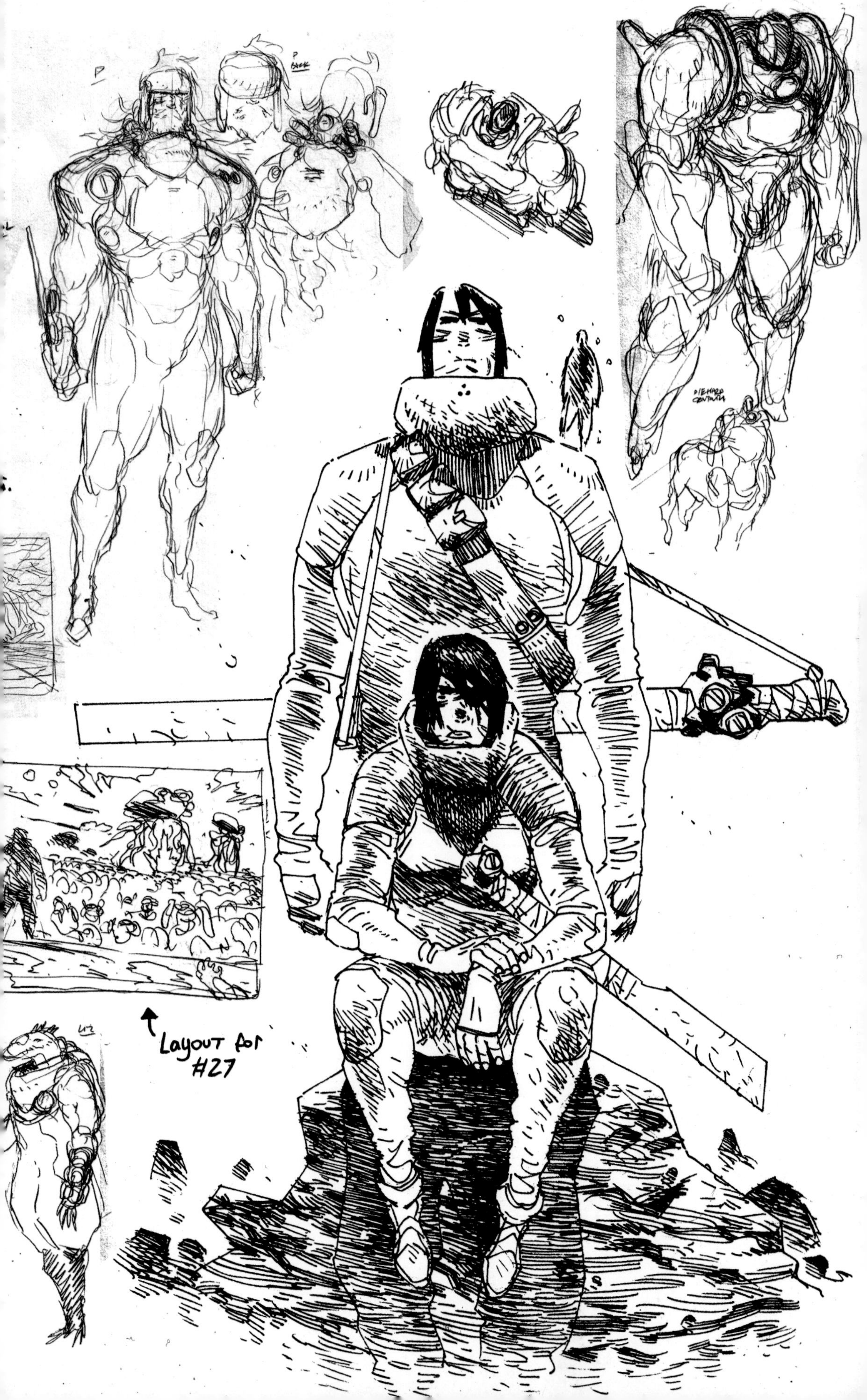
P
P BACK
DIEHARD
Layout for #27

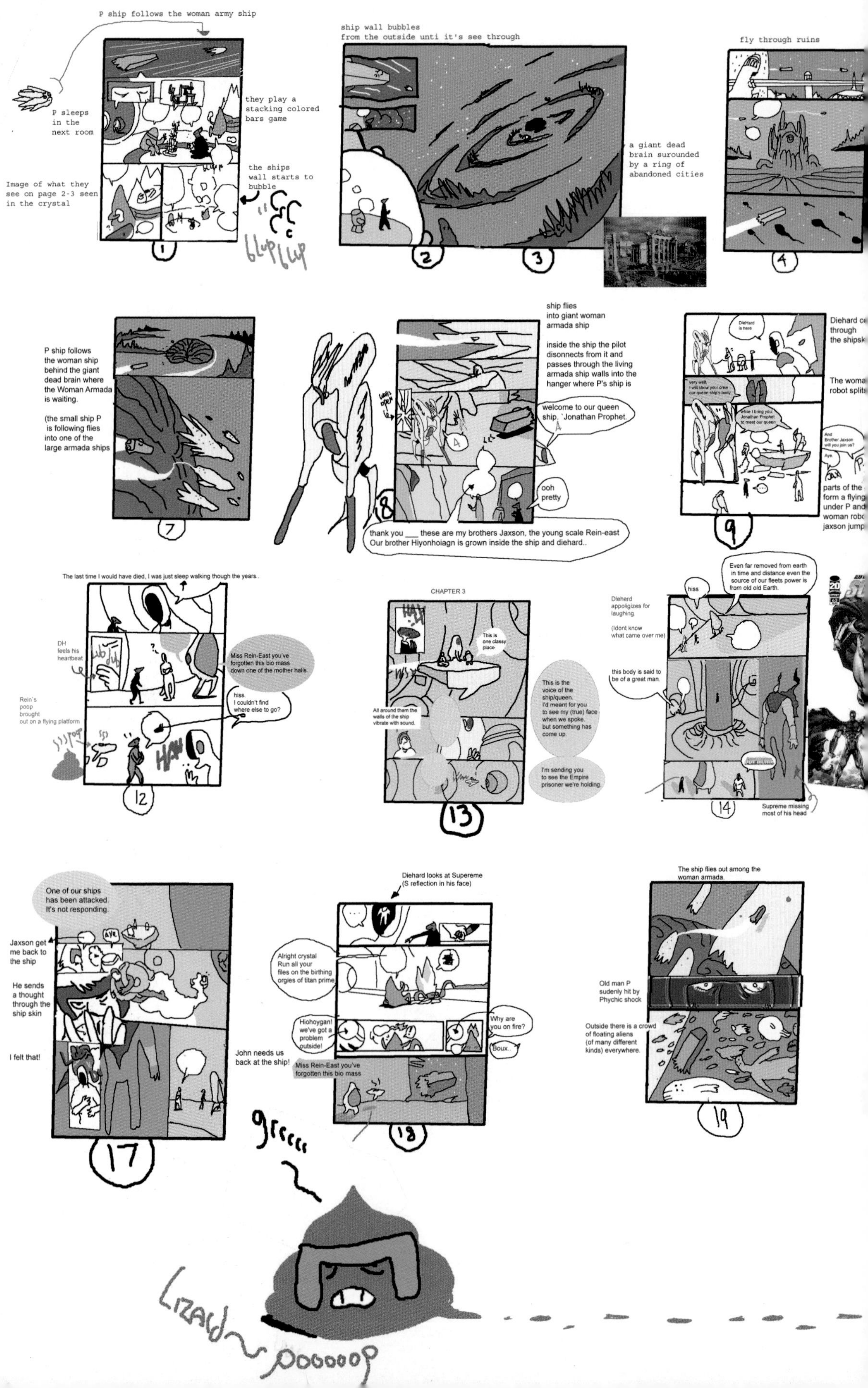

P ship follows the woman army ship
P sleeps in the next room
they play a stacking colored bars game
Image of what they see on page 2-3 seen in the crystal
the ships wall starts to bubble
blup blup
1
ship wall bubbles
from the outside unti it's see through
a giant dead brain surounded by a ring of abandoned cities
2
3
fly through ruins
4
P ship follows the woman ship behind the giant dead brain where the Woman Armada is waiting.
(the small ship P is following flies into one of the large armada ships
7
ship flies into giant woman armada ship
inside the ship the pilot disonnects from it and passes through the living armada ship walls into the hanger where P's ship is
welcome to our queen ship. `Jonathan Prophet.
ooh pretty
8
thank you ___ these are my brothers Jaxson, the young scale Rein-east
Our brother Hiyonhoiagn is grown inside the ship and diehard..
DieHard is here
very well, I will show your crew our queen ship's body.
while I bring you: Jonathan Prophet to meet our queen
And Brother Jaxson will you join us?
Aye.
9
The last time I would have died, I was just sleep walking though the years..
DH feels his heartbeat
Miss Rein-East you've forgotten this bio mass down one of the mother halls.
hiss.
I couldn't find where else to go?
Rein's poop brought out on a flying platform
HAH
12
CHAPTER 3
This is one classy place
All around them the walls of the ship vibrate with sound.
This is the voice of the ship/queen. I'd meant for you to see my (true) face when we spoke. but something has come up.
I'm sending you to see the Empire prisoner we're holding.
13
Diehard appoligizes for laughing.
(Idont know what came over me)
hiss
Even far removed from earth in time and distance even the source of our fleets power is from old old Earth.
this body is said to be of a great man.
Supreme missing most of his head
14
One of our ships has been attacked. It's not responding.
Jaxson get me back to the ship
He sends a thought through the ship skin
I felt that!
Aye
17
Diehard looks at Supereme (S reflection in his face)
Alright crystal Run all your files on the birthing orgies of titan prime
Hiohoygan! we've got a problem outside!
Why are you on fire?
Boux..
John needs us back at the ship!
Miss Rein-East you've forgotten this bio mass
18
The ship flies out among the woman armada.
Old man P sudenly hit by Phychic shock
Outside there is a crowd of floating aliens (of many different kinds) everywhere.
19
grrrrr
Lizard poooooop

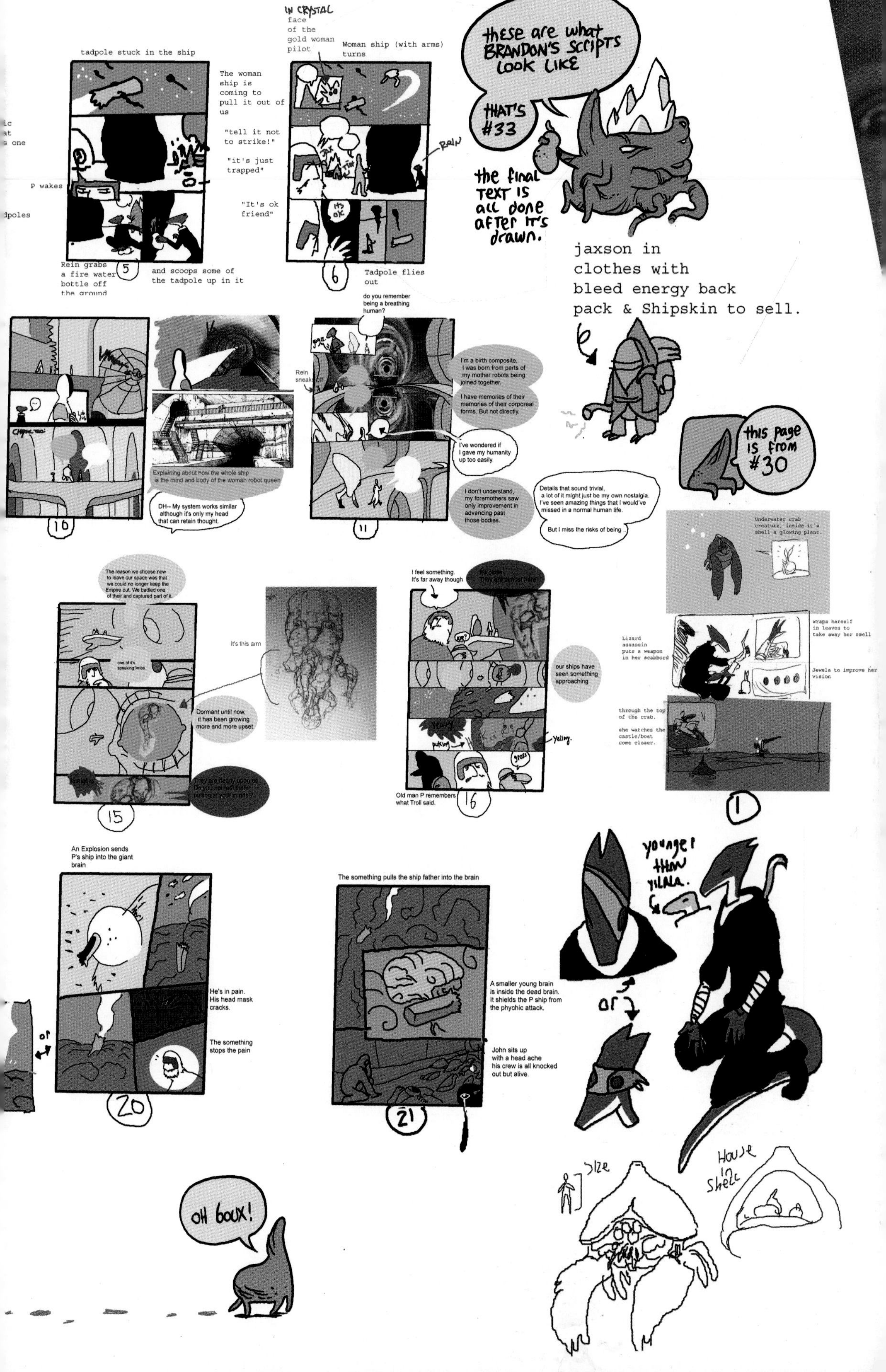

tadpole stuck in the ship
The woman ship is coming to pull it out of us
"tell it not to strike!"
"it's just trapped"
P wakes
"It's ok friend"
Rein grabs a fire water bottle off the ground
and scoops some of the tadpole up in it
5
IN CRYSTAL face of the gold woman pilot
Woman ship (with arms) turns
REIN
It's ok
Tadpole flies out
6
these are what BRANDON'S SCRIPTS LOOK LIKE
THAT'S #33
the final TEXT IS all done after it's drawn.
jaxson in clothes with bleed energy back pack & Shipskin to sell.
Explaining about how the whole ship is the mind and body of the woman robot queen
DH-- My system works similar although it's only my head that can retain thought.
10
do you remember being a breathing human?
Rein sneaks off
I'm a birth composite, I was born from parts of my mother robots being joined together.
I have memories of their memories of their corporeal forms. But not directly.
I've wondered if I gave my humanity up too easily.
I don't understand, my foremothers saw only improvement in advancing past those bodies.
Details that sound trivial, a lot of it might just be my own nostalgia. I've seen amazing things that I would've missed in a normal human life.
But I miss the risks of being ...
11
this page is from #30
Underwater crab creature, inside it's shell a glowing plant.
Lizard assassin puts a weapon in her scabbard
wraps herself in leaves to take away her smell
Jewels to improve her vision
through the top of the crab.
she watches the castle/boat come closer.
1
The reason we choose now to leave our space was that we could no longer keep the Empire out. We battled one of their and captured part of it.
one of it's speaking limbs
It's this arm
Dormant until now, it has been growing more and more upset.
They are nearly upon us. Do you not feel them pulling at your minds!?
15
I feel something. It's far away though
It's close. They are almost here!
our ships have seen something approaching
Yelling
puking
Yelling.
gross
Old man P remembers what Troll said.
16
younger than yilala.
or
An Explosion sends P's ship into the giant brain
He's in pain. His head mask cracks.
The something stops the pain
or
20
The something pulls the ship father into the brain
A smaller young brain is inside the dead brain. It shields the P ship from the phychic attack.
John sits up with a head ache his crew is all knocked out but alive.
21
OH boux!
size
House in Shell

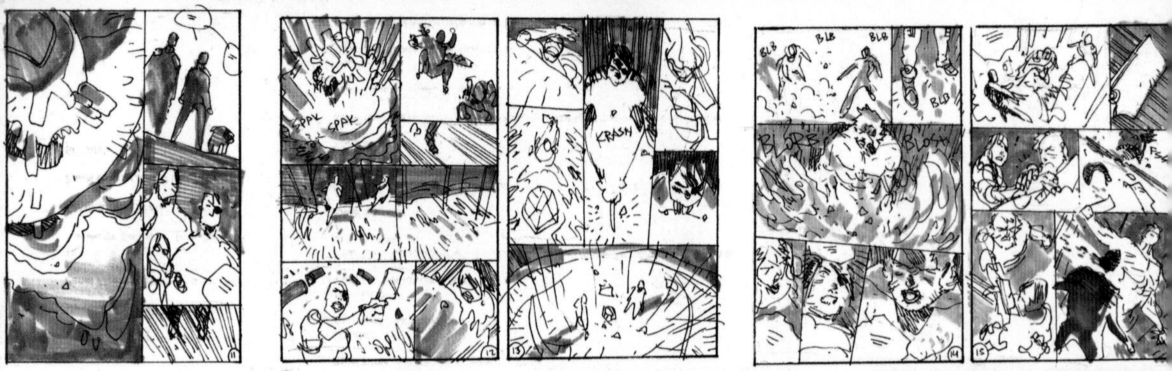
SPAK
SPAK
KRASH
BLB
BLB
BLB
BLORB
BLOSH

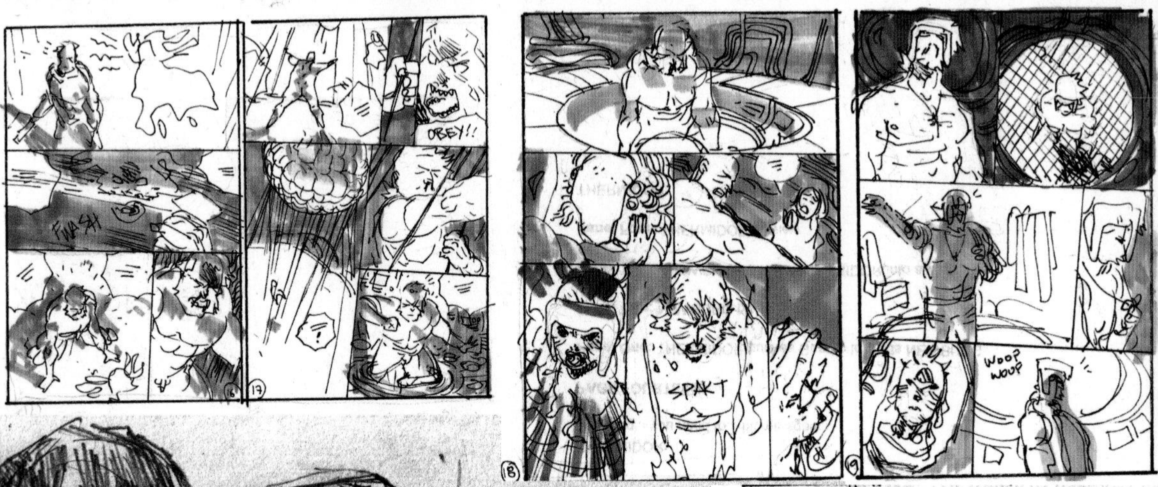
OBEY!!
FWASH
SPAKT
WOOP
WOOP

GIANNIS LAYOUTS FROM HIS 1ST ISSUE

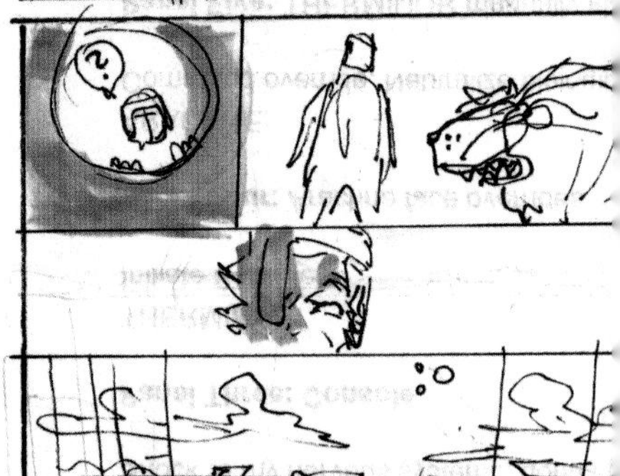

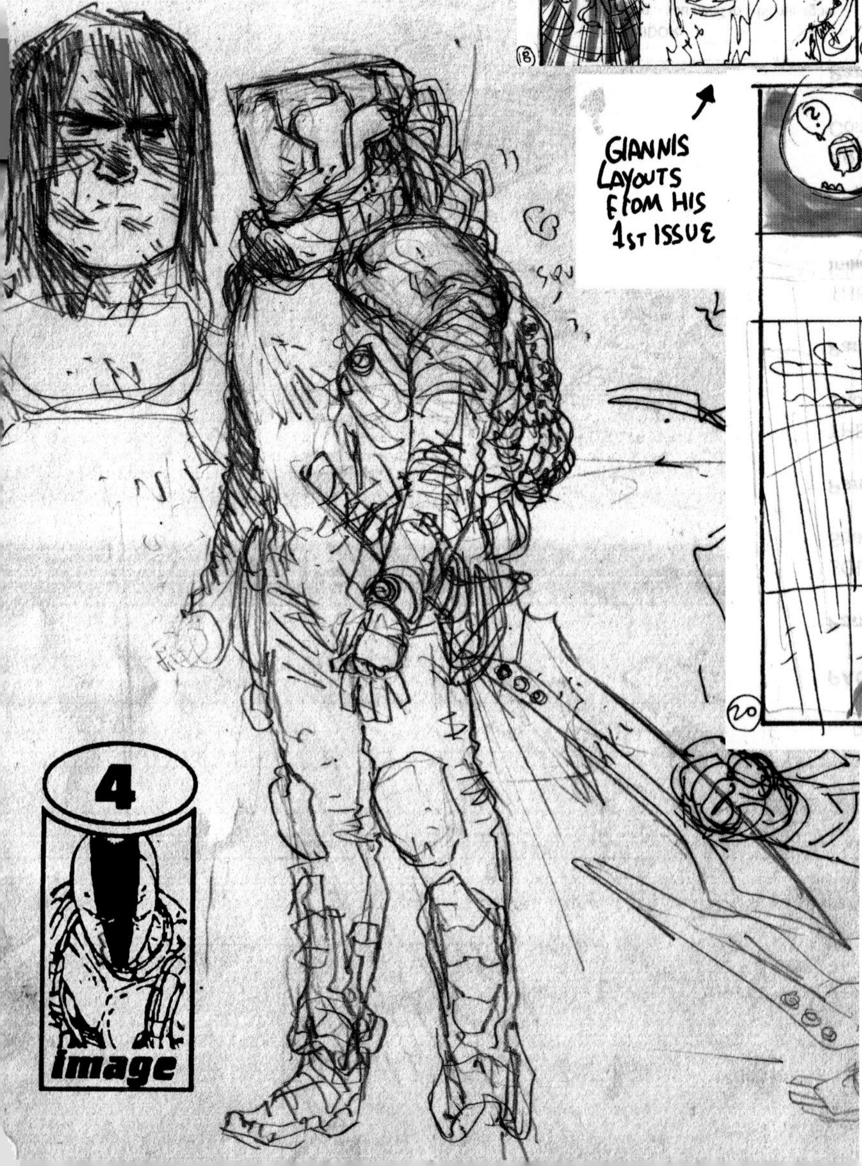

Earlier in the series we would send layouts back + forth. Eventually I took over doing most of them. for the sake of speed.

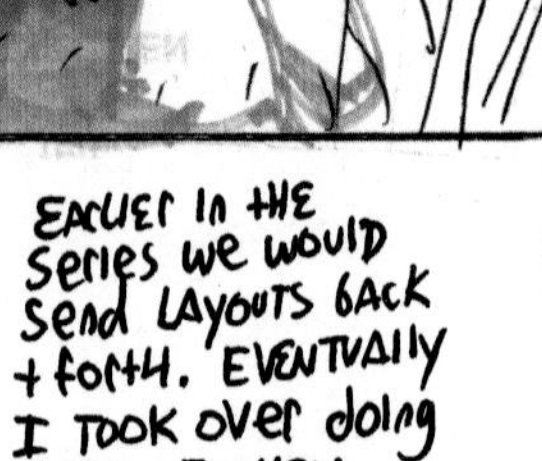
deadlines BANG.
brandon

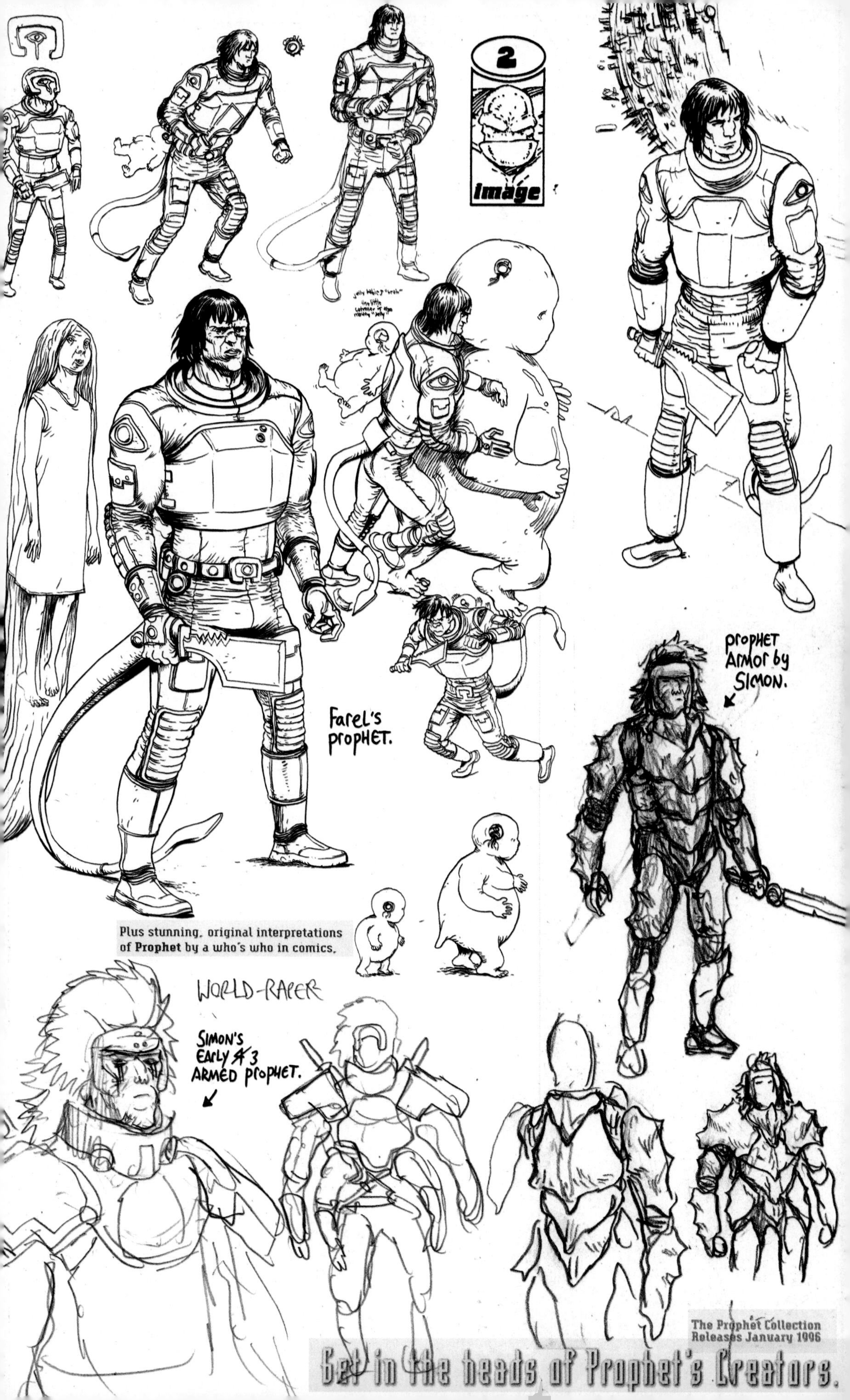
2
image
Farel's prophet.
prophet Armor by SIMON.
Plus stunning, original interpretations of **Prophet** by a who's who in comics.
WORLD-RAPER
SIMON'S EARLY #3 ARMED prophet.
The Prophet Collection Releases January 1996
Get in the heads of Prophet's Creators.

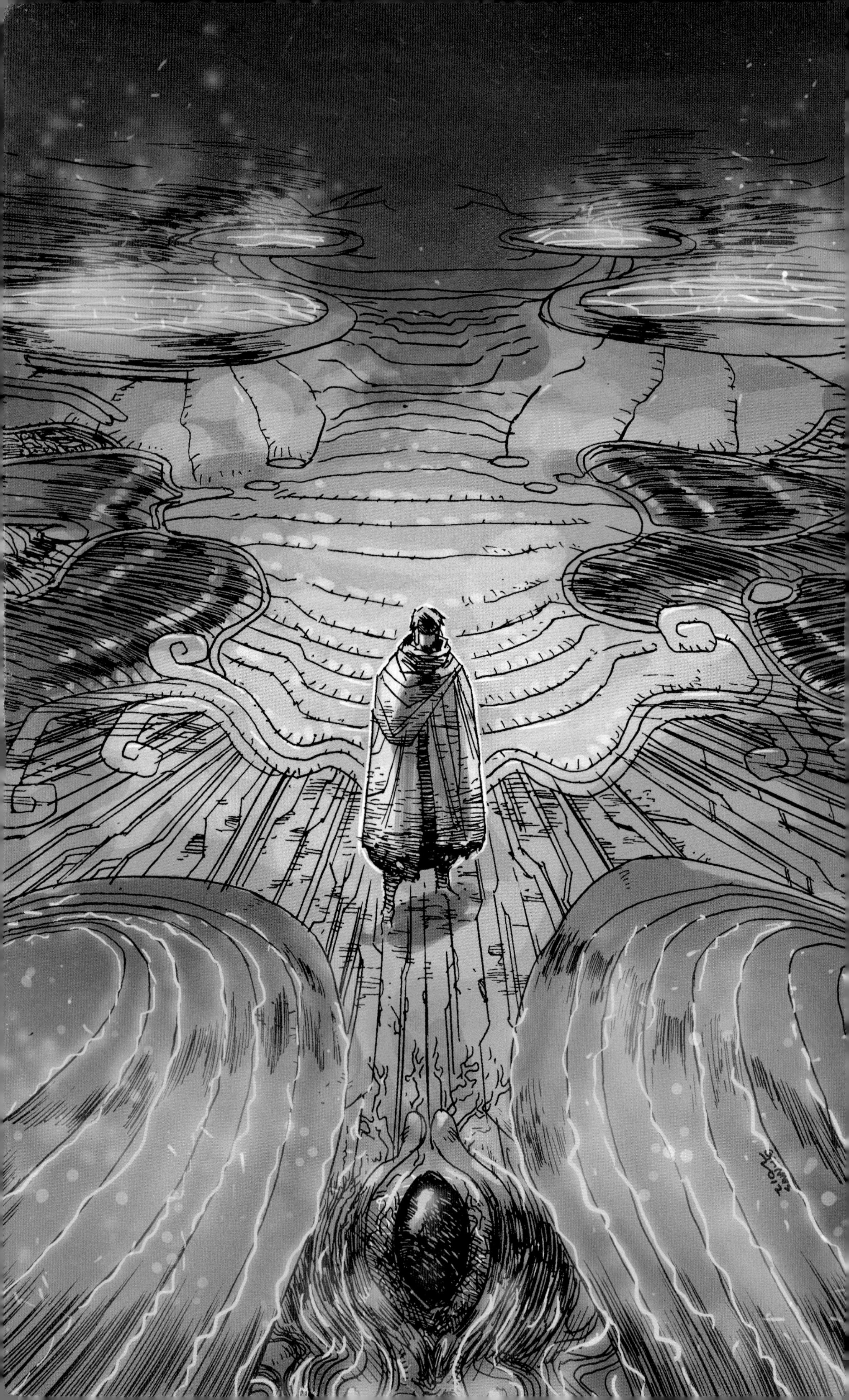